CARDIGAN SQUARE

Other Books by Alexandra Manners

THE STONE MAIDEN
CANDLES IN THE WOOD
THE SINGING SWANS

CARDIGAN SQUARE

by Alexandra Manners

G. P. Putnam's Sons
New York

Copyright © 1977 by Alexandra Manners

All rights reserved. This book, or parts thereof, must not be reproduced in
any form without permission. Published simultaneously in Canada by
Longman Canada Limited, Toronto.

SBN: 399-11918-3

Library of Congress Cataloging in Publication Data

Rundle, Anne.
Cardigan Square.

I. Title.
PZ4.R9425Car3   [PR6068.U7]   823'.9'14   76-57200

PRINTED IN THE UNITED STATES OF AMERICA

To May Hamp-Hamilton,
with admiration and best wishes.

CARDIGAN SQUARE

Chapter 1

$\mathscr{S}$able moaned in her sleep, moved drowsily, and was suddenly awake. The dark pressed down on her and the tip of her nose felt cold. At first she could not think where she was, or indeed, who she was. Drowsiness tugged at her, tried to pull her back into the region of dreams. She thought without quite knowing why of birds rising from stubbled fields. Crows and rooks, black and fluttering, their beaks stabbing at the early morning ground. She knew, even at that moment, that they were killing something.

Then, she remembered. Today was May the first. May Day. When it was lucky to wash one's face in dew. And she had banged her head on the pillow five times so that she'd wake up early enough to escape before the household awakened.

The day was windy. There was a moaning in the chimney and the trees creaked. The wildness of the weather evoked a response in her. There was only one place in this wilderness where there was a stretch of grass in which she wanted to bathe her face. That was on Hunter land. And Hunters did not like interlopers.

She smiled in the darkness. If they knew how often she invaded that forbidden territory. Even the dogs did not keep her out. They had come to know her by dint of her patient reconnaissance and assiduous cultivations. Now they ran with her, tongues lolling, as they crashed uncaring through thickets where the thin, rotted branches snapped as they passed by, plunging into the scummy lake where the lily pads had turned slimy with neglect. But they never stayed long in the decayed water. It was as if they sensed some evil presence there that drove them out, trembling and uneasy, to shake the thick green drops from their fur and to run on, dense shadows made real only by the sound of their progress, their harsh, panting breath. They had a facility for remaining almost unseen.

She had gone up to the windows of the house quite often when there was a celebration. They never drew the curtains, for they were certain no one could get within sight with the dogs on the grounds. Along the edge of the flagstones there were cold white statues draped in marble, their niches and folds invaded by spores of dampness so that they appeared leprous. One statue of a splendidly muscled young man wearing only a fig leaf had moss growing round the silly improvisation to decency, so that he seemed to have a pelt of soft green hair.

Once Morgan had glimpsed her and started up from the table shouting, "Brutus! Samson! Where are you stupid brutes? You are supposed to keep folk out, not let them gawp as if we were circus beasts. Brutus!" And Sable had run, laughing, filled with a delicious sense of power, Brutus with her, licking at her hand. Morgan had not really seen her properly, only a suggestion of her face close to the pane, her customary caution having vanished in a de-

8

sire to see more closely the silver and glass, the gowns of the women, and most especially the food. The fowl was sometimes dressed in its own feathers and this she disliked in spite of the hunger that came upon her at the culinary sights and the fine smells that escaped from the big, handsome room.

Thoroughly awake, Sable got out of the cocoon of blankets and stood up shivering. The wind was cold and capricious, banging at the door and lifting the rush mat like invisible fingers. It was the work of a minute to put on an old blue gown and thrust her feet into clogs. She could move like a wraith and was soon at the door where her cloak hung on a hook. She wrapped it around her and moved swiftly through the gradually lightening morning.

The piece of land her father farmed was small and she was almost immediately on Hunter territory. Through gaps in the shrubbery she could see a line of pearly light that was the beginning of dawn. She had to hurry if she was to be back for breakfast. Yet she did not want to hurry. The urgency of the clashing branches and swirling leaves excited her. The wind gusted up under the patched blue skirts and licked at her bare body, making her catch her breath with abandoned pleasure. She stretched out her arms, eyes closed briefly to capture the blustery essence of the morning.

The sullen glimmer of the pool opened up ahead and once again the ecstasy of living was spoiled as though a cloud had covered the copse. Brutus came, cowering, his eyes fixed on the dark scum as though he expected to see something emerge from it. He made a dismal little moaning noise that made Sable start to run, her heart banging and the rotten sticks snapping softly under her thick clogs. The shadow lifted once the pond was out of sight. It should be drained and cleaned as her father's had been, she thought. Strange that folk who were so very fine and dainty should neglect anything. Once the lilies had bloomed and the surface of the water had resembled the stuff of Jane Hunter's gown, the blue, shiny one she had worn last Christmas.

The ground rose into a steepish hill crowned with trees that overlooked the house. Below the tree line the grass, bleached in the early morning light, looked deceptively smooth. Sable knelt. A flicker of light touched a spider-web. Avoiding the web, she pushed her face close to the ground. A mushroomy smell came up from the damp soil as she twisted her head first one way, then another, feeling the sharp freshness of moisture on her skin.

She stood up, slaked of urgency, no longer caring if she was late getting home. The house below was clearly defined in an E shape. The gardens made definite squares and rectangles delineated by the smoky darkness of ave-nues and trimmed hedges. All around it the moor, a rough blur, seemed about to move towards the patch cleared from the complexity of stone, rock, heather, and bilberry as though to cover it afresh with a purplish stain.

The slope beckoned. Sable lay down and held her arms against her sides. She began to roll like a length of carpet, the breath knocked from her body, the world rocketing round her in flashes of sky, trees, rough grass. She found herself screaming with vertiginous delight, knowing she should remain quiet but unable to contain the outburst of exultation.

She came to rest with startling suddenness against some-thing hard and unyielding. Her eyes had closed; the wind was stroking her bare legs boisterously. She lay for a mo-ment deciding she had reached a stone and began languid-ly to sit up. But the stone was a boot that stretched up into knees, thighs, and very far off a face shaded by a hat-brim.

Sable became aware that her skirts had worked up al-most beyond the boundaries of decorum, that the unseen eyes could see what they would. She seemed composed al-most entirely of legs and a bare foot from which the clog had been hurled unnoticed in the reckless flight. She struggled to her knees, restoring the gown to decency, trying to assemble her thoughts through the dizziness that replaced elation. She looked around for the lost clog and Brutus came up, belly to the ground, and nuzzled at her bare foot.

"So that's how you do it. I often wondered," Morgan said. She could not tell whether he was indifferent or annoyed, but when she saw him bend down to cuff the dog, she found her tongue. "Don't hurt him. I made a friend of him. He still barks at anyone else."

"And I suppose you have Samson in your pocket, too?"

"He—does like me," she admitted, brushing the stalks off her garments.

"And what is there about us you find so fascinating? Why treat us as fairground spectacles?"

She could say something about admiring them in their fine clothes, about a desire to know more of the Hall and the family who lived there, but it could only sound false.

"Because it is forbidden."

He said nothing for a minute and she suspected she had disconcerted him by her frankness. Then he laughed. "So," he said, "our ghost is a skinny farm child. And as for you, you stupid animal"—he made a threatening gesture towards Brutus who bounded away—"go about the business you are meant for, or I'll have your hide! Now why are you here at this hour? You could hardly expect to see us so early. Or did you plan to climb the ivy to view us in our beds?" His tone had changed to one of displeasure.

Her heart had started to thud like a soldier's drum. If he were really angry he'd go to Father and she'd be beaten within an inch of her life. Father's hand was heavy.

"I should call at the farm," he went on. "Have this poaching stopped."

"I take nothing!" She was indignant.

"You take our privacy," he pointed out.

She was silent. It had not seemed like stealing. "It's May morning," she said at last. "There's no grass on the smallholding—well, not nice enough to wash your face in—"

"I'd forgotten what day it is." He reached out and tipped back her head, his hand clamped round her chin. "A defiant sort of face if I read it aright. I see no sign of contrition, young miss. Not that you'd know what contrition is—"

"Oh, but I do. It's—being sorry—"

Morgan Hunter frowned. "A queer sort of farmer's lass to know such big words."

She had never been so close to him. There was a heady triumph in seeing each pore of his skin, the wheel spokes radiating from the center of his pupils, the thick fringe of stubby lashes, the puckers of his lips, and the hair that grew down the sides of his face just in front of his ears. She realized suddenly that he could see her under the same microscope. She wanted to shrug herself away but his fingers were thick and strong. Her neck began to ache. "There's a man comes. He has books in his pack and he teaches me letters for a sleep in the barn and his food and drink. We found him one winter, near frozen. He'd fallen in the thorn hedge. My mother wanted me to do more than put a cross on a piece of paper."

"You mean Tom Dobbs?"

"Yes. Old Tom—" Though he was not really old. Just strange.

He released her chin and she wriggled her aching shoulders, relieved. "He was not always an eccentric—traveller, for want of a better word," Morgan told her.

She shivered suddenly, aware of her bare foot and the lack of any garment under the blue gown.

"Aye, and so you should shudder," Morgan said, noting her coldness instantly. "You've little on to keep you warm. The spring does not come because the calendar says it should."

So he had seen more than he should. Breathlessness overcame her at this realization. In a way he had stolen more from her than she had from his family. One's body was the most private thing there was. She had a brief memory of the youth with the fig leaf around which moss had taken root. The green pelt had looked oddly realistic in the dusk.

"Stay there," he ordered, not unkindly, "and I'll fetch your clog. I see it over there." He returned and gave it to her. "And now I will escort you from our land and I do not expect to see you here again."

"There's no need—"

"Oh, but I think there is. And since I came out to walk, it will give me purpose."

They began to climb the hill. She felt shabby beside him in his dark coat and breeches, the long waistcoat with its many small buttons, the fresh white stock. She liked the way his hair grew in a peak and was tied with a bit of black ribbon. Hers straggled in all ways, but it was abundant and much admired by village folk. If they could see her now—

She commenced to hurry, remembering breakfast. To help with the meal was part of her daily work.

"Has Tom Dobbs been here recently?" Morgan asked as they entered the spine of woods at the top of the slope. How well he filled his clothes, Sable thought admiringly. You could see there was flesh and muscle under the smooth cloth and not just emptiness as one imagined when one saw fine young people in church, no wrinkles or sweat, faces without expression. Morgan looked real.

"Tom Dobbs?" she repeated, "not very lately. In the winter. He left me some letters to practice and a book. I read better than I write."

"Read?" He seemed not to believe her. "When? Do you not work in the house and field?"

"I do both. Father does not allow me to skimp. I take a candle to bed."

13

"Yet still you find time to trespass?" he asked drily.

They were in the copse with its brown morning shadows and the pool lay close. "Would you have me work *all* the time?" she demanded.

He laughed again. "You are most direct." This time his amusement seemed kinder and she was quick to seize advantage.

"Please, don't tell Father. He'll beat me, and I do no harm. I'd not take one bird's egg, I promise you. That would be like murder."

"But how would you like it if I came up to your window and stared in at your parents and brothers at supper?"

The notion made Sable smile involuntarily. "There's nothing worth the trouble." She shrugged. "We are plain folk. The kitchen is for use and not ornament. There's nothing—exciting."

"And you think the Hall is?"

"Oh, yes. The statues, the way the ivy moves. The light streaming out over the flagstones—"

"And the fact that it is forbidden."

She said nothing. The pool was there now, sluggish and somehow watchful, as though eyes poked up through the thick scum. Sable began to quicken her footsteps.

"Do you find the pond distasteful?" Morgan kicked a branch away from the narrow track. For a moment they were very close together, his broad body shutting out the dull stretch of green. She looked over her shoulder. The pool was still and yet there was a suggestion of corruption about it, as though something had rotted there, long, long ago and had left something of itself behind.

"The dogs don't like it. They only go in if the sun shines." She evaded the question, preferring not to admit to her sense of disquiet. "I must hurry—"

"Back to a day's toil and a candle to read by. Does that satisfy you?"

"Not always." She was honest, yet she recognized her

14

disloyalty to her household. "But it is my life and that is mapped out for me."

"There will never be anything else?"

"Of course I hope there will be. When Chris weds, there may be changes. My room will be needed and there'll be an extra woman on the farm."

"So you'll be put into service?"

"Maybe. Father's spoken of it." The trees thinned out and she was close to home.

"What's your name?" he asked unexpectedly.

"Sable."

"Where would you get a name like that?" Morgan sounded surprised.

"It's short for Isabel. My cousin never pronounced it properly and it started as a joke. Tom Dobbs says there is an animal in Russia with my name. He says it's dark, like me."

"There is. Its fur is quite valuable."

"May I go? I am later than I meant to be."

"Before you go I ought to tell you that it is—indiscreet— to allow yourself to be seen half-naked, however accidentally. It might have been someone else who saw you. Someone less scrupulous. You do, I take it, know what unscrupulous means?"

"Yes."

"There's a danger in lonely places for girls of your age."

"Danger?"

"You live on a farm, don't you?"

"You know I do."

"Then have you no imagination?" He was staring at her now, the dark-spoked irises conveying a message she understood. When he saw that she did, he said, more gently, "If your brother takes a wife, come round to the Hall and see the housekeeper. Tell her I sent you."

"To the Hall?" she repeated, hardly believing the evidence of her ears.

15

"At least you'd be under our roof and Mistress Perkins would see to it you never had a chance to hang around the windows. Good day to you." He tipped his hat as though she'd been a lady and was striding through the copse before she remembered Father waiting, his brows drawn in anger. It no longer seemed to matter.

She began to run across the dark, furrowed earth.

Sable had expected life to change after that disturbing, but enjoyable, encounter. Almost immediately Chris would bring home the girl he meant to take as wife, they would shift into Sable's room, and she would present herself at Hunter Hall. But her brother bided his time in his slow, country way until she wanted to scream with impatience.

The work of the farm went on, the cooking and the baking, the feeding of hens and cattle, the mucking out, the ploughing, the sowing, the rhythm of crops—corn, clover, rye, barley, rape, and turnips. The hoeing and the harvesting, the patching of work clothes, the sewing of Sunday best.

As she grew older, she had less time for the things that mattered. Girls on the threshold of womanhood were not supposed to stand gawping as the red moon rose from a drift of grey cloud or the glow of the range beautified the bare, ugly kitchen with its cracked brown crocks and scrubbed table. Freedom became a rare, treasured thing.

She had not obeyed Morgan after the first week or two. The ache of deprivation became too great and she would let herself out quietly to run through the haunted spinney with Brutus and Samson and stand among the trees at the top of the slope to watch the house in moonlight.

Very occasionally, on a Sunday, she might see Morgan and his friends riding, wild and noisy, their coattails flying, the girls with plumes on their hats. His brother, Adam, was sometimes with him, tall and inclined to slenderness,

16

and Jane, the younger of the girls, was usually present. The elder, Charlotte, was rarely seen.

One day, passing the farm, Morgan had noticed Sable and had slowed down briefly to stare after her. She had gone to the house that night, drawn back to the window, but having first taken the precaution of smearing her face with mud so that she should remain unseen. The Hunters had company and the ladies wore sack gowns of silk brocade. These were so graceful with their trailing back panel and deep lace cuffs that Sable itched to own one.

Thomas Hunter, a grizzled version of Morgan, sat at one end of the long table and his wife, Sarah, at the other. Mistress Hunter was short with a tendency to plumpness, but she was by no means fat. Though not beautiful, her face showed spirit and determination, and her hair, still more brown than grey, had a lovely sheen. She addressed Morgan more often than anyone else. Intuitively Sable knew the younger son was his mother's favorite. Adam was seated behind a great arrangement of flowers and Sable caught only glimpses of fine, fair-skinned features and an expression of reserve. Jane, too, was fair and prone to curls and looked good-natured. Morgan was like neither.

The scene was so beautiful, with the gleaming fine furniture and the scalloped ceiling half lost in shadow, the arms bathed in candlelight and the illuminated breasts and necks, the fugitive glimmer of jewels, the pyramid of oranges and grapes of frozen velvet, that Sable again forgot caution, pressed forward, and half fell against the window. Heads turned in her direction, drawn by the thud against the glass. Samson, who had been lying by the hearth, bounded to his feet and rushed to the window, rearing up against the pane, tongue lolling.

As Sable got up, she had a glimpse of Morgan's face, the odd smile which told her that in spite of the mud he knew she was there. Thomas Hunter had half risen and was giving angry instructions to one of the powdered footmen.

17

She ran past the nearest statue and towards the hill where she was joined after a few minutes by the dogs. The breath sawed in her chest, but her body felt free and well able to outrun any servant dispatched by their master. The wood opened to receive her, the thin moon hurrying to keep up with her and seeming to wear an expression like that of a disapproving nun.

She laughed at the sight. But the amusement was struck from her by a sound from the copse in which the pond lay half-hidden—a soft, shuffling sound, lost almost immediately. The dogs had stopped, listening. Even the moon was still, bare as a thread, before making its escape behind a cloud, leaving the wood dark. A frog croaked, startling her. Again, the thing shifted. There was something sinister about the noise, as though some slimy, part-decayed object had crawled from the scum and pushed itself from its place of incarceration. It was unlike the dogs to hang back, but she knew they had never cared for the spot. The only place they entered the water was by the clearer stretch at the other side, and that happened in bright sunlight.

She took a step forward. The moon shot out again giving her a glimpse of a figure on the path, something quite shapeless and still. There was no going back, for Hunter had looked incensed and there could be trouble to face in plenty. If there was some sodden body in the pond, it would stay there. Ghosts were intangible, however unfriendly; one could run through them if sufficiently brave. Was she? She might require to be if there were sounds of pursuit.

Out of the obscurity came a grating whisper. "Who is't?" Silence. The figure moved and showed tufted hair, came towards her. "I thought it was you, lass. That laugh of yours, but I thought myself mistaken, for I imagined you in your bed along with the rest. I passed the house and saw it dark, so would not knock. And what's that on your face?"

Tom Dobbs! The dogs went forward without a growl.

They must be used to Tom. Sable remembered Morgan seemed familiar with this man. "Dirt so that I'll not be seen. We'd better go," Sable said. "I roused the Hall folk without meaning to, so we'd best not stay."

"Does your father know you go out?"

"No. He sleeps sound. They all do but me. I seem not to need so much rest."

They moved forward purposefully, the moon picking gleams from Dobbs' hair and eyeballs.

"Are you not going to scold me?" Sable asked, setting aside a branch.

"I'll not praise you. But I can understand. Freedom is important."

"I never stay out long, only an hour or so. My walks do no one any harm."

"There are sometimes those abroad you should not meet. That is my only concern. But all were meant to be free and that is what ails the world. Only a few have liberty. But it will change, you mark my words. No one can conceive the changes in store."

"Morgan Hunter says you were not always—" she blurted.

"A vagrant?" Tom suggested.

"Oh, no. He said 'an eccentric traveller.'"

"Same thing," Tom grunted, plodding sturdily, his shaggy head outlined against the moon. "He's right. He knew me from another place."

"What place?" Sable was intensely curious. Tom had said so little of his past and he had a manner in spite of his obvious poverty that commanded a respect one could not broach with questions. All her family knew of him was that he had little but the Bible he carried everywhere and an overpowering love of God.

"The Hunters go to the Lakes like many others. It's the fashion to love the rustic—so long as no one is asked to soil his hands. They are passionate for mountains, waterfalls, and the like. I lived there once."

19

"Did you have a house?" The dogs had gone back, unnoticed, and the man and girl were alone.

"Aye, I did, young miss." Tom increased his pace, stumbling on the ruts of the cart road.

"Where is it now?" She had a vision of it, broken and tumbled, open to the sky.

"Still standing where it always was."

She fancied she detected a note of sadness in his voice. "But if you're poor—couldn't you have sold it? Then you'd have had some money."

"I did. But I gave the money away."

"Gave it away?" She was incredulous. The shadow of the farm slanted over the barn and the hay shed and the rough moonlit fields.

"You'd best keep your voice down, young Miss Sable. You'll not want to be caught."

"No. But why?"

"All men are equal in the sight of the Lord. He told the rich man to sell all that he had in order to reach the Gates of Heaven—to give his substance to the poor."

"But does it help that you are now without anything?"

"There were families kept alive because of me, women kept from prostitution. And now the goodness in others reaches out to me in turn. I have a greater freedom than ever I had in my house. And my faith."

"But you still have nowhere to put your head tonight," Sable said practically. "Why did you go up to the wood? There's little shelter."

"To look at the moon through the branches. There are no birches elsewhere."

It seemed as good a reason as any. "I'll bring you some bread and cheese from the kitchen," she whispered. "And you must go in the hay shed. It's warm there. Come to breakfast. You know you'll be welcome."

"Did you practice your letters? Have you read the book I left?"

"Every day. Well—almost. There's much to do."

"Do you understand it?"

"Most. More and more. It's like finding another country." Her voice rose again with enthusiasm. "I think you'll be pleased with my progress."

"Hush!" Tom growled, "or you'll find your luck won't hold. And remember to wash!"

"I'll get the food. Some ale—"

"Nay. I drank from the brook. But bread and cheese will be welcome."

She opened the back door, thankful that the hinges were oiled, cut a wedge from the cheese that lay pallid and shining where the moon came in, took out a hunk of bread. Tom waited outside. "God go with you," he said very quietly and moved off towards the barn. She stood there until he was out of sight, reliving the excitement and the fears of the night.

After she was curled up on the mattress upstairs, the blankets pulled around her, she thought of Morgan's smile with its suggestion of complicity. He had expected her to return! He had never really said she must stay away. The words he had used remained in her mind. "I do not expect to see you here again." And he had not because her face had been daubed with mud! She found herself laughing softly and stifled the noise in her pillow.

The following day was Sunday, so there was not the usual urgency. There was still work to do, of course, but her mother always insisted that Sable did only what was necessary when Tom Dobbs called. "Her letters are important," she would tell her husband.

"What use to learn beyond her station?" he'd grumble. "Letters will not raise dough or bring cheese."

"Maybe not. But d'you not see how different she is when she finds out summat new?"

"Happen she does. But it's housework and farmwork

21

she'll make a living from. Her man won't expect her looking down her nose at him for putting a cross on a paper."

"Tom says it'd be a waste—"

"I like Tom Dobbs well, but some is born to crosses and some to lettering."

"They don't all have chances," Mother would retort, always on Sable's side.

Almost two years had passed, Sable thought, since the first time she had spoken to Morgan. Two years older, two years more aware, still driven out when the wildness took hold of her. Tom Dobbs had opened her mind and shown her things she wanted to do, but she began to fear she'd never experience them. The work she would be given at the Hall would be even less interesting than her tasks on the farm. Fires to lay, coals to heave, scrubbing, polishing, dishes and pots to wash, chamber pots to empty, and beds to make. Never time to stand and stare. Mistress Perkins was a martinet, she'd been told, and indeed she looked very unbending in church, and all the kitchen maids had red, ugly hands with peeling vegetables.

And yesterday she had heard that Morgan was nearly finished with the university at Cambridge and would be going away from home. Some of his friends were taking politics seriously and some like young Mr. Pitt and Mr. Wilberforce were thinking of seeking Parliamentary seats.

If Morgan followed their example—and his father had the money to subsidize a political candidate, so the locals assured one another—he'd be expected to live in London and she'd never see him again. Not that he was going to worry about a skinny farm girl who trespassed on his land and had the impudence to look in at Hunter occasions. But if she were to work her fingers to the bone at the Hall, she'd want the reward of a sight of him at least. Politicians were busy men who worked hard, and if they had recesses they went to their summer retreats to look at hills and water. Morgan would holiday where he always did, in the

Lake District, and he'd go out of her life. Why must people grow up? He was a man, she all but a woman, and intended, most likely, for some herdman or plowman in a neighboring dale. The prospect daunted her.

She frowned as her strong teeth bit into the bacon that was her Sunday treat. The thought of the future had taken the pleasure out of one of her favorite foods. The butter on the bread was thicker than the usual scrape because Tom was there and an honored guest. There were few guests at Highmoor.

Tom Dobbs was about her father's age, a short, broad-shouldered man, his hair rough, his gaze direct. Sable noticed that he had a bruise on his forehead.

"Did you hurt yourself?" she asked.

"Someone hurt me." He went on eating, his jaws moving rhythmically.

"Why?"

"Have you never noticed how folk attack anything different? Something they don't understand. Someone who is deformed, perhaps, or ugly. A blackbird pecks at the bird that is white. I was talking about God in a marketplace and boys threw stones at me. I am sorry for their ignorance." He laid his hand on the book that lay beside him as though he must not let it out of his sight. There was the mark of a healed gash on that hand.

"I'm sorry," she said, with new insight into the difficulties of his way of life.

"You must use your knowledge to better ends," Tom told her, finishing his bread. "You've been given the gift of an intellect. Use it wisely."

"There," Mistress Martin interposed, nudging Sable's father. "Did you hear that?"

"Aye, I heard." But he scowled. That he did not want Sable to be different was obvious. But her mother was not without influence. There was an obstinacy behind the plain, freckled face that would not let go of what seemed

23

important, a quickness of mind that was lacking in her husband and sons. Sable thought it a pity that her mother had not had some chance, that some past Tom Dobbs had not lain close to freezing by her door and tried to repay hospitality with teaching. What might her mother not have done? Would she still have married a farmer who could print only a cross and was happy for his sons to do the same?

Sable, despondent, could see her future stretch ahead without visible change. There would be the highlights of plow-match and harvest-end with its poetry, the mell cakes and the last sheaf, the rowan collars for the lambs in spring—rowans that were taken from the Hunter woods! There would be the occasional sheep-meets with their familiar junketings. Familiar. That was the word that oppressed her. What she wanted was the unexpected. She had loved every forbidden excursion to Morgan's house, but the one she would always remember was rolling down the hill like a hard-boiled egg at Easter and finding herself prisoner under his polished boot.

"Sable," her mother said, rising to clear the crocks. "Go fetch some catkins. You know they help at lambing and two or three of the ewes might birth today."

"Aye," her father agreed, the look of displeasure removed. Sable blessed his belief in superstition. She might have been struggling with reluctant cheese curds, but now she could walk by the river. Working in the kitchen at Hunter Hall would be less attractive than being in the open air, even if the autumn and winter winds took the skin off your face.

"I'll come with you," Tom said, picking up the worn Bible and putting it in his capacious pocket. "And should the ewes begin to lamb, I'll help you, John. It's as much God's work as preaching in marketplaces and no fear of a stone to my head into the bargain."

The day was as pleasant outside as in the sunlit kitchen. The blue sky was full of white, fluffy clouds and there were primroses by the hedge. The spring crop poked tender shoots out of the purplish soil and the small shadows of the clouds raced over the fells like rabbits playing.

"Did I remember right last night?" he asked when they were out of earshot of the house.

"That I had mud on my face and met you by the pond? Yes."

"And gave me supper and a bed I'd have had to wait twenty-four hours for, since I take nothing I am not first offered," Tom replied. "But that is not what I meant. I seem to recall you said 'Morgan Hunter says you were not always an eccentric traveller.' Now when were you in conversation with Thomas Hunter's son?"

"One May morning. I fancied to wash my face in their grass."

"And?"

"Morgan was sleepless and wanted to walk. He—he saw me and somehow we spoke of you."

"There must have been a reason for that."

"I—I remember now. He used a word he thought I'd not understand and he was surprised when I did. So I said you'd helped me."

Tom stopped by the willow where the catkins hung down like lambs' tails. "You'll get all you want and more here."

"Morgan ties his own hair, not like his friends. They have wigs."

"He'll have to do as they do in London. The guild of wigmakers is strong."

"You mean they can tell him he must have a wig?"

"So they say."

"And what of that freedom you spoke of?"

"I did warn you, young miss, that there would be

25

changes. The world will be vastly different when you are a few years older. Did you tell John you met and walked with Hunter?"

"No. But I was late that morning and I would have been beaten if Mother had not said she too liked to go out early on May Day and as there was no grass close by, naturally I'd have to go and look for some. She championed me as she always does."

"There's grass here."

"But the earth is all rumpled and shows through. And there are moles," she objected.

"What else did Morgan say?"

"That when Chris weds I could go to Mistress Perkins and ask for a post in the kitchen."

Tom gave a kind of grunt and asked, "And is that what you want?"

"At first," Sable said, picking catkins energetically, "I thought it was. A chance to be in that big house. But the more I read, the more I see it's a trap. I've listened to the women at market and outside church and it's clear I'd be more of a prisoner there than being at home. Only where else can I go? The parson's and the doctor's wives are well suited and their purse won't run to another girl. And if Chris weds, there's no place for me. Then Joe will follow Chris, for they seem to think what one does, the other must do. They are more sheep than sheep." She laughed and looked down from her perch, unaware of the attractive picture she presented. She had filled out since Morgan had called her a skinny farm wench. Her black eyes and dark brown hair were an interesting combination. But it was the intelligence that radiated from her freckled face that was her chief asset, that and her good white teeth.

"So you'll wed and tend geese," Tom said and took the bundle of catkins from her.

"Must that be all?" The light died from her face.

"There's no one you love, young miss?"

"No one."

"We'll see. We'll see, then," Tom muttered mysteriously, brushing pollen from the vast, frayed skirts of his coat. "I must go on a journey."

"But you've just come! You usually stay for a bit."

"I can't divulge more. In the morning I'll set off for Windermere. I've a friend there." And that was the most he would say for all her efforts to draw him out. But Sable was conscious of an excitement she found it difficult to control. Tom Dobbs's journey was on her behalf. There seemed nothing surer. She sang as she hung up the catkins that were meant to speed the safe birth of Highmoor's first lambs of the season.

Chapter 2

It seemed the greatest of coincidences that Chris should come in the following evening to say that he'd decided to court Jem Strong's daughter Pansy. Mistress Martin, who had been quiet all day after Tom departed so suddenly, forgot her disappointment in a mixture of relief and regret. Relief that Chris had chosen so sensibly, regret that she'd be superseded in her firstborn's life. But Pansy was a good girl, strong and loyal. She could ask no better daughter-in-law.

Sable had a shiver in her spine when she heard the news. It would take Tom some weeks to tramp across country and on to the lake. There would be the return journey. What if Chris decided to be cried three times in church, then marry Pansy Strong without wasting any more time?

Mistress Martin seemed to have the same idea, for she dressed herself very carefully one afternoon and departed on a mysterious errand. She came back, her cheeks very flushed and her head held high. Sable, who had been feeding the hens, made her way through the bustling, pecking fowls and said, "What is it, Mother?"

"That Mistress Perkins! Who does she think she is?"

"What has she done?"

"Well," her mother said angrily, tugging at her bonnet strings, "I was thinking that Chris and Pansy could be wanting your room and we must begin to think of *your* future, so I went to call on Mistress Perkins. It seemed the obvious place to go. But I didn't want to put you out as a kitchen maid, not with your lettering, only she don't see it that way. Asked if you were too good to consort with the lasses in the scullery where everyone begins. You should have heard the way she said 'consort,' with her long, sharp nose all screwed up. I could have *struck* her!"

"And was that all?" Sable was taut with anxiety.

"Not by a long chalk, it wasn't. Said a lot about tenant farmers putting on airs and said the Master was particular about the girls who applied for posts and how unheard-of it was for anyone to want something better for a farm girl who was probably as thick as a post and how she could get the pick of any lass between here and Hull."

She threw the bonnet onto the dresser with one vicious movement.

"So—they won't have me at the Hall?"

"No, lass."

Sable wondered guiltily what her mother would say if she knew of Morgan's offer of two years ago. It would salve her mother's pride to tell her now, but what kind of life could she expect under the thumb of a martinet who would be sure to hold it against her that she'd crossed swords with Mistress Martin and had lost? Better to say nothing and thank her lucky stars that she was still free to await Tom's return.

"What shall we do now?" Mistress Martin asked distractedly, fastening on her apron and putting her bonnet away more carefully now that her fury was diminished.

"Can we wait?"

"Wait? But you should be properly settled."

"Till Tom Dobbs comes back. Just until then."

"Why, what's he to do with it?"

"I think he has some idea—some place where there may be a suitable position."

"So *that's* why he went! I did wonder. It's not like him to go so fast and he usually does stay to lend a hand in return for his keep. I feel better now, child. Why did you not say? I'd not have worried so."

"He said not to, in case it didn't come to anything."

"Well, if it does, there's one person shall hear of it straight away," Mistress Martin said with grim satisfaction and poured flour into a large basin to start off a batch of bread.

Chris and Pansy decided on a summer wedding, which would just give Tom time to complete the double journey. Sable, remembering the large bruise on his forehead and the healed gash on his hand, was afraid he might not come back at all. If, as he said, people attacked those who were different, then one day the attack might be fatal and the preacher could lie dead under the night sky or under the sun in a market town. People could be so easily roused. Only recently, word had filtered through from London of the ghastly Gordon Riots which had resulted in the death of many. There had been dreadful demonstrations against Catholics and much damage to property, with prisons broken open and the inmates released.

Tom came back one hot afternoon. He looked brown and there were no visible marks of injury upon him though his wide-skirted coat was dustier and more threadbare than ever and his hair looked as if it had gone through a haystack. The big buckled shoes were cracking with use and Sable conjectured where he would get new ones. But Tom had a way of commanding respect and affection in spite of his oddness. He'd never need to go barefoot.

Sable ran out to greet him. He set aside the blackthorn stick and smiled at her excitement.

"I wondered if you'd really come. And here you are!"

"Surely you knew I would?"

"I couldn't help worrying. Those boys with stones—"

"The warmer weather must mellow them. It's been eggs and turnips of late."

"Don't you mind?"

"My pride does, but one subdues that." His eyes twinkled and Sable was immediately happy.

Mistress Martin, on her way back from the dairy, gave a cry of pleasure and began to run towards the house. "Why are you keeping him outside, Sable? Go in, Tom, and sit down."

When the guest was seated, his great bush of hair fired by sunlight, Mistress Martin could not contain her curiosity. "They say the Lakes are bonny," she ventured.

"Aye, they are. Very bonny."

Sable, perched on the wide window sill, her gown of faded pink grown too tight for her new, womanly shape, could stand the preliminary skirmishing no longer. "Did you see your friend? And is there any place for me? You see Chris—"

"I heard. There's talk in the dale," Tom said calmly, Bible on his lap where the light showed up its shabbiness and the fraying edges of the cover. "The lad's to be wed."

"Well, then?"

"I was teasing you," Tom told her, drinking copiously of the milk he was offered. "I have seen my friend—"

"A lady, is she?" Mistress Martin asked anxiously, doubtless thinking of the upstart Mistress Perkins. "It is a lady?"

"In every way. She is Lady Agatha Chryston of Knowehead, near Windermere."

Lady Chryston! Not even the Hunters were nobility, their position being built on trade. Sable's mother colored with emotion. Instinctively, as though she were in the great woman's presence, she hid her roughened hands in her apron. "She's not to be a scullery maid, is she? Our Sable?"

"Am I likely to want the girl to waste her opportunities? No, the reason I went so far is because Lady Agatha was a friend of my parents and she insists I remain on visiting terms in spite of my change of fortune. She is an unfortunate person, a woman of intelligence plagued by ill-health and surrounded by treasures she no longer enjoys. She has employed companions, but I fear she finds them either dull or uncongenial. She wishes for stimulation and never finds it."

"She sounds difficult," Mistress Martin observed doubtfully. "Downright difficult."

"She can be. But she's also kind in her own brusque way. She regrets, I think, that she never had children, but she inherited, alas, her father's looks and an unfortunate masculinity, a great impediment to finding a husband. She became suspicious of would-be wooers and could never be convinced that they might have more affection for her than for her property." He spoke as though he had the affection Lady Agatha had always doubted, Sable thought, as she tried to visualize the unknown woman. "But, she did marry late in life and was happy for a time."

"But what would my lass be doing? This Lady Chryston sounds to have servants enough."

"She has few. Her illness makes her almost a recluse and her tastes are simple. The house, I fear, is somewhat neglected, but what she has is a splendid library. The bindings may decay for lack of attention, but it is a place where the mind is important. The presence of a lively girl could do great good. Lady Agatha has lost heart since she was widowed."

"Will Sable be happy there?"

"I venture to think she'll be as happy there as anywhere. Of course it's too far off to do much visiting but I can bring news from time to time. You can rest assured, though, that your child will not be relegated to the kitchen. We talked of Sable for some time and Lady Agatha expresses interest in her. She'll have certain duties but there will also be time for reading and discussion, as much for the employer's benefit as for the child's. I left my friend with her spirits uplifted."

"And what if this Lady Chryston wearies of the lass? What then?" Sable's mother was practical.

"She would never see her destitute, if that's what you fear. She'd send her back or find her another position. But I doubt if the experiment will fail."

"Then I should be happy for Sable to go. What think you, child?" Mistress Martin smoothed her rumpled apron.

"I want to. But what about Father?"

"Yes. What about your father!" Mother and daughter exchanged glances and fell silent.

When John Martin returned from the field, Tom expressed a desire to see the sheep. They were gone for a long time and there was afterwards no real opposition to Sable going for a trial period to Knowehead. Lady Agatha had provided payment for the coach journey, since John would be hard-pressed to find such an amount.

Chris and Pansy went ahead with their plans to be wed and had the banns called in Daggleby Church. Sable looked around the pews for a sight of Morgan but saw only Adam Hunter, the elder brother, fair and abstracted. His was not an easy face to assess, she decided, disappointed that she was not to see Morgan before the departure to Windermere. Tall and reserved, Adam dressed quietly and had none of his brother's exuberant presence. His eyes and his mouth were sensitive and he was attentive towards his mother, she noticed, approving.

Tom Dobbs went away early next morning. Sable kissed him good-bye and thanked him for his efforts on her behalf. "I will see you at Knowehead," he told her, having given her copious instructions, then walked sturdily down the rutted track, his old dark blue coat still showing traces of past splendor, his leonine mane tamed with pump water and caught with a bit of ribbon from Mistress Martin's sewing box. The ribbon would drop out unnoticed, sooner or later, Sable knew. The buttons would fall, one by one, from the coat and surely his shoes would not take him five miles. He disappeared with a final flourish of his blackthorn stick, leaving the leafy lane curiously empty.

She went back inside to stitch a seam of the new gown she was to take with her. Sable would have loved a sack dress but had been told such a dress must be made of silk and was only for ladies. Mistress Martin, however, was not without ingenuity and had copied one of the Sunday gowns belonging to a visitor to Hunter Hall. She had memorized the dress from a vantage point behind a large tombstone in Daggleby churchyard as its owner dawdled down the path with eyes for no one but Adam. The material was modest, but there was no help for that, the color, a flowered yellow, making up for much the garment otherwise lacked. The petticoat under the open robe was of a plain maize shade, and there was a muslin bonnet to wear with it, the white enhanced with a yellow ribbon. Sable was to save her wages to buy another in Windermere.

The night before she was to leave home, she went to bed as usual and lay for some time watching the moonlit patterns on the floor. When she judged the household to be asleep she got up quietly, put on the old pink gown, slid her feet into the clogs, and went out. She ran, uncaring of the consequences, and stood at the top of the slope. The house, a confusion of deep blue shadow, was lit with oblongs of light. Farmers retired to bed early, worn out with hard work and the necessity of rising early. The Hunters had no such need. They would be dining now, the table littered with glass and china and half-filled decanters and flickering candles that softened and beautified the plainest face.

There was no sign of the dogs. They were, most likely, being fed in the vast kitchen. She must, Sable decided, have one last look before she went to her new life. A deep sadness came upon her, a feeling so raw and unexpected that she found herself in danger of crying. But it passed quickly in a flood of optimism. She was going somewhere better. The Hall would still be here when she eventually came back to visit her parents. And she could recall every step, every stone of the distance between Highmoor and this great mansion, every patch of lichen on those statues down there. Each window in its setting of thick stone. The shape of trees and clipped hedges in the gardens. How the moor still stretched out rough talons to take hold of this patch of civilization. She could see it any time she chose even if she was about to travel to the other side of the country.

Drawn like a moth to a flame, she began to descend the slope, her pale dress glimmering against the sighing grass. Quietly, she stole towards the frozen statuary, the wide, glowing window. The meal was finished and not yet cleared away, the chairs were empty, the remnants of food were still enticing. A footman moved out of a patch of shadow and Sable crouched behind the ivied niche until he had gone. Another window beckoned. She crept cautiously towards the yellow beacon and peered into the room.

Her heart bumped hurtfully as she recognized Morgan lounging against a marble fireplace flushed with pink from the fire's glow. There was someone else in the room, someone who was hidden by the fold of the heavy red curtain. Morgan laughed and beckoned with an imperious finger. A girl moved into sight, a tallish creature in ivory satin that was dimpled with the same pink shadow that lay on the marble surround. Sable had a glimpse of a profile she did not recognize, a cluster of fair ringlets, bare pink shoulders; then, Morgan's arms were thrown around the unknown girl and the room was suddenly still and quiet. Even the smooth satin folds of the gown did not move. Only the finger of the clock on the mantel crept on.

And then, Adam Hunter appeared in the half-open doorway, freezing instantly. He stared for a minute, his eyes bleak, then retreated, merging once more with the shadows, so that Sable was no longer sure if she had really seen him. Morgan, she thought stupidly, Morgan and a girl in white. But the thought hurt as she had not realized it could. When had her feelings turned to love?

To think too much about Morgan would do no good, Sable told herself. She must be sensible. Morgan moved in another world. He was bound to meet a girl one day who would claim his attention and affections, a girl of whom he would not be ashamed. Once having faced up to the unpalatable fact, Sable was surprised to find the knowledge bearable instead of bitter.

She did not sleep for long, but rose early to wash and brush her hair, to pack the last articles in the sturdy wooden box that contained her few clothes. Then she went outside. She had to swallow hard to keep down the lump that rose in her throat as the hens began to stir, imagining she had risen to feed them. She had come to know every feather, every comb, every bright brown eye. Her father knew better than to take one for the pot if she was there. It was always done in her absence, leaving a small gap in her life, another passing regret, for there was always another to take its place. On a farm one recognized the inevitability of change, arrived at an understanding.

Then, suddenly, everyone else was up, Chris and Joe looking at her awkwardly, knowing there should be some kind of farewell but not wanting to sound foolish. Mistress Martin bustled noisily, her tongue sharper than usual, and wrapped a parcel of food for the journey.

"And do put summat under your dress on Jem's cart seat," she admonished, pushing Sable onto a chair at the table and popping a larger than usual portion of bacon in front of her, a treat reserved usually only for Sunday.

"I will, Mother."

Chris began to tease her in his slow way, Joe joining in because he copied everything his elder brother did.

Only her father was silent, eating his way stolidly through breakfast, refusing to meet her eyes. Then he rose, rolled up his shirt sleeves, and walked to the door.

"Will you not say good-bye, Father?"

He hesitated in mid stride, then growled, "Good-bye," and was gone.

"He's upset," Mistress Martin said, seeing Sable's expression. "Tossed half the night. Thought he heard someone astir, but I told him he was mistaken."

Sable flushed. "I could not sleep either. It would be me he heard. It was not the boys. They snored away as they always do."

"We've good consciences, that's why," Chris said.

"And I have not?"

"You're a deep one," Joe told her, mopping up his plate with a hunk of bread and cramming the sloppy morsel into his mouth. "Well, this won't get the work done. Don't get too fancy up there in Knowehead, will you?"

Sable was gripped by a spasm of pure excitement. "Sorry I won't see the wedding but you want a bed to come back to, Chris, don't you? Not much use marrying, else!" She laughed as her brother turned pink.

38

She was tying on her new bonnet when she heard the cart arrive.

"Be a good girl," her mother said, turning a little pale now that the moment had come.

"Of course, I will."

"Send a letter by Tom. It'll take its time coming, the pace he travels at, but he can read it to us."

"I'll tell you everything." Her brothers shouldered the box and took it out. Jem Strong called out, "Come on, Sable. I've to get to York this morning! And you've a coach to catch. It won't wait for you."

Swiftly enfolded by her mother, hugged briefly by Chris and Joe, Sable found herself on the cart, her new gown protected by a large colored handkerchief hastily drawn across the seat by Mistress Martin. And then the big wheels were turning, the figures of her family and the shape of the house growing smaller with every revolution until they were completely gone. There was the immensity of the moor, a tantalizing glimpse of Hunter Hall from the other side, half-shrouded in trees and shrubs, then nothing much until the church spire at Daggleby and the little green where children played and dogs barked. There were hedge roses between the thorns after the village was left behind, and a drift of wild garlic along the river bank.

Jem said little. He was turning his business over in his slow countryman's fashion. Sable thought of the way Morgan had held and kissed the fine lady with the ringlets the previous night, remembered Adam stock-still by the door and the look of bitterness no one but herself had seen. Almost as if the girl in the white dress concerned him. But it had nothing to do with her. All it had achieved was to show her how wrongly she had behaved. Being rebellious and daring at fourteen or fifteen was a different matter from eavesdropping at seventeen. Morgan had been right. It was a form of theft and one which had done her no good.

Farm after farm and barn upon barn followed fields and

a great spread of plains cut into dreamy patchwork. Smudges of hazy copses and woods. An immense summer sky and York, shimmering in pale nebula, then coming into focus with its narrow streets and stalls around the market cross, children, wild and dirty, playing in the gutters where refuse stank in the hot sun.

The coach was already there, older and dustier than she'd imagined, the doors standing open. Jem lifted her box in strong, whipcorded arms and deposited it in the basket at the back. It seemed inconceivable that he would go, that soon she would be seated with strangers, going to strangers, to a place she had never seen. But it was the greatest challenge she had ever faced and she liked the change, pitting her wits against the unknown.

"Good-bye, lass. Good luck." Jem, a clay pipe stuck in his mouth, was flicking his horses into lethargic action.

She waved, watched him engulfed in a stream of folk and vehicles, then was conscious of the tide of noise and confusion that surrounded her. She was aware, too, that the new gown was noticed and approved. The excitement returned. How fortunate she was to be allowed this chance. The Lakes were conceded to be quite beautiful and Lady Agatha would never be dull if she fulfilled Tom's description.

There was a clatter of hooves somewhere, a man laughing. Something about the sound was very familiar. She was fifteen and rolling down the slope, staring up at a shadowed face. Craning, she saw that Morgan was dismounting some distance away, his mount's bridle tied to a rail while he spoke to a man who had emerged from an inn at the edge of the square. Sable watched him hungrily, glad she had not, after all, gone without a last sight of him, yet conscious of the futility of such thinking.

While she debated whether to wait or to go in search of the coachman, Morgan turned abruptly from his conversation and began to cross the busy square. He glanced at the coach impersonally, then noticed the fresh yellow gown and dainty bonnet. She almost enjoyed the stupefaction in his gaze when he recognized her. "Sable? It is Sable Martin?"

"Yes."

"But why are you here?" He did not ask why she was dressed as she was, but she knew that the question was there.

"I am going to Windermere." She wished, uselessly, she had not trespassed last night. The scene she had witnessed obtruded, spoiling the moment.

"Why?"

"To stay with a friend." It was not strictly true, but a friend of Tom's could just conceivably be hers if one believed in Tom's idea of a universal brotherhood.

"What friend?" How persistent he was and how pleasant his appearance.

"Lady Chryston," she answered and was perversely glad of his astonishment. "I am to be a companion."

"A companion?" She could have laughed at the way he repeated everything she said, only that glimpse of him with the girl in white still had the power to sadden her.

"To Lady Agatha? But she's so old—" He looked doubtful. "And strange."

"You know her then?" Sable asked quickly.

"Quite well. Knowehead is not far from our own house. But how unexpected!"

"Not at all. I have known for some time I was to go."

He smiled then and she did not know why. "It will be a big change for you. Are you settled in the coach?"

"Jem put my box in the back."

"Your fellow travellers will be snatching a meal before departure. Aren't you hungry?"

"No. And I have some food with me, should I want it. I'll be all right."

"You should sit inside then, out of the sun. How you've

grown." His look assessed her, half-amused, half-reflective. Did he recall the abandonment of their first meeting? She was sure that he did. But none of it mattered—could ever matter.

He held out his hand and she took it briefly. "Who knows?" he said. "We may meet again. Will you creep out of Knowehead to watch us at our play? Oh, I should not have said that! It was a child who wandered, and you are no longer that lawless creature. Good day, Miss Sable, and Godspeed." He tipped his hat and smiled, then strode off without a backward look.

She climbed inside the coach and tried to compose herself. A musty smell stole out of the battered seats and the square was filled with noises both gay and discordant. Screams proceeded from a black-mouthed narrow street and a dirty woman in a frilled bonnet threw slops into the gutter. Her head began to ache with the heat and the lack of sleep. Without realizing it, Sable slid sideways, her cheek against the window. The sounds and smells receded into a kind of peace.

She was wide awake again when they reached Harrogate which was very grand and flocked with ladies in elegant gowns, an impression spoiled somewhat by the very strong smell that emanated from the famous sulfur wells.

Her fellow travellers were loquacious and as she stared out of the window, her lips dry with summer dust, she heard how the one-legged man had lost his limb at Bunker Hill and how the father of the lugubrious gentleman in the stained waistcoat and untidy wig had fought at Quebec. A much-made-up lady with the purple feathers was an actress who regaled the company with a spirited rendering of "The Bunter's Wedding" at the next stop. The other woman passenger had helped to sew the wedding garments for the Queen. The King, the seamstress said, was more in love with one of the bridesmaids, a lovely lady called Lady Sarah Lennox, but he'd not denied his German wife her rights, since they'd produced no less than fifteen children.

Sable's heavy eyes closed again. She had no tales with which to divert the company, but it was fascinating just to listen to theirs. It had been generous of Lady Agatha to insist she journeyed as an inside passenger. Although it was at times almost unbearably hot, she was spared much of the dust that afflicted the outer travellers.

The only thing she found actively disagreeable was the inn at which the first night was spent, which smelt of sweaty garments and had bugs in the beds. Then the great county of Yorkshire again swam by in a pageant composed of richness and bareness, one minute plunged into a scene of foaming water and proud houses, the next of bald hills and vast silences where predatory birds hovered.

Westmorland was gentler, the landscape more minute, each dwelling a small tableau to be filed in the mind's eye. She was to be met at Kendal, and as the coach lumbered dangerously round narrow curves on the last stage of the journey, her anticipation once more overcame tiredness.

She descended warily, unsure of her reception. There was a castle, she noted, beyond the cluster of narrow streets and the usual clutter of a market town where business never really ends. Tracks ran off into uplands and the hills were quite close. The day's heat had brought the threat of thunder and the sky and the mountains to the west were divided in color by the barest shade of mauve. As though to compensate for the menace of a storm, the sun shone brilliantly so that the river was a sheet of silver.

There was a great clatter as her box was thrown from the basket to land on the none too clean cobbles. She looked about her uncertainly. All at once, there was the brisk clop of wheels, an excited shriek from two small boys seated on the steps of the market cross. A gig clattered and bounced over the smooth rounds of the stones, and in the driver's seat sat an enormous Negro, bare to the waist, his breeches of scarlet ingrained with a powdering of dirt from the dry road. He would have been an arresting sight without the red patch he wore over one hollow eye socket and the raised weals that marked his back. They were old scars, she decided, shading her eyes so that he would not be embarrassed by her scrutiny. Old, vicious scars that would never smooth into the purplish skin.

The gig stopped by the coach, the target of every eye in the street. People leaned from their windows to stare the better. How it must have hurt to be flogged like that, Sable thought, and wondered how he had lost his eye. The shadow of some past malignancy lay over the unspoken questions. A powerful black arm barred her way suddenly. "Is you Miss Martin?" The voice was deep and rumbling like the approaching thunderstorm, yet soft and not unkind in its dark center.

"I is—I mean, I am." Sable flushed, conscious that ears were strained to hear this conversation. A woman tittered, then was silent as the great, tightly curled head turned in her direction. His one eye had the effect of a Medusa.

"Then be so good as to climb in de gig. Am dat yo box?"

Just in time Sable stopped herself from saying, "It am." She nodded and the man bent down, swung it up as if it had been a toy, and placed it behind the seat. The wheels were huge and the shafts high, but there was a little step between horse and wheel. Sable lifted her skirts and put one foot in the stirruplike contrivance, then pulled herself up sharply to enter the neat little vehicle. From her point of vantage she could stare down at the broad, white body of the horse, the smooth, heavy haunches. Between them the man and the horse made a powerful combination.

The Negro sprang after her, light-footed and graceful for his size, then the gig was in motion, scattering the crowds of country folk who gawped and whispered. Sable was conscious of a sense of disbelief. Yet she knew that this was happening. Her fingers touched the smooth side of the gig, the cushion on the seat. Her body swayed with the motion of wheels rebounding over road and rut. Out of the corner of her eye she could see the crude scars as the man bent to adjust a rein. He carried no whip, as most men did, and she knew why. The whip was a symbol of brutality he could not forget. She pictured the end of the lash flicking his cheek and biting into the soft round of his eye and found her hands tightly clenched as she dwelt on his pain.

The dry road wound upwards. The shapes of the hills became abnormally clear. A soporific warmth came to meet her, then a drop of rain as big as a penny fell onto her skirt. The Negro interrupted his pagan song to pull at the rein and cajole the horse to go faster. Next minute, the gig was flashing along in a blur of wet greens and the hot rain fell faster. It seemed the most exhilarating thing Sable had ever done. She tried to picture her mother's face if she could see the new gown and bonnet as they now looked, heavy with water and plastered to her face and body as though she had gone swimming in them. She began to laugh and could not stop. The man turned, his own face split into a huge smile, then he went back to his driving as the gig lurched round a snakelike bend. A crack of lightning blanched the thin trunk of a birch, but Sable was unafraid. It was all part of a strange and beautiful experience she would never be able to describe to another person.

The heaviness had left the sky by the time the wide silver sheet of the lake appeared, and the birds were carolling with relief that the storm had been no worse. It was all calm and peaceful, totally unreal.

They stopped where the road seemed about to plunge into the lake. A wild little track shot off between burgeoning banks which the gig skidded perilously to enter, slipping a little in the mud as though to tumble backwards to the water. The big, patient hooves gained a foothold and

45

the vehicle was soon drawn towards the crumbling gate-posts of an overgrown drive, lush with convolvulus and drapes of ivy and huge pastel blossoms of hydrangea.

The house was rambling, without the dignity of Hunter Hall. It crouched in a welter of sodden green like a neglected woman taken to drink. It had a ripeness, a careless charm, but it was more that of a soiled but attractive bed robe than of a classic evening gown. It was too ornamented, peeling in places, yet it exuded an almost sensual hankering for attention. Roses sprawled cheek by jowl with foxgloves and willow herbs, and nasturtiums and marigolds rioted in unweeded borders. As everywhere in the Lake District, there was the sound of running water.

The Negro sprang down, again humming his pagan song. A thin woman appeared in the doorway, tall and peaky-faced, her skin leathery like that of the farmers' wives around Daggleby. Her expression was unfriendly and some of Sable's anticipation was dissipated.

"Are you the Martin girl?" the woman demanded, her face sallow against the plain dark gown and skimpy collar.

"Y—yes." Sable stood up, feeling foolish in her sodden clothing. She lowered herself onto the stirrup in a draggle of hampering skirts and slid to the ground, which showed traces of the heavy downpour. Large raindrops still clung to the dusty surfaces of windowpanes, glittering dully as they slid very slowly downwards to collect on the sills.

"You're soaked. Pity that heathen had not thought to shelter in Kendal until the rain was past. But it's too late now for regrets. Come in and we'll get you dry. Ben, you fool, bring in the girl's box."

Sable was ushered into a dim hall, cool after the heat outside, and conducted into a small sitting room filled with once beautiful chairs, their coverings faded into soft colors of rose and grey and cinnamon. The curtains were thin as old flags and a mirror with a dirty gold frame was dim and spotted. The Negro followed them, the box held easily on one mighty shoulder, then he set it on the floor and went away. Reflections moved in the marred glass, trembled on the worn carpet.

The woman went to a chest of drawers and took out a large towel. Like everything else it had once been expensive. There was a large *C* embroidered in one corner in washed-out blue thread. "Now get undressed; put on fresh clothing while I find a brush for your hair."

"I have a brush." She would not enjoy using one that belonged to someone else.

"Very well. Be as quick as you can, for Lady Agatha wishes to see you. I'll come back for those wet things." The tone was sharp, almost peremptory.

"Thank you."

Alone, Sable opened the box and took out the gown that had previously been the one she wore on Sundays. She towelled herself vigorously, the blood leaping under the skin invigoratingly, her cheeks glowing. Then she dried her hair and brushed it into damp waves and ringlets, thanking God there was a natural curl in it and that she'd not be entirely unprepossessing. The exhilaration of the drive from Kendal had all but gone, but she knew it would come back later. She was relieved to find that the thin woman was not, after all, Lady Chryston. How pretty all these muted things had once been. That chair had been scarlet, the other jade. And from the window she had glimpses of a mildewed terrace where a cracked fountain no longer dispensed water. There was a stone lion too, eroded with time, with traces of orange lichen in his eye sockets and in the tattered folds of his mane.

"Come with me," the woman ordered, crossing the room to pick up the discarded garments and stalking out again. Sable followed.

Somewhere in the distance, a voice shrieked. "Ben boy! Ben boy! Gadzooks! Hey nonny no. Hey nonny no." Sable's stomach muscles tightened. Could Lady Agatha be mad? But, no, Tom had described her as ill and suspicious of outsiders, but there had been no mention of insanity. He'd never have let her come if there had been anything to fear.

The thin woman pushed open a door disclosing a huge, shadowy room into which fugitive bars of sunlight ate like an acid. The brilliance burned holes in the carpet, which, like the one in the small room, was almost bleached of color, and in the velvets of the chairs and sofa. It touched the dulled surfaces of chased silver and china vases, candlesticks, a vast ornate tea jar and the great straggling chandelier that hung from the ceiling as though it was weary and would prefer to fall to the floor in a search for rest.

The remainder of the room was dim, for the windows were dirty and the garden grew right up to the glass. Sable could see no more of her employer than a seated shadow, the shape obscured by a rug that hung over the woman's lap and a shawl round the shoulders, as though even in summer she felt cold in her bones. Between the seated figure and the window hung a huge birdcage in which crouched a tousled parrot, the feathers very bright in contrast with that formless silhouette. It seemed that all the life in the room was concentrated in the bird and that the woman and the sad trappings of the room had died long since. The bird flew up onto its perch, screeching "Ben boy! Ben boy!" until Sable's ears rang.

"Quiet," the seated figure said harshly. "Quiet," and she lifted thickened fingers and rattled the thin bars of the cage. There were bird droppings on the floor, Sable noticed, and the cage itself smelt strongly.

Lady Agatha seemed unaware of either. Gradually, out of the gloom, details of her face became apparent, a hooked bony nose and long chin, dark searching eyes, a Punch-like face, the girl thought, remembering the fairground at York. "So, you're Tom's protégée. You look

48

lively enough. Tired, eh? A long journey at this time of year."

Sable hesitated, unable to decide whether she was intended to agree or to speak her own mind. "It was an interesting journey, my lady. And if I was a bit dry, the rain refreshed me."

"But you'd like something to eat and drink I'll be bound," the harsh voice said decisively. "Bring a tray, Annie. And sit down, Sable Martin, and let's have a better look at you."

The sunlight fell on the chair to which the girl was directed. She regretted, a little, that the new gown was temporarily spoiled, but she knew she looked clean and neat in contrast to the neglect that flourished all around her. "What will you want me to do?" Sable asked, distracted by the gleam of a spider web on the lower tier of the chandelier. "Tom said little."

"Well, my eyes are not what they were. Like my body, they show signs of wear and tear. I should like to be read to—quite often."

"I cannot promise to do this perfectly. Not yet."

"Tom says you are good." The gnarled hand flicked a scrap of birdseed from the lap rug. There were rings on the swollen fingers, stones that glittered in the dinginess like points of fire.

"Perhaps—for a farm girl. But I have not yet the knowledge—"

"You will have in time. If you reach a point where you falter, I will supply the word that evades you. You look unsure! I've tried governessy women and they were chill, unwilling companions with no animation, no desire to make the words come to life. I felt shut off even more from pleasures I once had. With you I hope it will be different. Tom says you've a great longing to better yourself. And it would not all be sitting reading with an old woman who will have days when she will carp and criticize. When my

49

bones are easier, I ride in the gig and you shall take me. You will learn to set trays and prepare meals for us. You can sew. That will be useful. I hope you may learn to write my letters. When I sleep in the afternoon, the library will be yours. There's the garden, such as it is. And in return, you'll get what you want. Flesh on the skeleton of an intellect. A fair exchange, I'd say?"

"More than fair."

"We could start with *Gulliver's Travels*. That should not be beyond your capabilities. *Pamela*? Perhaps not yet. There's *Roderick Random* and *The Vicar of Wakefield*. You've never read Oliver Goldsmith, I take it?"

"I've had no books but those Tom Dobbs brought."

"Of course not. I should have thought of that." Lady Chryston's face twisted with sudden pain. "Pass me that little bottle, child. And the spoon that lies beside it."

"This?"

"Aye. My hand trembles. Pour out a dose and give it to me."

Sable did as she was bid. The medicine was a dark brown color and looked unpleasant.

"And don't tell Annie I had it. She'll say I take too much. Put the bottle back just where you found it. That's it. I see we'll get on well enough."

Sable wondered if it was wise to take too much of anything that was a medicament, but she was there to take orders, not to argue with a woman who seemed disposed to befriend her.

Annie came back with a big silver tray with a rim round it to stop all the delicate china from falling off, a chocolate pot, cream and sugar, and a plate of little cakes.

"Good. Ratafees," the old lady said. The twist of pain had gone out of her face, leaving it smooth and relaxed. "All girls of your age enjoy sweet things. Put some sugar in your chocolate."

"I've never tasted sugar."

"Never!"

50

"We sometimes have cake made with honey. Had, I mean. Father has bees. But sugar is too dear."

"It's too dear in other ways," Lady Agatha pronounced, nibbling a ratafee. "Take one, child, do. When one thinks what the process of obtaining sugar amounts to, I cannot think why we don't give up the doubtful luxury."

Sable took a bite of her small cake. It was delicious and much sweeter than honey cake. Too sweet? She fancied it was. "What do you mean?" she asked. "About sugar."

"The cane cannot be farmed, gathered, and made into sugar and molasses without much labor. And to make a profit, the labor must be cheap."

"It sounds like farming," Sable said, sipping chocolate.

"Ah, but there's no one standing over your father with a lash, is there?"

"No." Sable had a disturbing recollection of Ben and the Negro's scarred back.

"England should hang her head with shame, though t'was the Portuguese started the whole thing. Sir John Hawkins began it here with a voyage or two, but Elizabeth the Queen sent him off with a flea in his ear and that was that. But once we had colonies, we needed the slaves and we plunged in as deep as Spain and Portugal. Our captains, taking our ships full of goods to Africa. Paying for human beings with trumpery articles—inanimate things—"

Lady Chryston took another cake and spooned more sugar into a second cup of chocolate, then, meeting Sable's clear gaze, she said, "I should be ashamed, I suppose, of my fondness for something so dearly bought. I always say I'll ban it, but it would be a futile gesture. There's nothing can stop it now, the slaving trade. The women, poor creatures, have other trials."

"What trials?" The whole story so far had seemed terrible enough.

"Things that you could not understand. Now don't look so mutinous! If I thought it would be good for you to

51

know, I should tell you. There are certain spheres in which it is a great disadvantage to be a woman at a man's mercy as you'll find out in God's time. Now, have another cake, child. Annie's not a bad cook when she's the mind."

"I'd rather not. Thank you."

"Don't blame you. Bad for the teeth and worse for the figure. Ben was a slave. With a master who was drunk every evening and became worse than a brute after a bottle or so. Not in the Indies, of course, or that would have been the end of him. In London. My husband found him more dead than alive in an alley outside the house and had him taken care of; he's been here ever since. Annie thinks of him as a heathen, of course. Her mind is small."

"He sounds—happy."

"I think he is. Tell me about yourself. Your folks. How you came to meet Tom."

Annie came back for the tray and cast a look at the brown bottle on top of the tallboy. She frowned a little as though she noticed it had been moved, but said nothing.

The sharp pools of sunlight had dimmed and softened like the colors of the old fabrics. The parrot had gone to sleep on his perch though his eyes seemed still open. A green lethargy stole through the big, now ghostly, room. Sable found herself telling her short uneventful life story without a need for haste or to get up to see to the cow or the hens or the necessity of washing the kitchen floor. There was only one point upon which she did not touch. She said nothing of her night excursions or of the Hunters. That was her secret and concerned no one else.

A peace descended on both the old woman and the girl, and when Annie, drawn back by the silence, came into the room, she found them both asleep. Annie scowled, displeased, recognizing compatibility.

Chapter 3

It did not take Sable long to fit into the ways of the house. Little of Knowehead was in use. Lady Chryston withdrew after her husband's death some years ago and dismissed most of the servants. Annie Gormley, who had been with Lady Agatha before her late marriage, remained, and a woman called Peg Morris, who with her stolid and backward daughter Mercy took care of what rough chores were necessary.

Annie complained constantly that Ben was shirking and unclean in his habits, that Peg and Mercy stopped working whenever they were left alone, but Sable noticed that their hands were always red with soda or from peeling the vegetables and wondered if the woman's disapproval was valid. Perhaps it was not entirely unfounded because the house showed so many traces of neglect, but it had been built for the usual regiment of servants and they no longer existed. Annie was probably unfair. There was only one person she cared for and that was her mistress, but it was an unhealthy affection.

This fact made Sable's position awkward. Lady Agatha had liked her from the first meeting and made no bones about it. Sable was what she needed, young, fresh, and stimulating, able to laugh, to please the old woman with her ability to grasp new ideas. The gratitude of her young charge, too, was heartwarming. She was strong, willing, and looked so attractive when animated. Life had returned to the old, crumbling house. Sable seemed not to mind that she went nowhere.

The seeds of jealousy were quickly planted. Annie resented Miss Martin and could not always conceal the fact. Sable was sorry; she had planned to like everyone and Annie's half-concealed dislike distressed her when it became evident and was forgotten when Annie was not there.

The old restlessness occasionally overcame Sable in spite of her almost immediate content with her new state. The doors of the house were never locked. Its isolation and the near impossibility of negotiating that wild bend into the drive except in broad daylight kept it safe enough. Lady Agatha took a sleeping draught, without which the arthritis would keep her awake all night, and Peg and Mercy shared the attics, sleeping the sleep of the dead. Ben had the room over the stable. There was only Annie who might reasonably hear if she crept out to wander the overgrown garden with its flowers washed white by the moon or stole down the track to the lakeside where the trout jumped on a fine night, where the clouds were puffed and distended into huge, heavily foliaged trees. There were birds, creatures that crept and padded and never showed as much as a whisker, and the small flitter of moths. It was intoxicating. The winter was a beauty she'd not forget.

Sometimes she missed the wood at Daggleby, but that was the past. Morgan still invaded her sleep, his face close as on the May morning he arrested her flight towards the lawns behind the house. She saw Morgan far more clearly than she did her parents or brothers.

Tom had come muddy and dishevelled as always with news from home. Pansy was to have a baby in late summer. Joe was walking out with Jane Biggs from the village. Her parents were much as usual and sent her their love and a pot of honey, hoping she was a good girl and making the most of her opportunity. Almost eighteen months had passed. It did not seem so long.

"Of course she is a good girl," Lady Agatha replied, stroking the bar of the parrot's cage and making shivers of elfin music. "She's all you said, Tom, and more. Tea, please, Annie." And Annie, dark-faced, went to fetch it while Sable pretended not to notice that ill-humor.

"I thought you'd get on well together. It's as well, for there's no place now for the lass at home. Joe's set on being wed before next Christmas. There'll be another grandchild next year. The little house creaks at the seams."

"Which is more than you can say of Knowehead. We rattle like peas in a pod. But I thank you, Tom, for bringing me the girl. There's cheer now where there was none after Davey died. Thank you, Annie."

Annie rattled the tea things sharply, lips compressed. Lady Chryston remained unaware.

"I'll write a letter for Mother and Father," Sable said. "I may have paper, Lady Agatha?"

"How could you write without?" The old lady gave her Punch-like smile and opened the cage door so that the bird could sit on her shoulder. The bright plumage accentuated more than ever the black-and-whiteness of the puffy face and musty mourning.

"Has that niece of yours visited you of late?" Tom asked, drinking his tea very neatly.

Sable looked up, surprised. There had been no mention of any niece until this moment.

"Clara? No. This place bores her to distraction. It's London she loves. Unless there's scandal and diversion, the girl's only half-alive, and what scandal could she find here where everything molders? No, it's the theatre and Vauxhall and supper parties that young minx adores. I may as well not exist. But she'll be sorry one day. You mark my words." Lady Agatha clattered her cup into the fragile saucer and seized another biscuit.

Annie, from her place at the door, showed silent comprehension. Sable could not think what it was all about, then, resuming her hunt for a sheet of paper, forgot.

"And have you converted many this last journey?"

Tom cradled a fresh cup of tea in sunburnt hands. The healed scar was still prominent. Why should good people be hurt, Sable wondered?

"A man and woman down at Skipton. A self-indulgent cleric at York. A maid or two—"

"It seems little for all the effort."

"One would have been enough."

The paper found, Sable settled down to write home, the voices of Tom and her benefactress a muted background, broken only by the occasional cackle of witchlike laughter from the old lady, laughter that made the girl smile. The letter proved more difficult than she had anticipated. Her parents would be disappointed to hear that the house was ramshackle, its treasures of silver tarnished, the valuable pots and vases dingy with dust that hid their beauty. The only things that sparkled were Lady Chryston's gems, the rings she changed every day for others, the necklaces she wore at dinner as a matter of course and not to impress anyone. Her Davey had liked her to show them off and she'd confided his presence often haunted the place, giving her the confidence of an afterlife. He remained, a kind memory, a benign shade, a welcome to the hereafter.

Neither could Sable divulge her night wanderings or her knowledge that Annie Gormley resented her. Her parents would not be reassured by a description of Ben. They

56

had an unfortunate mistrust of the unusual. But a description of her journey and of the big, odorous library where the book covers felt like dead skin and smelt of a thousand yesterdays might be entertaining.

The letter was finished, sanded, and sealed, ready to be picked up by Tom when he left. She'd been a long time over it, the smell of dinner was creeping along the hall. Sable loved this part of the day. Food served by candlelight and who cared if the dishes were cracked or the candelabra uncleaned? The shadow of elegance remained, reminding her of the lost splendor of Hunter occasions.

She had once broached the subject of cleaning the silver and hangings, but Annie had been so forbidding that she had kept off the topic afterwards. And the days passed so swiftly with reading and discussion, a ride in the gig when it was warm and Lady Agatha comfortable, the library in the afternoons, and tidying the borders and flower beds, though not too much or the careless charm would be lost. Sometimes she sewed and mended while Lady Chryston talked of her husband who had been in the East India Company. He had brought back spices, dyes and perfume, jewels and silks. Some of the materials had been used for the upholstery and curtains that still remained in the moldering rooms. The jewels were the ones she wore now and from which she'd never be parted. Chryston had had money and a position of his own, so she had trusted him where she'd always fought shy of involvement with other men. It was fascinating when she reminisced so, though she did not do it often. Only when the pain in her joints was less than usual and the sun warmed her to loquacity, reminding her of her golden years.

Tom went to wash his hands before eating and Lady Agatha stirred suddenly, her eyes heavy with pain. "The medicine, Sable. Get it now before Annie comes again. Please, child—"

Unable to contemplate the old woman's obvious torment, Sable went quickly for the bottle and spoon. It was unfortunate that Annie saw her leave the room, and that there was no time to conceal the draught. The girl passed her quickly, cheeks flushed with guilt, and ran to administer the antidote to agony. It was good to see the lines smoothed out of the drawn face, the return of a smile. "You're a good girl. Take it back."

Annie was in the large drawing room where the parrot's cage swayed gently in the breeze from the open window. The parrot cocked a sleepy eye and ruffled green and red feathers.

"Do you think you are wise?" Annie asked softly, a spot of red in each cheek like a daub of paint.

"Wise?" Sable replaced the bottle. "She asked me. She could not bear the discomfort."

"Or did you suggest it?"

"Suggest?" The girl felt cold. "Of course I did not suggest it!"

"There are regular times to take the stuff."

"There are no regular times to suffer! How could there be!"

"We cannot all be so clever," Annie sneered. "Worming your way in with smiles and artlessness. I never saw such cunning. But you'll be sorry one day. If the mistress dies, I'll say what I've seen. And you know the penalty for murder. You'll hang, my pretty one. Not so bonny tarred and black and hanging in a chain—"

"How dare you!" But Sable had a picture in her mind of a body swaying, crow-black and pecked by birds—

Annie shrugged. "Who's to hear? No one that I can see. I know what you want, of course. It's all her things that should go to Miss Clara. And don't raise your hand to me, Miss!" She took a step backwards and the fire-dogs jingled.

It took all of Sable's self-control to go out of the room and to return to the table for the evening meal. Distaste and panic fluttered inside her, turn about. Now that the enmity was out in the open, it brought no relief. Tom was back and talking to Lady Agatha, so there was no real need for much conversation on her part. But the anticipated food had lost its savor and she did little but toy with it.

"There's been no one looking for Ben?" Tom Dobbs asked suddenly. Sable forgot Annie in this new, intriguing departure.

"Not a soul. He's safe enough up here. Parksworth isn't likely to come this way. And few people know I have him."

"Only the whole of Kendal! Windermere, and Annie has an obsession about him."

"I cannot keep him a prisoner. He was that for long enough. Anyway, who's to know he was Parksworth's slave? One Negro looks very like another. Ben won't say."

"His eye?" Tom suggested. "Parksworth could hardly forget that."

"He never knew," Lady Chryston said harshly. "Sodden drunk as ever, administering a beating to kill a man, then Ben thrown out for dead. He'd not take it in. Davey was all for going back to thrash him in his turn when Ben finally told us his master's name. But he'd have asked for Ben back again once he was sober and he'd have had the law on his side. One cannot take another man's property. No, so long as Ben stays in Westmorland, he's safe. Oh, there you are, Annie. Why hover by the door? Fetch the pudding."

"Did Annie know about Ben's past?" Tom asked, when the woman had gone with the dirty plates. "That you took him from his legal owner?"

"No. I told no one."

"Not even Clara?"

"No one. A secret's no secret once it's out. But it's been years and no one's ever questioned the whys and wherefores of poor Ben."

"You must say nothing of this, Sable," Tom said seriously. "You know what it would mean."

"Yes. I do."

"Bless my soul! I'd forgotten the child. She's been so quiet. But I'd trust her." Lady Agatha's face, flushed with the effects of the potent medicine, was turned in the girl's direction. "You'd not want to push Ben back to that monster's servitude, would you, child? I've told you something of slaves, just how much I disremember, but whatever it was, you have the sense to keep it to yourself, have you not?"

"I'd never tell a soul. I promise."

"There's my good girl. I admit I find myself talking to Sable as I've not done since Davey passed on and she's been so silent this evening that I forgot her presence with that branch of candle between us. There's no end to the wickedness of people. Black boys bought as a diversion for some spoiled society wife and treated like pet monkeys, patted on the head and stuffed with sweetmeats, dressed in Oriental splendor. It's barbaric. I've said it before, but I'll say it again. I really must tell Annie that no more sugar is to come into this household. We'll use honey, instead, or figs or dates. No, Tom. Ben's become a part of the scene up here, and with Davey having his Company links, no one's surprised that I have a Negro in the house. There are others in Keswick and Ambleside, I know. Why bring up the subject so long afterwards?"

"We talked together in the garden and I remembered how he came to you. You were uneasy for long enough, wondering if Parksworth had put out a description. A train of thought , only."

"Thank you, Annie." The woman had returned with the pudding and the conversation turned to other things. Sable turned over the spotted dick unenthusiastically. Annie had spoiled her pleasure most decisively. She was glad when the long meal ended and she could plead tiredness and retire to her room. The thought of Ben's ill-treatment depressed her. True her father had beaten her for misdemeanours, but he was usually fair and had never allowed the punishment to overrun the boundaries of cruelty.

After Tom left the quiet of the household was disrupted only by a visit from Mr. Pembroke, Lady Chryston's solicitor, a stout little man with whom the old lady was closeted for much of an afternoon. From the library Sable heard the distant voices rise and fall, then the door open while Lady Agatha shouted for Annie to bring Peg from the kitchen. Annie came quietly, to be followed by Peg's clattering footsteps and the wheeze of her breathing, then the door closed again.

She heard them come out shortly afterwards and return to their own part of the house, then, just as she left the library, Mr. Pembroke emerged into the passage, a sealed envelope in his hand. He was shaking his head as though he were displeased. Sable smiled at him, but affected not to notice. Soon afterwards she heard his carriage leave and Lady Agatha called Sable to bring her a spoonful of medicine, as the interview had tired her and brought on the aching in her back and shoulders. "I'm unused to writing nowadays," she said.

Annie asked if she might go to Windermere in the gig the following day for some trimming for a gown and some household requisites. Sable noticed that she sat as far away from Ben as was humanly possible, as though the touch of him would contaminate her. Something about the proud carriage of the Negro's head touched the girl with its suggestion of splendor. He looked like a king. Annie's mean, pursed mouth and standoffish behavior must be quite obvious to him, but he affected not to notice.

When they returned, Annie looked pleased with herself, so she must have been successful in her search for the braid and buttons.

Lady Agatha found the warmer weather beneficial to her health. There were no more requests for extra doses of medicine, much to Sable's relief, for Annie watched her like a hawk, obviously bent on mischief. Trees and bushes burgeoned. Birds made nests and the air was filled with promise. Ben threw off his shirt to saw logs for the fire and went back to singing of Africa. Sable cleaned the birdcage and put protective mats on the floor, then fetched a great bunch of daffodils to fill one of the Chinese vases on the sill.

"We'll go out in the gig," Lady Chryston decided one day, slipping a diamond ring on a gnarled finger and choosing another from her shagreen box. "Annie, put some things into a basket for a picnic. And a bottle of claret from the cellar."

"Very well, my lady."

"We'll look for bluebells," the old lady said. "I've not done that in years."

The day was beautiful, the clouds massed in ramparts, their shadows scudding over the round hills, touching the water of the lake with dull fingers and swooping away again. Ben was left behind because there was little room once Lady Chryston was settled with cushions and wraps and Sable was quite used by this time to controlling the horse and gig.

They were trotting by Low Wood towards Waterhead and Lady Agatha was saying, "There's an old peel at Kentmere we must visit sometime. Fifteenth-century and built by some old follower of King John—" But Sable was not really listening. She was looking towards Rydal Mount and Grasmere, hearing half consciously the sound of other hooves, a shout or two, laughter. There was always laughter where Morgan was—

They took a corner and beyond the fringe of birches she could see a small cavalcade, the men neat in dark coats and light breeches, their hats shining, a lady or two in full-skirted habit and plumed headgear. They tossed remarks to one another across the narrow road or over their shoulders and seemed in no great hurry.

They drew closer together, seeing the approaching trap. Lady Chryston sat up. "Why, I do believe—! Adam. My dear Adam, it's been so long. Years, it seems—"

One of the figures detached itself from the rest and came towards them. Sable had not forgotten the last time she had seen him, standing in the half-dark at Hunter Hall while Morgan embraced the girl in the white satin gown, lips twisted with old resentments. He looked quite handsome today, in a cold fashion, sitting his mount, very straight-backed and unyielding. His grey eyes, too, were cool, though he smiled at the old lady and greeted her courteously while the rest of the troupe continued along the lake road, still chattering, one or two running assessing eyes over the gig and the girl in the yellow flowered dress that matched the sunshine on the bank.

Adam Hunter's gaze passed over Sable almost blindly. Quite certain he would never know her a second time, she sat very still, repressing a desire to shiver in spite of the warmth, unable to understand such lack of passion in a young man. It was as though he had seen nothing. Yet he was polite, his voice quite gentle, but conveying no sense of life or involvement. He could have been dead, only propped up on his horse to give a semblance of existing.

"What have you been doing? I live so cloistered a life," Lady Agatha said.

"I am now a Member of Parliament. An obscure constituency, before you become too excited, but nevertheless, a beginning. So I am installed in London."

"I imagined it would be Morgan who would reach Westminster. Those friends of his from the university, Pitt and Wilberforce—"

"A number of people have expressed similar sentiments, but one of us had to run the business and Morgan, living up to his name, prefers the sea and trading."

"His name?"

"He was born in Bristol in a house on the waterfront.

I'm afraid Mother cheated a little. Morgan means sea-born but he came, like the rest of us, in a conventional bed and did not, like Venus, rise from the deep. Father was there on business and Morgan was precipitate."

"And do you see Billy Pitt and William yourself? I remember them as a pair of merry young jackanapes— And now Billy has the seat at Appleby, and Wilberforce has made mincemeat of Lord Rockingham and spent nine thousand pounds into the bargain. He's too gentle for the game of politics. He'll not last, I fear. He'll continue to enchant his listeners and be drawn from the serious by the sight of a rose or a butterfly. When is he coming back to Rayrigg?"

"In the summer. He'll doubtless call on you."

"I hope that you'll all come. Morgan too. He's not here at present?"

"No. He's soon to start a voyage to the West Indies. Wants to see for himself how the business works."

"Tell him he's to lose a customer. I'm to strike sugar from my grocer's list."

"I'm sure that will make a hole in our fortunes!" Again he laughed that empty laugh.

"This by the way, Adam, is a young companion of mine. Sable Martin."

For the second time, Adam looked at Sable and on this occasion there was a degree more awareness in his regard. It was obvious, too, that he had never seen or heard of her before. Morgan had kept her secret. She wondered, a little maliciously, how he would react to the knowledge that she'd spied on him and his family in the past, that she had a hopeless love for his brother. That she was a farm girl—

Adam bowed slightly. "Miss Martin."

"How do you do, Mr. Hunter."

"The one thing the child lacks is young companionship," Lady Agatha said unsubtly.

Sable's eyes flashed alarm. Adam, surprisingly, seemed

to understand her reaction. "Perhaps when Charlotte and Jane are next here that would present a suitable occasion for introducing Miss Martin to our local society. Unless she hunts, our present company would be of little interest. All they can talk about is the length of a fox's brush and the height of a fence."

"Perhaps you're right, Adam. I had Tom Dobbs here recently."

"Oh, Tom. How is the old fellow?"

"Well, and still about his business of saving souls and doing good."

"He never comes to the house, though we do see him at Daggleby."

"D'you blame him? To call as a vagrant to the place that was once his? No one could expect that. D'you find it comfortable?"

"Extremely. Perhaps I should rejoin my friends. I'll not keep you from your excursion."

"Come for supper. You know where to find me."

"Sometime, perhaps I will." He tipped his hat politely and turned away, back erect and unbending.

"Au revoir, Adam."

Sable hardly noticed his going. So that was the connection between Tom and the Hunters. Their holiday house had been bought from Dobbs. It would be interesting to see it. Did the Hunters realize that their money had kept families with food and women from selling their bodies on the streets? Imagine Adam in Parliament fighting causes! What injustices would bring that cold man to any warmth of conviction? Even his courtesy seemed promoted more from a sterile liking for perfection than from a desire to flatter or please. And Morgan, he was surely as good as lost to her. It took two years to go to the Indies and back. Fool, she told herself, to hanker after the unattainable.

The picnic, shorn of some of its attraction, was pleasant enough and bluebells sufficient were found and tied in

65

bunches with tough grass, their stems pressed into damp moss to keep them fresh. The food was tasty and the claret banished the ghost of futile regret. They turned the gig, returning between the thin white birch stems and the new leaves in great good humor. The sun was dimmed and a frail light illuminated the pale sheet of the lake, throwing Orrest Head into sullen prominence. Sable was glad she had her cloak, for the day had changed and the gown was no longer warm enough.

Ben came out of the stable to greet them and to lift Lady Chryston from the high seat. How dreadful if he were ever found and returned to the master who had all but killed him! But no one could find out after so much time had passed. He was safe enough.

Annie was at the door, waiting to receive her mistress. There was a strange look of triumph on her narrow face, an unaccustomed color in her cheeks as she glanced at Ben.

"She's here, my lady. Just came this afternoon."

"Who's here?"

"Why, Miss Clara. Who else?"

Annie and Sable helped Lady Chryston inside, then the girl went to wash her hands and tidy herself for dinner. She changed out of the now rumpled dress, noticing that soil had marked the skirt where she'd knelt to pick the flowers. She must remember to put them in water, she thought. The moss would dry out.

She approached the dining room thoughtfully, hearing first Lady Agatha's voice, then a low rejoinder that told her nothing at all about the unexpected visitor. Sable had formed an unfavorable notion of Miss Clara from the snippets she had heard from time to time, but a sense of fairness told her she should gather her own impressions regardless of the viewpoint of others. How odd she had not written to give warning of her arrival.

66

"But I've already explained it was a whim, Aunt Agatha."

"You've said so often Knowehead bores you—"

"As a permanent residence, perhaps. But for a few days, that's different."

Sable saw a neat, narrow back encased in steel blue, a cascade of blonde ringlets, a white hand laid along the marble mantel. A long foot in an elegant shoe. There was a tiny trace of petulance in the voice she disliked.

"It's taken you long enough to feel so sentimental."

"Why, Aunt!" The voice was now reproachful. "You used to complain that I was lacking in family feeling when I stayed away. Now, you almost take me to task for coming."

Lady Chryston grunted. "Have you decided yet to settle down? You've been restless for too long. Have you come to tell me of an engagement?"

There was a distinct pause. "Not quite." The acerbity had become hardness.

"What's that supposed to mean?" Lady Agatha's voice was sharp, then changed perceptibly as she saw Sable. "Come in, child. This is my niece, Clara Caven."

The fair curls bounced as the slim figure turned. Sable stood frozen. She had seen that face before, those china-blue eyes. A knot gathered in her stomach.

"So this is your—companion," Clara said quietly.

"Friend," Lady Chryston amended. "Sable finds nothing a trouble. Is content to live at the back of beyond, as you so picturesquely put it. Doesn't want to go flying off to the nearest town in search of diversion—that's probably due to her farm upbringing. Reads voraciously and writes a fair script."

"A paragon," Clara mocked. "But then, Miss Martin has no real yardstick, has she, of scales of living? A farm hardly exercises intellect or stimulates thought—"

"Oh, neither does it stultify what is already there. Sable's no passive yokel, I can assure you. She's a good mind. The library's never been so much used."

Clara flashed Sable a glance that indicated that an inventory should be made of the books immediately, then allowed the blue gaze to continue over the neat gown and the luxuriant hair. She yawned delicately. "I hope supper's not delayed, Aunt. The journey was fatiguing and I'm tired and sharp-set."

"Annie is usually punctual. The only thing that might have delayed the meal is your unexpected arrival."

"Touché! Then a glass of wine while we wait." Clara turned towards the decanter and picked up a glass. "You, Agatha?"

"Only a little."

"Miss Martin?"

"Yes, please."

The deft hands performed the task gracefully then extended the glasses to each in turn.

"Thank you," Sable said steadily and drank, glad of the warmth that stole through her veins.

"We met someone you know," Lady Chryston said, setting down the glass with a little ringing sound, "only this afternoon. Adam Hunter."

"Oh, Adam."

"I daresay you've seen him in London now that he's in the House."

"From the gallery only. And very disorderly it can be," Clara murmured, laughing softly. "Members are like schoolboys much of the time, shouting and taking up inelegant attitudes. And as much noise and invective as a fairground. There's little polish—"

"I thought he was extremely taken with you at one time?" Lady Agatha probed. "Adam."

"Perhaps, to outward appearances." Clara shrugged but her eyes had narrowed as though she covered up dislike.

"A good catch he'd have been. The elder son of a well-to-do family and now a politician. I often wondered why he stopped calling. Did you have some quarrel?"

"Good heavens, no. Nothing so decisive. But I'm unlikely to go into a decline as a result."

"Time you found a husband. You're no longer a child."

"Neither were you, Aunt, if you remember, when you found yours."

Lady Chryston sat up straighter and frowned. "The circumstances were different. I had plenty of offers but I chose to wait."

"And what makes you think I have not?"

Lady Agatha could find no reply to this and the uncomfortable silence was broken by the apologetic advent of Annie with the soup tureen. Sable, watching, saw the strangest look pass between Annie and Clara Caven. She would not have imagined that Clara would have much time for a servant. But this glance implied complicity.

The meal passed with little conversation. Sable was constrained and Lady Agatha and Clara were occupied with their own thoughts. The visitor rose first from the table and begged to be excused. "Perhaps we could go for some excursion tomorrow?" Clara suggested. "Shopping to Windermere? In the afternoon, preferably. I do not rise early, as you no doubt remember."

"I don't know—"

"Oh, come, Aunt Agatha. I've come all this way and I'm all the family you have, just as you are the only blood relative I possess. You can't have forgotten! And if I've been remiss in the past, I beg you to forgive me. I was young and foolish and now wish to make amends."

"Well—" Lady Chryston's voice softened. "I can't say it doesn't please me that you show a change of heart. Perhaps I was too critical of youth and its vagaries. But the gig takes only two, now that I am so useless and need so many pillows."

"Oh, I'm sure Miss Martin won't object," Clara said easily. "You say she's avid for knowledge. There's always the library and I have some gloves that require attention and a gown that's dirty at the hem. I hope I may have use of the girl as personal maid while I'm here. I understand she fulfills this function for you. We could share."

Lady Agatha opened her mouth, then closed it again.

"Oh, I am wrong? I thought from what Annie said—"

"I do depend on Sable, it's true, but she's enough to do."

"With her afternoons free? Come, Aunt! It's obvious Miss Martin has an easy life. I hope she does not prevail on your kindness overmuch—"

"Of course I will help," Sable said. "It will not be for long."

"Did I say how long I was to stay?" Clara asked coldly.

"I thought you said—a few days."

"Did I?" The blue eyes mocked. "I have not decided. Indeed, the air entrances already with its suggestion of finer weather still. London is hot and dusty at present. It will be overpowering shortly."

"You did not find it so last summer," Lady Chryston remarked. "You refused my invitation."

"I was not there all the time. I had invitations. Young friends—"

"I should be the last person to keep you from them. I only wish you were settled."

"I shall be when the moment is right. I take after you there, Aunt Agatha. You cannot blame me for that? We are both women not easily taken in, presumed upon—"

Clara gave Sable a look obviously intended to convey that the last remark was for her benefit. Lady Chryston, being occupied with a scrutiny of the log fire, missed its implication.

"We are bound to be alike in some ways," she admitted. "Sable, put another shawl around my shoulders, dear."

Clara stepped forward immediately. "Let me. I intend to cosset you while I am here. And I'm sorry for my earlier snappishness, but the journey was undoubtedly tiresome and my fellow passengers unsalubrious. It was fortunate I was able to hire a curricle to fetch me out here. If I had been in Kendal half an hour later, there would have been no way of reaching you today." She placed the shawl around her aunt's shoulders and bent to kiss her. "And now, if you will lend me Miss Martin, she can assist me with my clothing and take my undergarments for washing. Will you be all right for half an hour?"

"Of course. Annie will be back in a moment."

"Come, then." Clara beckoned imperiously and Sable followed unwillingly. From the moment she'd seen Miss Caven she had known that the situation would change. Miss Clara was a person one could not ignore and around whom events happened. There was a word in one of the leather-bound books that described her. Catalyst.

There was a fire burning in the room Clara had been given and the long copper handle of a warming pan protruded from the banked bed coverings. Clara, her face yellowed in the meager candle-glow, grimaced. "Unfasten my gown and pray do not scratch me. I have slapped my own maid for less than that."

Why had she not brought her own maid, Sable wondered mutinously? Her fingers seemed stiff and useless. She knew she was being slow and irritating to the visitor.

"For heaven's sake, girl! Can you not make haste?"

"I was trying not to scratch you."

"And do not be saucy, my fine little madam! I've heard all about you, never fear."

"Annie has prejudices—"

Clara swung around. "How dare you give me your opinions! I am not as gullible as an old woman, as you'll soon find out. Not that you'll be here for long enough—"

Sable stared, the words imprinted on her mind. Surely Clara had not the power to remove her from her position? Only Lady Chryston could do that.

"Annie has enlightened me on many matters," Clara went on, now hatefully quiet. "She wrote to me after Mr. Pembroke's visit, when she and that kitchen woman were asked to witness a new will. She does have the rudiments of an education though her spelling is an affront. We all know who must be the new beneficiary."

"I don't know. How should I? No one told me. It—it isn't true."

"You must imagine us very gullible," Clara sneered. "And now that your plan has succeeded and you are to have what's mine by right, you try to accomplish her death. But Annie knows how you persist in pressing medicine on Lady Agatha and we can all imagine for what reason. I shall inform the doctor, of course—"

"It's lies! Lies—" The room felt cold in spite of the fire. "Lady Agatha will say that it is at her own request," Sable protested, white-faced.

"She will not because you'll have gone."

"I'll not go unless she says."

"Oh, but you will. You see there's the matter of Ben."

"Ben?"

"Oh, don't look at me with those great sheep's eyes! I know Parksworth, you see."

"But he imagines Ben is dead. That he killed him."

"Not for much longer if you stay here," Clara said grimly. "Annie overheard a most interesting conversation weeks back. She hates you, you know, more than she does that Negro. All these years with Lady C. and still at an arm's length. A servant only. Then you with your taking ways, taking in more than one sense, for the silly old woman, I fear, has put you in the place I was to have. Oh, it's true! And if you wonder why Annie prefers to have me as next mistress, it's because my aunt feels little affection for me. I'd not come between Annie and her useless devotion. She's jealous, my little bumpkin, and jealous women have unpleasant methods. If you don't remove yourself voluntarily, I'd go back and let slide a few innocent remarks in Parksworth's ear. About my aunt's so noticeable black man and where he was obtained. I'm not supposed to know the truth about him. Neither is Annie. Only you— So if you persist in remaining and later, Parksworth comes this way, you'll get the blame. You're educated sufficiently to write letters. You'll have done it for the reward. There's always a reward for a slave. There would be for Ben."

"I'll tell her now. What you've planned—"

"No you won't, my dear. I'm not like Annie. I've no love for my aunt. All that interests me is what she has to leave and that I'm the one she leaves it to. If you say anything, I guarantee my aunt won't live long enough except to change her will back in my favor. Annie will be quite willing to tell of what she's seen. The ever ready medicaments—"

"But, if she's devoted to my lady, she's not going to agree to having her poisoned."

"Naturally not, but if you persist in remaining she's going to think you did it. That should rouse her sufficiently. No, you are going to disappear of your own volition and after you've gone, one of my aunt's rings is going to vanish too. That should stop her hankering after you. Once you've disappeared, I'll be quite willing to wait for my inheritance and I'll conveniently forget where Ben came from—"

"You couldn't hurt Lady Agatha."

"That's where you're wrong. She's had her day, and if the truth were told, she's tired of living. I'd think of it as a kindness. She's not likely to be very perky after you abscond with her best diamond. I don't think I'd have to wait long. Now, will you finish undoing me?"

"I won't. You can get Annie to do it. I wouldn't touch you!"

"Don't make the mistake of revealing everything to my aunt. This place is isolated. She'd be dead before you

73

could tell anyone else. But you'd not benefit. A murderess cannot profit from her crime. I know something of law, you see. Annie will say what she knows, you'll be punished, and since I'm my aunt's only living relative, I'll only have to wait for everything to tumble into my lap." Clara shrugged. "And who'd listen to you anyway? They could check on Ben and Parksworth, but it wouldn't be very pleasant for the Negro, would it? I don't see that you have any choice. I know who'd be believed."

Sable went out of the room before she was tempted to do Miss Caven a mischief. They were only empty threats, she reasoned, crushing down the panic. Then she knew she could not take the risk of finding out. The medicine must be strong if it relieved her mistress's acute pain so speedily. There was, as Clara said, little choice.

She had known that evening when she saw Morgan kissing Lady Chryston's niece that the girl meant trouble. Adam's reaction then had made her influence plain. If only Tom Dobbs had been here. She could have talked to him. As it was, she had to plan her own future. And before morning.

Chapter 4

*O*ften Sable had cursed her inability to sleep at the prescribed time. Tonight she was glad.

Lady Agatha had retired, assisted by Annie. She called for Sable to say her good-night and the girl was stricken with misery to see that craggy Punch face on the lace-edged pillow, the eyes already sleepy and contented. "Don't worry overmuch about Clara," the old woman whispered. "She'll act as though she owned the place only for as long as it suits her. It never lasts. I know my niece. A week or ten days and she'll be off, then you and I will return to our old ways. Be patient, my dear."

A strong compulsion rose up in Sable to tell Lady Chryston the whole story, but Clara appeared, almost as though she had expected last-minute confidences, and remained to tuck in the bedclothes and offer hot milk which her aunt refused drowsily. "You may go, Miss Martin," Clara said firmly and sat down in a bedside chair. "There's no need for two of us."

Sable turned away from the taunting smile, the slim, shawled figure of her enemy. Clara would stay there all night if need be. She'd have no further opportunity to tell of Miss Caven's treachery.

Back in her own room she took out of the wooden box what clothing she needed most and wrapped it in an old piece of red blanket. She put on her plainest gown, and the cloak over it, then the stout shoes Lady Agatha had bought for her at the start of the winter. If she were seen walking alone, she'd pass for a Gypsy, and if she were in danger of starving, she could always whittle clothes-pegs to sell at back doors. It was not the first time she'd watched Romany folk in the spinneys around Daggleby. She must take a sharp knife as she passed the kitchen. Annie would be sure to notice it was gone but she was hardly likely to make a fuss, since she'd had her way and got rid of the thorn in her flesh. The world was a strangeness of varying blues as she let herself out of the house. She ducked swiftly between two large rhododendron bushes and stood quite still.

The black feathers of trees against the lakeside were blotted out suddenly. Sable held her breath. Then the broad figure moved and she saw a profile she recognized, the flattened negroid nose and full lips of Ben. He must have seen her from the room above the stable and imagined her to be a prowler. She had a moment's wild desire to step out, to tell him to run away or at least to beware of Miss Caven and Annie. But he would be in no danger if she left and it could be to Lady Chryston's advantage to have someone here on whom she could rely. He began his slow progress back to the house.

She did not move until twenty minutes had elapsed. The moon stared at her through gaps in the foliage and she was reminded of forays into Hunter land. But this was different. In the past there had always been somewhere to which she could return. Now there was nowhere. Even if

76

she could find her way back to Daggleby, there was no position open to her unless she went to Hunter Hall and told the housekeeper that Morgan had told her to apply for a post. Only he would no longer be able to vouch for the fact since he was due to set out on a long voyage and would surely be gone before she could reach the village. And she would find it impossible to explain to her parents why she had left Lady Chryston's employ. Somehow she must put as much distance between herself and Knowehead as possible; then, when she had found some suitable opening, she could send a letter home so that they would not worry on her behalf. Tom, on his next visit, would be sure to report her absence.

Once this was decided, Sable shouldered the bundle and began to walk in the direction of the Kendal road. Kendal was a place of activity, not that she'd be able to stay there with the threat of having stolen a ring hanging over her head. But there might be some farm cart bound for obscure country roads or a fair where she could mingle with the crowds.

She walked strongly for a time, then the weight of the bundle pressed down on her. It was still difficult to comprehend that she had been forced to leave the house where she had been so happy, so privileged. How disappointed Lady Chryston would be when she awoke to find out about her protégée's flight with a valuable piece of jewelry. But it was better than dying or being forced to watch the return of Ben to a sadistic master. No one could condemn the Negro to a life which would be trebly harsh. The God Tom believed in would protect her. Dobbs always portrayed Him as a benevolent character and not as a dispenser of hellfire, which was the general belief.

Sable skirted Windermere and it was when she was past Staveley and not yet at Burneside that disaster struck. She was descending a tussocky bank when her foot slipped into a rabbit hole and she fell forwards, the bundle dropping from her grasp. A violent pain shot up her leg. Sweat broke out on her brow. "God help me," she whispered. "What shall I do now?"

She sank down upon the bundle and withdrew her foot from the hole, wincing with agony. Staring about her, she realized her vulnerability in this bare stretch of country with not even a bush to give her cover. If a search was instituted at daybreak there was no escape. When no ring was discovered on her person, it would be concluded that she'd thrown it away or hidden it, realizing she could go no further. But Sable could not believe that Lady Agatha would want to have her charged with theft, however great her sense of betrayal. She was more likely to recall Mr. Pembroke—imagine her wanting to make Sable her heiress!—and revert to her original will, ignoring Sable's apparent deception. The old lady would suffer in silence, never allowing herself to become fond of another person for fear of similar hurt.

A rim of pink showed along the edge of the horizon. The girl, imbued with a sudden need for action, began to crawl towards the ditch that bordered the track below her. She wet a kerchief and bound it as tightly as she could bear around the badly swollen ankle. It was still painful to limp and she knew she could only go at a snail's pace, perfectly visible to anyone who passed by. She'd give anything for the first vehicle to be a farm cart. At least she could hold a plausible conversation with such a man and if he was kind, she'd surely be given a bed in a barn. Her foot needed rest.

She shouldered the red-covered bundle and hobbled slowly towards Burneside. She still had at least three miles to walk to Kendal and not until she was well past the small town would she feel safer. The rim of bluish pink grew broader and lighter. Green crept into the grey and the lake was bluer, reflecting the new color of the sky. Sable tried to move faster and nibbled at a crust from the pack. Her stumbling steps grew slower and her face whitened

with pain. She lurched towards a large boulder and strad-
dled it awkwardly, stretching the injured leg before her,
then removed the shoe.

It was some time later that she heard the sound of
wheels, faintly at first, the growing rumble seeming to
echo in the hills behind Staveley. Her pulse quickened.
Only the hardest-hearted would leave her sitting here with
a bandaged foot and no homestead in sight. Even if she
were thrown off at Kendal she'd think of some way to keep
herself until the ankle was mended.

A small coach grew out of the distance, the matched
grey horses fine and elegant, unlike Lady Chryston's stal-
wart white and the shabby gig. Sable tensed, sure at first
that the conveyance was about to rattle by, ignoring her.
Then she heard a sharp order and the horses slowed and
stopped, the coach swaying and creaking against the sudden movement. A head showed at the window. She was
aware of a face of pale severity and the gleam of fair hair
under a dark hat, lips that were set tight against the world.
A coldness rushed over her.

"Miss Martin?" he said harshly. "What has happened?
Why are you here?"

Sable looked up at the coachman who stared ahead as
though he were blind and deaf. But hear he certainly
could, and she was not prepared to make explanations in
front of him. It would be bad enough concocting a story
for Adam Hunter's benefit.

"You've hurt your foot," Adam went on, opening the
carriage door and springing down to confront her.

"I stumbled. It's sprained, I think." Her hand clenched
on the red bundle. His icy gaze made her feel so Gypsyish,
so lacking; yet, the beginnings of curiosity stirred behind
the grey eyes.

"I would be able to speak more freely inside the coach,"
she told him, glad that her voice betrayed nothing of her
inner turmoil. "You will assist me?"

79

He hesitated, taking in the plainness of her dark gown and serviceable cloak, the tinkerlike bundle in its threadbare wrapping of faded red.

"I could hardly leave you here. Yes, you'd best ride with me, I suppose. Jenkins, put Miss Martin's belongings in the coach." Adam bent to pick up her shoe just as Morgan had once retrieved her clog, then put his hands under Sable's armpits to hoist her to her feet. He could not have missed the bitten lip, the look of pain she could not repress. She was lifted up and handed into the vehicle to sink, thankfully, on green buttoned upholstery. Jenkins climbed back onto his outside perch and Adam joined her, arranging his wide coatskirts so that they would remain uncrushed. A careful man she thought, wondering how best to explain her predicament. A part of the truth would have to do. No real lies, just missing out what was too difficult to say.

"Well?" Adam demanded when she did not speak. "Why were you there? It seems strange to me—"

"It's not really strange," Sable told him. "A matter of a clash of wills or personalities."

"I can hardly believe that Lady Chryston could change so rapidly in her feelings towards you. Only yesterday I could swear she had a real fondness for you—"

"She had. It's her niece who took against me." Sable had forgotten that Adam knew Clara, so was unprepared for the jerk of a muscle in his cheek and a look of uncontrolled anger. "When we returned from our outing, Miss Clara Caven was at the house. She had been at Knowehead for some hours in conversation with Annie Gormley who has no great liking for me. And, unknown to me, Lady Agatha had changed her will in my favor. Miss Caven decided I had wormed my way into the household with this object in view and told me she'd not be displaced in this way, how blood was thicker than water. She suggested I leave before some situation was manufactured that would show me in a poor light. It was all very sordid and unpleasant and left me with little choice but to go. Then, on my way over the bank as a short cut, I put my foot in a deep hole. And there you have the tale of my departure."

Adam sat for a time, his profile carved in white and his mouth cruel. "I am acquainted with Miss Caven," he said at last, the tic in his cheek fluttering still and his gloved hand reaching up to cover the disturbance, "and with Annie. I find it completely in character that they should find your presence galling. I've half a mind to take you back so that Lady Chryston be told of the pressure brought to bear on you—"

"No! Please do not even consider it. I have made the break now, painful though it was, and since Miss Caven intends to stay for some time and I can do nothing about that, I'd rather not be the cause of a continued dissent. It would be extremely difficult and I suppose Miss Clara does have a grievance if her expectations were dashed. But I had no thought of personal gain. I hope you will believe that. I'd not want you to think me mercenary." For some reason she valued his opinion.

The cold profile did not change. "I suppose you are going home? Wherever that may be."

"Unfortunately that is out of the question. I had hoped to procure some post but now I have this stupid injury and cannot even produce a reference from my employer—" Sable shrugged. "I find myself at a disadvantage."

"I see." The grey eyes continued to stare ahead at nothing. "I know of no one who could care for you or employ you. Not here—"

"You must not feel obliged to make my problem yours." For the first time she wondered where he was going. There had been luggage on the roof so it seemed obvious he was leaving the Lake District. Was he going to Daggleby? Her heart thumped as she contemplated being put off at the village and seeing her parents and brothers. But what then? That seemed no answer. "Anyway, I'd prefer to put some distance between me and Knowehead."

"I can hardly abandon you," Adam answered without warmth. "I would feel I had behaved irresponsibly. I am going to London. Some pressing matter in my constituency. It might be possible to offer you a situation in my house. My sister has decided to look after my new household, since I have no wife and a hostess is necessary for the entertainment of political acquaintances. Charlotte has found she needs more help than I have so far provided, and you appear to have some sense of integrity, so lacking in many. Yes, a sort of companion to Charlotte could be the answer. Someone with the wits to take some of the load from her shoulders. Could you cope with this kind of life, do you think? There are constant visitors to a politician's home and they must be received with sympathy and intelligence. I will not always be there and Charlotte will have other calls on her time. You can, I presume, write letters? You express yourself well for someone so young, so I see that you've received an education."

Breathless, Sable tried to assimilate this astonishing proposal. Her mind whirling, she said, "I did, indeed do most of Lady Chryston's correspondence. And I had access to her library, which you must know is extensive." Extensive! How the words rolled glibly from her tongue. Words had always fascinated her, filling her thoughts, conveying their own pictures of delight or repulsion. Her mother would bask in this recognition of her abilities.

"I am acquainted with the house. I still cannot but feel that we should go back there—"

"No!" Sable said definitely. "I would prefer to be left at the roadside rather than reenter a place where I was so resented. It would be kinder to leave matters as they are. Are

82

you serious about offering me a position? Knowing so little about me?"

"I do not usually suggest things I do not mean to carry out."

"I didn't mean to question—"

"Well, then. Do you accept my solution of your problem?" The grey eyes were on her now, almost fanatically clear and bright in the morning light. She wished suddenly that there was a suggestion of warmth and humanity in him. Yet why should he be moved by a stranger? His was a properly clinical interest even though it chilled her. No wonder he had no wife. A woman would want more from a husband than frigid courtesy.

"Yes," she answered, still overcome by strangeness and a sense of unreality. "But there is one drawback—I doubt if I've enough money for the coach fare. Lady Chryston paid for me to go to Knowehead, and she gave me all I really needed in the way of clothes, writing paper, books, shoes, quills—. There was no real salary."

"Most of which you've had to leave behind, judging by the size of the bundle you carried," he hazarded.

"Yes."

"I will make myself responsible for the journey. It's only a matter of buying another ticket at Kendal where we join the long-distance coach. I fear you may have no recourse but to travel on top. Will this trouble you?"

"No," she answered, trying to subdue the pounding of her pulse. The throbbing of her ankle had gone up into her knee and her thigh and she felt a little sick.

"Very well," Adam Hunter said and went back to staring ahead at the buttoned upholstery, wrapped in his own empty thoughts.

How odd, Sable thought, pinching her good leg to see if she had not dreamed the whole thing. A flicker of pain shot through her. No, it was real. She was on her way to

London and she'd not needed to mention Daggleby or the worst of the threats Clara had made. It obviously paid to tell the truth even if only half of it was there.

The road began its series of narrow loops then plunged recklessly towards the roofs and chimneys of Kendal.

London burst upon her vision like a bright mirage. She had never seen so many people. Artisans bearing the insignia of their trade, snuff-colored gentlemen in tied wigs and tricornes, a one-legged seaman who had to scuttle in an ungainly manner from the scene of a near collision between two coaches and a sedan chair. Dogs and cats, pigeons swooping for food droppings and refuse. Raddled women and stout matrons. And shops—butchers and bakers and candlestick makers. A crone with flowers. Shouts, screams, bells ringing. And then the streets growing finer and the houses grander with pillars and porticoes, delicate fanlights. Carriages, trees in a park, the glitter of water. That, surely was a palace? Sable took a deep, satisfied breath.

An ugly man was haranguing the public from a temporary platform. He spoke against the King, holding a pamphlet in the air, and the crowd clapped and waved. "Wilkes!" they shouted. "Wilkes! Read to us from the *Essay on Woman*. We'll have none of Pope. We like not the King. His friends are never ours."

Sable's ears burned. Surely they must be apprehended for the slight to the Crown? The list of King George's mistakes seemed long and the palace could not be far away. It had never occurred to her that royalty could be so vulnerable, so open to criticism. The path through the congestion began to open.

She turned to look at Adam, but he seemed to have shut his ears to the cries of the populace. She was glad that they were not still in the long-distance coach with its dust and sweaty squalor and the enforced proximity with men with straying hands and nudging knees pressed against her own. But the long journey had accomplished some good, for the rest had been beneficial to the ankle injury which was nearly better, the swelling having diminished sufficiently for her to wear stockings and more delicate shoes. Adam had insisted on stopping at a Jew's shop, dim and cluttered, to buy her a box for her possessions. "It's better if Charlotte does not know you left Knowehead in so unorthodox a manner," he told Sable. "I will tell my sister that Miss Caven's appearance left you with insufficient to do and that I decided to employ you where you were more needed. My house will be besieged with working folk with grievances and troubles, some with letters and documents to support cases. There would be notes to take of your conversations with these members of the public. Histories to be filed with copies of the letters sent out. Anything more complicated than you feel qualified to deal with could be passed on to Charlotte or myself. Does the prospect daunt you?"

"A little," she'd answered honestly. "Why have you troubled yourself so on my behalf?"

"Because I've seen the damage Miss Caven can do. Had she not been involved, I might have taken your story with a grain of salt. A large grain, I might add. I'm by no means easily taken in. I will set you some test when we reach Cardigan Square, just satisfy myself as to your capabilities. If you fail, then I must rethink the whole business and put you to some more modest task."

"You have been kind."

"My dear Miss Martin, I am seldom kind. I dislike loose ends, that is all. It's no soft corner I offer you."

"I'm not afraid of work. Do you think Miss Hunter will—accept me?"

"She will probably object that you are too young. She's

85

conventional. But you cannot have been too young for Lady Chryston and I value her judgement. How old are you? Twenty?"

For a moment Sable was tempted to lie, then she knew that she could commit almost any crime but tell him an untruth. Adam Hunter bore all the hallmarks of disillusion.

"I am—younger."

His head swivelled round. "You surprise me. But I think Charlotte would prefer you to be twenty, so that's what I shall tell her. Is your foot better?"

"Much. I've done little but sit and that was the best cure."

"Good. I'm glad the box was big enough for your belongings." His eyes approved the yellow flowered gown into which she'd changed this morning. Intoxicated with excitement she went back to looking at the fine ladies in carriages and sedan chairs. She wanted to be taken out in such a chair herself, linkboys running alongside in the dusk with flaring torches. It might happen, though the possibility was remote.

The carriage rolled into a mews behind some large cream-colored houses. Black railing fenced off a flight of steps and a stone-flagged area into which a smallish window faced, sending out a glow of light. Wide black-painted doors opened to receive the carriage and pair. A face appeared briefly behind the piece of basement curtain.

"My box," she said, hesitating on the cobbled street.

"There's someone to take care of that. Come with me. A room will have to be prepared for you, and I daresay you're hungry?"

"A little. Thank you."

"Whatever for?" He propelled her up steps facing the mews and rang a bell.

"For rescuing me."

"You may live to regret it. You'll have little peace in this house." He laughed a little grimly.

The door was opened by a young man in livery who stood aside silently and closed the door after them. She was standing on marble squares. An enormous spiderlike plant stood on a carved stand with a shelf underneath. Its leaves drooped, making curved shadows on the painted wall.

"Miss Martin?"

She became aware that Adam Hunter must have spoken to her and she'd not heard.

"Come with me," he repeated with a trace of sharpness. "I'll take you to Charlotte and she can decide what's to become of you." He drew off the gloves and handed them to the footman, then began to walk quickly across the echoing marble towards a double-doored room. "Charlotte?" he called, on a note of interrogation.

The doors were opened inwards and the thin figure of Charlotte Hunter stood in the gap.

"Adam!"

"Some letters came so I decided I must come back. A letter to you would not have arrived more quickly."

Cool eyes, the same grey as Adam's, were appraising Sable. She stood a little defensively, aware of the dust in the folds of her cloak, a lingering twinge of muted pain in her foot. It must be the fault of these fancy shoes. She'd worn them too quickly. Pride always hurt.

"Oh," Adam said, "this is a young woman I brought to help you. She was with Lady Chryston, but Clara descended on the household and declared her redundant since she intends to look after the old lady herself. And I knew you'd have your hands full now that my constituents seem to have tracked me from home to home, and I'd had enough of Windermere—

"This is Miss Martin," Adam told his sister, his attention now centered on the letters which he riffled with thin, capable hands. "Have you another name? I never thought to ask."

"Sable."

"Sable?"

The girl hesitated, aware of her mistake. She should have said Isabel. If Morgan ever came here, he'd prick up his ears if she was mentioned. Of course, he had only to see her to remember. She thought, irrelevantly, of the knife that now reposed in the respectable box and with which she'd intended to whittle clothes pegs. She experienced a desire to laugh. How her future had changed. If she hadn't sprained her ankle she might have ended up in some Gypsy encampment or at an inn up to her elbows in soda and greasy dishes. "It's a shortening of my own name, Isabel," she explained quietly.

"How quaint," Charlotte murmured. "I must admit I had not expected—"

"Charlotte, the girl's here to help. Now isn't there a room next to your maid's? I seem to recall there was one unclaimed. It's been a long journey and I'm sure Miss Martin would appreciate being able to wash and hang up her clothes. Get her settled and then you can tell me of the most urgent matters accruing in my absence."

"Very well," Charlotte agreed. "This way, Miss Martin. I'll have the bed made up and some food sent to you." She glided up the wide, shallow stairs quite gracefully. She was inclined to plainness, but she moved well and her hands and feet were good. She opened the door of a high-ceilinged room with a pleasant fresco and fireplace of marble. The furnishings seemed impossibly grand, a bed with carved poles, some chairs Sable discovered later to be Chippendale, a pier table set against the wall that would make a good improvised desk, a lamp with pink glass, a big press facing the window, a mirror framed in gold-painted plaster.

"It's—a nice room."

Charlotte looked at her oddly. It must be a surprise to admit to the house not only one's brother but a complete stranger. Sable withstood the scrutiny without loss of self-possession.

"How is Lady Chryston?" Charlotte asked, obviously intent upon her own investigation into the newcomer who was to be more her concern than Adam's.

"She suffers a great deal of pain. But her mind is quite clear."

"Perhaps when you write, you would convey my good wishes?"

"Yes," Sable lied. There had to come a day of reckoning but it would not be immediately. She would have a breathing space. Perhaps she would become so indispensable that they would cease to care about her past or her omissions.

"Your parents?" Charlotte probed, running her finger idly along the mantel. "They'll be informed of your new position? They do not, I take it, live in Windermere?"

"No, in Yorkshire. That's where I was when Lady Agatha sent for me. She was unaware then that Miss Caven was intending to return to her. She did not need both of us. My parents are countryfolk and with two sons marrying, there'd be no place for me there. I have no alternative to making my own way in the world and I'll not shirk, I promise. I welcome work and should hate to be idle. I cannot say more in my own defense—"

"My dear Miss Martin!" Charlotte's face colored faintly. "Why should you think you require defending! And against what? It's just that I shall need to give some account of you, if only to my parents. Adam will never think to do it. And as he has his own secretary you will be under my jurisdiction, as he has pointed out. I must confess, had I had my own choice, I'd have chosen someone older and more experienced. But you may bring a fresh, uncluttered mind to the whole business and I could not fault Lady Chryston's judgement.

"A man in the public eye cannot call his soul his own and his way of life means that he's open to the complaints of all those voters who have grievances, warranted or otherwise. One of your duties will be to separate the sheep from the goats. You must learn to differentiate between the genuine and the false, the important and the trivial, the immediate—was that Adam calling?"

"I believe it was, Miss Hunter." Sable composed herself. As with Adam, she had told only part of the whole truth.

"I'll have water brought to you and I daresay that clatter on the stairs is your box on its way. I trust there will be room for all you have?"

Sable, with a glance at the huge press and the set of drawers, smiled. "I'm quite sure of that."

Charlotte frowned slightly, obviously not understanding the reason for her amusement. Then she was gone. Sable sank into one of the chairs and closed her eyes. How long did she have to make her own place in this house? At least Morgan would not be able to reveal her secrets. She had nothing to fear from that quarter until he returned from the West Indies. But the thought brought no comfort.

Chapter 5

*S*able became absorbed into the daily life of Cardigan Square with remarkably little fuss. Caught between the two strata of the household, she was thrown into the society of Charlotte Hunter's personal maid, Marie Claire, who had a small sitting room between their two bedrooms to which meals were brought. Adam's secretary, James Grant, had also been a friend of his at Cambridge and ate with him and Charlotte. Sable was intrigued by so many separate parts of a household. The kitchen staff were firmly entrenched below with butler, maids, and footmen.

Marie Claire was proud of her position and made few bones about her superiority. She'd looked askance at Sable when she first appeared, but the fact that the girl had been companion to a titled lady swayed the balance in her favor. But Sable found her empty both of humanity and ideas. Marie could sew delicately, launder and clean the finest garments, but her conversation was limited, and Sable spent a good deal of time in her own room where she could read and write and escape the stream of reminiscences of a not-very-interesting French background.

Sable's work was interesting. The very first caller was the mother of a thirteen-year-old girl who had been enticed into a house close by a theatre and deflowered by a drunken gentleman with a penchant for virgins. A surgeon on the premises performed operations on this girl and several others so that they remained "unsullied" for the benefit of other such roués. If it had not been for the fact that the girl had been left unattended by accident and had taken the opportunity to run out into the street and lose herself in the crowds, thereafter making her way home to Pudding Lane and to the arms of the distraught mother, Belle might never have been seen again.

Charlotte had been out, and Adam busy in the House, so Sable was left to deal with the case of Belle Briggs, to note the sordid details, to advise Mrs. Briggs to keep a strong watch on her daughter until the accusation could be proved. Adam had looked in after the woman had gone and his aloof expression hardly changed as the details of the child's sufferings were reported. He had read the written account and said, "There's no real corroboration. The child heard no names. She has no idea who took her to bed. The owners of the house go by Christian names only and London is full of Jacks and Sallys. They'll have taken fright with the victim flown and removed the rest to some other place. If it ever happened. Mrs. Briggs could have some personal spite against the owners of these premises. One can never be entirely satisfied—"

"But if you had seen their tears! You'd not have stayed unmoved," Sable protested.

"My dear Miss Martin, I know all there is to know of feminine tears," Adam said drily. "I was weaned on them in a household of women. I know never to accept anything at its face value. If I tried to take this case further without

92

proof, it would be a pointless exercise. I must visit the house in mention, see the child's home, listen to the comments of neighbors as to her character, have the child examined. There will always be one doctor to argue against another."

"But you will try, won't you?" she begged, her face pale. "They have only you."

"Oh, never fear! I'll try for whatever justice may be obtained in an unjust world. I point out only the mire of corruption that lies between the complaint and the redress."

"It's not easy—"

"Nothing is easy, Miss Martin." He ran his eyes over the neat handwriting and businesslike layout of her composition. "A quite journalistic gift of expression," he remarked with glacial approval. "But your heart must be controlled as well as your mind. Almost every problem that comes to this house will shock or harrow, and one must never become too involved." His look reinforced the verbal warning.

But, remembering the shivering child with her dark-rimmed eyes and the tearful mother, Sable did not see how one could remain so detached. If one had not the conviction, how did one acquire the tenacity with which to see the matter through to a fair or successful conclusion?

"There's never a guarantee for vindication," Adam went on, correctly interpreting her expression. "But I'd rather you were not in a state of perpetual hurt. At least I will always try. In this case I fear we'll fail. You see, the girl says 'a house near the theatre.' They all look the same. She ran out of it in fear and pain. She'd not stand staring at the facade for points of identification. It's days since she returned home. Her mother's poor and had to hunt around for her own Member of the House and walk to this address which is some distance away. Even if we chanced on the right building, the miscreants have had time to paper walls and paint cornices, shift furniture, do all manner of things

93

to confuse the child who'll falter and stammer with indecision, or they'll invent an old grudge, saying they employed Mrs. Briggs to clean laundry and how she was paid off for singeing the sheets and took umbrage against them. They could even provide evidence that it was the mother who procured the child for money and then took fright at the girl's distress."

The Briggs case ended as Adam predicted. Belle, when taken back to the street, became so afflicted with hysteria that she could not at first identify the house. When pressed to pick one, she could not reconcile the colors of the interior with her place of incarceration or recognize any of the seemingly respectable inhabitants, who were friendly and smiling, dissipating any suspicions that might have lingered, and who expressed indignation that appeared perfectly genuine, on Belle's behalf.

"Never believe the evidence of your eyes," Adam had advised, bitter over the failure to establish or apportion blame. "The child, if she's told the truth, which is likely, will be spoiled for life anyway. How can she have a rewarding relationship with a man after what's been done to her?" And he'd flung himself out of the interview room leaving Charlotte shaking her head over the unsatisfactory outcome.

"To think he started off skeptical," Charlotte said to Sable. "It was you converted him, I'm sure. I begin to wonder how we'd have managed without you, Miss Martin."

The compliment was enough to lift the girl's spirits from the trough of disappointment. There were not only failures. There was compensation even in the smallest victory.

It was about two months after her admittance to Adam Hunter's household that Sable heard a coach drive into the mews behind Cardigan Square, followed by a loud ring of the doorbell. Curious, she opened her bedroom door a fraction and heard footsteps on the marble floor, then

Adam's voice saying, "Great heaven, man, don't stand there looking like a ghost. Come into the study. Charlotte's abed and I think asleep. It's late." Then the footsteps, faltering, had made their way into the master's sanctum to be followed by a grumble of indecipherable voices, the soft clatter of a footman with a jingling tray, then more conversation that gradually petered out into monosyllables, then a prolonged silence.

Sable, wide-awake as always when others felt the need for sleep, was tormented by the unexpected event. This was a well-regulated household, predictable in its routine as the setting of the sun and the rising of the moon. Those faltering steps had pointed to illness or inebriation. But one did not resemble a ghost when drunk. A sick man arriving under conditions of secrecy aroused definite conjecture and Adam had sounded displeased as if the visitor was someone he disliked. When the study door was shut, their voices had risen a fraction in unmistakable discord. Now they were suspiciously quiet.

Sable crossed the hall noiselessly and looked over the rail. A lighted candelabrum showed an area of black and white marble squares, the pot stand with its cascade of pointed greenery shadowing the wall, an obscure painting. Then, with startling suddenness, the study door was flung open and Adam appeared, grim and white-faced. He called softly for the footman who had left the tray earlier, and the man appeared immediately as though he had anticipated the summons. Together, they went back inside the room. There was a dragging sound, then they emerged slowly, a man supported between them, his head hanging forward so that his features were obscured. Sable had a swift impression of broadness, a crumpled white shirt and stock, dusty shoes. She was just about to withdraw, seeing that they were approaching the foot of the staircase, when Adam looked up unexpectedly. "Miss Martin!" he exclaimed, surprised.

"I'm sorry," she said, aware of the fact that she was wearing only her nightgown. "I was awake. I heard—"

"Yes, yes," Adam said brusquely. "I thought someone would be disturbed but I'm glad it wasn't Charlotte. Could you put something on and help me? Fetch some water and a towel. Soap. Brush and comb. And do be quiet about it."

She ran back into her room and tore off the nightdress, replacing it swiftly by a gown. Tugging on slippers, she hurried beyond the baize door that led to the cavernous regions of the kitchen. The kettle was suspended over the embers of the fire and the water was warm. A swift glance showed her an earthen mixing bowl. Back in her bedchamber, she took up her own towel, comb, and an unused tablet of soap, then went softly along the hall to a partly opened door from which issued a thin stream of light. The footman emerged just as she reached it and cast his eyes down the demure gown, then raised them towards the ceiling. They'd hear all about tonight's doings down in the kitchen tomorrow. Ignoring the familiarity, she tapped on the door and stepped inside.

Adam raised his head from contemplation of the slumped figure in the chair. "I'm sorry I enrolled your help so summarily, but it seemed pointless to rouse maids when you were so wide-awake and at hand. The less fuss this causes, the better. I've sent for a warming pan, as the bed's not been used for a time. If I support my brother, could you wash his face and hands and tidy his hair? I'll see to the rest once the sheets are warmed and he's put to bed."

A rosy tide of color swept over Sable's face. Morgan was here and she'd not recognized him. There was no time to ponder over the where and how of the business. Adam tipped back Morgan's head, disclosing a crop of bristles and sunken, shadowed eyepits.

"He's had a fever. The ship was turned back to bring him ashore again in London. The fool decided to struggle here alone and all but collapsed on the step."

She fell to her knees beside the chair and began to wash the grey, unconscious face. This was not the young man she knew, so full of personality and animation. Carefully she soaped his skin and wiped it with the towel. She cleaned and dried his hands, then began to draw a comb through the tangled hair. Behind her she heard the footman reenter, the warm coals shifting inside the copper pan as it was thrust up and down and across the sheets.

"You have a gentle touch," Adam said in a repressed voice. "Do you think if Willy here, goes for the doctor, you could assist me further?"

"I was brought up with brothers. I'm no squeamish miss. I'll help. I'd be too excited to sleep now and it seems madness to wake someone who can."

"Stay then. Let's lift him onto the bed, Willy, and then you go smartly for Doctor Howe. It's lucky it's not far."

Morgan was placed upon the starched sheet and between them, Adam and Sable removed the soiled shirt and stockings. While Adam raised his brother firmly to a sitting position, Sable went on washing the limp body and patting it dry again, then covered it with a clean shirt that was lying on the press. When Morgan was ready, she lifted the warming pan and attended to the top sheets, then settled his now tidy head on the pillow after drawing the bedclothes to his chin. "There should be hot bricks in flannel. His feet should be kept warm."

"Can you—?" Adam moved his hands helplessly and shrugged.

"Of course. We used them at home." Sable smiled at him and surprised a look that perplexed her, composed as it seemed to be of gratitude and discovery.

Adam was staring out into the street when she came back, having found bricks and flannel in a cupboard and blown the fire into life with the bellows. She pushed the wrapped bricks under Morgan's unresponsive feet and looked at his face, uncaring in its stillness. "I thought I heard him speak," she said, disturbed.

"Oh, you did!" Adam had reverted to brusqueness, she noticed. "He had enough to say to begin with, then he grew quiet and—" he shrugged uncertainly, "collapsed."

"Exhaustion, perhaps. The fever seems past."

"We shall know soon enough. I think, Miss Martin, that everything possible has been done. I am grateful."

Once back in bed, she still could not sleep. The past crowded in on her mind, Morgan riding, Morgan in church with a gaggle of friends, Morgan dining by candlelight while she crouched with Brutus and Samson in the shadow of the naked statue. She remembered Morgan's body as she had so recently attended to its comfort, smooth and finely made, magnificently developed. Her hands traced the lines of her own breast and thighs, the flatness of her stomach. She drew her breath in sharply and turned over to press her cheek to the overwarm pillow. A great restlessness had possession of her, heightening her senses, driving away peace. She went over the steps of the relationship that had led, so astonishingly, to their presence under the same roof. More than once she crushed down the longing to steal along the hall to listen to what the doctor said, and again later, when silence took charge of the big house, she had to restrain herself from going to look in at Morgan, to reassure herself that he was not dead or dying. He was no business of hers and she could only antagonize Adam and Charlotte by interference on her part. Adam's newfound magnanimity would wither in the cold light of day. She had been there in a moment of weakness he now undoubtedly regretted.

She turned onto her back and stared at the dim ceiling with eyes that ached, whether with tiredness or grief, she was unable to decide.

The house was astir early next day, for all that it was a Sunday. The rustle of Charlotte's skirts and her cry of surprise, the bustle of servants, the rattle of the doctor's curricle—all disturbed the Sabbath calm. But it appeared that Sable had been right and there was nothing more wrong with Morgan now than extreme exhaustion following his feverish illness on the ship. The captain, aware of the importance of his passenger, had taken it upon himself to return to London, rather than have Mr. Hunter die during the voyage.

Sable, unable to bear the vapid remarks of Marie Claire, had busied herself with a pile of notes in her own chamber. The pier table was a confusion of letters and roughly jotted replies. There was one from a sailor, Jeremy Day, about conditions on the slave ship *Hyades*. This Jeremy Day had been so severely flogged during the final days of the voyage that he had been carried from the vessel and taken to the house of Quakers living close by. These good people kept a watch on the dock for abandoned slaves too weak for sale and no longer worth feeding and caring for, and it was during such an errand of mercy that Day was seen lying by a warehouse after his mates had reported his cold-blooded removal from the ship. The kindly treatment by the Quakers had wrought changes in the man's spirit and he had repented of his former insensitivity to the treatment of hapless Negroes by the crew of the *Hyades*. He gave sickening eyewitness accounts of what he had seen and done before religion caught him in its toils. He was prepared to name names and to divulge figures.

The letter had not been in its proper pile. It was Adam and James Grant who should have received this missive. Sable and Charlotte were allotted the female complaints, not that they were always milder and more pleasant than this. Either James or Charlotte had confused the destination of this badly written, much-blotted document. Maybe it was that the signature was hastily conceived and difficult to decipher and the name had been mistaken for Jessamy.

Sable's pity and horror at Ben's plight were restored by this tale of almost everyday behavior—if Jeremy Day could be believed. Then she remembered Ben's scars and the empty eye socket covered with the gay red patch as though he sought to minimize that nightmare, and she knew that the letter was truth. Adam might treat the diatribe with the same lawyerish caution that he'd used towards the Briggs case, but she would remain convinced of its veracity.

She went downstairs, the letter in her hand, and tapped at the study door. "Come in," Adam growled, unforthcomingly. She hesitated, wondering whether it was wise to intrude when the weekend had already been turned upside down and he had doubtless spent a troubled night.

"Oh, *do* come in!" he repeated.

She entered the panelled room with its shelves and shelves of richly bound books and leaned against the closed door, aware of the growing curiosity that tempered his previous asperity.

"Oh, I beg your pardon, Miss Martin. I have the beginnings of a devilish headache. You look remarkably fresh in spite of your labors of last evening—or was it this morning? You'll be glad to hear that Morgan will certainly recover with rest and care." A bitterness he could not conceal infused the words. "As usual, he has fallen on his feet."

"I'm glad," she said honestly, noting the haggard aspect of his face. "I should not have disturbed you, but this should by rights be yours. A bad signature—" She went to the desk and handed over the blotted pages. "It reads 'Jeremy Day.' A sailor. An unpleasant story."

He ignored the explanation though he took the letter from her. "You show little signs of wear today. How do you manage it?"

She shrugged. "I am obviously not made for sloth. Some are dormice, and others owls."

"And you are an owl? I have noted your management of your position since you came here and I can tell you that I am impressed, as is Charlotte, though she finds it more difficult to say. Do you think you will want to stay? Now that you've tasted the dubious delights of this way of life?"

"So long as you both wish."

"Charlotte says that when the recess comes and the flow of callers and letters subsides, she may wish to visit charity homes, prisons, seamen's hostels, and the like to study hospital conditions at first hand. She views schools with suspicion. She will expect you to go with her, I think."

"Then I shall go."

"There is nothing that displeases you?"

Sable thought immediately of Marie Claire and grimaced involuntarily. "No—"

"That means there is something, someone who is unkind?" Adam probed.

She shook her head. "No one is unkind."

"Uncongenial?"

He was quick enough to find the pith of a matter, she reflected.

"I suppose Mademoiselle Claire is limiting."

"I did not say it," she pointed out. "You draw your own conclusions."

His gaze returned to the letter. "Well, thank you for bringing this. I'll read it now. The sickroom is quite animated enough with Charlotte fussing like a broody hen. And I daresay my mother will arrive posthaste as soon as she receives the letter either Charlotte or Morgan may be concocting, doubtless at this moment. Now you'll imagine me niggardly and uncharitable—" His hand reached out towards the decanter on the table by the fire.

"It is not my place to condemn. But are you not glad—?"

"Glad! I thought I'd seen the back of Morgan, just between you and me. A year or two of calm in place of discord. I cannot pretend to fraternal devotion. And here he is, the voyage disrupted, the eternal prodigal son." Adam got up, the sheets of the letter scattered over the desk, unnoticed. "Forget what I am saying, Miss Martin. My natural caution has deserted me, but I'd be surprised if you betrayed confidences. We, all of us, now and again shed reticence in order to unburden ourselves. Please, if you have need, I hope you'll turn in my direction. Will you remember?"

The pale sunlight caught at her brown hair, glittered in her dark eyes. The moment was infused with a curious danger. She did not know if she wished to be committed.

"Please say you will?" he repeated.

"If there is need—"

"I'd not ignore it," he asserted.

She went out and just before the door closed she heard the sound of the glass stopper in the decanter being withdrawn, the greedy gulping sound of wine pouring into a tumbler.

Morgan was receiving visitors. The door to his room was forever open and the mews resounded with the arrival of conveyances packed with friends. "My dear Morgan," Sable heard Charlotte say. "You are suffering from exhaustion. You have been told to rest."

"Not any more," Morgan replied gaily. "Have I turned the house upside down?"

"You know perfectly well that you have."

"Is Adam very angry?" The voice was remarkably uncontrite.

"It makes his life difficult. And mine. There are the constituents—"

"Bother the constituents! I'm glad now I gave up the idea of politics. One sees so many long faces. Even Wilberforce has changed."

"William?" Charlotte's voice softened. "It has more to do with his own nature than with the House. He's the most charming young man I ever met—the most fun-loving mature. Except for you, Morgan."

"I have great recuperative powers, sister. Tomorrow I intend to get up."

"Morgan!"

"I must regain my strength and I'll not do it in bed. There is still the voyage. I intend to go as soon as I'm able even if I've to take another ship. You have no idea how the sea and the wind can take hold of you, how immense the sky is with no land to reduce it. And the islands remain to be explored. If I go soon, I may arrive for the sugar harvest."

"The whole thing becomes an orgy, so I'm told," Charlotte said disapprovingly.

"Then all the more reason for haste," Morgan replied wickedly. "I have been told so many times by Adam that I am degenerate that I'll end up believing it."

"You should be better friends," Charlotte reproved.

"Then that should apply to you and Jane also."

There was a pause, then Charlotte said, "Jane thinks of nothing but pleasure."

"I'm told we are alike," Morgan observed. "Everyone says you and Adam are so worthy—"

"I detest that word!" she cried.

"I agree. But laughter is so much better than overmuch sobriety. It makes the sun shine, magical things to happen. One stays young, though Adam does remark that he feels a sense of the ridiculous when he sees a man of middle age behave like a young cock."

"I must go to help Miss Martin. The letters were delivered half an hour since."

"Martin?" Morgan's voice grew sharp.

"The young woman who assists. Did neither of us mention her? Adam found her."

"If you did, I've forgotten. I once knew someone—but there can be no connection, not if Adam had anything to do with it. Well, go and get on with the good works, Charlotte, and send up some chocolate, if you love me."

If you love me. Sable fought down the inclination to apply those words to herself. Sable closed the door and tried to interest herself in her work. The doorbell rang again, was answered in a burst of laughter. The marble floor echoed to the tread of booted feet, then there was the duller thud of steps on the stairs, more laughter, footmen hurrying with refreshments for the callers. It was difficult, indeed, to concentrate with Morgan Hunter on the premises, especially when he had responded so unmistakably to the mention of her surname.

She had not planned to waylay him on the stairs, but their actual meeting could not have been better timed. Adam had left the house on Parliamentary business and Charlotte had decided to follow up a letter she had received that morning, concerning an alleged abuse of a prisoner held in Newgate. Sable, bound for the temporary sanctuary of her own room and moving silently to avoid the attention of Marie Claire, who was freed of her mistress's presence, was halted at the door of her bedchamber by a penetrating whisper. "So it *is* you! Please come here, Sable. Hurry. The place is alive with philanthropists and the opportunity may be lost if you delay."

She turned and he was there, leaning on a stick, his face pale, but infinitely better than on the night of his collapse. "You should be in bed—"

"Please, Sable. I'll return to it with pleasure, if you come."

She needed no second bidding. Within a minute they were inside the room and he was offering her the best chair while he set aside the cane with the clouded amber head and lay on the top of the bedclothes, leaning on one elbow and surveying her quizzically.

"Well—Miss Martin! I think you may owe me an explanation."

"Do I? This is your brother's house."

"You've grown up. I'd scarcely have known you. Tell me what happened to change you."

Sable told him the same story she'd told Adam. His face

104

changed when she reached the part Clara Caven had played in her departure from Lady Chryston's. His eyes became secretive and his mouth thinned. There was none of the open anger and censure that had marked Adam's reaction. But he laughed when she came to the point in her tale where she'd sat astride the big stone with a tinker's bundle and a sprained ankle and calmly hailed his brother's carriage. "How like you! I can see you sitting there, quite mistress of the situation. And Adam? How did he take it?"

"He was very—masterful. And a trifle grim."

"Did he—had he seen Miss Caven?"

"No. The first he knew of her presence was what I told him. He was all for going back to take up the business with her."

"And why didn't he?"

"I persuaded him not to. It would have accomplished nothing." Sable waited for Morgan to say he also was acquainted with Clara, but he merely lay there, smiling a little as he pictured her rescue. Her heart beat faster. He had all of his old attraction for her and there was an excitement in being here, at his bedside, where it was not impossible they would be disturbed by a servant with instructions to see to Morgan's comfort or to force medicine on him against his will. Not like Lady Agatha who begged for a bulwark against pain. How was she? Had she grieved after Sable left? Damn Annie. Damn Clara Caven.

"You look sad," Morgan said, sitting up. "An unusual expression for you. I connect you with rebellion, determination, ambition, and bravery. Some quality that has carried you from byre to gentleman's bedchamber." His voice changed. "You always wanted to be here, didn't you? From that first, titillating meeting, I knew. I remember the proud way you held your head in York while you waited for the coach. How you said, 'I am to be companion to Lady Chryston.' A pity it had to be spoiled for you. Now you are surrounded by worthiness, a commendable quality, but so dull. They make up for Jane and me, Charlotte and Adam, but I suspect you are one of us at heart, that you are drawn towards color and emotions rather than drabness and sterility."

"I do not see them like that! And I find the work interesting. It can be rewarding to put matters right for someone who has no idea how to set about it himself."

"So, you would make the world perfect. But you do like me, don't you, Sable Martin? Just a little?" Pale and haggard as he still was, he had the power to claim all of her attention and her honesty.

"I have always liked you." *Even when I saw you take another girl in your arms, I could not stop loving you, regretting you,* she thought.

"Help me eat these grapes." He leaned over and snipped off a small bunch from the large one and put it in her hand. *"Like.* Is that all, Miss Martin? I think you mean more than liking."

She ate a grape so that she need not answer, then another and another.

"I shall ask you again when they are all gone," he told her, his eyes filled with mischief.

"What good would it do either of us to tell you any such thing?" she asked. "Even if it were true."

"I shall be gone soon and then it may be too late." His voice beguiled her, lulled her thoughts of discovery. "I'd like something to take with me. A memory—" No mockery now, only an urgency that was real. "A pity I've not the strength to carry out intentions."

"Then it must keep for another day." She strove to keep her tones calm, amused. "And now I must go." She stood up firmly and moved towards the door.

"Come back," he said very softly so that she barely heard. "Come back—anytime."

She did not look back for fear she would no longer have the strength to go.

"Miss Martin," Adam said, coming into the interview room which was unaccustomedly empty. "That letter you brought me. From Jeremy Day—"

"Oh, yes. I remember it well." She forced herself to look alert, to listen intelligently.

"There was a case some time back. James brought it to my notice. There have been others, of course, but this letter revived the whole matter of slavery as the iniquitous thing it is. The letter arouses strong feelings of sympathy for men owned by others who abuse the privilege and treat them worse than beasts, and no one present in the vicinity of a fairground can say we are animal lovers. A hunted fox has a comparatively clean, quick end in comparison with what bulls, dogs, badgers, cockerels must endure in the name of entertainment."

"I have always thought so. And I know of such a Negro, beaten almost to death, then rescued only to fear being found—" Sable stopped, horrified. She had sworn to say nothing of Ben, and just because her wits were addled by Morgan's sorcery, she was made indiscreet.

"Such a man would lend great weight to any case against slavery—" he began.

"I have forgotten where he's to be found," she said quickly. "He may have died."

"Or you regret the confidence and fear for him," Adam said quietly. "Well, I suppose I must probe no further. I feel I should like to uncover such a case and bring it into the open but it would not be fair to the victim. Day's letter is damaging enough and could cause a stir, allied to previous episodes."

"Surely a beginning would be for English ships to refuse to carry slaves?"

"You hit the sore point immediately," Adam replied ruefully. "We need the colonies for the trade, we need cheap labor to grow and harvest, and if we refused to carry or employ slaves, the French would take over all such trade that the Portuguese and Spaniards did not first filch, and"—he made an expressive gesture—"England becomes steadily poorer and a bad standard of living for less fortunate people becomes a nightmare of deficiencies. I'm glad the responsibility of Hunter affairs still rests with my father and that Morgan will have a say. I should find it difficult to resolve my sympathies, I confess, were I alone in the matter."

Sable said nothing.

"Why, do you think, doI find it so easy to talk to you?"

"I can't answer that."

"I came in search of Charlotte, but it seemed not to matter that she was not here."

"She's with Morgan. Everyone was attended to and there seemed no need for both of us."

"She's fond of Morgan. Everyone is." *Except me,* Adam might have said. Instead, he continued, surprisingly, with, "I have thought over the matter of your place in the household. If James sits with us at meals, I really cannot see why you should not do the same. You are as much Charlotte's aide-de-camp as he is mine and you've proved your fitness long since. I think we can assume your probationary period to be over from this morning. I'll tell Charlotte of my decision."

"But Mademoiselle Claire?"

"She could have joined the rest of the staff, but preferred to remain alone. In any case I do not see that it concerns her. You've kept out of her way, haven't you? I'm not blind."

"Only because we seem to have—no point of contact." At one time, she thought, she'd have said "nothing in common." Words made their own differences in status, raised or cast down a person, made levels, separated.

"Then there are no bones broken. You'll sup with us tonight. If you wish—"

"I do wish—thank you."

"Good, until seven o'clock then, Miss Martin."

"Until seven."

Then she was alone, the excitement bubbling along her veins, her eyes shining. Adam was, quite unintentionally, helping her to see Morgan, be closer to him. Be careful, she told herself. Becoming on a par with James Grant did not automatically mean she could forget her antecedents. She would not have wanted to if it had not been for Morgan Hunter. But he knew everything about her and still he wanted her.

She dressed carefully for supper. She'd ironed the yellow gown and borrowed Marie Claire's curling tongs. The one piece of jewelry she possessed was a small jet brooch given to her by Lady Agatha some months after her advent at Knowehead, and this she pinned to one side of the low neckline. Morgan called this her milkmaid's dress, but it was the prettiest she had. Black slippers and purse. This would have to do.

It took all her self-possession to walk through the open doorway and into the dining room. There was no bright blaze of light, only the comforting glow of fire and candle. Adam rose from the high-backed chair at the head of the table. "Miss Martin will sit here," he said and one of the footmen pulled back a similar chair so that she might sit beside him. Charlotte, facing her, smiled vaguely as though her thoughts were elsewhere, and James, his eyes the color of pale gooseberries, inclined his head. He always looked studious.

"Where is Morgan?" Adam inquired of Charlotte, his irritation plain.

"He insisted he get ready himself and he's still weak."

"That's him now," James said, turning his head, and indeed, there were faltering footsteps on the stair, a slow progress towards the door, and Morgan framed in the gap, his handsome pallor offset by a wide-skirted coat of dark crimson and a waistcoat of white satin embroidered with green- and plum-colored silks. He leaned for a moment, smiling, one hand on the jamb. "Sorry if I kept you—" He could have made no more effective entrance.

"Help him, Willy," Adam said without waiting for his brother to finish. "And then you may tell Cook we are ready."

Morgan was duly settled beside Charlotte. Sable was intensely aware of him. She had not imagined that he would be here tonight in spite of his threats to be up and about so soon. His presence was both joy and torment. James and Charlotte had begun a desultory conversation, but the two brothers sat for a time in silence before Adam addressed the girl. "We have decided to visit Day," he said in his formal way. "James and I intend to go quite soon. I wondered, seeing you had read the letter first, if you'd care to come? Charlotte has enough on her hands with a sickroom and the household, but you've been out so little, I thought it might be a change for you."

"I should be pleased." It would be a reprieve from Morgan if nothing else. Sable remembered that soft, whispered invitation. She would find it hard to resist.

"You have not introduced me," Morgan said loudly.

"Oh," Charlotte murmured. "Do you not remember? Miss Martin."

"Of course. But you mentioned such intellectual accomplishments, I expected someone old and staid."

"Brains are not necessarily the perquisite of age," Adam observed pedantically.

"I am still surprised to see so young a woman who is so capable. Girls are not usually brought up to think, only to be decorative. Not that Miss Martin is not decorative, but to find she can read, write, form opinions, meet Adam's approval, then that can only be called exceptional. Jane could have done with taking a leaf out of her book. Does ambition drive you, Miss Martin? It would seem so."

"How did you guess?" Sable asked swiftly to counteract Adam's disapproval. "I never found that procrastination helped anyone."

"Procrastination!" Morgan's eyes showed delightful mockery. "You exude erudition."

"Not yet. But I shall. I was once advised to learn something new every day, and then, more importantly, to remember it." She challenged Morgan deliberately.

"And who dispensed this guideline to knowledge?" Still he had not given her away.

"Someone you know. Tom Dobbs." She breathed more easily, sure now of his allegiance.

"You know Tom?" Adam said, surprised.

"I have known him for years. He told me he knew you and your family, but it was only recently that I discovered you'd bought his house for Lakeland summers. Lady Chryston told me after we met that day of the picnic."

"A strange man," Adam said and pushed away his soup as though he were not hungry. Shadows of candlelight flickered in the frills of his stock and the lace at his wrists. In the half-light he looked almost as handsome as Morgan, only fairer and more finely drawn. Sable was always aware of some torment about him, a bitterness that spurred him on.

Morgan turned and smiled at Sable. "What think you of London, Miss Martin?"

"The contrasts amaze me. There's so much that is cruel and as much that is beautiful. There is nowhere like it. My first taste of it was hearing John Wilkes upbraid the King. I'd not realized at the time that the King had tried for so long to rid himself of the man. He's even been in prison, I believe, but created such havoc there with his multitudes of supporters they had to fabricate a law to show he was wrongfully imprisoned to save their faces and King George's. I could not help feeling a sneaking admiration for his impudence."

"Do you still have that admiration, Miss Martin?" Adam asked drily.

"Not really. It was he who provoked the Gordon Riots. And keeps American-English hostilities alight. No, I'd steer clear of troublemakers. It's only that some miscreants are more attractive or amusing than others, which gives them an unfair advantage." Sable looked directly at Morgan as she said this and was rewarded by his answering laughter.

"I should take you to see Mrs. Siddons," he said. "I've quite a fancy to see the lady—"

"If she goes at all, it will be in a party," Adam broke in abruptly. "Miss Martin is in my care while she stays here."

"Do you not trust her?" Morgan inquired innocently, leaning back in his chair and taking a deep draught from the glass.

"It's not Miss Martin I don't trust," his brother said shortly.

"Then it must be me. But I'm reformed, Adam. As I lay half-dead with fever, swamped in oceanic nightmares of delirium, I heard myself swear to put aside all bad ways if only I should come out of it alive and in my proper senses. You've not lain in a creaking cabin with the beams of the roof rising and falling, one minute almost resting on your eyeballs, the next soaring to a brown, shrouded sky where no clouds were set, your soul shrinking and expanding to the same rhythm. Waves of heat and violent cold, and a terror of being snuffed out, to close your eyes and never open them. It changes a man. And the light of the lantern flickering was the fire of hell—"

"Morgan," Charlotte broke in uncomfortably. "You know you play to a gallery. You exaggerate. There's been no real sign of a saved soul either in speech or action, so why pretend?"

"One coats pills with sugar to hide the kernel." He

shrugged disarmingly. "So it is with converts. One wishes not to embarrass one's nearest and dearest with applications of ash and sackcloth—"

Sable could not stop herself from laughing. James and Charlotte looked so sceptical, and Adam so weary. Morgan was incorrigible. And his beautiful coat was so far the reverse of the penitential cloth. The embroidered waistcoat dazzled. It could, of course, be an effect of the wine she had just drunk, but it was as though he had leaned across the table and touched her, recognizing her response to that touch. How obvious tonight the antipathy between him and Adam. It did not require much imagination to pinpoint the source of the enmity. Clara Caven. What had she done to Morgan's brother? Charlotte had never referred to Lady Chryston's niece, though she must know something of Clara's relations with Adam and Morgan. But Adam was a man who kept his own counsel. It would be unlike him to broadcast either deep joy or great misery even to his own family. It was not a subject, either, that Sable could bring up when alone with Morgan. Alone with Morgan. Her imagination, fired by wine, soared to dizzying heights.

"You'd be a fit stage companion for Mrs. Siddons," Adam was saying, for the first time this evening showing a spark of amusement. Sable was struck by the change in him. Divested of that weary anger he could attract. Wine could change a person as much as a severe illness. He'd been very kind to her but what would be his attitude if she showed her feelings for Morgan? She'd no wish to be forced to leave Cardigan Square, as she'd been ejected from Knowehead. Disturbed, she left the remainder of the wine and turned her attentions towards the food only to find that her inclination for it had deserted her. Chris had lost his appetite when he courted Pansy, she remembered. Already that seemed a decade ago.

113

She could not ignore Morgan, yet, in some strange way she was bound to Adam for his forbearance and loyalty. The worst thing she could do was to hurt him as he had been hurt by Clara.

Chapter 6

The docks were a hulk of dark buildings, their traceries of shrouds against the stars. Masts swayed and tilted with the pull of the tide and lantern light bobbed on the Thames water. Boats moved silently, searching for debris. Drunken figures lay on cobbles, like the dead, while others, less drunk, swayed singing or cursing all the world in general. The distant beauty of the reflected vessels was offset by the gangrenous shore, the tipsy revelling that filled the dimness of dockside taverns and occasionally burst out into shouts and cries on slithery pavements.

The streets were too narrow for the coach and Adam had decided to walk the rest of the way to Jeremy Day's lodging. With James Grant to one side and Adam Hunter to the other, Sable was able to enjoy the unusual experience without any real fear of the consequences. Now and again they had to move quickly to avoid the streams of ordure that were poured without warning from upper windows. She saw now why Adam had urged her to wear the ladylike clogs. They were not ugly like the ones she had worn as a farm lass, but they served to raise her from the mire.

"We'll meet none but draggle-tails and mud larks here," James said, covering his nose fastidiously. The smell of the river was strong and insidious, creeping inside house and shed, tavern and cloak, clinging with rank fingers to what it touched.

"Plenty of work for Charlotte if she's still of the same mind. No use having a foot in Westminster if one ignores what lies beyond the doorstep. Do you find you are put off?" Adam asked Sable.

"It's—it's exciting. I know I should probably hold up my hands in disgust and yet it—it thrills. The lights and the ships—wondering where they go and where they have been." Sable could understand Morgan's preference for the sea and its far horizons. "It's all so different from Cardigan Square and from Windermere." A lifetime, too, from Daggleby with its duck pond and barns, its limestone dikes and the great moorland tracts all white and purple with winter. She had a sudden longing to see her mother. But she had written as often as she could and she had her own living to make. There was no more she could have done. Tom Dobbs or the preacher would read her letters. Mother would be proud and Father doubtful, seeing pitfalls as he had always done.

"This is the street," James exclaimed, wrapping his cloak the tighter. The narrow canyon, full of gross shadows and smells of fish and of filth and of wet rope, closed in on them. Adam tripped over an inert bundle by a steep stair and fell against Sable unexpectedly. His hands fastened upon her arm, and for a moment they were bound in mutual need and support. She felt light and dizzy without his weight, as though she were set upon a turbulent sea after a calm harbor, her senses careering along at breakneck speed.

"What number was it?" Adam asked. "Was it five or eight?"

"Eight."

Adam knocked on the door. A baby cried fretfully, its thin wailing indistinguishable from a cat's. Someone grumbled, a chair was thrust back. Footsteps and a great bulbous shape in the doorway, a frizz of ghoulish hair. "Wot is it?"

"Jeremy Day. He lives here?"

"That psalm-singing hypocrite! I've not seen 'im for two days, the lying brute. Owes money, too. An' all that spouting of reform. A leopard don't change its spots. Wot d'you want 'im for, then?"

"I'd prefer to tell that to Day. You say he should have been here sooner?"

"Two days since. False swine." The thick lips parted to spit down the side of the stair. In the shadows the inert form twitched and subsided.

"That's not Day, is it?" James stirred the slumped mass with his toe. It groaned feebly.

"No. Saul West, that is. Used to be mates wi' Jeremy but he don't go along wi' Jeremy being a saint of a sudden. Though where he got the siller to get in that state, I can't think. Not a farthing to rub agen another usually—" The hateful voice was sharper.

"If Day comes back, would you ask him to call at this address? It's about his letter—You won't lose that paper, will you?"

"Don't I get nothing for takin' care of it for Jeremy? Could get lost, what wi' the nippers and all. Pick up anythin', that lot."

Adam produced a coin and the puffy hand closed over it voraciously. "You're a gent." A trio of round, pallid faces

117

showed behind the slatternly mother, one above another. She swung an arm and knocked them aside. One snuffled but the others had the sense to remain quiet. How wretched they looked with their hair all matted and there were sores on their lips.

"Poor things," Sable whispered.

The woman shut them from view. They stood uncertainly, Adam watching the sacklike form of Saul West for a moment, but there was obviously nothing to be had from him this evening. The man moved, snored and lay on his back under a patch of starlight.

"Gin drunk," James pronounced. "He'll not come round for hours. Odd how Day disappeared. If he's reformed you'd imagine he'd keep away from trouble—"

"No," Sable said firmly. "That's when most trouble starts. It did for Tom Dobbs. He said it brought out the worst in people. He was attacked, stoned, treated as a freak at the fair."

"That's true," Adam affirmed. "We can do nothing more about Day for the moment. Perhaps he will yet put in an appearance. We must wait."

"I'll come back and see West in the morning. She'll know where he lives." James indicated the cracked window at which Sable saw the face of one of the children staring out at them. She raised her hand, and, after a moment the child raised his, to be struck aside the next moment as the woman noticed his action. Her great bulk filled the small pane, shutting out the light. The child cried out in pain.

"I've a mind to have it out with her," Adam said furiously, one foot on the narrow stair.

"It would do no good," James told him. "She'll only destroy the paper you left and beat him the worse once we've gone."

"A pity it was a wild-goose chase."

"Not quite," James said. "At least we know he exists. That it's no crankish letter."

"We do not have the proof we require to make a case of it."

"We could advertise in the news sheets for the man who actually wrote the letter."

"Why, so we could," Adam replied in a better humor. "You'd best do that tomorrow. A pity, though, the evening's wasted. I feel cheated."

"I've enjoyed the experience," Sable said. "Except for seeing those children—But the river is splendid."

"Apart from the smells."

There were barges moored by the wharf and something moved beside them on the mud. Sable stared at dark shining figures that looked not quite human. She took Adam's arm and pointed. "Mud larks," he said. "A kind of beachcomber only it's not the clean finding of debris on a sandy beach by the sea. It's poking in the wet mud for wood and coal and suchlike. Not only children, either. I've seen old beldams with baskets and leaky kettles they use for scooping. Copper nails are best, but everything's grist to their mill. Bones. They can sell anything once it's cleaned. Sailors give them weevilly biscuits for the nails—they are usually lost from a vessel and can be used again."

"What are they doing?" Sable said quickly, glad of a diversion. "They've found something."

Faint lantern light outlined three of the glistening shapes that took on the semblance of seals or of beings that had climbed from the ooze, shapeless and deformed. She shivered. "Something large, I think."

"Oh God, it's a body. See? It must be. Legs, arms, a lolling head." James craned forward and the links of the chain grated. The thing, deposited by the foot of slimy steps, showed a pallid glimmer of a face. A lantern bobbed across the foreshore and was placed on a step.

"Poor creature," Sable said, still cold. The light wavered and the corpse seemed, horridly, to move.

"A sailor perhaps. It's easy to miss one's step in the dark

after a night on the waterfront. Or someone who cannot face up to life."

"I'd never want to give in!" she said violently. "To fight is better."

"Perhaps it wasn't an accident," Adam said. "Perhaps he did fight."

"Even that seems preferable. To fight and lose is at least dignified. But to stand aside and allow fate to overtake—"

"Aye, there's a distinction," James agreed. "I shall go down to see what I can do."

"Yes. I shall take Miss Martin back to the carriage. See that someone from the Harbor Commission is present."

"Don't wait for me. It could take some time. I'll make my own way," James said and set off down the steps.

Adam took Sable's arm and she turned away thankfully from the grim sight.

"I'm sorry the evening has not been a happier one. I made a mistake, I think, bringing you. It was against Charlotte's better judgement."

They reached the carriage, wrapped in their own thoughts, oblivious to the passing traffic of theatregoers and supper crowds bound for a meal and games of faro that could last the night. They were not so indifferent to the beggars by the curb, the vendors of hot peasecod, the men with skewers of cat and dog meat which they offered at mews behind the squares, the piemen, and the muted sound of muffin bells that carried for long distances in spite of the rattle of wheels and the clop of hooves. They seemed more the real life of London than those painted faces, spotted with black patches from brow to chin, that stared so emptily from coach interiors or the dim seclusion of sedan chairs and were escorted by the sweating, ragged figures of link boys, torches flaring as they labored to keep up with swaying vehicles and darted into gutters to pick up carelessly tossed coins as though their lives depended on it. As she supposed they did. There was something wrong with a world that allowed a favored few to gamble away fortunes while so many worked so hard and so discouragingly for so little.

They were almost home when the carriage took a corner a shade too abruptly and the conveyance drew to a halt, the horses plunging and rearing alarmingly in a noise of oaths and shouted voices. Sable was pitched across the seat to land with a thud across Adam's lap, her head striking the upholstery with unpleasant force.

"Fool!" she heard Adam say harshly as he grabbed her and sat her upright again. He put his head out of the window. She saw beyond his shoulder the window of the other carriage and the profile of its occupant, a pouched, dissolute face she disliked instinctively for its sensuality, its suggestion of corruption. The man turned, seeing her as she craned forward, her cheeks drained of color from the shock of the collision.

"Oh, it's you, Hunter," a wine-sodden voice said with a semblance of good humor. "Sorry if I forgot myself but you must admit it was part your man's fault." The degenerate gaze stole over Sable and quickened to an interest she found intolerable. "Still, there's no harm done. We've not met for a while, Adam, though I've seen Clara—"

"Clara?" Adam's voice was expressionless. "You mean recently?"

"Of course I mean recently."

"I imagined her with her aunt."

The man laughed, including Sable in that amusement. "Can you see Clara being content with a hermit existence? She told me she only went to put some filly's nose out of joint. A wench with ambitions to disinherit her. But playing the dutiful niece became a shade too exacting."

"So Lady Chryston is again without a companion?"

"Does it matter?" the man asked lazily, then shouted to his coachman. "Are the beasts all right?"

"Yes, sir. There's only a scratch or two on the doorpanel."

121

"Well, we'd not quarrel, Adam, over a touch of paint, eh? You must call on me. And bring your young lady—"

"I'm busy, Parksworth. I hardly think—"

"Oh, don't deprive me of the pleasure, man. It's not often one sees such freshness in the city, such enviable youth." Parksworth's laughter grated with its suggestion of lewdness. Sable, shocked into recognition of his identity, could only stare, for once dumbfounded. Ben's master. His name was unusual and Clara had mentioned she knew the man. He leaned forward, his hand on the edge of the window and she saw a scar on the back of it, pale and puckered into the shape of a distorted star.

"Do not let me keep you from your engagement," Adam said with icy courtesy. "I'll reimburse you with pleasure for any damage you've incurred."

Parksworth smiled and ducked his head towards Sable. The curls of his wig quivered with the movement. "Remember, little lady, that I invited you. You'll still be welcome even if Adam declines." He raised the scarred hand in a mocking salute. "Remember!"

"Drive on," Adam ordered roughly. "Goodnight to you, Parksworth."

Sable had one last, swift sight of the man's meaningful grin, then the vehicles disengaged and there was only the empty street barred with stripes of light from uncurtained windows, the long shadows of trees.

"I'm sorry you should have been subjected to two kinds of disagreeableness," Adam told her.

"It's all part of life's rich tapestry, is it not?" she replied with an attempt at humor.

Adam appeared not to notice. "But you'd never countenance accepting an invitation from him, would you?" he asked urgently. "If I happened to be away somewhere."

"No," she answered positively. "Not if he were the last man in the world."

"Good. And you're not hurt?"

"I'm not hurt."

"That's good too. I should not like you to be, not by anyone."

There was that note of inevitability in his voice that disturbed her afresh. If it were not so presumptuous she'd swear he liked her too well, Sable thought. And if he did, she must disappoint him, for her emotions were engaged elsewhere. And in a quarter where he would be bound to disapprove.

Her heart bumped uncomfortably. She must stop him, somehow, from becoming overfond. How, she could not decide, but it had to be done. Then the carriage stopped at the house and she knew she was reprieved for yet another night from all Hunters.

Charlotte looked pale, Sable thought, as she joined her in the interview room.

"Did you know it was Jeremy Day who was dragged from the Thames mud last night?" she asked.

"No! I went to bed early and I've seen no one this morning," Sable answered.

"James was there when the man was identified. It was not far from his lodging. One of the Quakers who once befriended him recognized the corpse."

"How did he die?"

"He—he had been beaten and thrown into the water."

"Because of that letter?"

"It might have been. Or he could have quarrelled with a former crony, a man called West. He took foolish exception to Day's redemption, it appeared. James was there for hours once he knew it was Day. I doubt if one could ever determine the manner or reason of his death without witnesses. And there are none."

"Poor man. He had a miserable life if all he says of sailors is the truth. They are treated worse than slaves. At least the slaves are worth money, but if a sailor dies, it's one man less to be paid. How dreadful to mean so little."

"Adam says there were children at the lodging, ill-treated by their mother."

Sable told Charlotte what she knew and took a note to investigate the matter. They were going through the correspondence when Belle Briggs and her mother were ushered into the room, Mrs. Briggs grim and Belle pallid.

"Oh, it's you again," Charlotte said surprised. "What is it?"

"Something Belle remembered, Miss Hunter. Mr. Hunter said not to hesitate to come back if she did."

"Of course. What was this something?"

"Go on, Belle. Tell the lady," Mrs. Briggs prompted, nudging the thin child.

Sable saw the already watery eyes fill with tears that Belle dashed, surreptitiously away. She was visited by a pang of strongest pity. "Come on, Belle," she coaxed. "It's not bad if it will stop other girls being so mistreated. Don't be afraid." And she reached out and took hold of the cold hand in her warm clasp, sensing the trembling of the girl's undernourished body. "Did you recognize something about the house?" she suggested.

"No, it was—" her mother began.

"You mustn't say, Mrs. Briggs. Hearsay won't hold up in a court. Belle must tell her own story."

"It—it was about that man. The first man—" The childish voice quivered.

"Well?" Sable prompted gently. "What about him?"

"It was something I'd forgotten," Belle whispered. "Only in bed last night I had a sort of dream—"

"Nightmare, you mean," Mrs. Briggs said vengefully. "You never heard such screams."

"Mrs. Briggs!" Charlotte reproved. "That's not helping."

124

"What was in the dream?" Sable asked softly, putting her arm round the suddenly hostile shoulders. "You could prevent dozens of girls from suffering as you did. Wouldn't that be a good thought? You would not have come today if you hadn't been brave enough to face the ordeal."

"I—remembered his hand. I saw it in the candlelight and there was a funny sort of mark on it." Belle sniffed and wiped her nose on the back of her wrist.

"What sort of mark? A birthmark, do you mean? A mole, a wart?"

"What's a birthmark, Miss Martin?"

"A red blotch."

"No. It wasn't like that. It was sort of—gathered. Like little pleats in a ring. Like he'd had an accident."

"What sort of shape? Round?"

"No. More like—pointed." Belle frowned unhappily.

"Could you draw it? If I gave you a quill and the ink?"

"Oh, no! I never used them." The girl looked pale and miserable, spent with the effort of imparting her remembered knowledge, afraid of the trials ahead.

"Well, if I make a few shapes on this paper, would you tell me if any of them resemble the wound you noticed?" Sable reached for a fresh sheet and made Belle stand beside the desk. "Is it this? Or this? That, perhaps?"

"No, miss. None of them."

"Perhaps, Miss Hunter, we could have a cup of chocolate and then try again? There cannot be so many shapes and it could be so important."

Charlotte rang the bell for the maid. "Would it be admissible evidence? We'd have only Belle's word."

"They could find those other children. Their combined identification would do, wouldn't it?"

"Perhaps. Yes, I see that it could be worth the trouble. Chocolate, please, Mary, and bring some biscuits."

The chocolate was brought and drunk with dreamy enjoyment by mother and daughter. Belle looked almost pretty, warmed, and soothed, her hangdog dejection half-forgotten. She watched, fascinated as Sable continued to make doodles on the sheet of paper, each stroke thick and firm. It was just as Sable was about to give up when Belle turned lint-white and gave a little cry. "That! That's it, Miss Martin."

The mark she had just made was something she had dredged out of a recollection of last night. An irregular shape like a badly made star.

Anyone could have a scarred hand, Sable kept thinking for the rest of the day. She had asked James what could have caused a wound that healed in that fashion and he said that a bullet might have done it. Soldiers, duellists, highwaymen, sailors, anyone used to arms might have received a similar keepsake. Just because she had disliked instinctively the man she had seen in the carriage last night, she must be fair. Parksworth repelled her and was capable of great cruelty. His treatment of Ben had proved that. And he had seemed attracted to her for her youth and freshness, but she knew she looked older than her years. Surely a man so sophisticated and experienced would find nothing of interest in a waif like Belle Briggs? Then she remembered how Belle had changed under the ministration of kindness and sweet chocolate. It was her harsh treatment that had altered her.

She decided she could only tell Adam of her suspicion but a messenger arrived to say that Mr. Hunter had been invited to dine with Mr. Charles Fox and would be home late. No one was to wait up for him. Charlotte expressed relief at the news. She had looked white all day and complained of a headache. "I shall go to bed now and hope to feel better in the morning. I fear it may be migraine. It's exceptionally severe."

"Can I do anything?" Sable offered.

"No, thank you. I have Marie. Leave those notes for to-morrow. I often think you work too hard, then, when you do go out for a change, you find corpses!"

"And that, of course, is to be deplored," Morgan said out of nowhere.

"How you startled me!" Charlotte cried, clutching her chest. "How quietly you move when it suits you."

"At least I no longer drag my legs with weakness. See? I can dance now." And he proceeded to perform a very stately minuet around the desk, humming his own accompaniment. The tiredness was almost gone from his face and his eyes sparkled with good nature.

"It's good to see you so transformed," Charlotte told him.

"Let me help you to your room," he suggested solicitously, and while Charlotte responded to this cosseting, he flashed a look at Sable that told her plainly he meant to make the most of the evening.

"James will be at supper, will he not?" she inquired of Charlotte.

"No. He says he means to visit a family friend since Adam will be out. Oh, dear. If I don't lie down soon I'll not make the stairs," Charlotte murmured, pressing a hand to her temple and closing her eyes. "You must all manage without me."

"Of course we will. You are not to worry," Morgan said soothingly. He was wearing the dark crimson coat and looking more handsome than ever. Sable was conscious of an almost pleasurable alarm. She watched the two figures climb the stair, Morgan's arm around Charlotte's narrow waist, her head on Morgan's shoulder. Where it would always have a right to be, Sable thought emptily. No matter what happened to them both, a brother and sister could never really grow apart if there was a fondness between

127

them as strong as there appeared to exist between these two.

She went upstairs to wash and met Marie Claire on the landing, her arms loaded with shawls and eau de cologne and sal volatile. Marie gave her a knowing glance as she passed and the girl had the uncomfortable feeling that the maid knew all about those visits to Morgan's room, innocent as they were.

Morgan was there when she went down to the dining room. She stared. He was sitting in Adam's chair and smiling at her expression of surprise.

"Should you?" she said doubtfully.

"Who is to know?"

"No one—I suppose."

"Then come, sit beside me."

"The butler, the footmen—"

"Will say nothing. They know they are well-taken-care-of when I am here. A greased palm works miracles."

"I hope he does not come back unexpectedly." She sat down and unwound her linen napkin.

"If he is dining with Charles Fox, how can he?" Morgan shrugged carelessly.

Sable move uncomfortably. The shadow of Adam seemed there between them, not to be ignored. "Now that you are recovered, I imagine you'll be going soon? Back to sea?"

"Quite soon. Will that please you?"

She said nothing and he seized upon her silence triumphantly. "You do mind! I'd begun to think you'd decided on Adam—"

"Adam! Why should I decide any such thing? Even if he had asked me—"

"So he hasn't."

"Of course not."

"Why ever do you think he brought you here in the first place? Why were you given such license? Assistant to Char-

128

lotte, supper with the master, your chair close to his, compliments and approval. He's head over heels in love with you. And the fact that Clara had you turned out of Knowehead couldn't have been more in your favor. Don't you understand? She toppled on those all too claylike feet and pushed you towards him to restore his self-esteem. Not that she'd be pleased about it. She'd be furious if she knew—"

"Was he in love with Clara Caven?" she brought herself to ask.

"Let's say he was in love with his own ideal of Clara. And he's a good catch for any girl, particularly a girl who cannot spend money fast enough and who has a rich aunt who refuses to die to please her."

"Poor Lady Chryston. Imagine knowing someone would prefer you dead."

"Adam never really looked at women till he met Clara. She can be deuced beguiling."

"You should know," Sable could not resist saying.

"What's that supposed to mean?" he asked sharply, then laughed. "Oh, I see. Those windows at the Hall. Never could resist our way of life, could you! And there you sit as if you owned the place. I'm damned if I don't admire you more than anyone I've ever known. Oh, good, supper. I'm famished."

There was little chance to say anything more personal during the meal but Morgan exerted himself to be charming and attentive and the wines were particularly good as though the butler had chosen the best of the cellar in the master's absence. Sable had a mental picture of Adam at Fox's table, his back very straight, his eyes empty. How could two brothers be so different? She realized she was a little afraid of Adam, she who had rarely experienced fear.

"Come to my room afterwards," Morgan said when the dishes were removed. "Please, Sable."

"I think Marie Claire knows I visited you. She's a curious

woman. She gave me the most searching look before supper."

"Bother French maids! But she'll be too busy with Charlotte."

"If your sister's asleep she won't be needed."

"Must the evening be wasted?" he demanded, crestfallen.

Fortified by food and drink, her reservations part-destroyed, Sable did not want to waste the evening either. Morgan, recognizing this, pounced before she changed her mind.

"What would you like to do more than anything?"

"Ride in a sedan chair," she answered without hesitation.

"Well, why not?"

"Could we?"

"Who's to care? The servants don't want us. Charlotte's got a migraine. Marie Claire is waiting with her beady eyes fixed on both our doors. James is boring some relative. And Adam is dining with politicians. When the cat's away?" He pulled her to her feet, laughing. "And Charlotte did tell you not to do any of those interminable notes. I'll find you a sedan chair if it kills me."

"Oh." The anticipation died from her face. "I've nothing to wear that's good enough."

"Does it matter?"

"Oh, yes. The real thrill would be to feel a lady, not a—" She stopped.

"Not a farmer's daughter pretending to be a lady?" Morgan supplied.

"Yes."

"Then I must find you something. Something—ladylike."

"How can you?"

"There are some things of Mother's up in the room I have. She left them when she came to inspect the house for

Adam. For damp and mice and all those things he should never have bothered about. She thought they'd be useful when she came next."

"I thought she would have come to see you before now."

"We decided that it was not worth the trouble to send for her, the worst being over before I reached London. She was not well herself before I set sail. It seemed cruel to worry and upset her when I soon must repeat the departure. It's an onerous journey from Yorkshire."

"I couldn't possibly wear anything that was hers."

"Why not? You'd have permission from me. Anyway, who's going to find out? Do you always imagine a Nemesis pursues you?"

"Not usually."

"I won't bring anything too compromising. A cloak, a fan, a pair of gloves—?"

She hesitated. "Nothing more."

He turned away from her smiling. The fire crackled after he had gone and she got up to look at herself in the oval mirror that faced the mantel. Such a beautiful mirror, clean and shining. Quite unlike the spoiled one at Lady Chryston's house in Westmoreland. A coach rattled by. Someone in a house across the street was playing a tune on a spinet while a young man sang. A cat cried mournfully from the windowsill. Overhead, a floorboard creaked.

"Here you are," Morgan said unexpectedly. She saw him reflected, his smile oddly distorted as though the glass were slightly flawed. There was something across his arm, a richness of dark green patched with white. In the moment before she spun around, she imagined he held the cat she had heard, but, facing him, she saw that the whitish object was an elaborate wig. The clouded amber cane was tucked under his arm.

"Now you can be all the lady you'd wish."

"How does one—?" She indicated the wig.

Morgan dumped the cane and the green velvet onto the

nearest chair and tossed the wig on top of them. "This is how." He pushed the hair back from her brow and from the sides of her face, then removed the ribbon from her throat to fasten the mass of curls compactly on top of her head. The white pyramid felt strange and looked stranger. Her eyes looked so large and black in contrast. He tipped up her chin, opened a little enamel box, and pressed a black spot high on her cheekbone. Then he took up the velvet which turned itself into a hooded cloak with narrow edgings of fur. It was so soft and light she hardly knew she had it on. The gloves were black like the huge feather and sequin fan that disturbed the candle flames as she flapped it to and fro.

"Now do you feel like a lady?" It was not like Morgan's voice anymore. The carefree smile had vanished. A thick silence encompassed the room. He took her in his arms and kissed her quite roughly. One hand strayed inside the cloak.

"The sedan chair," she said desperately.

"Damn the sedan chair."

"You promised. You said you'd find one if it killed you."

"But I hadn't seen you then, all dripping in forest green—so—damnably ladylike."

"Please, Morgan."

"Very well." He stood away, surveying her moodily, then took up the cane and his own cloak. He looked out into the hall. "There's no one about." She followed him, conscious of the soft swishing sound of the velvet as the folds rippled one against another. A faint scent stole out of the material. As they approached the front door a small sound made her turn and look towards the staircase. Marie Claire was standing near the top, her head craning in an effort to make out who Morgan's companion was. There was no recognition in the little, curious eyes and Sable had an impulse to laugh. Then she was outside, Marie forgotten.

* * *

The sedan chair was lined with green shagreen and smelt of patchouli and musk. Sable wondered how many other women had sat where she did now, where they had travelled and to what end. There would be secret assignations, women wearing towering wigs they wished to keep from rain and wind, women invited to some occasion beyond their station and unable to flaunt a carriage and pair. Men must have sat here too. Old men, young men in love, men like Parksworth who were both cruel and lecherous. Politicians like Adam—

The night was filled with the clop of feet on the road, the sway of the chair as it moved from right to left, the perfumed intimacy of this strange vehicle from which she saw torn fragments of flame from the linkboys' torches, the silhouettes of passing coaches and landaus, people leaving or arriving at houses, windows ablaze with candlelight across which passed elegant shadows. It was all so different from last night in that mean close by the waterfront with the mud-coated body taken from the Thames.

Morgan seemed to have vanished from existence. She knew he was in a second sedan, only a few yards behind, but the chair enclosed her in a private world where nothing intruded. The life she saw from it was transient, unconnected with anything before or after. Her body felt the movement of the conveyance as though she were on the deck of a boat with a canopy overhead. She saw, dimly, the sheen of the dark velvet, the lustre of the sequined fan on her lap. The weight of the wig pressed down on her, warming her face to unaccustomed color. She was happy and sad, proud and humble, totally disorientated. She would never forget tonight. It was the only thing of which she was certain.

She became aware that the movement of the chair was slowing down. It had stopped outside a large, pale-colored house from which light issued in amber floods. Morgan's face appeared close to hers, dark and smiling. He reached, helping her to alight, paying off the carriers and eager torchbearers.

"Where are we?"

"A gaming house. If you knew how much I wanted to come here all through that tiresome convalescence. Adam's such a wet blanket. And Charlotte—well, she's kind but she doesn't always understand that one needs something to excite. A stimulus."

"It looks very grand." Sable drew the folds of the cloak around herself and fidgeted with the black feather fan.

"And so do you," Morgan told her. "Come, you shall be my 'luck.' "

"Green is not lucky. So they say—"

He urged her up the steps. There were Negro flunkies in the hall, white-wigged, glistening in blue satin coats and pale breeches. A room lay beyond, dim and hazy, filled with small tables lit by candelabra. The tables seemed to float, small golden islands on a sea of dark carpet. Wall sconces and mirrors made attractive watery reflections across the obscurity of the ceiling. There was a buzz of conversation punctuated by bursts of laughter, the laughter as unconvincing as the entire scene.

Morgan seemed to know a great many people, all grandly dressed in glittering materials, all depressingly effete. Even the kindly glow of candleflame could not altogether conceal the coating of powder and rouge that made the female faces masks, and sometimes, regrettably, those of men. Some had as many as six patches set about their features, crescent moons, stars, circles, spades, and hearts of velvety black.

Each golden island was turreted with the white mounds of wigs in which pearls and diamonds rested, each well-worn throat was encircled with scintillating fortunes in precious stones, the metallic splendor of gold. Wrinkled hands set down a card here, held others in a tight fan while

134

eyes narrowed in cold concentration at variance with the overheated room.

Sable began to feel very warm but she could not discard the cloak. She put up the fan and swept it to and fro, disturbing the small flames and turning them to streamers of smoky fire. People addressed one another in mincing accents. Lady this and Lord that. The Honorable so-and-so. It was almost a shock to hear that some gorgeously plumaged being was a plain Mr. or Mrs. She wished they had not come. The chair was an adventure. This was tedious.

Morgan passed between the tables, obviously searching for an empty chair. A man and a woman rose, the woman saying pettishly, "and you swore we'd win! That we could not lose!" The man grunted ill-humoredly and set off across the plum-coloured carpet, the nagging lady in close attendance, and Morgan was seated in a flash, dragging Sable down to the chair so recently vacated. "You do not mind?" he asked conventionally of the three men remaining.

"Why, no. We'll cut you in." The man, more soberly attired than most in green and buff, his tiewig framing a thin, arrogant face, began to deal for four. Sable, immensely relieved that she was merely an onlooker, allowed her gaze to wander from the painted cards that weaved their incomprehensible patterns, the monosyllabic calls and replies, the scoop that lifted and set down, that pushed piles of coins around the table as though they were counters for children. Flunkies arrived with brimming glasses. She took one, in the hand that was not wielding the fan, and sipped tentatively. The liquid was sharp and sparkling and sent little bubbles shooting up her nose. She repressed a tendency to burst out laughing. Morgan had forgotten she was there. His whole attention was centred on the cards and on his three companions. A curious stillness lay over the table like a pall and she knew that to interrupt would be to bring down some form of censure upon her head, if not from Morgan, from one of the others. Figures crossed and recrossed her line of vision, all slow and stately, as though this were some grotesque minuet. Knee breeches, stockings, shoe buckles that glinted, pleating, ruching, ribbons, almost indecent necklines, weaved and vanished. She must be the only person in the room who was covered from neck to hem.

Gradually, Sable became aware of a figure that was familiar. Three tables away, a girl was sitting dressed as she had been that first night at Hunter Hall, in glistening white. Because she was in town, the golden hair was covered with the anonymity of a wig in which white flowers rested. The china-blue eyes had not yet discovered Morgan, but they would.

A great wave of violence and dislike swept over Sable. It was so like Clara to descend upon Knowehead, to sow her seeds of mistrust and deception, then to scuttle away again having left unhappiness in her wake. She could have had her inheritance if that was all she wanted. Sable would have stayed without an expectation of reward. Some of the heat of her reflections passed between this table and Clara's. The girl raised her head and encountered Sable's steady gaze above the protection of the fan. She frowned then caught sight of Morgan intent upon the game. Her expression changed. The pale eyes were flooded with reminiscence.

Damnation! Sable thought, flapping furiously with the ostrich fan. She'll not be fooled for long. She'll address me out of politeness or curiosity and what am I to say? He must speak for me. He brought me here.

But all the time she knew that she would speak for herself because of the strength of that feeling she had for Clara Caven.

Morgan's chair creaked as he leaned back. "Are you bored?"

"No, but—"

"If you are going to say that we must go back, you'll sound like Charlotte."

"Would that be so bad?" Sable saw that the man with the thin face was watching her with a flicker of interest she found unwelcome. Equally thin hands dealt the thick cards.

"I like your sister. But there is another, more pressing matter. Clara Caven is here. No, over there to your left."

"I see." Morgan did not seem overpleased and the girl was conscious of relief. "We'll meet that when it comes. Only another hand. Till I win—"

How many lips had spoken those same words, Sable wondered, holding the fan high so that Clara would not recognize her until it became inevitable. There was a man with her but he had his back to the table at which Morgan sat and all Sable saw of him was a broad brown-brocaded back and a curled wig that hung over his shoulders.

"My win, I think, gentlemen," Morgan said on a note of rising excitement.

"You'll not continue?" the thin-faced man asked.

"We must go," Sable whispered. "If anyone should look for me—"

"And who would look for you?" Morgan teased, well-pleased with his turn of fortune. "Do you think Adam will return and in his cups? And go so far as to forget himself?"

"Of course, I don't," she answered more sharply than she had intended.

"But you are worried," Morgan said quite gently and now he seemed more aware of her than of the painted kings and queens, the knaves and aces. "I promised you a sedan ride and you have more than you bargained for. Very well. We'll go. Thank you, gentlemen, and a good evening to you."

"Are you sure?" the thin-faced man said, his gaze roving

over the green cloak and the portion of face that was all Sable showed, his fingers caressing the cards.

"Quite sure. Come, my dear."

A satin-coated flunkey pulled back her chair and Sable moved away, Morgan at her back, the coins jingling in his pocket as though he savored the sound. Another minute and it would be too late for Clara to accost them. Sable breathed more easily.

"Good evening, Morgan. What a surprise," Clara said loudly. Bewigged heads turned. It was impossible to pretend one had not heard. Not that Morgan tried to evade the challenge. He smiled delightfully and placed a proprietary hand on Sable's forearm as though to establish quite firmly the fact that he was accompanied. The whole business was so effortless as to smack, undeniably, of past experience. Sable tried to tell herself the thought had not occurred to her, but, of course, it had and could not be forgotten. The heads were slanted once more towards the cards on the tables and each glowing, turreted island returned to its state of isolation.

"Clara."

"Is that all you have to say to me?" she said.

"I was on my way out. And you are attended—" He shrugged.

"When did that ever stop you?"

"I thought"—he paused—"that you had returned to your aunt?"

"I suppose Adam told you."

Morgan retained an enigmatic silence. Clara's cold blue gaze swept over Sable. She frowned again as though searching for the answer to a question, then she said, "Did he?"

"It could have been Adam." Morgan shrugged again and gave Clara the benefit of his entire attention. His look was no longer so detached. The satin gown was low-cut and Clara was pretty enough to send any man's pulses racing. "What made you think it could have been?"

"I—I called. He had just been there, so your housekeeper said. Though now that I come to think of it, he'd already left. My aunt, perhaps, though how she could have written, I can't imagine—"

"Is she completely disabled?" Morgan asked almost idly.

"No. But we should have known, Annie and I, if she'd wanted a letter sent."

"How mysterious. Why did you leave?" He made it sound unimportant.

Clara shrugged. "You know how shut off I feel up there. A week or two and I'm fit to scream."

"And what of the girl who was with Lady Chryston? Adam did mention her."

The golden islands shifted for the space of a heartbeat. The reflections of the great, heavy chandeliers with their carved prisms, licked across the carpet like tiny tongues of cool fire.

"Oh, that girl."

"Yes, that girl," he prompted softly, his hand tightening on Sable's velvet sleeve.

"I was forced to tell her to go. Not only had she influenced my aunt to change her will, but she was quite dishonest. We found articles to be missing, including a valuable ring. No. Miss Martin was a thief. A thief." The shrill voice condemned.

This was too much for Sable, who, without quite realizing how and why it had happened, stepped forward and slapped Clara, extremely hard, across one porcelain cheek. The sound ricocheted like a pistol shot. The buzz of conversation died. A ghastly stillness lay over the amber islands. All the painted, worldly-wise faces were turned in one direction like windblown leaves. They were worse than effete, Sable thought, terribly aware of Clara's animosity, the violent redness that marred one half of her features. They were debased, decayed, corrupt. The fine materials covered bodies that were soft as rotten fruit and as unhealthy, the powder and patches hid avidity and greed. And they all watched like vultures because one of their number was attacked. If it had not been for Morgan's grasp of her arm, she would be defenseless.

"How dare you!" Clara's voice grated over the cobblestones of hatred. All around them the self-indulgent eyes flashed with vicious amusement. Reddened mouths smiled. Sable thought of foxes after a kill. The whole room seemed briefly to be worm-eaten and mildewed, the splendor crumbled to show nothing that was not cankered.

"Who are you?" Clara demanded.

"This," Morgan said quite lightly, "is Miss Martin. The lady you just maligned."

The part of Clara's face that was not bruised became whiter than ever. "So it is you—"

The man in brown had risen to his feet unnoticed. Sable saw him properly for the first time. It was, inevitably, Parksworth. He came towards them without haste, but there was none of that crude bonhomie that had marked his demeanor towards Adam last night. Could it only be last night? Sable's heart jerked hurtfully.

"Why have you insulted Miss Caven?" he asked.

"Because she told lies about Miss Martin," Morgan replied, a little pale. "And Miss Martin, quite properly, took exception."

"I'm afraid I cannot treat the matter so lightly," Parksworth said heavily. "Because Miss Caven is with me, I must take the insult as though it were offered to myself."

"And because Miss Martin is my guest, I must act on her behalf," Morgan said incredibly.

"No!" Sable cried. "No. You must not—"

"Too late," Parksworth intoned and, stepping forward, he struck Morgan lightly with his glove.

140

Morgan's eyes grew wide and intent. Grim-lipped he said, "Where and when shall we meet?"

"My seconds will inform you." The hand with the star-shaped scar took Clara's white arm. "Come, Clara." They walked away. The silence was almost absolute, the flunkies carved from ebony.

"Come, Sable," Morgan ordered, breathing hard. The coins rattled again as they made for the door. She followed, disbelieving.

Chapter 7

The cool night air struck their faces as they emerged. "Morgan," Sable said. "Perhaps if I apologize— It cannot be too late."

"There can be no retraction. You saw how it was. The entire room listening."

"It's my fault that you are in danger—"

"What! From Parksworth! The only danger is that I'll kill him."

"I wish I had never agreed to this mad scheme," she said vehemently.

A pale girl stood on the other side of the street, singing "The Mistletoe Bough." Her pallor and her attenuation lent meaning to the words. Morgan tossed a coin to the singer but she finished the song before she bent to pick it up. It was the kind of tribute Morgan enjoyed. He did not seem unduly disturbed by the recent scene. He flourished the amber-headed cane and light shone through the yellow stone.

"You cannot mean you regret having made the most of the evening?"

"Not the sedan chair. But to engage in a duel because I find Miss Caven's accusations too much to bear."

Morgan hailed a sedan chair and looked around for another. "The business is just as much my fault. I insisted we went into the club where I was bound to see friends and acquaintances. I should have realized Clara might be there. I know she has a long-standing affair with Parksworth—"

"Is he married?" Sable asked, remembering Belle Briggs.

"Has been for a very long time. His wife, poor thing, has no say in his conduct. She lives much in the country where he has a house, though he's not above taking his doxies there when the spirit moves him."

"Did he know Lord Chryston?"

"Sir John had a town house near Chryston's, but they had little in common. There's a son somewhere. He quarrelled with Parksworth and I've lost touch." The second chair had arrived and conversation lapsed as they entered their temporary transport. The pale girl was singing another plaintive song and Clara and Parksworth were coming down the steps and looking around for his carriage. Clara had the collar of her cloak over her cheek and her eyes were hard and angry. Sable was glad when the chair was lifted and the gentle seesawing motion was resumed. Instead of the carrier's back and the outlines of street and house, she saw the painted cards with which the games of hazard and faro were played, the great mirror that reflected the gaming room so that the golden islands and the huge, icy chandeliers were multiplied into immensity. Painted faces, shifting patches, deft hands, fine coats, and exaggerated wigs. Clara, spiteful and censorious, dis-

144

pensing lies. Parksworth, suddenly imposing, saying those incredible words, "My seconds will inform you."

Adam would never allow it, of course. Like a cold draught, she realized that Adam must be told the entire story. He and Charlotte could hardly overlook the misappropriation of their mother's belongings, the enormity of the whole evening's happenings, culminating in that resounding slap and its dreadful aftermath. Was Parksworth a good shot? Instinct told Sable he would be. She would never ride in a sedan chair again if she lived to be a hundred. Or enter a gaming house—

Then the journey was over and the houses of Cardigan Square loomed high and imposing. "What if we are seen?" Sable asked, conscious of the borrowed plumes.

"The door will not be locked. I told Willy I might be late."

There was a light in the hall. Morgan closed the door behind them quietly, but that did nothing to prevent the confrontation with Adam. The study door was flung open and Adam stood in the gap, pale and furious, his look of accusation more for Sable than Morgan.

"Before we say anything we will be sorry for," Morgan began, "shall we not treat the entire household to the story?"

"Very well," Adam said grimly. "Come into the study."

Once there, the shelves of frowning books seeming somber and critical, neither knew how to begin.

"Is that not my mother's cloak?" Adam asked coldly.

"It was I suggested Sable borrow it. Just as it was I who asked her what would please her to idle away an evening when we were beholden to nobody."

"Idle away! That's typical of you, Morgan!"

"Just as it's typical of you to lose sight of the fact that pretty young women like beautiful clothes and romance. I would not say that your own evening out with Sable was so successful."

"Always the same, Morgan. What someone else has, you covet."

The brothers faced one another, breathing hard, both expressions implacable. "I take it you refer to Clara? You never had Clara. No one ever has Miss Caven. All you had was an illusion. A meeting, an invitation to the Hall. Introductions. A chaste wooing with only boredom at the end of it. Is that what you call having a woman?"

"And I presume you call taking her to bed having her?"

They had forgotten Sable's presence entirely. Adam seemed, for the first time, entirely flesh and blood, his clear eyes flashing, his mouth splendidly condemnatory. And Morgan was smiling provokingly, his unaccustomed pallor admirably offset by the dark plum color of the handsome coat, his waistcoat glinting in intricate splendor.

"Well, isn't it?" Morgan challenged, evoking pictures of himself between the sheets with Clara. "How else could one phrase it? Without being reduced to the language of the cow byre?"

"No, I do not agree," Adam replied, that weariness coming over his face, so that he looked his normal self. "There's more to possessing a woman than behaving like a farmyard cockerel. I beg pardon, Miss Martin, for any unseemly outburst on our part. We are used to being in opposing camps, my brother and I. What has incensed me is that he knew I wished him to leave you alone—"

"And are her wishes less important? She wanted to come, Adam! Look the fact in the face before you lose sight of it in a sea of excuses—"

"Did you?" Adam asked abruptly.

"Yes," Sable replied honestly. "You see, I have known Morgan a long time."

"You mean—before that night? Before he arrived?"

"Long before. Since I was old enough to walk." She unloosed the strings of the velvet cloak and took it off. Removing the wig, she released her hair so that it sprang around her face in rumpled curls. She told the whole story

146

of her origins, her forays into the grounds of the Hall, Tom Dobb's schooling, Lady Agatha's unstinting help, and her disappointment and frustration when Clara ruined that promising relationship. "I told you no lies," she ended. "I could not tell you how grateful I felt when you rescued me from that stretch of moor with only that bundle to my name. I should have whittled clothes-pegs had you not taken me with you, or"—she shivered—"been found by tinkers or highwaymen who would have used me unkindly. Morgan was a friend who knew all about me and who had kept my secrets. To go with him tonight was foolish and I think I knew it all along. But he meant well and I've brought him nothing but trouble—"

"Trouble?" Adam questioned sharply. "What trouble?"

"Parksworth has called me out," Morgan said without preamble.

"You fool! What cause had he?"

Morgan described the incident. "A saint would have wanted to hit Clara for her accusations which I, for one, do not believe."

"You did not steal a ring? Other valuables?" Adam asked Sable. "I must ask, I'm afraid."

"No," she answered steadily.

"Then I can see you were provoked. But how, Morgan, can I condone you duelling with Parksworth? It's as much as my position is worth."

"His seconds will undoubtedly present themselves. He struck me and I had no choice."

"What a mess," Adam remarked bitterly, "and all because you must idle away a few hours of your life. I could regret you were laid low with the fever—that you ever came—"

"That changes nothing," Morgan replied, shrugging. "It has happened."

The clock chimed lugubriously. A log settled in the hearth.

"I suppose," Sable said, "that you will want me to go?"

"Go?" Adam looked as though she had taken leave of her senses. "Why should you go? You are guilty, perhaps, of a degree of concealment I find I cannot take too seriously because you appear to have the mistaken idea I'd deplore your background. Neither will Charlotte condemn you. I confess I appear to have gone about with my eyes shut while at Daggleby, though Charlotte did say she noticed a familiarity about you. It's late, Miss Martin. I should try to get some sleep."

"Yes, go to bed, Sable," Morgan said.

"I'm sorry—" she began.

"Nothing is your fault," Morgan told her. "It's all mine."

"No—"

"But, yes!" He almost shouted the words and she saw that he looked deathly tired.

She could still hear their voices after the door was closed and she was climbing the stairs. There was a crack of light under Marie Claire's door and she realized only now why Adam had known she and Morgan were out. Marie had put two and two together and made four. Marie would have pretended she was being helpful after Adam returned from that dinner engagement.

It was not until she was in bed that she remembered she had said nothing about the scar on Parksworth's hand. She was exhausted. It could do no harm to leave the matter until tomorrow. It was too tenuous a clue to be of much value.

She was on the verge of sleep when she heard a tap against the door. In spite of her weariness—a state brought on, she suspected, more by the shock of the imminent duel than from any other cause—she roused instantly, knowing who stood outside. She saw Morgan as she had that long ago May morning, handsome in black and white, his hair held back with a ribbon, pretending to be stern where she now knew he was amused. Morgan riding, Morgan staring at her as she worked in the fields around her father's farm. An ox roasting at Daggleby to mark some occasion and Morgan laughing as the great carcass browned over the flames and his friends craned to see it the better. Morgan who might die because of her action tonight.

She lay, scarcely breathing, her body tensed. But the summons did not come again.

Charlotte's migraine persisted the following morning and she remained in bed. A palpable atmosphere hung over the house, infecting the entire staff. The maids were agitated as they cleaned and garnished, the footmen surly, Marie Claire vinegar-faced and bossy.

Sable, as she went downstairs, could hear the Hunter brothers in the study, still arguing in low, furious voices though the gist of their conversation was inaudible. There was only the odd word here and there that sprang out like jack-in-the-boxes. "Selfish as ever!" from Adam. "Grudging," from Morgan, and "do you so badly want to be old?" "Hurt your mother," which was Adam again. "Play God!" Morgan shouted, then banged out of the study and hung white-faced and angry against the jamb of the interview room, surveying Sable with accusing eyes that brought back the memory of last night, then strode upstairs.

Adam came next and did not look at her at all. He fixed his gaze on the edge of the desk and said, "I must attend the House. You must cope with things the best you can."

"Of course. He's in no real danger, is he?"

"Morgan? He appears to think not. But I know Parksworth. He's a good shot. Too good for my brother, I fear."

A little thrill of panic ran along her nerves. "But Morgan said—"

"Take little notice of that," Adam commented tartly. "I'll find some way to botch the affair, never fear." His face was bleak and she knew there was no kindness in him for all that he implied he would help. "Could you not have trusted me entirely, Miss Martin? If Morgan could know, why not me? What is there so special about Hunters besides money? We're glorified shopkeepers."

"It does make a difference. But now that I know you better, I'd not make the same mistake again."

"Does anyone really know another? I doubt it. Though Charlotte always seems an open book. Are you sure you can manage?"

"I'll do my best."

"Very well, Miss Martin. There's Willy with the carriage. We'll talk further tonight."

There was an emptiness after he had gone that she tried to fill by busying herself with the heap of letters, the pleas, and the ill-written information on subjects of national concern. To the matters Charlotte would wish to take in hand she attached neat memoranda. Gradually she became immersed in the work, glad of the necessity of using her mind to some useful purpose, secretly rejoicing in the knowledge that she had done better than anyone could have anticipated, with the possible exception of Tom Dobbs. With the thought of Tom her stomach churned uncomfortably. Perhaps at this moment he was at Knowehead, frowning over the story Lady Chryston would have to tell, shaking his shaggy head, the light searching out the dustiness and shabbiness of his greatcoat, the pockets bulging with the weight of the Bible, with objects found at the roadside on his eternal journeying in search of souls for God with bread and cheese for solitary dinners.

She heard James Grant go out, his tread unmistakable, since it betrayed a certain hesitancy that matched his careful thinking and dislike of self-commitment. There was a certain spinsterish quality about Grant that she knew amused Morgan. She did not hear Morgan, only looked up some ten minutes later to see him back in the doorway, that pale tautness of anger gone, replaced by a secret mockery that sent her pulses racing.

"Why did you pretend you were asleep?" he asked soft-ly.

She tried, without success, to convey lack of comprehen-sion.

"You know perfectly well what I mean," he said with false severity.

"I was—very tired."

"Will you always feign exhaustion?"

"What am I expected to say to that?" She riffled papers energetically, wondering privately how she would find their proper order when they were needed.

"Of course, there may be very few times I could repeat that request," he said with a lapse into solemnity. "Parks-worth is more able than I imagined. His seconds are sure to arrive before long. No doubt, at this moment he negoti-ates."

She made a sudden sharp movement. The pot of sand was overturned and the quill fluttered to the floor. "Don't say that!"

Morgan bent to retrieve the pen.

"But it's true. And you could make it worthwhile. I'd not mind extinction if there was a memory to take me." For a moment he looked young and curiously afraid.

Sable experienced a sick terror. "Oh, Morgan! Morgan."

He held out his arms and she ran into them, her eyes brilliant with unshed tears. He held her tightly, hands clasped across her back as though he would never let her go. She closed her eyes and the tears were squeezed out to make their slow, painful course down her cheeks. She nev-er cried, could not remember ever having done so. Now misery swept over her in wave after wave of despair. May mornings, the galloping figures that marked the hills around Daggleby, the dogs with their lolling tongues, the lichened statues, the lit windows of the house, so deeply imprinted on her mind, flashed by in bright images forev-er lost.

"I had not realized he was such a wizard at the draw," Morgan said, his voice muffled against her hair. "He's never looked a marksman, but that obviously signifies nothing."

"I should not have been so hasty," she whispered, conscience-stricken. "But it never occurred to me what might follow that blow. It seemed a matter between myself and Clara. If she had struck me, I'd have accepted that as my due. But that you should pay! I cannot forgive myself." She choked upon the last words.

"It would not be so bad," he said, very low and intense, "if you were kind to me." His mouth moved across her brow, down her wet face. "I think I always wanted you. That morning you tumbled towards me—you were desirable even then, but you were a child and I'd not take advantage. It was in York I knew we'd have encounters one day. You by the coach in that yellow gown. It was difficult to leave you." He returned to kissing her, and his hands slid down to her hips where his fingertips dug into her smooth skin and set her trembling. "So—you'll not shut your ears tonight when I knock at the door? Say you won't."

Deep in a confusion of guilt, self-reproach, and a quite heady sensation of sinking in dangerous quicksands, she answered. "No. No, Morgan—"

"You'll let me in?"

"If that will please you."

"Please me! Go to bed early. I beg you."

The doorbell rang loudly. Rang again. They stayed, clasped in one another's arms, listening to the slow footman's tread, the cold sharp voice that said, "I'm here on behalf of Sir John Parksworth. Is Mr. Hunter at home? Mr. Morgan Hunter?"

Morgan's arms fell away to hang slackly by his sides. His features had grown sharp and wary and his mouth had set into lines oddly reminiscent of Adam's. In spite of their differences of character, they were not unlike.

"Morgan?"

He seemed not to have heard. Then he swallowed, set back his shoulders, and went from the room.

After he'd gone, she returned to the documents, thankful that no constituent had arrived in person, and she heard James Grant return from his short errand, the murmur of voices from the study, the footman passing the door with a clinking tray. Willy had never learnt how best to carry one. Her gaze focused on the paper she held. There were the drawings she had done for the child, Belle Briggs. The shape of the melted starfish lay there obscenely, reminding her of unimaginable horror, the child pinned down, the strong hand with its telltale decoration. Had it been Parksworth? He was sufficiently cruel. His behavior to Ben confirmed that. For the first time Sable realized fully that Clara still could have her own revenge for that incautious blow. She could tell what she knew of the slave.

Sable got up and began to pace the floor. She should have voiced her suspicions about Parksworth yesterday or before Adam went out this morning and she must certainly do so when he came back. Perhaps the scar might be some lever to stop the nightmare that threatened, though she could not yet see how it could benefit Morgan. She returned to the desk and lifted another paper.

Across the hall the study door opened and Morgan said in a strange, cold voice that frightened her, "I will present myself there at the time and place you suggest the day after tomorrow."

There was a click of heels, the noise of the street quite loud, then a bang and a resumption of silence. She waited for Morgan to return, but he did not. Two nights left to give Morgan what he wanted. Her hand trembled against the closely written sheet.

Adam returned in the early evening. Charlotte was still

prostrate and confined to her bed and this gave Sable the opportunity to broach the subject of Belle Briggs and her later testimony and the scar on Sir John's hand.

"Great God! And how are we to connect the two? One child's word—and if you recall, her reactions were so confused at the house she pointed out that the case was thrown out—against a man of Parksworth's stature. We've traced no other child to bear witness. We do not even know if it was Parksworth. Scars are ten a penny."

"We could confront him with Belle."

"How? Drive up to his door? His butler would never admit us or the child."

"Outside somewhere?"

"You mean, spy on him? Watch for him to leave or enter? We could be there all day and never set eyes on him. Think of the ordeal for the Briggs girl."

"There's one place we'd see Sir John."

"Oh?" Adam raised his brows. "And where is that?"

"Someone came today to arrange the details of—the duel."

"The devil, they did!" he shouted. "I told Morgan he must send a message to the House if there were any such move. Where is he?"

"I've not seen him since. But I heard him say the day after tomorrow."

"Where?"

"I heard nothing more. And I think he has gone out."

"Then Morgan intends to keep it secret from me." Adam had whitened visibly.

"He might tell me," Sable told him quietly. "If I went about it the right way."

"And I would not?" Adam challenged coolly, then shrugged. "You're right, of course. The more I bluster and try to show my authority, the more he rebels. It's not easy to see when someone you've known all your life passes

154

out of reach of one's jurisdiction. And I presume," his lips twisted a little bitterly, "you've reason to expect an opportunity for finding out?"

"I think so."

"I'll not ask what it is," he replied stiffly. "I think I'll take supper in my room. I take it you'll tell me tomorrow?"

"If I can persuade him."

"You had better, Miss Martin. My mother will find it hard to forgive me should I fail to prevent this encounter."

"He may divulge the meeting place if I promise to keep it from you. Then, if we could take Belle with us, that could create some diversion and Parksworth, if he is the man, could be put off even if he insists upon satisfaction—"

"You have it all worked out in that clear little mind."

"You make it sound an accusation," she reproached.

Adam relented. "It was not really meant so. I seem not to have the knack for happy relationships. I'll tell the butler there will be only two for supper downstairs. And, Miss Martin, I will ask you to visit the Briggs to borrow the child. James could go with you. And Morgan, naturally, is not to know."

"Very well."

He hesitated, seemed about to say more, then turned from her abruptly. She heard him go upstairs slowly and heavily as though he were tired in body as well as in mind.

Marie passed Sable in the passage outside their respective bedchambers. She smiled thinly. Sable had an impulse to take her to task for telling Adam she had gone out with Morgan the previous evening, but, remembering the shocking scene with Clara at the gaming house, she refrained. Mademoiselle had been piqued that Sable was invited to dine with the Hunters while she was not. It was as simple as that and not worth the trouble of enlarging into another fracas. She was sick of disputes.

155

Morgan was already there when she went down to the dining room. He had not changed so she presumed he had just returned to the house. The plain dark coat made him look more elegant than the more showy plum-colored one, and she liked the folds of the high, white stock against it. He did not smile as she entered, only looked up moodily and said, "Is Adam in?"

"He was tired and will sup in his room."

"Thank God." Morgan brightened. "I feared I should be lectured. Subjected to unwelcome questioning."

They were silent while food was brought and served, and claret poured to accompany the meat. Morgan dismissed the waiting footman and drank deeply, refilling his glass almost immediately.

"Where is it to be?" Sable asked, staring at the plate before her with repugnance. "The duel."

"It cannot be in London because of Adam. And Billy Pitt may come to hear of it and there would be another confrontation. He's extremely opinionated."

"But—where?"

"Need that concern you?" Morgan was suddenly unfriendly.

"Of course it concerns me. Since it was I who placed you in your present position—"

"What good would it do you to know?"

"I could at least think of you—"

"Shall we not speak of it? I have made practice shots today and they were poor."

She stared at him, appalled. "You must not give up!" she cried. "You speak as though it were all settled. That he wins!"

Morgan made an attempt to rally. "He cannot be fit. He does not live wisely. Only I had that fever and it took its toll. But it is not only that. I have an oppression—"

"You are young and I should know that you've recov-

156

ered. That was no puny embrace you gave me. My ribs still ache." She forced her voice to lightness and was pleased to see him respond.

"You did not object?"

"Not in the least. I am like you. Always I knew that the first man to love me would be you."

"The first?"

She nodded.

"I can't say the same." He shrugged disarmingly.

"Men are different. They are allowed wild oats. Though I must confess I think it an unfair segregation."

"I cannot touch this dish."

"Nor I."

"Then go upstairs. I'll come in half an hour."

"Be careful Marie Claire does not see you. She's turned unfriendly. Not that I'll take it to heart, for I never really liked her."

"She reminds me of a bun with two niggardly currants in it. Set rather close together."

"Please, don't make me laugh. I'll never be able to stop."

"You are beautiful. In the strangest way." He came and stood behind her, his hands stroking her hair, moving to her neck. "Your skin is quite light but everything else is dark. I never saw such huge, black eyes and your lashes are so thick and strong. And you have a little bump on your nose—"

"I quarrelled with my brother Joe and he struck me harder than he meant." Sable had a sudden image of her mother rolling up her sleeves to start the baking, of her father's stern profile. What would they think of what she contemplated? The touch of Morgan's fingers was very seductive. His hands had reached her breasts, cupping them, rubbing them so that she was conscious of an intolerable pleasure.

A noise outside sent them apart, studiously avoiding one

157

another's eyes. Willy came back, his knowing gaze on the half-eaten food. "The pudding—"

"We will not require the pudding."

"Very well, Mr. Morgan."

Sable took the opportunity of escape. Her heart thudded so wildly it seemed to reverberate like the sound of a gong. Her body still tingled with sensuous pleasure. From the window of her room she could see that there was a party in progress in the house opposite. Every window glowed with light and the sound of music stole from the rooms where the silhouettes of many people moved.

Her bedchamber seemed doubly quiet because of the atmosphere of gaiety that prevailed across the street. Carriages drew up, deposited their burden of cloaked women and tall-hatted men. Sable experienced a moment of intense isolation. It was almost as though she were back at the windows of Hunter Hall, shut off from its splendours by much more than barriers of glass and a curtain of ivy. She felt lonely and unsure and the shadow of the day after tomorrow lay heavily over her.

She got into bed, and overcome by the enormity of what might happen, began to weep silently. It was so that Morgan found her a few minutes later.

She woke very early. The room was cold with the approach of autumn and the sky beyond the window was a sharp, deep blue. For a moment she thought nothing but the color of the sky and the coldness of the air, then the recollection of Morgan came, scoring her mind with intermingled pain and pleasure. Sometime after she was asleep he had gone.

Sable shrugged herself up against the tester and pulled the bedclothes over her bare shoulders. The whitish pool on the darkness of the floor was her nightgown, taken off very expertly by Morgan and tossed aside. He seemed to have forgotten his misgivings over the coming encounter with Parksworth, kissed away the uncharacteristic tears, and told her not to worry. And strangely, her fears had been lulled. He had even made her laugh, not too loudly because of Marie Claire. To be diverted in the isolated world of a bed that contained the man she loved was a joy indeed. She regretted that he had not said goodnight—or should it have been good morning?—but that showed consideration.

Last night she had been weak and fearful. This morning she was strong and fulfilled. She would not allow Parksworth to kill Morgan and must work all day to this end.

She rose, washed, and dressed, brushed her hair to neatness. Downstairs, the maids were already busy, laying fires and cleaning hearths. Daisy fetched her a cup of chocolate and some bread and butter to the interview room. She ate and drank without noticing the taste of the food as she took out the file on Belle Briggs and read through the child's statement very slowly and carefully. She had imagined she was over the shock of distaste that had engulfed her at first hearing the child's story, but the sharp edge of revulsion was not blunted.

Sable threw the papers down violently. No joy, no laughter, in the bed that Belle Briggs had shared.

"Good morning, Miss Martin."

She had not heard Adam come into the room. His face was pale and pinched and she had an instant of compunction as though she were responsible for that strain. But it was not so. She owed him gratitude but nothing more. The clear eyes pierced her. "Did you find out where Morgan is to meet Parksworth?" He closed the door behind him.

"Yes." It had not seemed real last night when she had coaxed and cajoled until Morgan had told her. Now, with the story of Belle on the desk before her and Adam's face as long as a wet week, the imminence of Morgan's peril was back into perspective.

"Where?"

159

"One of his seconds, Geoffrey Bland, has a house at Englefield Green. It is to be in the meadow behind the house at eight o'clock in the morning."

"I see. One thing troubles me—"

"Yes?"

"The child. We should need to wake her mother in the small hours and she has other children."

"I hadn't thought—"

"It would be better if you were to bring her here tonight."

"But Morgan would know."

"Not if I were to keep him out of the way while you smuggled the girl inside."

"The servants—"

"She could stay in your room. You could plead an indisposition so that you could be there and see she did not stray or make any sound. Lock your door. Then there would be no chance of disturbance."

Sable said nothing. Morgan was sure to come again tonight. If her door was locked against him he would think she did not want him. And she could not explain.

"Of course, if you have changed your mind," Adam said distantly, "you have only to say. It could be a wild-goose chase. Parksworth might well be innocent and the sight of the child would then leave him unmoved." He shrugged. "It must be your choice."

It came to her then that he might know all about last night. The deep, warm embraces. Morgan's lips against her flesh. Their soft, repressed laughter. This might be a way to separate them. But he could not know. And it was important to find out who had violated the child. If she could shake Parksworth it would be worth any misunderstanding.

"Of course I have not changed my mind. I have thought of little else. You see the papers there. I've read them all again and sickened a second time. No, if it is to uncover that man's wickedness I'd sit up a month with the child. I find I hate him more than I thought possible."

"Then you've made up your mind he's to blame? Or is it because he threatens Morgan?"

"There's another reason. Something I know to his discredit." She chose the words carefully.

"Can you not tell me?"

"I can tell no one."

"Why?"

"Because it could harm someone who does not deserve to be hurt."

"I could not quarrel with such a reason." The acidity that had permeated his tone with the mention of Morgan had gone.

She wished Adam were not so upright. It was made more difficult to deceive him as she knew she must if Morgan continued under the same roof. "Tell me what I am to do," she asked.

"This," Adam said and proceeded to outline the plan.

Charlotte came down after Adam went. She was still looking unwell with huge dark circles round her eyes. Sable put away the file, as Charlotte was to be told nothing at this stage either of Belle and Parksworth's scarred hand or the incident with Clara. Adam had been very definite on this point.

Morgan had looked in halfway through the morning, very handsome in tawny brown and a high, black stock, the clouded amber cane under his arm. The color leapt to Sable's face. He looked disappointed that Charlotte was there. Remembering Adam's strictures, Sable wondered if she could not visit Morgan's room instead, but Mrs. Briggs had said the child had nightmares, screaming out in her sleep. She could not leave the poor creature alone, not even for Morgan Hunter.

Morgan remonstrated with his sister for getting up too

soon, told her she must not do too much, conveyed a secret look to Sable, and said he would look forward to seeing them both tonight.

Sable felt in low spirits after he had gone, but she forced herself to be useful to Charlotte for most of the day, then was glad when Charlotte decided to rest in her own room with Marie Claire to minister to her. It would make it easier to leave with James in the carriage, as she had been instructed.

Cloaked and bonneted, she left the house with James half an hour later. The carriage rattled and bounced, sending dogs and people flying from its path. The fine houses gave way to meaner streets of dark shops and bosomy women who hung from upper windows enjoying the remnants of sunshine on sooty cobbles and the sight of their neighbors about their business. A flyblown butcher's, a candlemaker, a smithy with bellows blowing and a red flutter of sparks, the smell of a burnt hoof. The acrid odor reminded Sable of the village where she was brought up and she wondered if her letters and parcels had been received. Her body felt strange and new as though she had been a snake and sloughed off the old, familiar skin to reveal a new maturity. All day she had wanted to lower her eyes in case that disturbing newness should reveal itself too plainly.

The carriage stopped and was surrounded by vociferous boys, watched by almost every person in the street. James fended off the most adventurous and cleared a passage for Sable so that she could broach the subject of Belle with Mrs. Briggs. The room where the woman received her was distressingly furnished, mostly with pallets and blankets, a bare table and a complete lack of refinements. The farm had been a palace compared with this. And yet, Mrs. Briggs had been brave enough to seek out her Member of Parliament when one of her children was abused.

The younger Briggses huddled against the darkest part of the wall, the smallest whimpering with the strangeness of the visit. Belle, big-eyed and pallid, tended to the child mechanically.

"You want Belle to go with you?" Mrs. Briggs was astounded.

"Only for the night. You want us to identify the man, don't you?"

"Men, you mean," she said bitterly.

"That's asking too much. But the first. We could find him, I think."

"Dunno if she'll go. She's scared to be away from me now."

"She had courage enough to come to Cardigan Square last time."

"Yes. She did. Belle? Do you want to go with Miss Martin? Sleep in her bed?"

"I don't know, Mam."

"You'll be perfectly safe, Belle," Sable said gently. Her heart gave a great flutter as she thought that they could not force Belle to accompany them and that if she did not, there would be no need to lock her door this evening. But her hatred of Parksworth seemed, unaccountably, stronger.

"All right," Belle said, pressing her pale lips together as though to suppress a cry.

Her mother put an old cloak around the child's shoulders, held her close. "Be a good girl. Do as you are told."

"Yes, Mam."

The whole neighborhood, it seemed, saw the child enter the carriage, scowled as the coachman flicked his whip at the more persistent urchins, pressed forward threateningly as the vehicle gathered up speed. Even the mangy curs did not seem to like them, Sable thought, putting her arm round Belle's thin shoulders, rejoicing in the feel of that slight body slowly relaxing against her own, enjoying the wonder that came into the frightened eyes as they dwelt on the interior of the conveyance with its buttoned upholstery and the swinging lamps that were newly lit against the onslaught of dusk.

Sable and James smuggled the child in between them when they reached Adam's house, and then James himself fetched them a tray laden with food that made Belle's mouth water visibly. Poor scrap. Sable had not realized she could feel so maternal. They ate together after Belle had washed in the flowered basin on the marble stand and dressed in one of Sable's white bedgowns.

She said her prayers after the alfresco meal and giggled when she was shown the closestool, then lay down, her gaze fixed on the bed-hangings. "It's like a house"—she said of the bed, keeping her voice low, as Sable had instructed—"with a roof. How lucky you are."

"Yes, I am."

"Good night, then, Miss Martin."

"Good night."

She fell asleep after a time, but Sable saw that the sleep was not a peaceful one. Every now and again Belle moaned dismally and twitched, pushing and plucking at the coverlets as though she fended off some unwelcome visitation or sought to hide herself from something she feared.

The candle guttered, made whispering noises. Sable took one of the child's hands in her own and sat waiting. There was no party in the opposite house this evening and there was only the sound of the wind moaning ever so softly down the chimney and the distant clop of hooves, the grumble of wheels. Even the house was quiet apart from the murmurs of the distressed child. The small fingers struggled to release themselves and a beading of sweat broke out on Belle's forehead.

Sable sat rigid. Another noise now, small and furtive like a mouse in the wainscot. The scrabble of nails on the door-panel. Silence, then another tap. The door handle turned very slowly. The door creaked. "Sable? Sable!"

She looked at Belle. She was asleep. Unlikely to wake in the next hour. Sable felt deathly cold. Every instinct clamored for her to get up, turn the key. But she could not do it. "I know you're awake." Again the whisper, sharper now. "Sable. What's wrong? What have I done?"

Still she did not move. Then there were footsteps, light and self-important, stopping outside the door.

"Miss Martin is indisposed," Marie Claire said with a note of pleased malice. "I'm afraid she will not answer."

"Mind your own business!" Morgan said furiously.

"I thought I was helping."

"Damn your help! I don't require it."

"Good night, then, Mr. Hunter." Marie did not sound put out. She pattered in the direction of her own bed-chamber.

"Good night," Morgan said viciously. And then the silence descended and remained unbroken as the quiet of a tomb.

Hours later Sable heard the carriage enter the mews. As Adam had predicted, Morgan, moving quietly, let himself out of the house, and the carriage drove off. She watched him from a window across the landing; cloaked, booted, tall-hatted, he swung himself into the vehicle with an ease that showed his new fitness. There was a creeping mist that concealed much, reducing the big houses to blurs, the trees to shadows.

Time to rouse Belle, to feel a twist of pity for the tired face, the apprehensive eyes.

"He won't—touch me?"

165

"Of course not. I shall be there with Mr. Grant and Mr. Hunter."

"Why do we have to get up so early? Go into the country?"

"He's a difficult man to find. This morning, we know for sure he'll be there. All you have to do is look at him and tell us if he's the one. We must hurry, my dear. There's a long way to go. Be quiet, my darling, we must rouse no one. There'll be a hamper in the carriage and you can breakfast on the way. There's Mr. Hunter coming. Will you be warm enough?"

"Yes, Miss Martin."

Adam in redingote and James in dark cape waited outside. Adam picked up the child and they descended the dim stairway, stole cautiously across the black and white marble where the big plant crouched threateningly on its stand. A few more minutes and they were seated, riding over the wet cobbles, for the morning was dark as well as misty, and Sable was opening the basket to offer Belle milk and cold fowl and buttered bread. Neither she nor Adam wanted food, though James accepted chicken, but she was glad to join in with a drink of brandy from the silver flask with the ornate Hunter *H* chased on one side in a creeping of ivy leaves.

The signs of civilization died away and the carriage bowled along through a network of grey hedges and menacing trees that started off pale and watery, then loomed dark at the moment of passing and reached skinny arms to catch at them. The sky grew lighter, but remained vague and colorless. Then the visibility improved a little; the spikes of the hedge were accentuated, webs glittering between them. They caught glimpses of farm windows lit, the bulk of cattle standing in islands of opalescence, a gallows tree at a crossroad with its chains clanking dismally. The horses galloped tirelessly like the four that belonged to the horsemen of the Apocalypse.

Belle ate hungrily as though she'd not seen food for a month, spilled a little of her milk with the motion of the conveyance, and looked as though she were about to cry over her carelessness.

"It's not your fault," Sable said. "Anyone could have done the same." The child was fearfully pale and obviously dreading her ordeal. How terrible it would be if she were wrong, Sable thought, and Belle had been harassed for no good reason. Still, she felt the pain of having denied Morgan, of sending him out on this macabre errand with no grain of comfort. The morning's grimness crept into her heart and lodged there like a stone.

"Bland's place is over there," Adam said at last, poking his head out of the window to shout directions to the coachman, and disturbing a scattering of rooks. Their nests in the elms resembled dark and unhealthy growths.

"We'll leave the coach here," Adam ordered. "It's no good if we are seen. That's the front of the house, so if we take this bridle path, we should arrive at the meadow. Go slowly and stay by the avenue. The trees will give us cover. I see no one yet, but they are probably in the house, Geoffrey and Morgan and the man who drove him here."

"Parksworth?" James inquired.

"He cannot have arrived. See, there's one carriage in the drive, but not the second."

They walked slowly, Sable holding Belle's hand, their long skirts brushing the moisture on the pallid grass. The line of great beeches glistened dully. She could see the meadow now, a flat, milky sea around which the trees writhed in varying shades of grey.

"Here," Adam directed. "Sit the child in that hollow between the branches, then she'll not tire so quickly. Are you all right, Miss Martin?" His tone was quite impersonal in contrast to the kindliness with which he had addressed Belle. Perhaps he had heard Morgan last night. He could hardly have avoided hearing Marie Claire.

Sable nodded, not trusting herself to speak. The wind disturbed the grasses gently, made the old branches creak. At first she thought the sound of the wind sharpened, but then the rumble became perceptibly louder. The coach came out of the obscurity, a low-moving blur that took on shape and color. Black horses trotted funereally, their breaths rising in pale clouds. The lamps were still lit, emitting a faint yellow glow against house and shrubbery. Indistinct figures appeared and were joined by others and the far-off voices echoed queerly against the thinning pall of mist.

Belle wriggled on her perch in the tree. Her eyes were enormous and her skin grey above the dark cloak. Stretched knucklebones betrayed her nervousness. Sable forced herself to smile, all the time seeing the small black figures that now reached the far side of the meadow. They seemed to walk so slowly. Six, no seven of them. There would be two seconds apiece and the doctor. She could make out Morgan now, taller than the others, his stride defiant. She wanted to run from the gloom of the trees' shadow, to tell him she was sorry but Adam's restraining hand was on her arm holding her cruelly tight.

"No, Miss Martin."

She stared at Adam with a hatred of which she was unaware and he accepted that antipathy apparently unmoved. "Please, Adam—"

"No."

The murky figures were all in a huddle by this time, poring over something in a long box. Morgan was taking off his cloak and handing it, together with his tall hat, to a second. Another man was marking the ground, counting paces. There were pistols in the long box. She hated their long, sinister shapes. A smell came out of the earth, a cold dampness with a whiff of decomposition.

Adam released her to lean, trembling, against the moist

bark. "I beg you to stay there, Miss Martin, while I take the child." He was lifting Belle Briggs from the tree, holding her close to his chest while she buried her face in his shoulder. "He won't touch me? He won't? He won't touch me?" the child reiterated.

"No," Adam said harshly. "He will not."

He walked away, tall and erect, his redingote sweeping the drifts of meadow grass. The riding coat made him appear supernaturally long, Sable thought, her palms wet with fear for Morgan. The party in the meadow had seen Adam now and indistinct faces were turned in his direction. She began to run after Adam. Belle saw Sable and held out an entreating hand. Behind her she heard James's hurrying step.

The faces took on shape and feature. They were like mourners with their black clothes and frowning expressions.

"A moment of your time, Parksworth," Adam said loudly. "Time, time," the echoes were thrown back from house and tree. "Time."

"Damn you, Hunter! What do you want?" Parksworth shouted, his gaze averted briefly from the priming of the pistol he had chosen.

Morgan was staring at Sable with a mixture of accusation and disbelief. "You told him."

"I could not help it," she whispered.

"I hope you are satisfied," he answered bitterly.

Parksworth, his face contused, was very close to Adam now, near enough to see the network of broken veins in his cheeks, the holes in his nose that were like the pits in a strawberry. He lifted his hand to his mouth and the scar was plain.

"Do you recognize this man?" Adam said. "Please look at him."

Belle turned her head. She saw the hand first and her

169

eyes flew open with the shock of recognition. Then she raised her eyes and saw the pitted nose with the veined skin on either side. Her sudden jerk of fear made Parksworth take a step backward. The child gave a little choking cry. Her eyes rolled upwards to show only the whites. She became limp in Adam's arms.

"What's the meaning of this charade?" Parksworth demanded thickly. "I came to meet your brother, not his entire household."

"She knew you," Adam said very softly.

"I don't know what you mean."

"She remembered your hand."

Parksworth turned grey.

"I know nothing of this," Morgan insisted. "Sir John and I have urgent business and I'll thank you to take yourself off, Adam."

The seconds whispered behind their hands and the doctor looked cold and uncomfortable as he set down his bag of instruments.

"You still wish to call out my brother?" Adam asked.

"Your charade can make no difference," Parksworth said more easily. "I find your attempted diversion incomprehensible, as do my friends. I'll thank you to take Mr. Hunter's advice and return from whence you came. What you should hope to achieve is beyond understanding."

"Oh, you'll know that well enough in due course," Adam replied. "Come James, Miss Martin. We'll wait for you, Morgan." And he began to retrace his steps.

"You may wait for ever," Parksworth asserted, his voice a fraction high.

"I could not help it," Sable said again. "Do you understand?"

Morgan said nothing. He looked chilled. Then his hand went out to take his own pistol, his gaze dismissing her as if she were of no account.

"Miss Martin," James called sharply.

She began to follow Adam, her blurred gaze fixed on the row of great beeches that made up the avenue. The trees wavered, then were still. There were voices behind her but she was too numb to comprehend what they said. A shout. A silence. Then a shot. She stood frozen. Nothing happened. A long time afterwards there was another shot. Another silence.

When she looked, there was a black shape lying very still and the doctor, his flying cape birdlike, skimmed the milk-white grass. She could not see the face from where she was, then the doctor knelt down and she could not see the body either. And then she heard Belle screaming.

Chapter 8

The field became for a moment nebulous, the trees round its perimeter whirling in shrouds that loosened and blew away, bringing the morning back into focus. Sable felt sick and shaken. The dark figures that converged upon the body and the kneeling form of the doctor had no faces. It was as if her eyes would not recognize them in case she did not see the face she sought. Then, just as terribly, their features were all Parksworth's, poxed and bloated. Behind her the girl's screams died to whimpers.

Adam gripped her arm. "Are you all right?"

She stared at him mutely, trying to change his eyes and his mouth into Morgan's but they refused, obdurately, to alter. There was a pain in them she recognized.

Someone said, "I think I killed him. What shall I do, Adam?" The world reeled.

"You damned fool, Morgan. You damned, headstrong fool—"

"What should I do?" Morgan was very pale. "There's bound to be trouble—"

"I said there would be. But recriminations won't help. This is what you must do. Go straight back to London—you came by carriage, so you have the necessary transport. Then go to the office in Blackwall and see Caparty. Tell him the *Janus* must leave sooner than scheduled even if he hasn't all the men required. He'll get seamen at the first port of call. And you must be aboard when she sails. You'd have been going anyway. With luck the whole thing will blow over—in time."

But he can't go, Sable thought. Not like that, not without a proper good-bye. Only, of course, he could leave, drop out of all their lives, because he had killed Parksworth and once the news was out there must certainly be repercussions. She wrestled with the realization, unable to come to terms with it, seeing Geoffrey Bland come towards them, his face pinched with cold. "There'll be trouble with Parksworth's seconds—"

"Yes," Morgan snapped. "Adam says I must go. Lie low. Not that I want to—"

"It's good advice," Bland said, rubbing his chilled hands. "Something before you go, eh?"

"He has not the time," Adam insisted. "For God's sake, Morgan. Don't wait. I'll stay."

"I still don't understand what you are doing here—"

"I'll write to you at Sierra Leone. Explain everything."

"I'm in a fog. The *Janus* will sail? There'll be no problem?"

"Say it's Father's orders," Adam said inexorably. "Caparty won't argue with that. If I can, I'll come later today but I do have other calls on my time and I've wasted much today already."

Belle had stopped whimpering. Out of the corner of her eye Sable saw James with a protective arm around the girl's shoulders. Belle's initial terror had given way to a stony-eyed impassivity. She was looking at Parksworth's body on the misted grass, its stillness mirrored in herself. Belle had not said that he was her ravisher. But he was. There could have been no other reason for the child's reaction. Sable was glad he was dead, that he could do no more harm. She felt incapable of pity.

Morgan stood for a moment, as much a mourning figure as the kneeling men in the dimness of the meadow. There seemed no trace of color in him. He was black and white and grey, cold and unsure and looking at her as though she were someone he had known a long time ago. Sable became aware that Adam still grasped her arm, that Morgan saw this as an outward sign of some inner possession. She had, after all, told Adam what was meant to be a confidence between lovers.

"Good-bye," Morgan said, his voice very low and intense. "I should not waste any more of your valuable time on me." Then he turned away abruptly and began to hurry towards the house, Bland almost running after him.

Sable, too, wanted to run but Adam would not let her. His hand clamped her wrist cruelly hard. She could only stare impotently after the tall, striding figure that was quickly reduced to a blur, that reached a gap in the clipped hedge and vanished.

"Morgan—" She was hardly aware she had spoken.

"Belle needs you more," Adam told her, his manner hard and unsympathetic. "It was your idea to bring her and the shock was great. See to the child and I'll go to Parksworth." He released her and a tingle of pain shot through her arm. Sable rubbed at it futilely then walked as though in a dream towards James Grant.

James relinquished Belle with what appeared to be relief. "I should take her to the house," he advised. "Bland's wife will surely give her some brandy. I'll stay with Adam."

Belle moved close to Sable like a small animal whose security was threatened. Sable responded to the token of

175

trust. They walked together through the watery land-scape. "Miss Martin—"

"Yes?"

"That was—"

"It was the man?" Sable prompted, listening for the sound of Morgan's departure.

"Yes, Miss Martin. But he's dead now, isn't he?"

"I think so. Thank you for coming. It could not have been pleasant."

"He'd have shot Mr. Hunter otherwise, wouldn't he?" Again there was no note of questioning. "Don't cry, Miss Martin."

"I'm not crying. I'm just sad. But it will pass. Everything passes."

"There's a woman at the door of the house."

"So there is. Come, child. I feel like Lot's wife."

"Who was she?"

"A woman in the Bible. She was told not to look back but she insisted upon doing so and turned into a pillar of salt."

"But how could that happen? No one can change people into something else."

"Would you like to know more? Hear other stories?" Sable asked mechanically, one small part of her senses still hearing that diminishing sound of the carriage. It would not hurt so much tomorrow, the day after—

"Yes, Miss Martin."

"If ever I have the authority, I'll employ you. Would you like to work for me?"

"Yes. I don't think I want to get wed like me Mam. I'd rather not."

"You'll change."

"You can't change people," Belle said with tough perti-nacity. "I don't like men."

"Only some men, surely." Sable shivered, recognizing a bleak honesty.

"None of them. I can't hear that coach now. Can you?"

"No. It's—quite gone."

They were at the main door of the house and a young woman in a green gown and ivory lace fichu was beckoning. "I'm Cecily Bland. Please come inside for some refreshment."

Belle's gaze was riveted to the pretty dress, to Mrs. Bland's clean rosy face and brown ringlets. She pulled her cloak tighter round her thin body as though she recognized her own plainness, her own shabbiness. Charlotte Hunter must have some gowns she did not want, Sable thought. She'd be after them when they got back to Cardigan Square. To a house that was empty of Morgan. Don't think of him. Think of Belle, of Jeremy Day, of Tom Dobbs. All those persons who required Adam's help. She had put Morgan out of her mind before and life had not been entirely barren. She could do it again.

Cecily chattered all the way to the bright little morning room where candles were lit against the misty darkness. After a minute Sable decided the flow of talk was to combat a natural nervousness. It could not be every day that a man was shot to death in one's paddock. There would be the disposal of the body, the return of all those black-clad figures with their damp cloaks and dew-wet boots.

"I confess that I was not expecting you," Cecily said, dispensing tea with a dash of brandy and plain biscuits, since no one felt like eating anything more substantial.

"No," Sable agreed. "It was—that Adam hoped to stop the duel."

They sipped at their tea a little awkwardly while Belle admired the furnishings. James said nothing.

It was with a certain relief that they greeted the opening of the door and the advent of the seconds and Adam.

"Where is the doctor?" Cecily asked, rising to her feet.

"With Sir John," her husband replied. "No, my dear. No tea. We'll have something stronger." He crossed to a cabinet on the wall, taking out a decanter of spirits and some tumblers.

"How are you?" Adam asked Belle, appearing surprised

by her composure. Since she had seen Parksworth's body she had acquired a new strength.

"I'm—very well, sir."

"It was as we thought," Sable told Adam, wishing that he had not that look of Morgan about him. "We can speak of it later. Of Parksworth—"

"I see." Adam's eyes were ice. And yet there was a touch of fire behind them. Sable had considered him capable only of a cold anger. She saw that she must become used to this unexpected facet of his character. "Yes, Miss Martin. We'll discuss the matter further."

"Sir John?" Cecily Bland asked. "Have you made arrangements?"

"Parksworth cannot be moved," Geoffrey told her, taking more brandy. "Doctor Dalrymple will stay with him until he recovers or—" He shrugged.

"You mean—" Sable began, "he is not dead?" The affair had new complications.

"He's alive, but barely so. He'll have to be strong to recover from the wound. I had him put in the blue room," Bland told his wife. "But you are not to worry. A nurse will be brought in. Two, if necessary."

"I will pay whatever costs are incurred," Adam said. "Since Sir John was injured by my brother and is no concern of yours, the bill must come to Hunter's."

"You should let him die," Belle said stonily. Every face turned in her direction.

"My dear!" Cecily was shocked. "One cannot allow— It would be wicked."

"There are many things that *are* allowed," Belle replied. "And they are also wicked."

"I think we should go," Adam said, setting down the tumbler. "Thank you for your hospitality, but I have much to do. Please keep me informed of Parksworth's progress." He turned to Sir John's seconds. "You, I presume, will notify his family."

"Of course. But don't think that's the end of the matter—"

"Very well. Come, Miss Martin." Adam bowed stiffly.
"James."

Sable followed, Belle close by her side.

It was not until they were seated in the carriage and
some distance from Bland's house that Adam said, "The
child's right. He should die. But we cannot play God."
Then, seeing Sable's expression, he went on, "and if you
think that is what I have done, then I must live with the
knowledge. And should Parksworth's days, indeed, be
numbered, then perhaps Morgan has done something
noteworthy, long though it has taken him to do it."

Charlotte was angry that she had been told nothing of
the affair. She could be outspoken since James had eaten
earlier and gone out.

"It was to spare you distress," Adam explained tiredly
over a very late supper.

"What an ordeal for Belle," she pointed out.

"Strangely enough, she seems none the worse for it," he
commented. "It was as though the sight of him struck out
much of the terror."

"I thought it drove the fear deep inside her," Sable said
sharply. "And if it has, I will take the blame. She seems
harder and less pitiable, I agree, but something in her is
spoiled."

"You cannot both be right," Charlotte commented. "I
wish there was something I could do—"

"There are two things," Sable told her. "If a post here
should fall vacant, it might be offered to her. She could be
trained without much difficulty. And if you've any surplus
clothes, I'm sure the whole family could benefit. Mrs.
Briggs would go to a deal of trouble to convert them. She's
a good mother." As soon as she had spoken, she wondered
at the change in herself since she left Knowehead. She an-

179

swered back at Adam and addressed Charlotte as an equal, and neither evinced any surprise.

"I can certainly provide some gowns. Marie Claire may be disappointed, but she has already had a fair number."

"The Briggses need them more," Sable insisted, a twist of misery inside her adding to acerbity. "And there are those children at Day's lodgings. Perhaps your friends might supply more."

"You do not expect that woman to alter gowns to fit those mites?" Adam said. "She'd sell them for gin. To take food and watch them eat would be as much as one could do in that quarter."

"Perhaps you are right."

"But to see Morgan shipped off in that way. As though he were a criminal," Charlotte protested, reverting to her original complaint. "How could you, Adam?"

"I thought it for the best." His face closed up.

"And you actually saw the ship sail?"

"I told you, the *Janus* was better prepared than I imagined. They were able to put out late this afternoon."

"Short of crew?"

"Four only. But they can be got at the first port."

"If only—"

"Charlotte! Speed was the essence of the operation. I missed an important debate to see our brother safe. I should prefer less recrimination. He was to go. He has gone. Now for God's sake can we forget the subject?"

"If you say so, Adam."

"I do say so."

"May I be excused?" Sable said, unable to bear more. "I had little sleep last night."

"Certainly. I had intended to suggest," Adam responded, "that you should lie late tomorrow."

"Of course. You should rest. We could manage without you tomorrow."

"I would prefer to be busy."

"As you wish." He was as he had been at that first meeting at the lakeside, all cold courtesy and rigidity. As though he were dead yet still moved, spoke, saw.

There was a silence as she left the room. Once outside she could move no further. She had never felt so before. It was frightening to be without motive or volition, lacking strength.

"I cannot imagine what Morgan was doing with the Martins' girl," Charlotte said. "I knew I had seen her before, yet never connected her with the farm."

"Does it matter?" Adam asked. "Does she work any less well?"

"You know she does not. She's the cleverest girl I ever met. I could trust her implicitly to do the right thing. Between them, Dobbs and Lady Agatha have turned the sow's ear into a creditable silk purse. But Mama would be bound to feel differently. Is that why you sent Morgan packing? To avoid the situation you may have envisaged?"

"And which situation is that?"

"Morgan is not notorious for his constancy. He takes fancies—"

"I made Morgan go because there are bound to be rumblings—a politician's brother in a fatal indiscretion—"

"Oh, not fatal!"

"I fear it will be. You did not see Parksworth. I'd not give a fig for his life."

"And Miss Martin?"

"Nothing has changed as far as I'm concerned. I want her here."

"And Mama?"

"I will handle Mother, never fear."

"You are quite sure you are being wise? Where Miss Martin is concerned?"

"She has done no harm. She is barred from her own home, from Lady Chryston's. It would be cruel to turn her loose on an unsympathetic world."

"There are other posts—"

"No!" Adam shouted. "I refuse to hear of it! You need say no more, Charlotte. The subject is closed. Now there's that matter of inviting some friends from the House. I've been remiss. I've accepted several invitations and not returned the hospitality, though it was difficult with Morgan's rowdy cronies here at all hours."

"Some of whom are your own colleagues," Charlotte pointed out a little waspishly after Adam's outburst. "But you're right. If you care to give me a list, I'll see Cook about a menu."

Sable regained enough strength to drag herself upstairs. Adam's implacable refusal to allow her to leave, his restraining arm at the Blands' paddock, added up to a loss of freedom. The house seemed for the first time to be a prison, her bedchamber a cell.

She lay awake for a long time in spite of her exhaustion, hearing Marie Claire's finicky footsteps in the sitting room next door, faint laughter from the house across the road, then the firm tread she knew to be Adam's. But it was Morgan's footsteps she longed to hear. Morgan holding her— loving her. She could hate Adam for banishing him. And yet, somewhere in that hatred lurked a shadow of pity.

"Did you find Saul West?" Adam asked at breakfast. They had all been quiet after the events of the previous day and his voice broke the silence like a blow.

"No," James said. "I found no trace of him and though I asked at Day's lodging I had little help there. Though I could not help but see the outline of two men at the back of the room, and they were seamen judging by the shape of their hats."

"Had he been back since the night we saw him?"

"She said she'd not noticed, but it seemed she spoke for the benefit of those men. A harridan if ever I saw one, Day's landlady, doxy, wife—whatever she is."

"We'll go again. Oh, and Charlotte, there's the list of guests for Friday."

Charlotte ran her eyes over the lines of neat, strong writing. "I see you've invited William Wilberforce. How does he find time for politics with a business to run?"

"The same way as I do. He has Abel Smith to deal with the financial side. The man's perfectly capable, from a strong banking family. Better by far than William, who is fairly addicted to pleasure and popular, since he's attractive, young, and a good catch, though he keeps women at a distance in spite of the charm, I notice."

Sable saw Charlotte flush and her hand tremble very slightly as she straightened the guest list. It was not the first time she had reacted in a similar fashion to the mention of the gay Mr. Wilberforce who sang very delightfully and could be distracted by the sight of anything that was frail and beautiful, by butterflies and flowers, sunsets. How different he was from Charlotte, who obviously adored him in spite of her seniority and the seriousness of her outlook.

"And there's Mr. Fox, Mr. Sheridan, Billy Pitt, Mr. Pepper, Mr. Denham, Mr. Isaac Milner, Mr. Arden, Mr. Eliot—is that all?"

"I think so. And we must head off Pitt if he gets on his hobbyhorse about the oversetting of all that Lord Chatham achieved. He detests the American War of Independence, but what's done can't be undone. Pitt's father was betrayed, there's no doubt, but I'd not have him make a meal of it over supper. Oh, and there must be some good wines. If Morgan can order them in my absence, I see no reason why they cannot appear at table in my presence."

Sable sat perfectly still, her face expressionless. The reproof rebounded on her since she had partaken of the offending claret. How cruel of Adam to chastise her for what Morgan had done. The cold emptiness of the previous night washed over her in runnels of despair. Morgan was at sea, every minute of this abominable day blowing him further away.

Charlotte and Adam discussed a possible menu, she interested, Adam not much concerned, then finally impatient. "That surely is your province, Charlotte. That is why I have made you mistress of this household. Since I have no wife. Yet—"

"I only thought—you know their tastes—" Charlotte was red with mortification.

"They have most of them been to Hunter Hall. Their tastes are unlikely to have altered radically."

"No, Adam. I am sure you are right."

Sable was angry. This was a bitter Adam she had imagined, erroneously, to have softened of late.

"What," Charlotte began timidly, "do we say, should anyone call from Lady Parksworth? They are bound to send for her. She could scarcely ignore our part in her husband's injury."

"Hm," Adam grunted. "I'd debated about that. I cannot stay from the House more than is necessary. Any inquiry should be referred to me, of course. An appointment can be made, either here or at Parksworth's home."

"Very well. I thought of what you said, Miss Martin, concerning Belle Briggs. It would seem a kindness to give her a position if only to stop her brooding on the past. She's sure to send her mother some of her wages so Mrs. Briggs would not suffer. When I think of her watching the players and that dreadful woman approaching—"

"I've thought of something!" Sable sat bolt upright. "Belle said she heard the chaunters. A girl who sang 'The Mistletoe Bough.' I heard that girl, I am sure, the evening—the evening—" Her face paled. She could not go on.

"You mean the evening you went out with Morgan," Adam said clearly. "There's no need to be coy." His fingers drummed on the table top.

"Very well. She was outside that gaming club. I'd know

her again and it's possible she's often outside the theatre. She could remember the woman who enticed Belle away. Or have noticed which house they entered. Perhaps Parksworth will die, but the whole unsavory business will go on if we cannot stop those others."

"There certainly seems a lead to follow," Adam said after a minute. "You are most observant, Miss Martin."

"And I loathe injustice," she said more sharply than she meant.

"Well, you cannot complain you have had that here," Charlotte broke in with more spirit than usual. "Adam has been exemplary in his treatment—"

"I made no complaint," Sable answered quietly. "The injustice I referred to, as you must have known, was that to poor Belle Briggs. And others like her."

"I'm sorry," Charlotte said. "It has all been so upsetting. My indisposition. Morgan."

"Morgan will enjoy himself," Adam retorted drily. "When does he not?"

Then Adam went on more pleasantly, "Since I am to give suppers more frequently, I think a gown or two for Miss Martin will not go amiss. And as a bonus for her quick-wittedness over the Briggs case and the clue of the chaunters, we'll attend the theatre. I suggest you take her this afternoon to your dressmaker. At least three gowns, I think, with the accessories, naturally. To go on my account."

"I had already planned—" Sable began uncertainly, "a gown, from my wages."

"It will be my pleasure. Oh, and a cloak. The autumn approaches. Perhaps like my mother's, only in a shade you prefer." Was it his intention to be hurtful as well as satirical?

"You sound as though you are making up to me for some disappointment," Sable could not restrain herself from commenting a little bitterly.

"Do I?" Adam's expression was enigmatic. "Why not try to think of it as an exercise that will bring me some satisfaction? And to you also, I hope."

"You are kind," she replied conventionally.

"Then that's settled," Charlotte said with relief. "We'll go after luncheon."

"Come, James," Adam ordered, preparing to leave the table. "We'll decide what we are to do about Saul West and that letter of Day's. Your advertisement hasn't yet borne fruit. I think something more decisive must be done. Oh, and Charlotte, Friday is only two days away. Perhaps, if a gown cannot be got ready for Miss Martin before then, you might provide a substitute? As a temporary measure."

"Well—I may have something." Charlotte did not sound enthusiastic.

"Good." And Adam swept from the room leaving the room as quiet as the grave.

Madame Yvette's was a solid establishment, extravagantly draped, filled with scurrying figures carrying bolts of variegated materials, huge sharp scissors, measuring tapes, pins, and pieces of chalk. A vast, pouter-pigeoned matron stood in an open cubicle in her whalebone stays, the compressed flesh bulging above and below, reminding Sable of a butcher's shop.

Sable had a moment of purest panic. She had not imagined the process to be so public. A wafer-thin girl passed with an armful of blue green silk, that, had it been embroidered with peacock eyes, would have been the loveliest thing she could have seen. Then, she remembered that, compared with the women who were arrayed in alcoves in various parts of the huge salon, her body was made in proportion. Morgan had considered it exquisite, had wanted to touch and kiss every part of it. She'd not been alive before that night. Being without him was a kind of death.

"Miss Martin!" Charlotte said a little crossly. "Madame is speaking."

186

"Yes," Sable murmured, and came back to the present with the ghost of Morgan's touch still on her flesh. She could not care what they thought of her calico shift and petticoat. She was clean and that was what mattered most. Her eyes followed the splatter of peacock silk with a twist of desire. Adam would not care that she wanted it. He'd be glad to have her in his debt, she knew that now where she had formerly suspected it. But she must not take advantage of the feeling he had for her. That would be as bad as whoring.

"Miss Martin's figure is enviable," Madame Yvette remarked, swathing her in dark blue. "The open-robe gown, I think—" She had a habit of baring and clenching her teeth that intimidated.

"The sack dress?" Sable ventured, remembering her impossible dreams.

"Out," Madame Yvette said in a tone of snipping scissors. "Quite finished."

"But they are so pretty."

"You'd be decidedly unfashionable," Madame commented with a bulldog snarl of which she was probably unaware.

"One only—"

"Perhaps you'd better humor Miss Martin," Charlotte interrupted. "She has a mind of her own and after all, it is she who's to wear it. Did I not see you admiring that kingfisher silk?"

"Surely something plainer?" Sable muttered, embarrassed to have been caught out so openly. "I'd not want to present your brother with a bill that was too high."

"I am sure Adam meant one for special occasions," Charlotte went on.

"Mr. Adam? Then this is perhaps his fiancée?" Madame inquired with a look that meant business.

Charlotte flushed. "No," she answered hastily. "Not Mr. Hunter's fiancée."

"Not yet, eh?" Madame pursued with a knowing smile.

"Well, then. We must make sure you look your best so that he makes up his mind the quicker."

Someone sneezed daintily. Another seamstress said, "Good afternoon, Miss Caven. Will you come over to this cubicle, please? Madame will not be long."

Black eyes and china-blue met and held, both filled with an anger neither could hide.

"Charlotte," Clara said coldly and passed on with a swish of skirts, a whiff of musk.

"Clara," Charlotte murmured.

She must have heard all that stupid business of her being Adam's fiancée, Sable thought, all the pleasure gone from the sight of the bright bolts of silks and satins, taffetas, muslins, and velvets. Staring into the pier glass she could see Clara's silhouette at the long, curtained window of her own alcove, the small hands plucking at the green gloves she carried.

"One kingfisher sack dress," Madame murmured with satisfaction. "One dark blue open-robe gown with matching stomacher and underskirt. One—was it the brown striped with black? Ah, yes. Very chic. Now the cloak with fur trim. Have you a preference?"

"Not green." Sable would remember Sarah Hunter's cloak till her last memory was gone. "I think black with a brown edging."

"Very suitable, particularly with the darkest gown. And with your coloring."

"Will you be long, Madame?" Clara asked loudly. "I have not much time."

Madame looked up surprised. "Why no, Miss Caven. Marie. Give Miss Caven a glass of wine while she waits. Will you not sit down?"

"I prefer not. I have not come on pleasure bound. I am here to buy mourning."

"Mourning? Well, Cecile will be pleased to show you blacks for the short time I'll be occupied," Madame said soothingly, her sharp teeth well under control in respect for Clara's dead.

Oh, God, Sable thought, her spirits plunging, it would not be Lady Chryston, would it? But if it were, Clara would be triumphant. As it was, she scowled darkly. It must be Sir John Parksworth. Morgan said there was an affair between them and Parksworth's money would stop with his death. Again her glance collided with Clara's and the unspoken message in Miss Caven's was "murderess."

The sack dress, incredibly, was ready for Friday afternoon. How many poor girls had sat up for two nights to sew the many seams, Sable wondered guiltily.

Sable and Charlotte had returned to Cardigan Square in a chastened mood and next day, Adam was heckled in the House for having allowed his younger brother to engage in a duel and had been closeted with the Prime Minister for some considerable time, coming home pale and quiet, disinclined for conversation in the evening. The matter could not have helped further his career.

The gown had arrived this morning, and as there was little official business on hand for once, Charlotte had told Sable to spend the afternoon bathing and washing her hair in readinesss for the supper party while she visited Cook to see how the preparations for the meal progressed, then made her own toilette with the aid of Marie Claire.

The degree of Charlotte's nervousness told Sable that Adam's supper party meant more to her than she would admit. She was rarely flustered unless her brother showed displeasure or acerbity. Sable steeled her heart against Adam, remembering how he had kept her from Morgan. Her wrist seemed even now to feel the grasp of that strong hand. Like the blood that Lady Macbeth in Shakespeare's play tried to wash away, it could not be eradicated.

Upstairs in her bedchamber Sable took the dress from its extravagant box. It had been tied with a blue-green ribbon that echoed the colors of the changing silk of the garment. Laying it across the counterpane she began to undress. Her body seemed strange and new to her since Morgan had possessed her. She studied its pale, gleaming shape in the mirror, immersed in contemplation of how each intricate fold, bend, curve, thew, and muscle flowed into one simple entirety. She closed her hands around her breasts and imagined his lips upon them, the burden of his head. Then her imaginings became a torment and her body trembled. She rubbed her hands down her thighs, uselessly, then turned her back on the sight of her own nudity.

She had known the gown would be beautiful, if only for its color, but the low rounded neckline that surrounded an area of milky breast like the sea round a white cove, the fitted sleeves that were flounced from just above the elbow in cascades of fine lace, added to the rest. Turning sideways she saw the long panel that hung from neck to floor. She had never seen a more attractive gown at Hunter Hall. The misery of Morgan's absence receded. It would not be the last time they would see one another. If she kept her place, took care never to antagonize Charlotte or Adam or his parents when they came, she must have a second chance.

Two maidservants and Willy in his navy-and-gold livery brought a small hip bath to set in front of the fire and big copper pans filled with hot water. This was undreamed-of luxury, since she had been so far expected to stand on a towel and wash herself bit by bit with a cloth, using the water in the bowl on the washstand. Had the thought originated with Charlotte or Adam? Sable did not care. With her back pressed against the high curved back of the bath, her knees bent, and the water swishing gloriously below them, her spirits rose by the minute.

She rested for a time, as she had been instructed, after

190

washing her hair. The firelight soothed her, dulling the sense of deprivation that the memories of Morgan had brought. It would all come right in the end.

A maid brought her tea and little cakes she had no appetite for, then a little later Marie Claire tapped on the door to inform her she ought to dress. There was a vinegary tone to her voice that made Sable smile inwardly. She thanked Marie sweetly and began her preparations.

The first sound of a carriage stopping outside the house brought its own excitement. Masculine voices in the hall below, Willy and the butler tap-tapping across the marble squares that were set out in a facsimile of a giant chessboard. Lady Agatha had taught Sable the rudiments of chess, but there had been no time to instruct her in the finesse. Sable thought suddenly of Ben, who had been Parksworth's property. To whom would he now legally belong? Lady Parksworth? Or the son Adam had once mentioned, who had detested his father so much that he had gone to make a life of his own. Neither sounded the kind of person to be vindictive about an escaped slave. It was so heady a realization that Sable danced around the bed, then tried to compose herself sufficiently to await Charlotte's summons.

The dining room was very grand. Sable had thought it impressive when they had eaten supper en famille, but with the best china out, the flowers, the snowy napkins folded into shapes of water lilies, the wines glowing through prisms of crystals, the smell of apple logs pyramided to perfection, the candles scenting the warm air, there was the flavor of evenings at Hunter Hall. The centerpiece of a huge bowl of fruit pleased her sense of color. The house had not been so alive, apart from those forays upstairs by Morgan's friends, and those had been impromptu, the gaiety kept behind Morgan's closed door as though it were unwelcome. If only he would come downstairs now, the skirts of the dark red coat swirling, the satiny front of his embroidered waistcoat throwing back the candleshine. His intimate smile—

Adam's guests were mostly young. Lord Chatham's son, Billy, was there, tall and thin, his nose sharp as his brain, his eyes taking in the whole room in one sweeping glance in which there was more than a shade of arrogance.

Charlotte, looking younger in a rose-pink gown Sable had not seen before, her hair much ringletted—a style Sable regretted for it took away Charlotte's own distinction—was talking to William Wilberforce. They made an odd pair, she a foot taller and William looking like a mischievous choirboy, only his voice mellifluous and reflecting his true age. Isaac Milner kept close to Wilberforce, very heavy-faced in contrast, his brows well marked, his frame giving the promise of great broadness.

The others were a procession of faces she never did distinguish in particular that evening apart from Mr. Denham who had red hair and a poxed skin and had recently returned from India, and Mr. Sheridan who had remarkable wit.

Adam had placed Sable to his right. He had been talking to Denham when she had entered the room, whereupon there had been a sudden hush. Sable, conscious of her lack of ornament—she possessed one brooch only which did not go with this dress—flushed faintly and looked about her for rescue. Adam turned round to discover the reason for the inexplicable hush and saw her hesitating near the door, the intense black of her eyes catching the dancing flames of the candles, the dark cloud of her hair melting into the obscurity of the wall behind her, the rest of her encased in the shifting green-blue of the new gown, except for the deep neckline. The hands that escaped from the lace flounce were slender and bare of rings.

"Ah, there you are. Gentlemen, may I introduce Miss Isabel Martin?" There was a babel of introductions out of

192

which Sable was aware only of Adam's expression, no longer cold or censorious but imprinted most unmistakably with a desire that filled her with unease, then was lost behind a barrier of reserve.

"Why, you sly dog, Adam!" Pitt said. "Where did you find such a goddess?"

"At Lady Chryston's," he answered. "You could have found her for yourself had you gone to the Lakes."

"Miss Martin," Wilberforce said. "I know Knowehead."

"Lady Agatha spoke of you," Sable replied, taking her place beside Adam and aware of Charlotte's chagrin that William showed her interest.

"What did Lady Chryston say?" William inquired, perched on his chair like a well-scrubbed youth.

"I think—I believe she was surprised you'd taken up politics. I imagine she thought you too gentle," Sable answered.

"He has enough obstinacy for a thousand mules," Milner said. "Lord North won't have all his own way. But now that Dunning's motion is passed that the power of the Crown ought to be lessened, I fear North may have had his day. It's gratifying that Tories with all their built-in privilege can be overset by the Josiah Wedgwoods who batter their way from practically nothing by dint of brain, application, self-faith, and pride of craft. He makes pots, but *what* pots! A hundred years, two hundred, and people will look and wonder, put them in safe places, and maybe throw back a thought across the centuries to a yeoman's son who did something unique. Became someone not because he was born in the right bed. North must be decidedly unsure. Was he too bad yesterday, Adam? After all it wasn't your fault Morgan was a fool. They say there was a girl at the bottom of it. Not that that's an original story. Who was she? Anyone who could get the better of the Caven must be an Amazon."

Adam turned white. "Lord North has his job to do. I

193

stepped out of line and I have no one to blame but my-self."

"And Morgan?"

"At sea. There was a ship of the Hunter Line and he was due to sail anyway. Fortunately he was recovered from that illness. But shall we not touch on the matter? We are meant to enjoy ourselves. Denham, I rely on you to enter-tain us. You should have much to say of India."

Denham was grateful for the opportunity to shine and told countless entertaining tales of India.

The women were expected to withdraw with the termi-nation of the meal. The butler brought the port with an os-tentatious gesture and Charlotte rose to her feet.

"Shame!" one of the unidentifiable young gentlemen said as Sable followed suit. "At times I feel the decanter is eclipsed."

"Hear, hear!" Denham supported, clapping his hands slowly.

For a long, triumphant moment Sable hesitated, her smile radiant, the moving green-blue of the dress tantaliz-ing as it showed first one then another curve and indenta-tion of her body. She knew that their eyes followed her as she walked out with perfect composure. It was strange to be certain that no other person would in future have the power to intimidate her. If the King himself were to ad-dress her, she felt she would have an answer.

Charlotte went upstairs with the briefest of good-nights, but Sable could not sleep. She left her door open so that the talk and the laughter flowed upwards to hang about her bedchamber in little eddies of sound. They talked of royalty, of the poor state of France, of the price of timber and tea, of America. They discussed members who were not present. Adam sounded so different she could hardly believe it.

At some point she must have fallen asleep, for she woke out of a doze to find herself still in the sack dress and stretched across the counterpane, her eyes heavy and blinking in the light of a candle.

She sat up hastily, her mind briefly hazed, half wondering if Morgan had slipped ship and come in search of her. But it was Adam standing there, his coat removed, his stock undone as though he were half-ready for bed.

"Your door was open," he said quietly. "I wondered—"

What had he wondered, she thought with a trace of bitterness? If he was entitled to what Morgan had had, now that he was gone? If the open door was a signal?

"I forgot it," she said without expression. "I must have been more tired than I thought. As you see, I am not even undressed."

"You did well," Adam told her, as though he did not want to go. "They liked you—"

"Thank you for telling me my door was open. Perhaps you would close it as you go out?"

There was the longest silence she had ever known. He was so still, his upraised hand so steady, even the candleflame held captive. She shivered suddenly, breaking the unnerving spell.

"Good night, Miss Martin."

"Good night."

It was dark when the door shut behind him and now she was wide-awake, a curious pain plucking at her senses, the triumph and the assurance gone.

"Morgan. Oh, Morgan," she whispered. "Morgan?" But she could no longer picture his face or any part of him. The sea had him and would keep him, take him to burning lands and places of poison green and parched yellow that were evoked by Ben's songs of his homeland. She could not remember. Could not, or would not. The night was terrifying in its emptiness.

Chapter 9

In the three weeks since the successful supper that had gone on into the small hours Adam had grown whiter and quieter. She had not too far to look for the reason. He had expected something of her that he had not from Clara Caven. It was her body he had imagined she might give him out of loneliness or ambition or because, once aroused, she might be unable to resist the opportunity of physical satisfaction, now that Morgan was not there to pleasure her, as he had—indeed he had. Even as she had furtively washed the blood from the sheet next morning, she had not remembered the initial pain. Morgan was an expert at rousing and satisfying even one as inexperienced as herself. That conversation between the brothers had been so revealing. Chaste wooing and boredom were his way, Morgan had told Adam scornfully. Farmyard cockerels were his brother's way Adam had retaliated. Perhaps he had had enough of chastity and would find out for himself what existed on the other side of the coin. Not that he could still be virgin. Sable found herself studying him curiously, unable to come to any conclusion. He was such a contained man. She had it in her to be sorry for Adam, but she was not there as an experiment for some recently aroused desire for self-fulfillment and he should not have expected it.

A curious giddiness overcame her as she leaned across the desk to take a note from Charlotte. Charlotte was speaking to her, but her voice made only noises without meaning. There was a hollowness in Sable's ears like the sound in a shell.

"Miss Martin." The words echoed, rebounded, soft and insistent. "Martin—"

"I'm sorry," she murmured, the paper suddenly becoming clear and familiar. "Yes, I will file it." Charlotte's meaning was once more mercifully plain, the odd moment gone.

Charlotte looked at her sharply. Adam had gone in that strange interval and James was halfway to the study. "Shall we have a dish of tea, Miss Martin? You really do look tired. I sometimes think you need not be so dedicated."

"I like to be occupied," Sable answered. One had less time for self-pity, for regrets. They were emotions she despised and would go on thinking contemptible. She'd prefer to be like Lady Chryston, disregarding her pain which was considerable and wearing her diamond rings to please a dead husband she refused to mourn because she believed his essence to remain in the house they'd shared together. Using her mind rather than have it rot with neglect. Spirit was the thing. Anyone else would have taken to their bed years ago. Not Lady Agatha.

The doorbell rang. The butler crossed the hall. There was a confused buzz of voices. Sable and Charlotte exchanged glances.

A light tap at the door, then the butler appeared, saying, "It's Lady Parksworth, Miss Hunter."

"Lady Parksworth! What does she want? And Adam not here." Charlotte was flustered.

"It's not Mr. Adam she wants. It's Miss Martin."

"Miss—Martin?"

"I took the liberty of putting her in the morning room."

"Me?" Sable was amazed. "What—Oh! She blames me. For her husband's death."

"You do not have to see her," Charlotte said.

"She'd not have come if she were not determined," Sable replied more calmly than she felt. Only three weeks ago she had thought she could hold conversations with the King if there were need, but that was all wine-headiness and the courage that came from the admiration of men on a special occasion and knowing she looked her best.

"I will come with you—"

"No, Miss Hunter. She asked for me and indeed she has a right to her say, poor woman. It was my doing."

"Very well. But I will be here if you need me."

Lady Parksworth was standing by the window when Sable went into the morning room. It was dull outside and not much light infiltrated the chamber. All she had at first was an impression of a small, dowdy figure in black, whose face was hidden by the brim of a bonnet beaded with bits of jet, the outline clouded by the softness of a sable plume.

The girl's stomach muscles were taut. What did one say to a woman who had widowed?

The little figure turned. They stared at one another over a chasm of secret thoughts.

"I am Isabel Martin," Sable said.

Lady Parksworth moved forward and sat closer to the fire where the meager flames illuminated her lined face in a desultory fashion. She had large blue eyes, set now in a host of wrinkles. Her soft skin was crisscrossed, too, with a

199

mass of spidery lines. But her bones were good and she must once have been pretty. She gave the impression of looking much older than she was and of being, ironically, well aware of the fact. "You are wondering what he saw in me," she said unexpectedly.

"No—" Sable was startled out of composure.

"Oh, go on. You were," the pretty voice urged with an undertone of ugliness that saddened Sable inexplicably, making her aware of a life of sterility that had been bounded by self-hatred. "I don't mind you admitting it. I may as well say that you are not what I expected. Younger. Not degenerate as I half imagined when I heard your name coupled with that of Clara Caven. Ah! I see that you hate her too. Some women have elements of badness, but Miss Caven has them all. She's like the kind of the dish the Borgias excelled in. The delicious potion with gall at its center. What she touches is immediately made unhappy or warped. You think I'm jealous, don't you? But I'm not, Isabel Martin. My husband married me for my money, despised me, robbed me of my son who could not bear to be where he was so I must lose him also.

"Do you know what I did when they came to tell me Parksworth was finally dead? I could not stop laughing. Every time I thought of it, I began to laugh again. Not madness, child. Relief. As though a stone were rolled away from the sepulcher of my lost identity. But, oh, how it hurts to try to find oneself and then know that it's no longer worth the effort. That the truth has gone."

"Oh, please!" Sable was immensely distressed. "You must know that is not so. You've not given it sufficient time. There must be detachment after a while. You'll see more clearly then."

"Why, I do believe I like you, Miss Martin." The light laugh was not so false.

"I am quite prepared to accept the blame," Sable told her. "Everything began with that slap to Clara's face—"

"It should have been with a holy-water sprinkler," Lady Parksworth remarked, unmoved. "Ah, I see you do not know what that is. A barbaric weapon of long ago, a kind of iron ball set about with spikes that one swings from a chain with all of one's strength."

Sable was astounded that one so small and delicate in appearance could be so bloodthirsty. But remembering Parksworth, she could understand the slow erosion of the finer feelings. The descent into loathing, culminating in the pit of despair.

"But I am sorry—"

"I am not! Neither do I expect platitudes from you. I am glad John is dead and my primary purpose in coming here, since I understand Morgan Hunter is no longer in the country, was to thank you personally for administering that blow that led to my freedom from servitude. I must now try to find my son—"

"To thank me?"

The small, crumpled face smiled a little bleakly. "I'm well aware it is not usual. But then, I have not led a pretty life and squalor leaves its own hard shell." She opened the reticule on her lap and took out a necklace of great beauty, all gold links and faceted stones of enormous brilliance. The soft, wrinkled hands held it towards Sable. "I brought you this more tangible token of my appreciation. Will you accept it? Please—?"

"Of course, I could not! For a man's death?"

"A satyr's death. He had hideous ways—"

During all of this unbelievable confrontation Sable had forgotten Belle Briggs. Now the previous revulsion flooded back so that she could more easily understand this woman's apparent derangement. She must have been married to Parksworth for a very long time. She had a grown-up son who had cut himself adrift—a son she had loved. What scenes had she not witnessed! What cruelties—

"There is one thing I would take," she said, suddenly sure of herself and of her temporary power over Lady Parksworth. The opportunity might not come again.

"And what is that?" The woman dangled the jewels against the firelight, half-mesmerized by their fire and richness.

"There was a slave once in your husband's employ—a black man called Ben."

"Ben? What could you know of him?" The woman's voice sharpened and she dropped the glittering cascade of the necklace back inside the bag on her knee.

"He didn't die—"

"Oh, but he must!" Lady Parksworth's face had whitened. "It was appalling what John had done to him. No one could live after that." She frowned. "But you must have been a child at the time. Five years? Six? How would you know?"

"He's still alive. Mutilated, but alive—"

"Tell me."

Sable sat in the chair facing her unexpected guest. "This is how I know." When she had finished she said, "You may guess what I want. A paper signed by you to say that Ben is no longer your property, but Lady Chryston's."

"Not yours?" There was a strange note in the woman's voice.

"Oh, no! I could never own a person. But Lady Agatha does not think of Ben as a possession any more than I do. The thing that would make her happiest is to know that Ben is safe. Not hunted. Never in danger of being removed from — sanctuary, I suppose you would call it."

"And that is what you really want? Nothing for yourself?"

Sable shook her head. Lady Parksworth seemed to see nothing macaber in offering a reward for her husband's removal. In spite of her aversion for Parksworth's actions Sable's skin crept.

202

The small figure rose. Soft, crepey fingers dangled the reticule invitingly. "No?"

"No."

"I will have a paper drawn up regarding the slave," Lady Parksworth said, "and have it sent to Lady Chryston. You will receive a copy."

"I'd prefer it if you need not mention that I had any hand in it," Sable told her. "Let her think you found Ben's bond while clearing your husband's papers—"

"But I have to tell her, don't you see? How else should I have known he was alive and where to find him?"

"Oh. I do see."

"Either I can ignore the fact so that she spends her days never quite sure that he can be recalled—recognized—"

"Or happy in the knowledge that he's free," Sable supplemented thoughtfully.

"Much better, would you not agree?"

"Much. Oh, and Lady Parksworth, it may please you to know that Clara Caven will be furious to discover that a lever has been removed. She discovered Ben's secret and threatened me with the power to use her knowledge. We are old adversaries."

Lady Parksworth smiled for the first time. All the tiny lines in her face were crisscrossed in malevolent amusement. "Then my action is all the sweeter. I'm glad you told me. It goes without saying that if I can ever help you, I will."

"Thank you. I will not forget."

They took a last look at one another, each probably thinking they had never met anyone to match one other for peculiarity, and Sable sure that Parksworth's widow considered her a fool for rejecting personal gain. Then she rang the bell for the visitor to be shown out.

It had been a strange morning.

"She wanted to what?" Adam demanded at supper, incredulous.

"To thank me for being the means to his death," Sable repeated. Charlotte had retired with another migraine, so there was not so much need for circumspection.

"The woman's mad," James remarked, intent on his meat.

"Her life must have been hell," Sable defended.

"You told her nothing of Belle?" Adam asked, tilting his glass so that the contents were swirled gently from side to side.

"It seemed not a subject one could discuss with a widow. Why add to her distress?"

"She would never have contemplated suttee, that's obvious," James said. "Lit the pyre, mostlike, and danced around it like the Witch of Endor." It was unlike him to joke, if one could call it a joke.

"I was sorry for her."

"And that was all she came for?"

"She did say she regretted Lord North's reprimand and—" she could not resist saying it, "that she wished I had used more than my hands to strike Clara."

"What did she suggest?" Adam asked curiously.

"A holy-water sprinkler."

James gave a shout of laughter that was quickly stifled by Adam's lack of support. He dabbed at his lips with his napkin and excused himself.

Alone with Adam, Sable cast about for her own excuse but he forestalled her by asking, "Why did you really leave your door open the evening Pitt and the others came?" The wine shivered in his glass as he continued to twirl the stem. "You didn't really forget. I've never believed in that explanation."

"No. I thought what a pity it was that Charlotte and I had been banished and I could hear that the dining-room door was open to let out the warmth, so I listened. I didn't hear all of what was said, of course, but every now and again it became noisy and my bedchamber was filled with opinions, knowledge, jokes—Anyway, that is why you found me as you did. I wished I had been a man for the occasion, but the next best thing to involvement was to pretend I was still there." She accepted the offer of claret in her own glass and played with it as he had. "Then I—fell asleep."

"So that is the kind of life that would appeal to you."

She raised her eyes to his. "Why, yes. What's the use of knowledge one never uses? But to discuss, to argue, to listen, to make a point that is applauded for its boldness or truth. To decide the fate of great personages, the events in countries far off. It's—it's like a game of chess with no end—"

"Chess? You play?"

"Lady Agatha taught me the rules but she had not the time for the refinements—"

"I have never known anyone like you," he said in a low voice and now his tones were a little slurred. She had not previously known Adam the worse for drink. "You must come to the gallery of the House to hear a debate. I will arrange it."

"I should like that."

"Charlotte's migraines," he said, seemingly inconsequential. "They do tend to prevent her being what I envisaged. A permanent support in a public man's household. Someone strong who is always at hand. She does well, but what if I had expected her support tonight?"

"It would have been unfortunate. But I'm sure she regrets it as much as you do."

"No doubt. But the problem remains."

Sable spoke without thinking. "You should marry—" Then she bit off the words abruptly.

"I had thought the same. I had even thought of a—possible wife."

"Then that could not possibly concern me," she said decisively, seeing the intentness of his gaze upon her. "I thought I would leave you now. There is a book I wish to read before sleep."

Adam rose and barred the way to the door. He looked very tall, his body broader than formerly, his mouth set in obstinate lines. Sable, in the brown dress with the stripes of black, looked small beside him, not as lovely as in the silk sack dress she had coveted, but unusual enough with her pallor, her intensely dark eyes, the shadowy brown of her loosened hair, the pale traces of summer freckles.

"That business of the theatre. The chaunters—" he said.

"The girl who sang 'The Mistletoe Bough.'"

"Yes. We must do it. Attend the theatre—she could be there. If not, we'll go again—"

"I should be pleased."

A pause.

"Is there anything else?" Sable asked.

"You know damned well there's something else," Adam grated, and seized her by the shoulders in a grip that bruised. "Damn the theatre and Charlotte. You said yourself that I should get a wife. And you knew as you said it that it was you I wanted."

"No—"

"Be good enough not to lie." He had dragged her close enough towards him for her to feel the heat of his body, to sense the urgency of his desire for her.

She opened her mouth to say that she loved Morgan, but she was not allowed to utter a word. Inexorably he ground his lips against hers as though she were an enemy. His knee pushed her legs apart as though he meant to take her against the wall like a doxy on the waterfront.

And then, as suddenly as he had taken hold of her, he released her so unexpectedly that she fell back, shaken and disbelieving. "It was not the way I meant to propose to you, Miss Martin," he said almost formally. "But I hope it will not prevent you from thinking about the matter."

Then the room was empty and there was only the steady

thump of his boots on the stairs, the tick of the clock, the beat of her own blood. It seemed an age before she could bring herself to move, to slither along the wall in case of an enemy at her back, to stare around the hall, bemused.

If it had been an unusual morning, the evening had been quite singular.

She had imagined it would be difficult to look at Adam next morning, but it had not been as hard as she feared. She had felt squeamish on first rising, as though she had eaten something that disagreed with her, and looked paler than usual. The thought of breakfast did not invite, but it would have been cowardly not to put in an appearance. She suspected her indisposition to be brought on by nerves and was determined to vanquish them at whatever cost. Men taken the worse for drink often did things they later regretted. Her body remembered, with a curious insistence, the moment when he forced his knee between her thighs, spread-eagling her against the wall of the dining room.

He obviously had no such memories. He had eyed her dispassionately, bid her a perfectly ordinary good-morning, commented that Charlotte was still poorly, but had Marie Claire, so there was no need for worry on that score.

"Miss Martin, why don't you take the carriage and which of the maids you prefer and Willy will fetch the bundle of cast-off clothing Charlotte promised the Briggs family." He took five sovereigns from his waistcoat pocket and put them on the table. "Then you will buy as much food as you can out of that and take it to the mites at Day's lodging. Insist that you stay to watch them eat. Make some of your purchases in flour and such things that would last a time."

Sable's spirits rose at the thought of the change in routine and the prospect of air was welcome. Today each part of the house seemed unaccountably close.

"It will take all day," she said almost gaily.

"All the better. You've been out all too little. I realize that now. I—I must see about those tickets for the theatre. We will make up a party."

So he had not forgotten! She had not realized he could dissemble so expertly. Perhaps this was his method of apology, to ignore all but the more pleasant aspects of an encounter. To hand out his treats of fresh air and diversion and never refer to the happenings that had led to bruised shoulders and smarting lips.

She tried to catch his eye, but already she was dismissed and he in conversation with his secretary. What if she were to call his bluff and tell him she had thought over his so-called proposal? He'd be certain to disremember that.

Adam gone and Marie Claire too busy to be a nuisance, Sable threw off her initial lethargy and sent for the youngest and least-privileged maid to accompany her on her errands of goodwill. Daisy would have few treats and had to work hard for her living, performing the tasks that Sable had once expected to be hers at Hunter Hall.

Once in the carriage, Daisy, her round, rosy face polished like an apple, stared around her in delight. "Oh, miss!" she kept saying, "oh, miss!" As though Sable had waved some magic wand, when all they were doing was to dispense charity. One day, perhaps, everyone would have enough of everything as a right.

They passed the carriage of the Marquess of Rockingham who was tipped to become the next Prime Minister and Sable related the tidbit of news very gravely to a shining-eyed Daisy who could think of nothing else to say but another ecstatic, "Oh, miss!" It was all very heart-warming. One day it might be Adam Hunter who would be first Minister.

The street where the Briggses lived was as mean as ever, crowded, noisy, and odorous. The roast-chestnut stand made a brave onslaught against smells and grime with its glowing charcoal and sizzling, browned nuts. Sable stopped the carriage and bought a bag for herself and Daisy and a large one for Belle's brothers and sisters.

The clothes delivered and seized enthusiastically by Mrs. Briggs were soon distributed among members of the family, who divided their attention between dressing up and chewing mouthfuls of chestnuts. Neighbors stared in at the streaked window to see what was happening.

Belle alone took no part in the unusual festivity, hanging back in the darkest corner of the room, her eyes lackluster.

Sable went to her. "What is it, Belle? Look, this is the gown I thought would best become you. The blue is the same as your eyes—"

"Is he dead, Miss Martin?"

"Dead?"

"That man. The one who was shot."

"Of course, no one has been here since then! We should have found a way to tell you, but Mr. Hunter's house is such a busy one. Yes. He died a few days later."

"I dreamed he came last night. It seemed so real."

"He can never come to anyone. You must forget him, hard though it is."

"People look at me in such a queer way. I cannot bear the thought that they know. What he did. And those others— It makes me remember all over again. Even Mother—"

"Miss Hunter did say she'd look into the matter of employing you. But it would be just the same there, wouldn't it? You'd know that we knew. What you need is a place where you are just another girl who is prepared to work. No different from the next."

"But I am different, aren't I," Belle said bitterly. "Still it would help to be thought like any other servant."

"I'll see what I can do. Try to keep two of the gowns.

209

You'd need them if you were to take up a post. And I can let you have a cloak and buy you shoes. The country would be a good place. It can be—very healing."

"The country, miss?"

"The place I took you to the day of the duel. It's not always like that, all grey and morning mists. I promise I'll come back soon with good news. Miss Charlotte will understand if I tell her your feelings on the matter. I know how it can hurt to be looked at—reminded—"

"I wish—"

"Yes, Belle?"

"That I were like you. Good—"

Sable could think of nothing to say. She moved away almost blindly, the sounds of the Briggses' revelry muted into a soft mockery. Belle obviously imagined her to be some worthy virgin when in reality she was self-willed and had already given herself to a lover. There was nothing good about her.

She forgot her own deficiencies when she made the coachman, Jim, stop at a big shop on the way to the docks, keeping Daisy close by her, as the thoroughfares were thronged with sailors and gin-merry doxies and poor drunken creatures, bunched and misshapen or huddled in rags that were certain to be verminous. A pennorth of gin brought dreams and near oblivion. Even if Adam did disapprove and would like to ban the stuff from Holland, was a total awareness of one's bodily misery any better? Even the wrong kind of happiness, however temporary, seemed preferable to no happiness at all.

A parrot screamed on a seaman's shoulder, reminding her of Lady Chryston. The thought made her smile, and the smile was taken as encouragement by a tall, swarthy man who had just emerged from the ship chandler's at the corner. He stood still, watching the girl and the servant disappear inside the dry-goods store to add to the commodities already purchased.

He was still there as they emerged smothered in parcels, with the coachman carrying a sack of flour and a side of bacon. "We'll get no further by carriage," the dark, attractive girl was saying. "We'll go the rest of the way on foot. It's up that lane there and I believe it's the third yard on the left. We can send the little boys back for the rest. Can you manage that lot there, Daisy?"

"Course, I can."

"You better stay with the carriage," Sable told the coachman. "I'd not trust any of these folk with a penny whistle. And don't look so worried, Jim! It was Mr. Hunter's idea. He must have thought it safe enough. Come, Daisy. Watch you don't trip over those barrels, child. Yes, it's up this lane and let's pray they'll save the slops for later. I don't quite fancy a splash of something unmentionable over my cloak or yours. Now, under this arch and there's the house, up those crumbly steps. Aren't you glad you live in Cardigan Square? Imagine living here always."

The walls still ran with damp and the smell of rotted fish seeped everywhere. There was someone in the house, for there was a feeble glow of tallow dip and something small and stunted shifted across the window. There was a tiny skittering scuffle in the yard and Daisy gave a little scream. "Oh, miss. Rats—"

"Stamp your feet," Sable advised. "Noises will keep them off." And she rapped at the peeling door. It was not opened straight away, but she could still see the light at the window, so she knocked again, this time more loudly. The door opened a crack and an eye appeared low down in the gap.

"You remember me," Sable said warmly. "You once waved to me from the window. Is your mother out?"

"Yes."

"Well, could you let me in? The weight of all these pies and bread and oranges is dragging my arms from my body. I thought we could all take supper together. I'd meant it to be tea but I've been so long in the shops—"

The dim lit room opened up suddenly in front of her with its smells of damp and neglect, dirt and urine.

"Oh, miss—" Daisy breathed at Sable's shoulder. "Oh, them poor souls."

"We must sound cheerful," Sable said. "This is to be a celebration they'll remember to their dying day and Providence has ordained that the ogress is conveniently away. She'll be in the nearest gin shop, I daresay, and long may she remain there. What's your name, boy? Davy? Well, Davy, you and the rest will go with Miss Daisy Bank—why, Daisy, it had never occurred to me how appropriate your name was! Has it any significance, I wonder? You'll go with Daisy to fetch the rest of the food and I'll put the table ready. Off you go. It will take no more than quarter of an hour and here's a piece of pie for each to eat on the way."

She could hardly bear to see the grubby hands pushing the unexpected treat into mouths covered with numerous sores brought on by neglect and ill-feeding. Neither could she fail to see the marks of brutality, the half-healed bruises, the way the children walked crouched as though even in the woman's absence they must avoid the blows they expected. They scuttled down the eroded steps like the rats in the yard, all matted hair and grey skin that could not have been washed in a month of Sundays.

It was quiet without Daisy and the children, so she cleared the things from the table quickly, then was amazed to find that there was a baby in the rickety cradle in the corner. It was so pale and still that she imagined it to be dead until she bent down and detected the smell of gin that hung around its mouth and found it to be faintly warm under the grisly rags.

A small sound behind her made her start up with a quickening of the blood. She had half expected to see the toadlike shape and frizzed head of the abominable landlady but it was a man's outline against the dusk, the torso powerful in seaman's sweater, his hair tied in a queue at the back of his neck. He said nothing, only stood with his hands planted on his hips and his legs apart.

"She's not here," Sable said, suddenly dry-mouthed. "You should come back later." The thought came to her that if he did, then all those little creatures would see what their mother and these transient visitors did with one another. Their lives were made up of one squalor after another, each worse than the last. Her sickness turned to anger. "On second thoughts, take her somewhere else to appease your lust! Why should her children be brutalized. Go away, for they will soon be back."

He moved one leg to kick shut the door. There was not much light from the tallow dip but enough to see the thin lips stretched in a grin. Then he came forward, lifted the table she had just cleared and pushed it against the door. Advancing, kicking carelessly the parcels of food in passing, he came up to Sable. Snatching at the switch of hair that hung over her shoulder, he yanked her to him, then thrust her down on the uneven floor, his hands fumbling with the fastenings of his breeches. There would be no kisses, no lips on her breast or her bare body. Only the unspeakable use of her as between one animal and another.

She tried to rise but he flung himself upon her ignoring her scratches and struggles, she all the time aware of the smells that rose from the sour earth and some slight scratching like mice in a wainscot, a tiny snuffle from the gin-drugged baby in the cot. He dragged up her skirts as far as he required and tore crudely at the barrier of her underclothes. She tried to calculate how long the children and Daisy had been away. It could only have been five minutes. He had been waiting in the obscurity of the yard. She knew now who he was and where she had seen him. Outside the ship chandler's close by the carriage. They would still be gone ten minutes. Long enough—

She seized upon the part of him nearest, the rounded

213

part of his throat that partly obscured her mouth and bit at it. He laughed softly as though this were a stimulation he had not expected and arranged her as he would, ready now to enter her at his pleasure. It would be no use to scream. In a backwater like this and with the landlady's life-style a cry for help would go unnoticed.

"Please," she said, "please. I have money. Leave me and I'll give it to you—"

It was useless, of course. Another second and he'd touch her with his nakedness. A body that had lain with whores. Probably diseased— It was this last thought that sickened her most. She did scream then, pulled her body from side to side, screamed more and scored fingernails down his hard-skinned cheeks.

There was a shout, a crash upon the window, a heavy something that struck the floor and rebounded onto the seaman's head. A stone, greened with slime. The coachman's voice, hoarse with rage and fear of what Adam Hunter was likely to say if he returned with Miss Martin raped, shouted, "The Runners are coming! You were seen to enter." And the yard, incredibly, was now awash with scurrying figures, though most were rather uselessly the children who'd not have the stamina to hold the man for arrest.

Her body was, suddenly, light and free as the sailor bounced up with an oath and began to put his breeches together. He shifted the table in a panic and pulled out a knife which he held out straight in front of him.

"Be careful!" she screamed to those outside. "Take care!"

The door was pulled open on an inrush of clammy air and the man plunged outside, falling heavily from the top of the worn steps and arousing shrieks from the tattered little boys surrounding them.

Sable got to her feet, fighting nausea. It was the worst thing that had ever happened to her. Only, by some miracle, it had not really happened. But the thought remained branded on her mind that but for that stone through the window she'd most surely be degraded. It was as though she now felt everything that had not occurred in a series of abominable pictures that went on and on in a compartment of her mind.

Daisy rushed into the room. "Oh, miss! Oh, miss—!"

"It's all right, Daisy." Sable was white-faced, but now had her skirts decently covering up the marks of the recent battlefield. "There was really nothing to make a fuss about. I am grateful, though, for the diversion. It made it easier to get rid of him. It was the woman he expected and it was difficult to explain I was not in the same line of business. How did you get back so quickly?"

The children stole back, grey and anonymous. She could not tell one from another, girls from boys. The coachman, Jim, followed, his eyes everywhere but on Sable. He must have seen everything from the window. "I thought I should not let you and Daisy go alone, Miss Martin, in spite of what you said. So I paid someone to stay with the carriage while I followed with the rest of the things. When we got here and tried the door I knew something was wrong for one of the boys said he'd seen a man in the corner outside—but he's used to that and thought little of it. Then I took a peep"— he cleared his throat diplomatically—"and thought the mention of Bow Street Runners wouldn't come amiss. And out he came near spitting me with that knife, but I was expecting it, thanks to you. So, all's well as ends well as you might say."

"Thank you." Her eyes met his at last with a sense of shame and silent obligation. Then, seeing the row of small, frightened faces she cried, "and now we'll have that celebration. We'll put this clean paper from the parcels on the table. And there's a cooked goose somewhere—" There could, quite easily, have been another sort of cooked goose, but she'd not spoil their pleasure with such foolishness as to let them down at the pinnacle of enjoyment by becoming influenced by a nonevent. She became brilliantly gay.

But when the feast was set, and the flour put away for future use, the big side of bacon dangling from the hook in the ceiling like a hanged man, she went outside into the yard and retched up her insides far enough away not to be overheard. She felt terribly ill, as though it were not all reaction from the narrow escape. But, wiping her mouth with her kerchief in the pallid aftermath, she could not help but rejoice in the sounds of festivity from the room where the children laughed, probably for the first time in their lives. Daisy sang and the boys thumped on the table in time to the words.

The thought of Morgan was quite unreal. She had taken out her private memories of him as an antidote to the beastliness of an hour ago, but they left no impression of joy or of hope. It was Adam who obtruded, strong and indomitable, who had enjoyed the same power the seaman had, but who had not used it. There was a shuddering gratitude in the reflection.

The letter from Lady Parksworth arrived next morning. It was written on thick, expensive paper and was sealed very grandly with an insignia of a prancing bull with a garland of flowers around its neck. A peculiarly appropriate design, Sable could not help thinking. Parksworth and those poor, fragile girls—

"You look sick as a cat," Charlotte said, breaking into Sable's private nightmare of yesterday. She sounded piqued that she had not been told of the letter's contents. But Ben was Sable's secret and no business of anyone else's.

"I do feel a little indisposed. We are a pair, are we not? Your head and my insides!"

"Yes. I suppose we are."

Adam came into the room unannounced. Sable had not

seen him at breakfast and had been immensely relieved. "So you've recovered, Lotte. And how did the day go for you, Miss Martin?" Sable was surprised to detect a trace of relaxation around his mouth and the expression in his eyes was quite human.

"Very well. Mrs. Briggs was overcome with the gowns, but Belle has come to realize the difficulties of living with other people's knowledge of her—her position. She could be happier in some quiet country post with employers who would not be aware of her past. I think I sympathize and agree with that."

"I'll file that for future reference," Adam said with a ghost of a smile. Charlotte for the first time showed signs of jealousy. Sable, having fallen foul of Annie Gormley, was not unaware of this quality. She must be even more careful in her relations with Adam's sister, and yet it was so constraining not to be allowed to voice the truth as she saw it and seemed so unnecessary.

"And the Day children—if they are Jeremy Day's—had an afternoon and evening to remember. Their mother was not there. She had not even come back by the time we left but we prevailed on a neighbor to keep an eye on them. I'm afraid I had to use the remainder of the last guinea to bribe her."

The odd little smile was accentuated. "It was given to you to use."

"And Daisy enjoyed herself greatly."

"Could you not have taken Florrie, the upstairs maid?" Charlotte inquired coolly.

"Now, Lotte," Adam said gently, obviously enjoying the repartee for a change. "Too few pleasures make hard work of youth. But soon we are to have our turn. The recess. I've a notion to go to the Lakes. Windermere is so lovely in autumn—"

"Windermere? Not home? Not the Hall?"

He shook his head. "I'll ask Mother, Father, and Jane to

217

meet us there, I think. And I should like Miss Martin to see Tom Dobb's house. But before that, we must try to attend the theatre. How would Thursday suit you, Lotte?"

"Thursday?" Charlotte looked blank. "That day will be no different from any other."

"Very well. Thursday it shall be. You did, I think, Miss Martin, express a wish to see Mrs. Siddons, did you not?"

Sable shook her head. "No. It was Morgan. Don't you remember?"

The gentleness went out of his face. "Perhaps," he agreed distantly as though the topic no longer interested him. "I'll arrange a box. James will make a fourth."

"Will James go to the Lakes?" Charlotte asked.

"No. He'll spend the recess with his family."

"I shall stay here," Charlotte said, her expression still displeased. "I—I do not feel like making such a long journey. And there are matters that may arise. In any case the servants take advantage when the master is away. Or the mistress." This with a glance at Sable as though to reinforce the fact that she was not yet superseded.

"But I had thought to have all the family together—"

"Morgan will not be there," Charlotte reminded with asperity.

"But everyone else—"

"Is there any particular reason for such a gathering?" Charlotte asked directly.

"Very well," Adam conceded grimly. "I see you are adamant. It would have pleased me, but you choose to be difficult. I'll not argue against you."

"Difficult? You know I have not been well—"

"Indeed," Adam said thoughtfully. "I do remember. And it seems that perhaps I have expected too much from you, my dear. There must be a reason for those migraines and I feel that you have too much responsibility. That it cannot agree with you—"

"Oh, but Adam!" she protested. "I did not intend—"

"I mean it, Charlotte. You must have less to worry you, then you will feel better. After the recess I may make changes. In fact I am certain to make some, so you can begin to relax now from this moment. I feel hungry and supper can't be far off, so I'll wash and change my coat. Please leave us, Miss Martin. There's something I must say to my sister first."

Sable picked up the letter from Lady Parksworth and Adam's gaze rested on the seal, then rose to ask a silent question. "It came from Sir John's widow. Arising out of that interview after his death," she said.

"So you did have some request?"

"It was—private."

"Then I'll respect that privacy." But Adam was undeniably curious. Sable could see it in his face and experienced a small moment of triumph at disturbing his composure.

She went to her room and chose the dark blue dress to wear at the evening meal. Not that she was inclined for food and Charlotte would be sure to sulk over Adam's plain speaking.

Only Adam was in the room when she went downstairs. They sat down formally and still had not spoken when there was a light tap at the door. Marie Claire entered, her eyes seeming to gleam with a suggestion of complicity that Sable found disturbing. "Miss Charlotte will have a light supper in her room," she announced.

"Is there any particular reason?" Adam asked.

"A headache—"

"Very well, Mademoiselle Claire." His fingers tapped the table top.

"I was distressed," Marie went on with a portentous look at Sable, "to hear of your dreadful experience. I hope it was not too late."

"Too late?" Sable asked.

"When Jim threw the stone through the window. He seemed unsure."

"What the devil are you talking about?" Adam demanded, dangerously quiet.

"Why the visit to the waterfront, of course. When Miss Martin was alone—Jim was very concerned. Daisy too. They saw it all through the window. And the door barred!"

"Kindly leave us, Mademoiselle," Adam requested icily. "Tell my sister I'm sorry she's indisposed."

"I hope—I hope I've said nothing amiss?" Marie Claire murmured slyly.

Adam said nothing. The door closed very quietly after the French maid.

"What did she mean, Miss Martin?" His face was so pale that she was afraid. He exuded such an aura of repressed violence.

"It was all very unfortunate," she began.

"Do not prevaricate," he warned.

She told him the story then, dispassionately, as though it had not been the unspeakable occurrence it was, all the time watching his face change from cold distaste to a blazing fury.

"And was it?" he demanded when she had finished. "Was it—too late?"

"Whatever I say, you'll not believe me!" she cried. "And it is of consequence only to me."

"You know that's not true. You know how I feel—"

"But it is not how I feel. And I see now you'd be continually beset by doubts, imagining me having been had by some sailor I never saw before. Perhaps allowing him the privilege—"

"I said nothing of the sort!"

"Your eyes said it for you. Oh, I know you'll say it did not enter your mind, but it did. I watched the moment. And it was not pleasant."

"Then I retract. If you say it did not happen, then I do believe you."

"Would it matter so much?"

220

"You know that I want you. That I intend we marry—"
A coal crashed in the fire and sent a shower of sparks skimming up the chimney.

"And you know that I love Morgan."

"Morgan—" His mouth assumed bitter lines.

"Yes, Morgan."

"He's faithless—"

"I know."

"He's had many women."

"I know that too."

"He's almost certainly forgotten you already."

She was silent now, thinking that this was probably the truth. It hurt.

"I would not forget you so easily—" His voice had softened.

"You seem not so constant as you'd have me believe. You imagined yourself in love with Miss Caven, did you not?"

"Imagined was the operative word. She seemed something I quickly discovered she was not. I was unused to women and she set out deliberately to ensnare me. Then Morgan came home. I had not realized it could be so painful to find out that I meant nothing to the first woman I allowed to come near me. I became—hard. I admit it—"

"How do you know you will not feel the same about me? There are things about me you don't know. Will never know—"

"It seems suddenly not to matter. I've employed you for some time now and never caught you out in any smallness, any discrepancy in my image of you—"

"I can't pretend to love you."

"But you might—some time—"

"I'd not want you to build up false hopes. Anyway, your family won't think me much of a catch."

"I'd allow no one to influence me in my choice of a wife. And I've no need to marry money, thank God."

"I think I should look for another post. I begin to feel

like a bone thrown to dogs. You and Morgan. Now you and your sister. Then it will be you and your mother—"

"Don't tell me you couldn't vanquish the lot! That's the quality that draws me most towards you. Courage. Valor. Honesty. Added to which you are disturbingly attractive—"

Was she courageous, valiant, honest enough to tell him that she had slept with his detested brother? She knew she was not. It was the one thing that would turn him against her and she couldn't do it. Morgan would come back. He might still remember—expect to find her waiting. And like a fool she would.

"Don't place too much store on that image you have of me. You could be wrong."

"I'm prepared to wait. Please stay. Charlotte will not be difficult. We talked—"

"Well. I do like my work—"

"And you'll come to Windermere? You've no need to be afraid. I should tell Lady Chryston the truth."

"There was something I did not tell you."

"Oh?" The fire crashed again like a judgement and the sparks were reflected in his eyes.

"Lady Agatha was often in great pain and prevailed upon me to give her—laudanum, I have since discovered it to be. Annie Gormley noticed this and told me I could be arrested for murder. Both she and Clara held it as a threat against me. I hate to think of Lady Agatha being controlled by such people. Annie has an obsession about her mistress. I have always been afraid since that if I went to make my peace, as I should like to do, and Lady Chryston died, however innocent it turned out to be—"

"Dear God," Adam said. "They left nothing to chance, did they? I think I should have a word with Lady Agatha's doctor about the matter. Annie should be got rid of."

"I wondered if Knowehead would not be a good place for Belle. She seems an intelligent child and no one need know about her past. She'd not mind the occasional sight of you or me. Of course there would still have to be some older woman, but there must be many decent, kind widows with a mothering instinct."

"I'm sure you are right."

Sable wondered for a moment if Adam was being ironic. It was sometimes difficult to tell. "Then we could try to put matters right? If you knew how I have longed to see Lady Agatha—"

"You do not relinquish your affections lightly, do you?"

"No."

He sighed and she knew it was because of Morgan. And then supper was brought and there was no more chance to plan, to ask searching questions, or to demand impossible answers. They sat there, almost like man and wife, eating and drinking, exchanging occasional quite ordinary remarks, receiving only formal answers. But must it be so to be wed? Could it not be exciting? Challenging? It could, she decided almost immediately, and she'd not settle for less. And then she thought of the night of Adam's proposal and was aware of a shiver of desire or of unease. She found it impossible to decide which it had been.

Chapter 10

The days had passed quickly. A Quaker had come to say that he had written the letter for Jeremy Day and testified to the repugnance that had motivated the complaint. He had been horrified by the belated news of Day's beating and drowning. The captain of the *Hyades* could have had wind of Day's conversion and of the resulting letter to Adam Hunter. Saul West might have let out the facts in one of the waterfront taverns and been paid for the information. He'd been drunk insensible for a week before he disappeared and had been seen with men from the *Hyades.*

Sable was glad that the journey to Westmorland had not been delayed. She hated discord of the niggling kind. A good blast of released emotions suited her much better with her liking for challenge. She had achieved the kind of relationship with Adam that was easiest. Both had expressed their feelings and their hopes. He knew she wanted to wait until Morgan returned. There would be no more pressure brought to bear on her.

His parents and sister were not to come immediately to Windermere, as Jane wished to hold her birthday party at Hunter Hall first. But the proprieties were to be preserved, for Belle was to accompany Sable to the house near Knowehead. Bays, it was called. It was not large, Adam said, more like a farmhouse with dormer windows, beamed ceilings, a rambling garden with views of the lake and hills.

They had gone to the theatre just before the departure, Sable in her fur-edged cloak and the sack dress drawing admiring looks to the box where they sat, Adam very distinguished in black with a high, white stock and the candlelight on his pale hair. If she slid her eyes very quickly towards him, then away again, she could imagine he was his brother. She had the impulse to reach out and touch him, the resemblance seemed so great, but it was only the effect of light and shade, the unaccustomed smile that softened his mouth. Who would ever dream it could be so cruel? Or that those arms and legs could act so crudely at the height of passion. Like the sailor—

There was a wildly colorful back-cloth and an appreciative audience, and the evening had a magic of its own. But there was no sign of the chaunters as Sable emerged with James and the Hunters to walk to the carriage. The pale girl who sang "The Mistletoe Bough" so sweetly and plaintively had chosen some other playhouse for her night's work and there was no chance of questioning her until after the projected holiday.

The journey to Windermere was enlivened by the presence of Belle, who seemed to throw off some of her premature age and melancholy under the excitement of being transported from her sad surroundings. Sable had assured her that no one would be aware of her circumstances. She'd be accepted as a little Londoner, like any other

Cockney, and must not look back into the past at what could not be undone, but forward to a brighter future. It was noticeable how she bloomed during the dusty pilgrimage, her blue eyes wide at the differing sights. Just as she herself had been two years ago, Sable thought, with a memory of Morgan at the coach stop at York and of herself in her yellow gown.

She had felt a little indisposed during the few days in the coach. It seemed that her indisposition still dogged her. In the glass at the inn she had looked pale and heavy-eyed and, once, the flying countryside had blurred and shivered leaving her vaguely disquieted.

She was never quite sure when she had realized finally what ailed her. It was probably when the carriage that had awaited them in Kendal had stopped at the door of Bays and she had swayed and all but fallen into Adam's waiting arms. There was a rush of sickness to her throat, a memory of something that had not happened since she had washed the blood from her sheet the morning she woke to find Morgan gone back to his own room. She stood, face blanched, her head pounding, aware of Adam's concern. Oh God, she thought. One night only, but enough to give her a child. A child whose father could not possibly return until it was over a year old. Who could meet some other woman on his travels and give Sable no other thought. Who could come back with a wife. Morgan would be a popular guest in the homes of West Indian sugar planters. There were bound to be presentable daughters. Rich, beautiful daughters. And Morgan had never lived like a monk. He would not begin to do so now merely because he had bedded a farmer's lass on an isolated occasion when she had wanted to comfort him and he had needed comfort. She had desired that as much as he.

A plump, bustling woman appeared, greeting Adam with a rosy-faced pleasure, directing the disposal of boxes and trunks, clapping her hands to summon a pair of shy little maids in spotless gowns and aprons, their hair smooth under white caps, and instructing them to bring chocolate and refreshments.

"Oh, no, not chocolate," Sable said quickly. "Not for me." Her stomach revolted at the thought of its thick sweetness. "Tea, I think. If it is not too much trouble? But Belle would like chocolate, I know, wouldn't you, child."

Belle nodded, overawed now that she was inside the rambling house with its odd levels, the steps that rose to one door, or descended to another, both out of the same room, the impression of comfort that prevailed in the padded furniture and the cushions that sprawled everywhere, the warmth of the thick curtains that framed deepset windows with their views of the lake.

Nothing had changed. A hundred years would pass and the hills and water would look as they did now, stern and beautiful, Sable thought, divesting herself of her cloak and sitting in one of the chairs that faced the dusky panorama. Thank God it was evening. It would not seem strange to ask to be excused after supper. She would, presumably, be given a room of her own as Adam's guest. She must be alone.

Mrs. Crabbe drew the curtains and shut out the austerity of the view. An oil lamp with a pink shade cast a benign glow on all the comfort of rosy cushions and red curtains. Yet, for all the semblance of cheer, Sable was cold and could summon up no leap of anticipation. She could not think what she was to say to Adam for the duration of the stay, how she was to face Thomas and Sarah Hunter. And there were her parents awaiting a letter that they expected would fill them with renewed pride in their unusual daughter.

Sable drank her tea, glad that Belle was already well occupied with a lengthy and pleasurable survey of the room with its many small treasures of silver and porcelain, of pewter and copper, her thin little hands held out to the blaze of apple logs. She was also relieved that Adam and Mrs. Crabbe had much to say to one another.

And then Mrs. Crabbe was gone, taking Belle with her to see her room in the attics, and she was alone with Adam who bestrode the cheerful fireplace like a colossus, radiating good humor as he never had before. Sable shivered. The hand that held the delicate cup trembled for all her efforts at composure.

"Tired?" Adam inquired gently.

"Very." She could not bring herself to say more.

"We'll go to see Doctor Hughes tomorrow—"

"Doctor Hughes?" Sable half rose from her chair, startled. Could he have guessed? But he could not. His tone was perfectly controlled. Perfectly friendly.

"We were to speak to him about Lady Chryston. I cannot have you threatened."

"Of course. I—had forgotten."

"And then we'll see Lady Agatha."

Warmth and feeling returned to Sable.

"Oh, I should like that. There's no other woman I liked so much."

"Then that's what we will do tomorrow. If you are not overtired."

"I won't be. I feel better already."

"Good." His eyes studied her face as though he wished to imprint her features on his mind. Quite unconsciously, she made a disclaiming movement; then, realizing what she had done, pretended to remove some speck from her gown. She would have to tell him, but she had not the heart to ruin his first evening at Bays. Adam worked too hard to have his holiday spoiled before it was begun. They would get the matter of Lady Chryston settled first, and then she must disclose her secret. She could go out of his life without doing so, but that would be to leave him with useless regrets. Only the truth would free him from his obsession. But not yet—

Doctor Hughes agreed that Annie Gormley could be an undesirable companion for Lady Chryston, were she to stay permanently. "I have noticed her unwillingness for Lady Agatha to receive visitors. More than once I've heard her send one or other away. And as for the laudanum, perhaps it was indiscreet of Miss Martin to administer it quite so readily. The old lady does not complain, so I do not always receive the true picture. I will find something else to alleviate the pain between her prescribed doses. But to say what Annie did about Miss Martin being sent to the gallows betrays a derangement I find disturbing. However distressing it is, she must be replaced."

"We would have to find a woman quickly—"

"Oh, I think I could solve that problem without difficulty. I lost a patient only this week who leaves a widow in most impecunious circumstances, a good, cheerful woman. She'd soon have all the gloom and cobwebs removed. Not before time."

"I believe Annie has a sister. It's not as though she had nowhere to go," Adam said. "But I blame Lady Chryston's niece more. She encouraged Annie in her unkindness and we cannot so easily dislodge Clara. Still that's a problem we must meet in its own time. No use crossing bridges—"

"Then you'll go this afternoon to prepare the ground," Doctor Hughes said, rolling down his shirt sleeves and looking thoughtfully at Sable's pale face. "Much will depend on the old lady herself. She's used to Annie and the woman's got a hold after these past years."

"When she hears what I have to say she'll be amenable enough," Adam replied confidently. "I know Lady Chryston. There are things she'll not tolerate."

"You look too white, young miss," Doctor Hughes said unexpectedly. "In fact—" He stopped abruptly as though on the verge of indiscretion, then turned away to replace some instrument in his capacious bag. Sable's heart beat faster. It would be difficult to fool a man used to the sight of breeding women. But she'd been introduced as Miss Martin. He might imagine it was Adam who was to blame. There was irony.

They returned to the carriage, Sable shamed, Adam determined. There was a slight mist overhanging the lake and the leaves were orange. Orrest Head had retreated into a phantom silver that caught one solitary beam of light that struck it like an arrow. She stared out at the autumn countryside and felt once more the strong spell that was laid upon her when she first came here.

The carriage spun wildly as they took the bend that led to Knowehead. Sable was tumbled into Adam's lap and felt his arms close around her in a more than proprietorial way. She tried to struggle free but he would not allow her to do so. Then she became still and let him do what he would, thinking that he would desist at her lack of either enthusiasm or cooperation. But he chose to interpret this as a triumph and fondled and caressed her, surprising a response that she condemned instantly as verging on whoredom. She could not be in love with both brothers, and to find that her body reacted to Adam made her aware of an inconstancy she detested and feared.

"I knew you'd not fight against me for ever," Adam said thickly. "You must feel something." His fingers teased at her breast under the cloak, while the other hand fell to her thigh and stroked the inside of it. She must stop him and there seemed only one thing that would accomplish that.

"I am to have a child," she said coldly and distinctly. "Morgan's child. I cannot think why you have noticed nothing. Doctor Hughes knew immediately. He was quite abashed, poor man, because he almost blurted out the truth half an hour since. So I'd be obliged if you'd stop pawing me, since I feel sick enough already—"

He was so still that she knew she had gone too far. His hands stayed where they were, one on her thigh, the other round her breast, for what seemed an age. Then they fell away, made themselves into fists. He raised his head and stared at her, the rocking of the carriage unnoticed by either.

"Why, you bitch," he said softly. "You bitch. I thought you were different in spite of the occasional moment of doubt. Bitch!" And he lifted one hand and struck her across the side of the head so that her very brain shuddered. The dark shrubbery and the thin grey of the sky ran into one another, made a puddle of mouse-colored nothing, then came back into sickly focus. Her eyes felt heavy with a pain that seemed more than merely physical. There seemed nothing to say.

The carriage ground to a stop and still they had not spoken. Ben's grinning face appeared at the window, his eye widening almost comically as he recognized Sable. He still wore the red patch and it looked incongruously gay in contrast with the grey of the day and his prune-colored skin. "Miss Martin," he said in his deep voice. "Why, Miss Martin."

"I expect you are surprised, Ben," she said, trying to disregard the waves of pain that attacked her skull, thankful that it was not her face Adam had struck, for she could not have hidden the mark. "I hope Lady Chryston is well?"

"De poor lady am sick," he said, the smile disappearing. "She am sad since you gone. Bad-tempered."

"Will you tell your mistress that Mr. Hunter is here? It would be better if you mentioned only my name," Adam told him. "To begin with."

"Very well, Mister Adam. Dat Annie—she won't let Miss Martin into de house—"

"Go on, Ben," Adam said sharply. "Annie is not the mistress here."

The black face vanished. Sable bent to pick up her reticule and was afflicted with a sudden hurtful dizziness. She was aware of falling forwards, of Adam catching her ungently and pushing her back in the seat, then dumping the bag on her lap.

"I'm sorry," she said tonelessly. "I should not have told you like that."

"Why not before we left London?"

"I didn't know. It was during the journey—"

"Are you sure?"

"Certain. I can't think why it had not occurred to me before."

"I should not have hit you—"

"I brought it on myself," she said in a low voice. How bleak his eyes were. He was imagining her with Morgan. Picturing them in bed together on every conceivable occasion. She wished she had used another adjective. Conception was too simple—too permanent.

"It was not like that!" she cried.

"Then how was it?" he asked grimly, and started to smooth his gloves with obsessive care as though nothing else mattered but perfection.

The carriage door opened and Ben was there, beckoning conspiratorially. "Dat Annie am busy so she can't say stay out. Please to come, Mr. Adam."

Adam descended, then turned to help Sable alight. The pain in her head had steadied to a dull thumping and her back teeth ached. She could not meet his eyes knowing how he would look—all dead and dried up inside, as he had after Clara. He would remember Marie Claire blurting out the incident at Day's landlady's house, the table barring the door, and the seaman lying on top of her. He would remember she had sent the children away with Daisy, that she had mentioned seeing the man previously outside the chandler's. Perhaps Adam would imagine she'd encouraged him. But Ben was there and there was no opportunity to tell him of that one night before the duel when Morgan could have died. The only night she had been with a man. It had been a kind of obligation.

Quite suddenly she knew she could not face Lady Chryston just yet. "Go without me," she said, still looking anywhere but at Adam. "I'll walk round the garden and you can call me when you've said all you must. I know it's cowardly of me and I detest cowardice, but I couldn't do it."

"Yes. I quite understand." Cold. Dispassionate. Remote. And she had done that. She heard Adam's footsteps cross the hall and saw Ben go to attend to the horses. Turning, she took one of the overgrown paths round the side of the house. The massed shrubs enclosed her in dim, green tunnels. There was a soft dampness in the air that refreshed her skin, soothing away some of the awful finality of the scene in the carriage, though the dull grinding remained to remind her of the violence of Adam's repudiation.

The scent of chrysanthemums rose up like the smell of funerals. She had a sense of irredeemable loss. There would be no more Cardigan Square. No more stimulating political suppers, no lying on her bed with the door left open so that she might savor the masculine aftermath with plain speaking about other Members or of the peccadilloes of the royal family, past and present. Her steps grew slower, more difficult.

She emerged from the path and found herself at the back of the house with the abandoned fountain even more lichened, the lion more moss-grown, a few sad flowers waving on slimy stems. The windows looked dirty and secretive as though webs were overgrowing the whole place.

That had been her window, the one from which peered a thin, malevolent face. She could not restrain a gasp. Annie had not looked like this even on her worst days. She had deteriorated quite unmistakably during Sable's long absence. Perhaps that was why Clara had left so quickly. They stared at one another for what seemed eternity, then the white face vanished.

234

Sable was conscious of a quickening of alarm. Annie was not averse to eavesdropping and Adam had been in the house for some time now. Perhaps the woman was already aware that her days at Knowehead were numbered. Sable began to run back the way she had come, the damp greenery brushing her face, tangling in her dark hair. She entered the still-open front door in a rush, then saw Annie standing in the shadows. She stopped, irresolute, then called, "Adam? Adam!"

Annie moved. There was something in her hand, something steely, glinting dully in the obscurity that shrouded the foot of the staircase.

"Adam!" She knew that this time she screamed and that he would come. Annie knew it, too, and came out of the gloom, the scissors held open, the points like little teeth. "You meddling girl!" Annie said very softly. "We never wanted you to come back. We are quite happy, Lady Agatha and me. We don't even want Peg and Mercy now. And the heathen does the shopping or fetches Doctor Hughes when she is not well. He must stay because I cannot leave my mistress. I can never leave her. Never, do you hear?"

Annie was quite close now and the scissors looked as though they had recently been sharpened. Too late to run.

But the gap of the doorway was suddenly filled; someone plunged the hall into dimness. "You be behavin' yo'-self, Miss Annie," Ben said and pushed Sable aside. She fell against a small table, knocking a plant to the floor in a welter of soil and broken earthenware fragments. Annie gave a high-pitched shriek and threw herself at Ben, the scissors plunging into purple flesh.

Adam appeared with startling suddenness as Sable still scrabbled on the floor in the litter of earth and crushed stems. Ben cried out and thrust at Annie just as Adam came up behind her and grabbed at her arms. The sharp, pale face twisted with a terrible rage. Blood spurted from

Ben's arm, soaking into Annie's prim gown, dropping in huge spots onto the floor and onto Sable's outspread skirts.

"I have her now," Adam said tightly, his wrists clamped around Annie's forearms squeezing inexorably so that the fury turned to impotence and pain. "You must put a tourniquet on Ben's arm at once. Can you do that?"

Sable scrambled to her feet. "Yes. Yes, I've done so before, when Joe cut himself with the scythe." And she lifted up the hem of the gown to tear at the stained petticoats. Annie dropped the dripping scissors and went on saying terrible things as Adam maintained the pressure on her arms. Everywhere there was blood and Sable thought she must be sick, but Ben's need seemed greater. She placed the thick band of linen around his arm and began to tighten it carefully. The gouts lessened and she tied the strip in place, aware of Ben's grey, confused face, the swaying of his great body. His eye closed and he slid quite gradually to the floor, his back against the jamb of the door.

There was a sound that obtruded into the new, repressed silence. The rumble of wheels, the sound of boots springing to the weedy gravel, Doctor Hughes's voice calling, "Ben. Ben? Where are they?" Then his dark silhouette against the grey of the afternoon.

"Oh," he said. "I feared it. Some intuition. So I followed."

Annie had started to scream in a high, searing fashion. Sable thought she could not bear to listen, but there was no escape. "Hold her still," Doctor Hughes said. "Can I rob you of some more of your petticoats, Miss Martin? Yes, from the hem. The material is strongest there." And he proceeded to fasten Annie's wrists in spite of her struggling and the bared teeth that tried to bite him as he bent to his task. "We must lock her in her room for the present, then put poor Ben to bed. You go to Lady Agatha, my dear. Mr. Hunter and I will manage now."

"Are you sure?"

"Quite sure."

"Ben—"

"You must not try to lift him," Adam said sharply. "Do as Doctor Hughes says."

Sable obeyed, her head unpleasantly light and still aching from Adam's blow. The sound of Annie's shrieks receded. Then she was at the door of the room where the chandelier seemed to drag down the center of the ceiling and the parrot's cage hung, still rusted, still containing its burden of bright feathers, the sharp yellow eye. The sight of the hunched figure in the chair aroused in her a storm of emotion she could not contain.

"Oh, Lady Agatha. Dear lady—" She was running across the faded carpet, and then she was on her knees, her head taken to the black, musty lap in gnarled hands on which the ever-present rings winked and flashed in the meager firelight.

"Sable." The old voice was husky. "I'm—afraid."

The girl raised her head, wondering. "Afraid? You?" The thought was incongruous.

"Just lately—"

"Don't worry. Adam will take care of things. Doctor Hughes. And me. I'll stay for a time if you'll have me."

"Adam told me why you went. I never believed that story. But you had gone—"

"I had no choice."

"And I know something else. Ben brought me a letter. Annie would not have let me have it. But he came when she was not with me. It was to tell me he was safe and it was all your doing. I knew it was a good day when you arrived out of the thunderstorm. Lady Parksworth said you'd take nothing for yourself—"

"Let's not talk about it. I'll put some fuel on the fire and make you something to drink. Read to you. And there's a little girl I fetched from London you must meet. And a

237

good housekeeper the doctor found. Knowehead is going to be different."

"And Adam? Morgan? There's a story there, I imagine."

There was a long silence, then Sable said, "Tomorrow. I'll tell you tomorrow."

"You're sad—" The stiff old hands moved over her hair.

"It won't last. Any more than your sense of fear. We must cure one another."

"Tomorrow—or the next day," the old woman murmured.

Tomorrow. When she was ready—

It had been easy to remain at Knowehead without arousing comment at Bays. What could be more natural than Miss Martin taking care of her old friend in her hour of need? Everyone began to remember instances of Annie's increasing strangeness, after she was taken off to Bedlam. Sable had terrible pangs of guilt for her part in precipitating Annie's irrevocable breakdown. It was as if she and Adam had tried to play God and their efforts had backfired most dreadfully. But Doctor Hughes said that Annie's mind could have given way at any moment over any situation that involved Lady Chryston. Even Clara's return might have destroyed her reason.

Belle was sent over in the carriage to join Sable and three days later Jenny Wilde, the widow the doctor had recommended, arrived to throw up her practical hands in horror at the state of the house. Peg and Mercy were reinstated to cope once more with the heavy work and to help them turn over Ben while he was confined to bed with a fever after his wound had become septic. Now he was still weak, but on the mend.

Adam came to visit Lady Agatha who thrived under the new regime and was now teaching Sable the finesse of chess moves, since she had so ably mastered the mechanics of play. He said little to Sable except to inquire after her health, and then they listened to Lady Chryston's tales of her late husband and of the East India Company.

Near the end of her story she stopped and addressed Sable. "Sable, my dear, are you well? You have suddenly become very pale. Adam, take her out into the garden for some air before the child faints. The shock of Annie's attack must have been very great. And she's been untiring in trying to transform the house into order with Mistress Wilde. I will have a nap while you have your walk."

Sable found the wildness of the garden echoing the stress of her own feelings. She was uncertain of the future, ashamed for having goaded Adam into striking her. And she had still not told Lady Chryston of her condition. She did not want to fall in the old lady's estimation now that the bond between them was so much stronger. Lady Agatha was of the old school that prized honor.

"I'm sorry you have been cumbered with my presence," Sable said, breathing in the sharp air with relief.

"I have been wanting to speak to you alone. This gives me the opportunity."

"Oh? Have you heard from Morgan?"

"There will be no news of Morgan till he reaches the sugar islands."

"What was it you wanted to say."

"The child. It's a Hunter—"

"Oh," she said, unable to resist the dig. "So you've decided it's not a sailor's by-blow—"

"I never thought that," he answered grimly, his cold gaze on the lake. "But if the child is Morgan's, then it should have the advantages of being born into the family without stigma."

"Its father cannot be here to do his duty. Not that I'd want duty from Morgan," she retorted.

"Life could be very difficult for you—"

"I'm not afraid of a challenge."

"But would it be fair? I think of the baby. He's entitled to his birthright."

"But he cannot have it, can he," she said sharply, aware of the validity of his arguments. "He'll have to be a bastard Martin. We cannot expect Morgan to be blown back a second time by the winds of fate. And I could not blackmail him into giving up his freedom. I would only marry him if that was what he wanted above all. I think I have grown up in the last weeks so I understand now that Morgan prefers freedom—"

"You've not told Lady Agatha?"

"No. I thought I could but when I tried, I was ashamed."

"Then marry me now. We could wed in secret and there are plenty of seven-month children. Oh, I'll expect nothing of you! I just cannot see you encumbered and the target of jealous tongues without wanting to give you the protection of my name. And it would only be fair to the child. He should have his rightful place. He's entitled to his name—a proper birth certificate. A father of sorts. And afterwards, if you want to be free, I'd not stand in your way. Though I hope you'd stay. You'd be an asset as a young politician's wife and you said you liked the life—"

"You paint an attractive picture, Adam." Subconsciously, she used his name. "But it's I will have the best of it. Respectability, though there'll be calculations when the child appears. People are not fools. But they'll imagine we were fired by our proximity in Cardigan Square. We would have had every chance. I'd have all the advantages and you—nothing."

"It would not seem nothing to me. Think about it. I can get a licence quite quickly and we could be married with only a pair of witnesses. Lady Agatha and Doctor Hughes, for instance. Or, if you prefer it, complete strangers. A fait accompli—"

"I wish you had not asked me. I have not forgotten my unkindness to you—"

"And I, mine to you. But we must do it quickly if at all."

They continued to walk down towards the water and the light dazzled her eyes. She felt tired and confused and the temptation to allow someone to direct her future was suddenly overpowering. However hard she tried, Morgan's face would not appear in her mind. If it were not for her pregnancy, Morgan could have been no more than a dream. A life with him would have been a succession of episodes like the evening at the gaming club, a variety of excitements that had no meaning for her. She saw very clearly the whitened, effete faces with their velvet patches, the sickness in their eyes. She saw Morgan in bed with Clara, knowing he was taking her from Adam, yet not really caring for his brother's feelings. She thought of every aspect of Morgan that had disappointed or disquieted. But the only thing that had real meaning was the child she carried and the knowledge that his future rested with her. She could make him happy or miserable, rich or poor, wanted or unwanted. The Hunters would welcome a grandchild, love and care for him. It was, as Adam said, the child who mattered.

He stared at her, reading her expression, recognizing the moment the battle was won. "You'll do it."

"I'm so tired—" He thought the battle won, but she thought, irrationally, it was lost.

"We'll do it on Sunday."

"Oh, Adam! Are you sure?"

"It's for the child. Remember?"

"Yes." She knew then that she would do as Adam directed. It was not fair to him, but he seemed not to mind. And it need not be permanent. He had said so. They were free to do as they wished after the birth. The child was a Hunter and should be recognized as such.

241

He took her arm as they began the climb back to the house. She must become used to Adam at her side. It was not real. But it was never going to happen. Dreams. Mirages.

Her nights were torn with dark nightmares and misgivings. Adam must think a great deal of her for setting aside his anger so soon. She knew that he would be kind and fair to the child who would take his name and that he would accept him as a father. She would never know how Morgan would have received the news, but intuition told her he'd have felt shackled, unwilling to face the responsibility. Already he would be diverted by the sea, the ports of call, the society invitations that were bound to ensue during the long voyage. He had had her now, as he had intended all along. The childhood promise was fulfilled and he was done with it. She knew it and deep inside her the hurt remained. If he had really loved her, he'd not have left her behind. There had been nothing to stop her going with him. He could have snatched her away from Adam's restraining hand—

Her face grew ravaged and Lady Chryston was concerned. "There's something on your mind, child. What is it?"

"A decision I have to make. At least, I have taken it, but—"

"You don't know if you do the right thing. Is that it?"

"No."

"It has to do with Adam, of course. I'm not blind, you know, not yet. He loves you, child, if that's what worries you. I've seen him look at you. And he did rescue you from—well, neither of us will ever know the answer to that. From what he has told me, you'd make him the proper wife. I'm certain any prejudices Mrs. Hunter may have will quickly disappear when she meets you."

"He seems to love me too intensely."

"My dear child! Is that the only fault you can find? A fine, handsome, well-endowed man loves you intensely and you can only complain? You disappoint me, Sable. There must be a million wives who wish their husbands loved them more."

"But I don't deserve it."

"Then there's something else?"

"Nothing I can speak about."

"There's no one I should like so well for you to marry."

"Then you would not mind if it were to be here? Tomorrow?"

"So that's why Adam's been flapping about between here and Kendal like a distracted hen. I knew there was something! Of course, it must be here. Morgan may have the charm—I never knew anyone more taking—but Adam has the integrity in that family. You're fortunate, Sable, you've the right brother. Morgan's a fly-by-night but he does draw one to him with miraculous ease. A secret wedding at Knowehead! Chryston and I wed secretly, oh, not because he was ashamed of me for all that I had no looks to speak of, but neither of us could bear the usual circus. We were both private people."

"Adam is. A private person."

"You'll be good for him. Teach him to laugh. I must get Jenny to make a cake. I won't say what it's for, so you needn't worry. Now go and wash your hair and do all the things brides do and if you need your nerves calmed, we'll play chess later after supper. And you'll have a posset to make you sleep, my pretty. I have to thank you for that little Belle you brought with you. She's sharp as a needle and I'll have her reading in no time."

Adam came to find out whether Sable had broached the subject of the wedding and to receive the old lady's approval. He looked relieved that the matter seemed settled and held out his hand to clasp Sable's, but she had a sudden image of Parksworth's hand with the puckered scar and flinched away from his touch. It was quite stupid, she thought, but Belle had come into the room and she thought often of Belle being forced by someone she did not know, never mind love. Relations with a man needed some sort of affection, but liking seemed not enough for such intimacy. Nor gratitude.

In the quiet of her room Sable prepared the mixture of chestnuts and other good things in which to wash her hair, then sat in the firelight, drying it with one of the worn blue towels. She had the hip bath brought out and sat in it for a long time as though requiring to wash away some indefinable uncleanliness. She had thought of marriage, as all girls do, but she had imagined it would be at Daggleby with all the villagers and farmers crowding the seats and her family there. But if she waited for that, there would be the small betraying bulge to draw the attention of the lynx-eyed matrons if not the others, and she minded Adam being the target of the disapproval that should be hers.

Then she supped with Lady Agatha and they played a game with the onyx chessmen which, not unnaturally, Lady Chryston won. Sable was glad of the posset. Her inability to sleep was more accentuated of late.

She woke late, but thankfully refreshed. The sack dress hung upon its hook in readiness. Of all the clothes she would ever have, this gown was the one she would love most. Once she had risen, a great restlessness possessed her, a sense of being tossed on strange and turbulent seas with no end or beginning.

Unable to eat, she almost ran down to the lake, for in the water and the harsh crags there seemed permanence. A long way round the curve of the bank was the stretch where she and Lady Chryston had met the huntsmen and the mounted ladies the first day she ever spoke to Adam. The first man had been Adam. And then the hot tears

244

pricked at the backs of her eyes, for in her case the first man had been Morgan and the memories flooded back where of late they had refused to come at her insistent clamoring. They were all recollections of gaiety, of color, of young irrepressible emotions, of excitement. She would never be able to go through with the ceremony because there was no rightness about it.

Regardless of what might come next, she began to walk away from the house, her eyes fixed on the lowering sky, the ashy slopes of the hills. A sharp little wind ate through the folds of the cloak and the red leaves began to whirl and twist, scuttering across the path, floating on the leaden surface of Windermere. Her body felt heavy though it looked little different when she had seen it naked in the pier glass after her bath. Pregnant women were renowned for broodiness, she told herself. This ache could not last for ever.

She did not notice the carriage at first. Then the moving darkness intruded upon her line of vision and she knew as surely as though she had seen through the solid frame of the vehicle that it was Adam with Doctor Hughes and the minister.

He leaned from the window as he had the day she sat on the rock with the red Gypsy bundle, but this time he smiled, and somehow the smile touched and comforted her. She would not need to pretend with Adam.

He descended, handing her into the carriage as though she were something of value. He'd every right to despise her but, that first violent reaction over, he ignored the shabbiness that now seemed to cloak her relations with Morgan. No matter how she tried, the magic was gone. A resigned calm encompassed her. Then she wondered if he knew she had been running away. A sideways look showed her the ironic twist of his mouth that said that he understood.

Once back at the house, she went to change into the silk

sack dress and to brush her hair into some sort of order. She was outside of herself, looking down at a white-faced stranger, cloudy-haired, neat-figured in kingfisher blue that changed color each time she moved or twisted a fold. There was no Sable Martin. No past. No future.

Belle, chosen to attend her, her blue eyes large with a bewildered pleasure that made Sable catch her in her arms, came to fetch her, carrying a little posy of white chrysanthemums for the bride and orange-brown ones for herself.

"You look lovely, Miss Sable. But too white. Ain't you got no color? Mister Adam will think you don't want to get wed. And he's the best man I know. There ain't many."

"It's a sobering thing, marriage. Rub my cheeks for me, Belle."

"There you are, miss. Now you look a treat."

They went to the big shadowy room where the birdcage was, cleaned for the occasion; the chandelier sparkling, the firelight and candlelight catching winks from anything that shone. Adam looked very tall, very reserved, immaculate in dark suit and white stock. Lady Agatha, resplendent in her best black and more diamonds than ever, her Punch-like profile grinning crocodile fashion, was the only animated figure in the room. Dr. Hughes fidgeted and cast a few looks at Sable's waistline but she knew there was nothing yet to see.

She had a moment of panic when the ring was slipped onto her finger, and her responses had been slow, as though she were unwilling to speak them. She had watched herself become somebody else. Isabel Hunter. There was her name on the paper beside Adam's. Sable Hunter. The unreality returned, stifling the gaiety that rang ever so slightly false, the blushing entry of Jenny Wilde with the cake and the wedding refreshments, the sight of Belle gathering the posy to her breast, her gaze on the new gown she wore, blue as her eyes. Doctor Hughes tossing back brandy, Lady Agatha beginning to nod. A signal from the doctor. Then alone with Adam.

"What—next?" she asked, conscious at last of the weight of the ring, of the remnants of the feast.

"What would you like to come next?" he asked, eyes shadowed.

"Somewhere no one knows us."

"The carriage is here. We can go where we wish."

"Anywhere away from here."

"Very well. Gather a few necessities. I'll be waiting."

She went first to Ben with a piece of the cake and a glass of wine. Then she tossed brushes, nightgown, and day gowns into a heap and seized her cloak, said her good-byes to Lady Chryston now installed in bed, kissed Belle, and climbed back into the coach assisted by Adam now in his redingote. Then the conveyance was lumbering down the uneven drive past the misty confusion of shrub, flower, and weed, the lake glimmering below under the first of the stars.

She was never quite sure where they stopped. She only knew that she was weary, that the wooden stairs creaked as the maid preceded them with candle and warming pan, that there was a strong smell of chops cooked not long ago.

The room was not large, but the bed was. Draped in red, it seemed to fill all but the smallest area. The shadows dipped, then climbed the wall.

"Let me unfasten your gown," he suggested, then his fingers were at the hooks, not so firm as usual, the warmth of their tips branding the smooth skin below. The gown opened, slid downwards, and made a dark blue pool around her feet. He performed the same service with her stays and petticoats, then turned away to stare out of the window at the Lakeland darkness. Shivering, she put on her nightgown and got between the sheets. The red roof of the bed gloomed in a penumbra of shade. She waited, but Adam never came. At some moment just before she

247

fell asleep, she heard the sound of the stopper being taken from a decanter. She tried to rouse herself to say something, but the drapes of the bed seemed to close in around her shutting her away in oblivion.

It was dawn when she woke. The room startled her with its strangeness. The curtains remained undrawn and there was a line of pinkish violet along the horizon against which unfamiliar masses of black hillsides and tattered trees obtruded.

The red ceiling lowered angrily as though reproaching her. She lifted her hand to push back her tumbled hair and saw the ring on it, clean and shining. Very new. She remembered Adam and sat up hurriedly. He was lying back in the big wing chair, his head at an awkward angle, the redingote pulled up to his chin.

She was conscious of a flood of shame and self-recrimination. Her own selfishness was so apparent that she recoiled from the knowledge of it. Adam had done everything for her. Given her child a name, shielded her from unkindness and malice, sacrificed his future, stayed from the bed to which he was entitled because he had promised her he'd expect nothing. And like the mean, egotistical bitch she was, she had taken everything he offered.

The weakness, the broodiness seemed lifted from her and she was herself again. Strong. Full of hope. Filled also with a longing to repay Adam in some small measure.

She climbed out of the bed and went to the chair, barefooted, her hair adrift, the nightgown crumpled from her disturbed sleep, the tossings and turnings, the unquiet thoughts.

"Adam?" She touched his arm and was startled by his reaction. He was awake almost instantly and sitting upright, his eyes staring into hers almost without recognition. "Adam. You must be frozen sitting here and it's still early. Come to bed."

"I did not want to disturb you—"

"Well, as you can see, I'm wide awake. You can't disturb me now. And the maid will think it very odd for a husband to occupy a chair."

"Not really, my love." He grinned unwillingly. "An inn is a place where one sees every facet of life. Love. Hate. Indifference—"

"Well, I'm not indifferent. I've behaved stupidly of late, thought only of myself. But I've exorcised myself of dreams. I promise you, I have."

"Perhaps you have. For today. You've a kind heart, Sable. Why do you think I love you?"

"I saw their futility. And it seemed so unfair— Come, Adam. You can't truthfully say you are warm or comfortable."

"No," he admitted.

"Well, I'll go back and warm the sheets. And that will give you time to undress."

"Then you must take it upon yourself what happens once I join you," he warned, only half joking.

"I woke up and realized I was your wife. It was as though I woke from more than one dream. I thought you deserved more than a stiff neck and no comfort."

"Oh, God, Sable. Don't play games, I beg you." He was pale now, tugging at his stock and the buttons on his coat, flinging the garments onto the chairback.

She said nothing, only sat up against the thick, downy pillows and watched him undress. He was slimmer than Morgan. The thought slid into her mind unasked, unwanted. There was a grace about him, an indefinable elegance. He pulled back the covers when he was naked and turned towards her. "You were running away—"

"That was yesterday."

"And today?"

"It seemed there was something cruel about all take and no give— But I have not what I should have given."

"I won't say there is not a fleeting regret." The hands that lifted the folds of the nightgown were suddenly stilled.

"Don't think of it. I could have kept it from you. It's not the first time you asked me to marry you. At least there has been honesty between us."

There was a long pause, then the gown was pulled over her head and thrown to the floor. A pinkish light filled the room, though the bed was still shrouded in greyness. His long, slanting eyes glittered. "I knew you'd look so." The hands were on her body, pressing her back onto the mattress. His mouth abused hers as though he punished her for the long wait. His knee separated her thighs as if he were as experienced as Morgan. There was no pain this time. Only an urgency that consumed her and a glorious outpouring of expectation that made her shiver with an unsought delight, made her clasp him to her as though he were, indeed, a lover.

And then he had withdrawn from her, the anticipation dashed, her nerves screaming for fulfillment.

"I'm sorry," he said drily. "But Morgan has put up his own barrier. It seems that I cannot—not while it is there."

"Oh, Adam." She felt she could burst with the remnants of the feelings he had aroused still tingling within her body. But the paleness of his face, the unmistakable disinclination to resume his lovemaking was too apparent to dismiss as inexperience or inability. She should have left well alone—waited till he made the first move. She had forced this humiliating situation upon him.

"I do apologize—" His tone was formal as though she were a stranger.

"There's no need." She must not allow him to see her disappointment. "I believe it is quite common for—failures in early marriage. Next time, perhaps, it will be different. Try to rest so that you'll be ready for breakfast."

They lay some distance apart, both looking at the red roof of the bed, both bodies taut. It was some time afterwards that Adam's eyes closed and his frame relaxed. She leaned on one elbow and stared down at his sleeping face, the crescents of fair hair that fringed his eyelids, the relaxation of his mouth. Her own body was alive and quickened to the memory of what he had done—and left undone. Her arms folded around her body as though to contain this new, unlooked-for feeling. There would be problems enough in store, but she could not regret them. Capturing Adam would be far more difficult than the appropriation of Morgan, but there could be more of a prize at the end of the battle.

She sighed and watched the pink fade from the sky to leave a new day.

Chapter 11

She woke up when the maid pushed open the door with the breakfast tray. Sable, perfectly possessed as though she had been married for years and was used to this situation, sat up and told the girl to leave the tray on the bedside table.

Adam shrugged himself up against the bed tester, avoiding her eyes. Then he reached across to take his coat from the wing chair and she had a glimpse of his back, smooth and well muscled, the long indentation of his spine shadowed. He took two small packages from a deep pocket and tossed them onto the red-and-white counterpane.

"The smallest is from Lady Chryston," he said unemotionally, "and the other is from me."

"Why didn't she give it to me herself?" Sable asked, picking up the little box.

"I think she may have thought you'd refuse it. But you must not disappoint her, Sable. She thinks of you as a daughter she never had, I think. And it's a thank-you for what you did for Ben."

"Oh. You know about that."

"Yes. It was Ben you meant when we talked of slaving and a need for its abolition."

"You see why I could not say more at the time—"

"Of course. I—I think you very exceptional," he said in a low voice.

Except that you cannot make love to me, she thought, remembering this morning, then saw that he remembered too. His mouth compressed. She looked away, quickly. Opening the box she saw what must be the most beautiful of Lady Agatha's many rings. "Oh! She mustn't. It must be worth a fortune—"

"Try it on. She cannot wear it herself. Her knuckles are permanently swollen."

Sable put it on beside the wide wedding band. The stones winked back at her almost as though Lady Chryston were there, smiling and challenging her to refuse it.

Adam's box still lay there on her lap, longer and broader than the other. She hoped he had not given her anything too valuable. There was a locket inside it, chased gold on a thin chain. A large *H* was inscribed in the centre of the oval, surrounded by small twining stems and leaves. *H* for Hunter so that she would always be reminded she was his wife.

"It's lovely." She made to close the box again, but Adam said, "I don't want you to keep it in the case. I should prefer you to wear it. If you turn away, I'll fasten the catch."

She did as he told her, aware that his fingers trembled slightly, conscious too of his warm nakedness against her back. He pulled the chain taut, clicked shut the fastener. For a moment his hands stayed on her shoulders, then they fell away.

"Thank you, Adam." She faced him again with apparent pleasure, but with an incipient misery gnawing at her, threatening to become greater as the day wore on. "Shall we have breakfast? It grows cold."

The tray resting on his knees, they ate little, but drank copiously of the thin China tea, then rose to dress. As he had undone last night, he fastened her now into her underwear and gown as a new husband would, but she thought of what might have been and was not and thought she must tempt him once more to see what might be the outcome. But he could not welcome a second faux pas and it would be wrong of her to invite the catastrophe. It seemed that the picture of Morgan having been where he desired to be was something Adam found too repugnant. He'd feel differently later on, she was sure. Then the certainty left her and she was sad, her hand reaching for the locket where it rested on her breast as though this contact, small though it was, was all she could have of him for the present. Perhaps for ever—

He noticed the action, as he seemed to see everything she did, but made no attempt to come near her, to ask anything of her, however unimportant.

"I cannot help but think of Charlotte," she said, "of her reception of this news—"

"Charlotte? I would not find it my business to prevent her marrying where she will. Why should she condemn my choice?"

"I think she might."

"It's of no consequence," he said. "You are my wife. It's done. Now you are the mistress of my house. Charlotte will have to accept that."

"She—she won't stay."

"That's her business then. I'm grateful she assisted me and I shall tell her so. But I have James and I have you—"

Morgan's words seemed suddenly to resound in the quiet bedchamber. The future must become a series of compromises if it was to be worth living. And she was now a politician's wife and helpmeet. At least that was an area of

255

his life she could invade at will, in which she could shine. She had done well enough already. Even Charlotte had admitted that and she had been hard to please of late.

She thought unexpectedly of Hunter Hall. Now she belonged there. The wide windows, the statuary, the pond, Samson and Brutus—they were hers as much as any Hunter's. There was one thing she would do first of all when they went to the Hall as they must sooner or later. She could not repress a smile.

"What has amused you?" Adam asked, fastening his many coat buttons.

"When we go to Hunter Hall, will you promise me something?"

"If it's in my power."

"I should like to invite my mother to tea and have Mistress Perkins attend her personally."

"Some old grudge?" Adam asked, unbending.

"Yes." Sable laughed then, enjoying the future encounter. "It would give my mother so much pleasure. And me—"

"I'd like to hear of this past clash," Adam said, seemingly diverted. "I know little enough of your youth. And you need not be discreet. I've long detested Mistress Perkins."

"Mother went to her once, pleading my cause, and she called me 'thick as a post' and 'putting on airs.'" Sable giggled and their eyes met and sparked in mutual amusement. "I cannot wait to see her face!"

"Pray that I am there at the moment of undoing," Adam agreed, grinning.

Sable sobered. "But there's something troubles me. Not your father, or Jane. But your mother may resent me. Charlotte must have written. And she could have had some great expectations for you. To find us wed so secretly—"

"As I said before, it's no one's business but ours. Anyone

who disapproves can stay away from Cardigan Square as far as I'm concerned. And I'll visit no house where you are unwelcome. Mother must make her choice, but if it's to make you unhappy, then she must do without my company."

"I won't let you cast off your own mother. I must make her approve of me. Will you tell her?"

"Tell her?" Adam had buttoned his coat and raised inquiring eyes.

"About the baby? That it's Morgan's?"

He frowned, his whole face darkening. "I'll tell no one. And neither will you. Do you think I want it broadcast?"

"No—"

"No one must know. The whole point of our marriage was to make the child ours, was it not? Of what use, then, to tell my family otherwise. If they choose to think I anticipated the ceremony, that's a rod I'll gladly bear. But as we'll be in London when the child's born, no one need know exactly the details of its haste. Daggleby and London are a long way apart. So long as it's born safely, the news of its arrival need not be sent immediately. It's of no concern to anyone else, is it?"

"No." If his cold, concise instructions fettered her, then she'd not show it. Of course Adam would not want it known that he was cuckolded before the marriage lines were written. She must have been mad to expect it. But there were people who might guess. Charlotte, Lady Chryston, Marie Claire, Morgan—

Her face flooded with color. Morgan could be a problem. He'd not really care who knew it if would hurt Adam. "You are perfectly right, Adam. We'll keep the date to ourselves. For your sake."

"And now?"

"We must go back to Bays. I'm sure you've already caused sufficient conjecture in that quarter."

"Very well." He pulled on his gloves with great exactitude, held her cloak so that she could put her arms inside it. Then he opened the door and called for service. Sable looked back from the doorway at the rumpled bed. She was a wife if one could call it that. But she knew now with a great certainty that it was not the kind of wife she wanted to remain. Adam had roused something in her that had surprised and delighted her. To a point. It was what lay beyond that point that tormented her, for she could not bear to think that it might never be reached. Morgan had pleasured her, it was true, but it had not been the same. She might have felt as much with any personable man.

She took her gaze from the red hangings of the bed and followed Adam downstairs.

Bays was in a ferment when they got back. Mrs. Crabbe rushed out the minute the carriage stopped outside the house to say that Mr. and Mrs. Hunter and Miss Jane had arrived and were at supper after having had a rest. "They look forward to meeting Miss Martin," she said with a curious look at Sable's possessions on the coach seat, then, her eyes riveted to the rings on the girl's hand, she gave a sudden gasp.

"Why, Mr. Adam! And no one with any idea—"

"I'll go and break the news," he said. "You take my wife to my room—our room—so that she can prepare herself for what must be an ordeal. But I'm perfectly sure, my dear, that you are well able to cope. I have not forgotten a certain occasion at Cardigan Square when you were the toast of the evening. Applauded by Pitt—"

"I'm nervous, I admit."

"Well, I'll prepare the way. Go with Mrs. Crabbe. And do not become flustered. They can find no real fault." His voice was deceptively gentle.

"No visible fault, perhaps," she said, then regretted the

258

remark when she saw his brief anger. "All right, Adam. How long shall I give you?"

"Come when you are ready."

"Half an hour?"

"As you wish." He took off the long redingote in which he looked so distinguished and went off in the direction of the dining room. Mrs. Crabbe, oozing suppressed excitement, led the way to Adam's room, a large oak-beamed chamber containing a bed with yellow hangings that was not nearly so intimidating as the one she had occupied last night, some large, dark presses, and a polished oak floor upon which a few scattered rugs rested. A masculine room without so much as a flower vase.

"I'll send your things up and a girl to help. There's plenty of room in them presses, Miss—Mrs. Adam, begging your pardon, but it was that sudden. Mr. Adam don't have many things around him, not like young Morgan or Miss Jane. A couple of parrots, them two—all bright feathers."

"I don't have much either, so his room will change little," Sable said. "But some flowers, I think, and a fire."

"Didn't know what to do when he didn't come back last night," Mrs. Crabbe said, obviously longing to be enlightened.

"I'd better not keep them waiting too long," Sable said firmly.

"Of course not, Mrs. Adam."

Mrs. Crabbe's feet were heavy on the stair, then came a procession of lighter steps, girls bearing clothes and brushes, a pot of chrysanthemums. The fire was blown up with bellows into a comfort of red and gold, the brown-and-black dress laid out. Sable washed, brushed her hair, changed her gown. There was silence as everyone went. The rings glittered on her hand. She took out her wedding lines. They had not vanished like fairy gold. Her name was

259

still there in spidery writing. Sable Hunter. The full enormity of the occasion rushed over her like a wave, then receded to leave a false calm.

She went downstairs with her back straight and bit her lips to give them a pretence of color. The door was part open and as she approached, she heard Mrs. Hunter say, "But surely we could have met her? Such unseemly haste."

"I was not disposed to wait," Adam said in chilly tones. "You forget that I'm a grown man, Mother, with my own life to lead. I need not ask for directions from anyone. And the distances between us preclude speedy communications. You'll not look far for the reason for my haste when you see her. One can lose what one wants by hanging back and allowing others to take the prize. It did happen once before, not that I regret it now." But there was an all-too-evident bitterness in the quiet words that struck home.

"I cannot say I am happy—"

"Sarah, as Adam points out, the thing's done," Thomas Hunter put in. "And I have a respect for Adam's taste. At least he picked his own wife, a privilege not afforded to many."

Mrs. Hunter was silent. Theirs had been an arranged marriage, Sable thought uncomfortably, and Thomas's reminder could do her little good in that quarter.

She went into the room. She had heard enough to know how the land lay. Jane was the first person she saw, very fashionable in blue and cascades of ringlets, a small beauty patch on one cheek, and a glitter of stones around a slim neck. The spoiled young eyes contemplated her with composure. Next to her was Thomas, thickset and grizzled, his brown coat straining over an incipient paunch, his stock untidy. But there was a respect in his eyes that showed his admiration for Sable's ability to capture his son. It was Thomas, she had been told, who came from ordinary stock, but whose aptitude for work and business had enlarged and improved the firm his father had begun earlier

260

in the century, increasing the number of ships in the line and the opportunities for trade with almost every part of the known world.

Sarah Hunter stared at her almost unseeingly with cool grey eyes that reminded her of Adam's. There was a distinct resemblance between mother and son. Jane and Morgan seemed a mixture of both parents, were more colorful, lustier, more extroverted.

Then Adam was at Sable's side and his arm was around her. "This is Sable," he said and now there was life in him, a kind of perverse satisfaction. "I told you she was beautiful, did I not? And you see I was right. She's clever. But there's more to her than that. She cares. She feels for situations and people. She'll care for you if you let her. And that will be your privilege, I can assure you. Jane, will you not greet her? Father? Mother?"

Jane rushed round the table and gave Sable a perfunctory hug, then stepped aside to allow Thomas to come near. His look assessed her kindly, with an acceptance she found encouraging. He took her hand and shook it with rough enthusiasm. "He could have done worse. If you saw some of those painted little madams we've had sniffing around at the Hall—"

"Of course," Sarah said very clearly, "you already know the Hall quite well."

"Very," Sable said as clearly, feeling Adam's hand tighten on her hip. "I hope there will always be cordiality between us, Mrs. Hunter, surprising as you may find Adam's choice of a wife. And all of you will be welcome at Cardigan Square."

Sarah sat down again without touching Sable in any way. "You had better join us at table. We've almost finished—"

"She wished to make a good impression after a fair journey," Adam told his mother. "And what does it matter if she's a little late this once. One does not get wed every day. Mrs. Crabbe, will you send some more of that special wine?

And if you will bring the staff, I should like you to toast my bride. Now, Sable, this pie has not spoiled and you must be hungry. There you are, my dear. Jane, pass the chutney. Father, you have the ham in front of you. Please cut some of it. Suddenly, I'm famished."

It could almost have been a family supper at her father's farm, Sable thought, then knew it was very different. Her mother would never have looked at her, as Sarah Hunter did now, without the slightest trace of feeling. Anger gave her courage.

"How were my parents when you saw them last?" she asked her new mother-in-law.

"I believe Mrs. Martin appeared quite well at church. She had her daughter-in-law with her, the farm girl from—oh, I forget where—"

"Tenby Farm," Sable supplied without a tremor. "In the next valley—"

"They both appear to be breeding—"

"Who? My mother and Pansy?" Sable affected surprise. "I thought Mother past it."

"I meant your other brother's wife." Mrs. Hunter ignored her husband's smothered snigger.

So Charlotte's letters had encouraged an interest in their lowly neighbors, Sable thought, half-amused.

"I will be able to see them at last when we visit the Hall," Sable said calmly, spearing a slice of ham. "I've missed them this long while. I think I will ask them all to tea."

Mrs. Hunter stopped in mid bite.

"An excellent idea," Adam agreed before she could speak. "At Christmas, perhaps. That's the family time. Ah, Mistress Crabbe. Allow me to give you each a glass of wine. And the girls. Jane, Father, Mother? A toast to Sable." They all drank, only Sarah's lips barely touching the glass. She should not have tormented her with the threat of the entire Martin clan at one sitting, Sable thought. It would be more fun to visit them at the farm except that Mother must have her revenge over Mistress Perkins, whatever happened.

Everyone talked, rather obviously after the servants left, of Hunter matters while Sable ate her supper, conscious of covert looks from Jane and her mother-in-law. Sarah noticed the beautiful ring and could not help remarking on it.

"The ring. It is exceptionally fine."

"It was a gift from my friend Lady Chryston."

"I see. I had heard you had been there. There was trouble with a servant—"

"She—was ill." Sable, quite suddenly, lost her hunger. She saw Annie deranged and shrieking, saw all those gouts of blood. She clenched her hands and tried to combat the ensuing dizziness.

Adam's arm came around her waist. "Some more wine, my sweet. It has not all been honey and lotus-eating of late. We've had worries enough in London, too. Morgan—" Belatedly conscious of his indiscretion, he raised his eyes to see the expectancy in those of his parents and sister. Morgan's reappearance and second departure were to have been kept from his mother.

"What of Morgan?" Mrs. Hunter asked in a tone that brooked no refusal.

"I suppose I must tell you. We did not wish to worry you." And Adam proceeded to tell the bare outlines of the tale of Morgan's fever and of the duel.

"You mean you allowed him—?" Mrs. Hunter began ominously.

"It was my fault," Sable broke in. "Adam has met most of the repercussions himself. Bills for nursing Parksworth. A severe reprimand from Lord North. But you cannot blame Adam for what happened. If I had not struck Miss Caven, who asked for all she got, then the situation would not have arisen. You must censure me, Mrs. Hunter, though, in my defense, I never foresaw such an outcome—"

"Sarah, you know what a baggage Clara turned out to be," Thomas said loudly, remarking his wife's angry pallor. "As far as I can see, both Adam and Sable behaved creditably. Imagine your own feelings had you been accused of theft before a roomful of people—"

"The situation certainly would never have arisen."

"There are episodes in everyone's life that are downright distasteful. Bad—" Husband and wife looked at one another over the remnants of the meal, Thomas's eyes full of unmistakable meaning. Sarah's gaze fell after a time and she said little more except to assure herself that Morgan had recovered after the fever. "I should like to have seen him," she said in a low voice that held the traces of recrimination.

"No use crying over spilt milk," Thomas told her. "Morgan goes his own way. He does it pleasantly, I'll give him his due, but none of us would stop him and well you know it, once his mind is made up. He'd get around the devil if there was need—"

"I don't need a homily over my son's character," Sarah answered.

"*Our* son's character, my dear. It takes two to get a child. Now I think we'd best leave the subject of Morgan, for on that we never agree. You seem to have got yourself a spirited lass, Adam."

"Pitt admired her greatly and he is not normally renowned for his kindness to the opposite sex. In fact, she outshone the whole table at the last political affair and not only visually!"

"You've changed, Adam," Jane told him.

"Have I?"

"You need a wife who can hold her own with the likes of Pitt and Fox," Thomas observed.

"I should have thought breeding and wealth as much an asset," Sarah murmured.

There was a silence, then Adam said quite pleasantly, "I think we should have a tour, Sable and I. She's still trying to become used to me, never mind an entire dynasty. Now that I've introduced you, you won't mind if I carry her off again? I've a notion to have her to myself for a spell. So we'll be off tomorrow."

"How long—?" Sarah began.

"Till the fancy takes us to come back. You'll be here for a time, I expect?"

"A few weeks," Thomas told him, "now we're uprooted."

"Then that's settled. Come, Sable. We promised ourselves an early night."

"So we did. Good night," Sable said, perfectly composed, a smile for Thomas.

But once outside the room, she faltered as they climbed the creaking stairs to Adam's bedchamber. "She hates me—"

"Mother does not unbend easily. But I was a fool to let it out about Morgan—"

"At least they know. I think your father likes me."

"Don't let them intimidate you, any of them."

"I just wish it were different."

The fire still burned in the big, low-ceilinged room. The thought of bed was attractive.

"Flowers," Adam said, surprised. "I never had those before."

"It was a notion I had—"

"Then they must stay. Go to bed, Sable. I'll sit by the fire for a time. There's something I must work out—"

"Don't—don't do what you did last night. Sit in the chair—"

"No."

"Help me with my gown?"

265

He did as she asked but he did not linger over the task, as he had done last time, neither did he watch her climb into the bed. He drew the chair close to the fire and leaned back in it comfortably, his boots stretched to the mantel, feet crossed.

She lay for a time, watching the firelight and shadow, growing pleasantly drowsy. Then she awoke with a start to find herself in an unfamiliar darkness, a hand on her body stroking her back, the curve of her hip. It hurt her strangely to feel that he required to caress her so secretly, to wait until she slept. But she gave no sign that she knew. Adam loved her in his own fashion and she must wait until he loved her in her way.

"Where are we going?" Sable asked as they drove away from Bays next morning.

"It's a secret," Adam told her.

"Have I been there before?"

"Not really."

"Do you think your mother will mind us going so suddenly?"

"Married couples make up their own minds. She was—not kind and I meant what I said."

"Tell me where we are bound for?" The sky was a vivid blue, patched with white clouds and the leaves shimmered orange and gold. The spaces between the trees dimmed to grey and purple. And the hills—she could not describe them. She only knew she was happy.

"You'll know when we get closer." And that was all he would say.

It was pleasant proceeding across country in this suddenly golden weather with the blackberries huge and succulent in the hedges, staying the night at whatever inn was provident. Not that the pattern of sleeping was any different. She was expected to go first, then much later, and sometimes smelling of wine or brandy, Adam would come, she sometimes still awake or half waking, disturbed by his entry to the bed and sensing the warmth of his body, aware still later of those furtive caresses, sometimes the weight of his arm around her waist or cupped under her breast.

He was never there in the morning. He would be outside or standing by the window staring at the awakening world, a contained stillness about him that made him seem far away. A stranger.

It came to her one day that this was much the journey the coach had taken from Daggleby to Kendal. There were crags, valleys, stretches of river she recognized. But she would not spoil Adam's surprise by a premature disclosure of her certainty. Each morning she expressed her ignorance of their location, pressing him to tell her their destination, enjoying his amused smile, his laughing refusal.

They skirted Harrogate—purposely on his part, she realized—so they were closer to Hunter Hall than she expected. She had thought to see the spa again with its sulfur fumes and fine ladies with parasols as well as the woods and flowers.

The first sight of the Hall struck her with a violence she had not expected. One minute she was looking at the dark mesh of trees, then there was the great house, the hill rising behind it with its porcupine of birches and rowans. Adam had brought her by every byroad and lane in order to avoid any previous familiarity before he was ready. Her senses were bound by the growing wastes of the rocky heather, the spreading bilberry. Her vision blurred briefly. She saw Adam's smile.

"Oh, Adam—"

"I thought it time you saw your parents."

She turned towards him and pulled him towards her in an access of excitement and pleasure, then was intimidated by his sudden stiffness, his determined stillness. Gently he detached her clinging arms and bent towards the window. "Nothing changes," he said, indicating the house and the moor. "It will never change."

"No," she said, too brightly, hurt by the rebuff. "It will always be the same."

The big ironwork gates were opened and they were travelling up the long, winding drive. She wondered how soon she could visit her parents. The day drew on and she would be expected to be introduced to the household, to unpack, to dine with her husband. It could not be before tomorrow.

She had never been at the front of the house. The door, set inside a porticoed porch, was enormous and painted a shining black. The tall, wide windows glittered in the last of the extravagant sunlight, so that the house seemed to be on fire. Servants appeared quickly and Adam held out his arms to help her to descend. They would not recognize her, of course, not immediately.

"Please bring all the members of the household," Adam directed, once they were in the vast hall. "I would have them meet my wife." And he took Sable's hand and pulled her towards him so that they stood side by side at the foot of the stairs.

There was a great hurrying and scurrying before the lines of footmen, bootboys, scullery maids, housemaids, and parlormaids, along with the housekeeper and the butler stood half-awkward, half-curious under Adam's calm scrutiny.

"Why, Adam!" Sable said loudly. "I think I have been misinformed. These young girls look far too intelligent to be described 'thick as posts,' don't you agree? Someone has been unkind." And she went first to the lowliest of the servants to shake their hands and ask them details of their homes and families, continuing up the ranks until she reached the previously awesome figure of Mistress Perkins. "You have a great responsibility to these young people," she said. "I like to see a staff happy as well as fully occupied, don't you agree? I sincerely hope these girls and young men have time to visit their homes and are not always kept nose to the grindstone."

Mistress Perkins did recognize her. The grim mouth dropped open in stark amazement, then closed like a trap.

"I should like to see some sort of rota prepared, Mistress Perkins, of time allotted to the staff for private recreation. Don't you agree, Adam?"

Adam's face was a study in conflicting emotions. "That seems a worthwhile idea. Yes. Perhaps we can see some kind of document tomorrow."

"I take it you can write?" Sable asked of the housekeeper.

The harsh face colored unattractively.

"Oh, you do not? Then you can attend me in the morning room after breakfast and I will do it myself if you will supply the names."

Her gaze swept the attentive ranks. "I will always be available if there are any problems. Complaints. Injustices. Do I make myself clear? So long as I am here, that is."

"Yes'm." It was like a Greek chorus with undertones of amusement.

"You may return to your duties, then. Pray show me to my room, Mistress Perkins."

"Very well—ma'am." The last word was, not unexpectedly, grudging.

They followed the woman upstairs, Adam controlling his expression with difficulty. Sable could see him out of the corner of her eye, his mouth twitching. The landing opened out into a fine gallery where musicians once had played and a honeycomb of doors and passages were arrayed.

"We were not expecting you, Mr. Adam—"

"Well, there's time to see to the fire and the comfort of

the room. The bed must be aired. I'd not have my wife die of a chill on her first visit."

Mistress Perkins surveyed Sable bleakly. If looks were weapons she'd be stone dead on this landing, Sable thought and smiled.

Alone in Adam's room, which here, like the one at Bays, showed a masculine disregard for fripperies, she could not help but roll on the bed in helpless laughter, then sat up, suddenly sober.

"Oh! I'd forgotten your mother. Will she—can she resent me even more for undermining her position, do you think?"

Adam chuckled. "I don't imagine my mother will hear a great deal of the recent routing of Mistress Perkins. But it was I backed you up, remember, and I stand by it."

"You are too good to me," Sable said, "and I wish—I wish I could be as good to you."

"I have what I wanted—" His face was now serious. Resigned. The laughter gone.

"Have you?"

"Have I not just said so?" Adam said. "But we must not waste time in a premature rejoicing over the defeat of a tyrant. I can't understand why Mother keeps her, except that the place is adequately run—"

"As a prison might be," Sable interrupted astringently. "Everyone knows her strictness."

"No matter. We must present ourselves for the meal. May I suggest the sack dress? There's nothing becomes you so well. And the locket would show well with the scooped neckline."

"You had better look your fill of it, since it may not meet on me next month," she said ruefully.

He said nothing, only went on changing out of his travel-creased suit and into a fresh one, as though he had not heard. But he could not play the ostrich, ignoring the

270

changes that must take place. The first triumph of arrival had waned and she was disinclined for the evening ahead, disappointed by his silence and abstraction.

The excitement returned when they were downstairs in the magnificent room she had seen so often from the outside. On an impulse she went to one of the long windows and stared into the garden.

"Oh, Adam," she murmured. "I've been so foolish. If only I could undo—certain things."

"We can never do that. Come to table. No one will bring anything until you do."

The table shone like warm orange satin, the candleflames blooming on it, shivering, contracting, expanding, like exotic sea creatures. The white marble mantel was carved into shapes of fruit and flowers and white doves, while real fruit pyramided in the center of the bare, lovely table was reflected in its warm depths. Strange to think that though none of this was now forbidden, there was something nagging at its center like a maggot that would destroy the perfect whole.

"I have talked to Wilberforce," Adam said out of an echoing void. "He says he must use his position for more than mere self-advancement. But he's like most of us, feeling our way through a fog of injustices without taking hold of anything really substantial."

"I should like to see you do something for the Belles and the Bens of the country. You've helped those in particular—"

"You mean you have—"

"Both of us, then. But I mean the great masses. I'd still like to smoke out that den of beastliness to which those children are drawn by promises of plumcakes and comfits to find—rapists!" Sable said the last word so forcibly that the approaching footman wavered, recovered himself manfully, and was rewarded with the warm smile that was her greatest attraction. She turned back to Adam. "Yes, it must be slavery that will be your special battle. Of the spirit and the body. Promise me, Adam, it will be that?"

"It's you should be standing up in Parliament." He filled her glass almost to the brim and she took it thankfully, for the room seemed cold in spite of the fire.

"I will watch you instead. And clap and stamp my feet when you make your best points. And scowl at those who would put you down."

"Oh, Sable."

"Shall we go out for a little? Walk in the grounds? It's too early to retire and I confess I am stimulated by so much that is new. Come with me, Adam."

"Well. If it will not overtire you—"

"You forget. I'm a farm girl. And it seems a fine night."

"Fetch Mrs. Hunter's cloak," Adam ordered. "And my redingote."

"And leave the lights on at the back. I've a mind to climb that small hill with the wood on top and look back at the windows," she added.

They let themselves out onto the terrace. It was as she remembered it, splotched with the yellow glow from windows, the ivy trembling and swaying, the marble figures softly irradiated. Adam had not taken her arm, neither did he say anything at first.

Sable pulled the cloak closer around her. The moon was abnormally large and gold as a guinea. The hill seemed steeper than it used to be and the night was full of tart scents and small sighings, rustlings and silences. An owl drifted, dropped, and the peace was rent with death agonies that left the silence thicker than before. Something that was alive when she left the house was now torn to pieces. The thought was an ache that grew stronger as the summit was reached and the trees receded to the milieu of the pond.

272

The dogs came, tongues lolling, exuding friendliness, just as she remembered the pond. "Brutus," she whispered, then "Samson. You've not forgotten. I remember one night, Adam, when your father had the keepers after me. I had mud on my face so that none of you would see me. It was a wonderful night."

"You are an extraordinary creature."

"Can we go as far as the pond?"

"If you wish. But no farther."

She experienced the same feelings as they approached the scummed water and the dogs dragged their tails and were quiet in the brooding hush that surrounded it.

"What happened here?"

"Who told you anything happened?" He was close to her now and the moon was ahead, crisscrossed with thin branches as Lady Parksworth's face had been with fine wrinkles.

"I—know." She shivered.

"Someone drowned. A long time ago. They never found the body, for all their dragging. It seems the water's surprisingly deep."

"Who was it?"

"A cousin of Mother's. A young woman. A young widow, actually, of Irish descent. She visited the Hall frequently from the time of my parents' marriage. They never spoke of it except to warn us as children not to be too venturesome. The reeds can pull at one. Come back, Sable. I can see you are cold." He did put an arm around her then and she turned from disturbance to pleasure in the contact.

"How horrible, just to vanish—"

"Yes. She was very beautiful. I found a miniature in a drawer and showed it to Father. He said it was Aine—"

"An odd name." She was intrigued and horrified by the crystallization of her intuition.

273

"Tomorrow, I imagine, is the scene of the triumph. You will want a note sent to your mother, I presume? The tea party—" It appeared he wished to change the subject.

"Oh, yes. A note on Hall paper would be so lovely. But—I forgot—she cannot read it." She was crestfallen.

"Then a verbal summons would be more appropriate. Do you intend to ask them all?"

"They could not possibly all come together. Farming is hard work. No, I will ask that Mistress Martin call to see Mrs. Hunter—to take a dish of tea. Imagine her surprise, then, to find it is me." She laughed again, the sensation of haunting gone.

"I can see the excitement will keep you awake. We'll have some mulled sack. That should close your eyes for you."

They stood at the top of the slope, looking down at the indigo bulk of the house, the yellow rectangles. The huge moon was half behind the forest of chimneys.

"This is my favorite view of the house," Adam said, bending to clap Brutus on the flank. "One sees the Elizabethan shape of the place and the gardens all laid out almost like a map."

"And now I am a part of it. A small part—"

"Small? When you have reduced Mistress Perkins, made her admit she is unlettered. Won over my Father—"

"But not your mother or Jane—"

"Give it time. You must give everything time. We cannot have all we want on a plate like John the Baptist's head. Or would you have that too?"

She stumbled on the hillside and fell towards him. His arm tightened around her until she could scarcely breathe. Then he picked her up and carried her as far as the foot of the slope. Her ribs hurt after the rough caress, but she could not regret it.

"Adam—" The light from the windows flooded the flagstones, showed her his tall, dark shape.

274

"Well?"

"Must you always wait so long? At night—"

"There's always much to think about."

"You could think just as well in bed. I'd not distract you."

"Wouldn't you, my sweet?"

"Not intentionally."

"I see you have grasped the point as you always do. And we want no more repetitions of recent disasters, do we?"

"But, Adam—"

"No, Sable. It will be as it was. It's more dignified." His tone was cool now as the night air. They entered the house in a thoughtful quiet. Damn dignity, she thought with a tinge of desperation. Damn, damn, damn dignity. There were more important things.

She watched her mother's approach from the window, the curtain screening most of her face. Mistress Martin hurried up the path, her face anxious, self-conscious in her Sunday best. She disappeared from view when she neared the flagstoned side entrance.

"Bother! I should have had the footman tell her to come to the front door," Sable said aloud.

Adam looked up from the book he was reading. "The poor woman would have been petrified," he remarked, amused. "Let her become used to matters in easy stages."

Her back to the fire, Sable took up her position. Adam laughed. "I do believe you are more nervous than your mother must be."

There was a tap at the door. It opened to reveal the bristling figure of Mistress Perkins who had spent an uncomfortable morning helping Sable to compile the list of servants and their projected spare time and who had to welcome Mistress Martin in person to meet her temporary mistress this afternoon.

The room was dark except for the corner where Adam

read. Sable's figure against the firelight was a mere silhouette. "Mistress Martin, ma'am."

"Thank you," Sable said gruffly. "You may go. Have the tea sent directly." Her voice sounded strange, even to herself. Her mother entered warily, her gaze anywhere but on that figure by the fireplace or in the direction of Adam. But as soon as the door closed upon the housekeeper, Sable flew across the room and flung her arms around the sturdy body encased in the neat grey gown. "Mother. Oh, Mother, Mother—"

Mistress Martin's face turned pale. "But, the message said—"

"The message was perfectly correct," Adam said, rising. Sable seemed unable to speak just at the moment. "Now I must leave you to have tea with my wife."

"But Adam—"

"You'll discover more to say without my constraining presence, I daresay. You know where you can find me if you want me."

"Well, Mother," Sable said when he was gone. "I hope Mistress Perkins was polite to you when you arrived."

"To tell the truth," Mistress Martin said, "by rights I should have lain dead on the step. But it's some prank, isn't it? You couldn't be wed to a Hunter." She sat down suddenly in the nearest chair. "But Tom did read us your letters about how you'd gone to London to help Miss Charlotte. I thought it was Mr. Adam's mother I was to see with some news of you from there."

"I hope I didn't worry you. But I wanted you to be able to have your own back on an old enemy. She won't be going on about my stupidity and oafishness now, will she! I wanted her to feel small for once. I'm not very nice, am I."

"Oh, Sable. It's exactly like you—"

"To be 'not nice?'" Sable teased, enjoying the return of country color to her mother's cheeks, the older woman's unashamed appraisal of the grand room.

276

"No! To be full of surprises. And to mind that that woman humiliated me once. But maybe I did expect too much in them days. It was just that you seemed special."

"But of course I am special! Am I not young Mrs. Adam?"

"Funny," her mother said, "but if I ever had to imagine you with one of the Hunters, and I'm not saying I did, mind, it would have been with the other one. Young Mr. Morgan."

"Oh." Sable was not laughing now. "Do you know, Mother, I think it *did* cross your mind? How strange."

"Of course, it didn't! Not really. But we all have our dreams and he was a bonny, happy lad."

"Yes," Sable said, "he was." It was as though she spoke an epitaph.

"I was disappointed you'd to leave Lady Chryston's. But Tom told us her niece had come back. Tom's here. In the barn as usual. It's where the next baby will have to go, too. The place won't hold any more—"

"I'll prevail upon Adam to have a few more cottages built. One for Joe, one for Chris, and there must be others needed. It'll give some local work for the young ones nearly ready to start. Then they won't all be running off to York and Hull."

"Would he?"

"He has a lot of influence with his father. But Tom! How opportune. I long to see him. I'll go back with you. We'll take the carriage. Ah, Mistress Perkins. I trust the tea is really hot? I had thought to see it before this. And you will be sure to send some in to Mr. Adam?"

Mistress Perkins glowered.

"What pretty cups," Mistress Martin said, ignoring her old adversary. "So dainty. Not like the ones at home—"

"I had a lovely home," Sable defended, "and I can't wait to see it again. I hope these scones will be light. And the cheesecake does look a trifle overdone. Is there no plumcake, Mistress Perkins? My mother's partial to the rich fruit. Please see if you can find some."

The door closed ungently. Mother and daughter looked at one another and laughed.

"I promised myself that for a long time," Sable said. "But she'll be rid of me and my disturbing ways shortly. Adam wants to go home soon—"

"Home?"

"Cardigan Square."

"But, his holiday—"

"He says politicians take too much time off. He maintains problems don't go away while they disport themselves in the country. The truth of the matter is that Adam likes his work. And so do I."

"How did they take it?" Mistress Martin asked curiously. "The Hunters?"

"The womenfolk didn't like it. But old Mr. Hunter's on my side."

"Always did have the men on your side, our Sable."

"Except for Dad."

"He is really, only he don't like to show it. Didn't want you educated in case you got hurt. But you haven't, have you? Done truly well, you have."

"No. I didn't—get hurt. And if I have done well, I suppose you have the credit. And Tom Dobbs." Sable reached forward to pick up a plate and Lady Chryston's ring glittered on her finger. She remembered when that same hand had scrubbed tables and floors, brought cheese, planted and gathered about the farm, picked rowans at lambing time. It was not true that she remained unscathed, but Sable accepted that this was a necessary part of living.

Her mother went on talking between sips of tea and nibbling the dainty fare, her compact body relaxed, her bonnet nodding every now and again when she made some point, her gaze still wary as though this room and everything in it might quite suddenly disappear.

Mistress Perkins came back with the plumcake and sent a maid to replenish the teapot and see to the fire. It was all quite pleasant and almost familiar, as though they had done this many times before and would again.

Her mother would never forget today. A warmth spread through Sable's body, leaving no cold crannies to reproach or torment her. This afternoon was the culmination of Mistress Martin's life and she'd go back to her farmhouse with her prestige enhanced, the envy of her neighbors and acquaintances for the remainder of her time. Every now and again, when Sable was at the Hall, they'd have tea together as they did now and to the devil with Sarah and her disapproval! Thomas would uphold her.

Adam came when he felt they had chattered their fill and was very courteous to Mistress Martin. Indeed he was not distant at all, and cracked a few homely jokes to put her at her ease, approving of Sable's plan to take the carriage and some gifts over to Highmoor Farm.

"I'll let you go alone this time, my sweet. I'd feel redundant. But you must ask Tom to come here before we leave."

"You'll not take her too soon?" Mistress Martin said anxiously.

"I must confess, I itch to return to a proper routine. But we'll stay another week or so, then take our time on the return to London. There are places I'd show Sable. Places that have meaning—"

"And I want to see them," Sable told him. "I wish only to please you." The message behind the words did not escape him. Some color came to his face, though he quickly turned the conversation to other channels, then sent footmen scurrying for comfits and sweetmeats, for gifts of game and fowl, for the gowns Sable had decided to give

279

Pansy, her newest sister-in-law Jane, and her mother. There was a handsome watch for her father and pipes and tobacco for her brothers, gowns and shawls for the babies and ivory teething rings. All of which preparations Adam watched with an indulgent eye, then prepared to return to his study. And to the brandy decanter, Sable thought, with a twinge of despair she quickly banished. She'd not allow Adam to become besotted with drink. It was borne upon her that she had come to love him to distraction, that she would do anything to have him as a lover as well as a husband by law. Yet, already she had wrought important changes in Adam. He was no longer a figure more dead than alive. He had animation, some purpose, no longer sat astride a horse like an automaton. He could joke, see the amusing side of most encounters, want to touch her even though he waited till she slept. It was almost enough that he found her desirable.

Chapter 12

*A*s Sable had expected, Charlotte did not stay more than a day or two after their return to London. She was very quiet after Adam told her he and Sable were now married. It was almost unnerving having to remain composed under the intense scrutiny of both Charlotte and Marie Claire, and Marie had an unpleasant habit of allowing her small, dark eyes to roam around Sable's midriff as though she suspected what only Adam knew.

Daisy was undisguisedly happy with the advent of the new mistress and Sable made a private pact with herself to advance the child in easy stages to become her personal maid. In the meantime Adam could cope quite well with the more complicated fastenings of her grander gowns and it was one way to make him touch her, however unsatisfactory the brevity of such encounters.

She was well aware that she roused Adam in bed and occasionally would turn, apparently sleep-drugged, to invite his embrace. But though he would kiss and caress her, he would not go so far as to possess her, and, if he suspected she had awakened, he would become quite still. Sometimes she would make small, languorous noises and wind her arms around him, pressing close against his body, but he obviously imagined her still thinking of Morgan and did his best not to respond.

One evening at a supper at Cardigan Square presided over by Sable, Adam's friends began to tease him about becoming a father.

"You've wasted no time, you old dog," Eliot teased, eyes sparkling with mischief.

"With such temptations," Denham countered. "Who could resist?"

"Will you make him a politician or a businessman?" Pepper asked, oblivious of Adam's small frown and his disinclination for the usual cheerful thrust and parry of the now familiar gatherings both Hunters seemed to enjoy.

"You jumped the gun," Pitt accused with his brittle smile, "but one would think you unnatural, had you not. You've been undeservedly fortunate, my dear Hunter."

Wilberforce, seeing Adam blanche, reprimanded Pitt. "How can you be so forthright? I'm sure you would not really question Adam's honor. Nor that of his wife—"

To all of which, Sable merely laughed and nudged Adam to do the same. No one would think it worth a mention next time and it was not. Her pregnancy was accepted, arousing no more comment until the evening the group met to discuss Lord Rockingham's succession of North and how his high opinion of Wilberforce could only be to the advantage of both them and the vast county of Yorkshire. It was then that they all became quite touchingly considerate of her condition, rising to aid her on the slightest pretext, bringing small, premature gifts for the coming child.

Daisy had progressed well to become upper parlormaid

and was poised to become personal maid after the baby was born. Sable began to concentrate more and more on the life within her and Adam resorted to the dressing room where he was less aware of her tossing and turning, yet available should she need him. Sometimes she would lie for a long time, aware of the candlelight through the part-open door and the rustle of pages as he read his papers or indulged in a book, waiting for the flame to be snuffed out so that she could say good night. This was a moment she never cared to miss.

They had been to Drury Lane to see Mrs. Siddons one evening when Sable looked out of the carriage window to see a figure she recognized.

"Adam!" She gripped his arm. "The singer. Over there on the corner. That girl—"

The girl seemed to know only "The Mistletoe Bough," for she rendered it now as on each other occasion with piercing sweetness. Sable remembered Morgan throwing his careless bounty, the girl finishing her song in tribute before bending to pick the coins from the gutter. And as her thoughts went back, Morgan's child stirred and she was conscious of an onrush of faintness that made her lean back against the buttoned lining of the carriage.

"I'll fetch her," Adam was saying, oblivious of the child's assertion of his place in her life, his paramount need of her. He sprang from the vehicle and hurried across the muddy roadway between coach and sedan chair, women picking up their skirts from the filth and men deep in discussion about the play or the state of the country.

Sable's stomach subsided. Adam appeared at the side nearest the pale girl who looked faintly wary as though well-used to propositions from affluent-looking gentlemen. Her expression lost some of its cynicism as she saw Sable, slightly bulky now under the evening cloak.

"Get inside," Adam directed. "You'll be paid for time lost, never fear."

"You'll take me somewhere," the girl objected. "I been taken before—"

"This lady is my wife," Adam said testily. "Why should I—?"

"They all say that. Sometimes wives ain't enough, even if they're pretty as this one."

"I've been looking for you for some time," Sable told the girl. "Have you eaten recently?"

"Not yet. Got a pig's trotter at 'ome—"

"Then, perhaps a supper room," Sable suggested, registering the famished look in the girl's pale blue eyes, noting the hollow cheekbones. "You know them better than I do, Adam, my dear. Come sit beside me, what's your name?"

"Betty, Ma'am. Betty Davies."

"Betty. I've seen you before. Some months ago. In that same place."

"I thought I might have noticed you," Betty said, relieved. "You have the sort of face you don't forget. Begging your pardon for doubting your husband, but it ain't the first time I been asked inside a carriage, then promised things you don't never see. Just thrown out after a fumble as though you was dirt. And no thanks, neither."

"Oh, dear," Sable said softly. "I can assure you nothing of the kind is likely to happen to you this evening. My husband is a Member of Parliament and we wish your help—"

"What sort o' help, Ma'am?" Betty's foot was arrested on the step.

"A poor child suffered some similar trouble, only she was less able to take care of herself. Thirteen years old, and small for her age. Spoiled for a normal, happy existence. I feel very strongly about it. She mentioned you when she told her story and I thought you might have noticed others. I can assure you she was not the only one."

"It could be dangerous, telling on the likes o' the folk you mean."

"You would not feel—dirt."

284

"No," Betty answered, her face paler than before. "I could end up feeling nothing at all."

"We'd protect you—"

"I don't know, Ma'am. You don't know what they are like—"

"Oh, but I do! They are monsters."

"Even if you found them, there'd be others in two shakes o' a cat's tail." Betty shivered. "They'd know who blabbed—"

"How could they know?"

"They could see me now—"

"Then get inside. You could pretend my husband wanted you for—what was it you called it—a quick fumble?" Sable suggested, not without irony.

"Oh, Ma'am! He don't look the sort now I've had a good look at him. Aw'right. I'll listen. And I am hungry, so I won't say no to a good feed. But nowhere too posh for it ain't only the common lot you're looking for— There's gents too."

"I know that."

Betty mounted the step and sat in the far corner of the coach while Adam joined Sable and called for the man to take them to the Golden Cockerel club where a good supper could be had in reasonably reputable company. Once there, he insisted on a corner table where little light penetrated and ordered a meal of oysters and beef and apple tart at the sight of which Betty Davies brightened visibly.

They talked little until they had eaten and were content, Betty venturing cautious looks around the room, keeping her old cloak drawn close enough to hide part of her face.

"Now," Adam said, pushing a glass in her direction. "There's a house close by the theatre for men with a penchant for virgins—"

Betty looked confused. She had probably never heard of either.

"A liking for very young, unused girls," Adam went on.

"One of whom managed to escape. Her mother came to me for aid. But the house she took us to seemed harmless enough—"

"I remember when they scarpered," Betty said gleefully, her glass empty and held out again invitingly. Adam replenished it and waited. The room was filling up now with couples from the theatre and other places of entertainment. The pale girl, flushed now with food and drink, pushed back the hood of her cloak and became bolder. "I'd no thought that you was to blame, o' course, but I do mind it. She was furious—"

"She?"

"Oh, come," Betty said. "A bite o' supper and I'm s'posed to tell you? I'll not be able to work Drury Lane till the stink blows over. And there's nobody that generous for just a bit of a song. Only for—" She stared at Sable, her pale eyes wide. "You know what I mean."

Sable realized she could hardly feign innocence with that betraying bulge, not that she was at all ungainly. "We both know what you mean, Betty. I'm sure my husband will not be ungenerous."

"Of course not." Adam, having received the cue, fumbled in his pocket and produced two sovereigns which he laid by his plate. "One," he said, "for only a little information. Both for names and to have the house pointed out by you when we leave this place."

"I should need five to go away where I'm not known. And I s'ould have to go. People work together around the theatre. One 'elps another in a manner o' speaking—one could be missed."

"You mean," Sable interrupted, her voice suddenly sharp, "that you help send those children—"

"Oh, no, Ma'am! But other business can be put someone's way. Folks that are willing. I'd not force anyone. But boys are wanted by some and they make a living that way.

And you needn't look so fierce, Madam! Folk like you never need to sell anything. It's all give to you on a plate. My brother Billy don't eat unless he goes with some dirty old man and some not so old. All worlds are not so pretty as yours—"

"No," Sable said in a low voice. "That's all too plain. But it's not you, I blame. You're as much a victim as Belle—"

"Belle? Oo's she?" The drink was taking effect and Betty's voice had risen. Curious glances were coming their way.

Sable, finding the odorous warmth uncomfortable, tugged at Adam's coattail. "I think we should go. It's perfectly obvious we are questioning the girl and I'd not like to know I'd put her in danger. A friend of ours," she said soothingly to Betty as she rose to her feet. Betty got up, too, swaying slightly, but not too far gone to remember the money she was promised. "Five," she insisted. "It has to be five—"

"Very well," Adam assented. "As soon as you show us the place. There's the two for the moment, as our act of good faith, for you've told us nothing yet."

The thin, dirty hand closed over the gold pieces avariciously. Wide, pale eyes gleamed with a mixture of excitement and cupidity, then changed to contain a trace of fear. Betty, again cautious, raised the edges of the hood to cover her hollow cheeks and hung behind Adam like the frightened child she probably still was at heart.

Outside, the narrow pavement was crowded. Adam cleared a way through the crowd for Sable and Betty Davies as linkboys ran by, their torches casting a shimmer of red-gold light over humans and conveyances alike and along the gleaming flanks of patient horses. It was all very noisy and Sable's head began to ache.

Betty crouched in the carriage, licking her mouth nervously. "It's back the way we come," she almost whispered

287

and jumped as someone bumped hard against the side of the vehicle, making it lurch.

Adam gave the coachman directions. "Now, Betty," he said firmly and took out three more sovereigns. "The names of the persons—"

The thin figure stiffened.

"Oh, but you must," Sable told the girl. "Now you've gone so far—"

"I don't know—"

"If you could have prevented your brother—"

"I couldn't leave Billy behind to be got at. We'd have to go right away. Brighton maybe. There's a living to be 'ad there with the Prince and all his cronies liking it so much. It's a little London I 'eard say."

"I think I could find you both a place," Sable said, remembering Lady Parksworth and her offer of help if it were needed. "There'd probably be stable work for the boy—"

"He do like 'orses, Ma'am."

"And what of yourself? Would you be prepared to perform household tasks? There'd be good food in the country. Respectability. You could forget what's past."

"Don't know as I'd like the country. I been in a town all my life. Used to it—"

"Well, it wouldn't do any harm to try it, would it?"

"No—"

"What's the name?" Adam said and jingled the coins seductively. "And which house?"

The carriage picked its way slowly through the sordid nightlife of the theatre district. Shabby women opportuned passing men. The coach lamps glimmered on a thin, white face, a childish body covered in little more than rags. A man watched but made no immediate move.

"Deb. Deb Miller," Betty said suddenly as though the sight of the ragged child had roused some chord of feeling. "She's the one who looks out for them. Takes them back—"

"Where?" The dingy housefronts all looked depressingly alike, but here and there one could see an attempt at decency, clean curtains or a painted door, a step that had been scrubbed.

"There!" Betty cried out as though she feared to say the word.

It was one of the dirtier houses, the windowpanes uncleaned, the strips of curtain a greyish green. The door, once brown, peeled leprously. A pane in one of the lower windows was cracked, giving the effect of a giant spiderweb.

"There's a man you'd best look out for—Davy, he's called. Davy Jerrold. 'E's a big man with a beard and 'e's not particular what 'e does. Carries a knife. There's others, o' course, but Davy and Deb, they're the worst. She looks so kind too, does Deb. Friendly—"

"You must say nothing," Adam told the girl.

"D'you think it likely?" She laughed discordantly. "Ain't much to look at for all your lady wife was so kind about my face. It'd not be even that for long once Davy had a whiff o' someone talking—"

"I know you wouldn't let it out, not unless you spent the money on drink. It loosens the tongue. So leave the gin alone, Betty, till I have the place visited."

"The Runners, you mean?"

"The Runners. And others. Some to watch the back. Others posted in front," Adam said, his eyes fixed on the house with distaste. "What we really need is a decoy. Catch them red-handed—some fresh, innocent girl, quite young, brave enough to invite that woman's attention by watching the theatre crowds. And you can forget that look of eagerness, my dear Sable. There's no one would take you for untouched goods now. But I appreciate your devotion to

289

duty. There's one springs to mind, a child who'd do anything for you—"

"You mean—Daisy?"

"The same."

"But—the danger if anything should go wrong—"

"I agree there is an element of risk but there'd be good, honest proof."

"Yes. But I'd not forgive myself if Daisy were harmed. I'm particularly fond of that girl."

"I'd make sure she had protection. In any case, she would only be allowed a very few minutes in the house before we followed."

"Yes. I know you'd be careful." Sable was conscious of a premonition of disaster. The plan, she knew, was perfectly sensible and there was no one better fitted than Daisy, so young and fresh, to carry out the essential part of attracting this Deb Miller. Pretty enough for any fastidious lecher—

"Can I go now?" Betty asked anxiously, breaking into her train of thought. "I'm known round 'ere. And there's someone I promised to meet after I done singing. I got to be there or it'll look funny."

"Will you be at the theatre each evening this week in case I want to talk to you again? And you must think over my wife's offer of work. Think well. There's your brother to remove from his present—depravity is the only way I can describe it."

"Yes," Betty answered, grabbing the hood so that only her frightened eyes showed in the round of shadow. "Every evening, same as tonight. But don't take too long, will yer? My nerves wouldn't stand it if you was to take too long to do it."

"I won't take any longer than I can help," Adam promised. "And don't rouse any alarms. Just be yourself. Say nothing even to Billy."

"No, sir. This corner would be best. There's the money, Sir. You haven't forgot—?"

"I haven't forgotten. Thank you, Betty." Adam handed over the rest of the sovereigns, and the girl scrambled down to be lost almost immediately into an obscurity of hurrying figures, plunging horses, and revolving wheels that splayed up the evening's muck over stockings and skirts.

"I feel I should like to go home and take a bath," Sable said unsteadily.

"It does leave a bad taste in the mouth. Home!" Adam shouted to the coachman, and the vehicle gathered speed. They sat together unnoticing now of the teeming streets, the cloud-swept darkness of the sky, where only one dim star showed above the ragged chimney pots.

For two days Sable scarcely saw Adam. The weather had lost its pleasant crispness and was dark and sullen and there were few callers. People seemed inclined to stay inside their homes just to keep warm. Christmas had come and gone long since and they had not gone back to Yorkshire because of her pregnancy. That Autumn visit was only a bright memory in a period of stagnation.

But it was not stagnation! Though she had no part in it, much was happening. In spite of the fact that she did not regret the coming of the child—it had become too real, too much of a person to be deplored—Sable felt inhibited by being kept from anything but cosseting and cautions. Adam fussed as though it were his own. She had had to fight for every particle of independence of late. As if sitting behind the desk in the interview room would tire any ordinary woman.

She kicked at the tapestry footstool in a sudden frustration, just as Adam came into the withdrawing room.

"Do I have a mutiny on my hands?" he asked, lowering himself into a chair and stretching out his long legs.

"Oh, Adam, I long to be myself again. Being six months with child does not really agree with me. I think I shall always find it so."

"Indeed?"

The oblique reference to the bearing of future children had not been lost on him, she noticed. His flash of mischief over upsetting the stool had been quenched most decisively. He must find her tiresome and unattractive now, and the next month would see her become even more bulky. She could not hope to resume her previously abortive attempts to win Adam for many weeks yet and the knowledge accentuated her feelings of uselessness and deprivation.

"You must curb those restless pangs, my dear."

"Then you have noticed?"

He laughed, good humor restored. "You are not subtle, love." The endearments came easily enough, but they were only words. She longed increasingly for action to implement them.

"We—we are to take action tomorrow," Adam said more seriously, as though he had read her thoughts.

"Action?"

"Over Betty Davies's information."

"Oh." Her heart bumped hurtfully inside her rib cage. "Daisy was very brave, I thought, when we asked for her cooperation. I still feel that we are making her a kid tied in the jungle to attract the tiger. The kid is apt to end up with its throat torn out before the spears reach their target."

"I talked with Betty last night. The fact that she and Billy are still unscathed means that she's not suspected. There's nothing to alert them. I will be there to follow the child. The Runners will be out in force. A formidable body. There will be the woman Miller, Jerrold, the doctor who attends the girls, and not many more, or Betty would have known. Two perhaps at most to guard the place. Belle Briggs mentioned one who spent his time upstairs and the description did not fit Jerrold."

"What if she's not there?"

"Deborah Miller? She's been at the theatre nightly of late. A dearth of prospective victims apparently since the weather precludes much night wandering. She goes always at the same time—before the evening performance."

"But what if she picks some other girl?"

"Then we'll still act. But intuition tells me Daisy will attract attention. She has that wholesome, well-scrubbed look that makes her so suitable for their purpose."

"I cannot help worrying. Even in a short time—"

"They'd do nothing. After all, it's her virginity that's her chief asset. They won't cast that away too readily."

"No—"

"Then don't look so worried."

"I'm thinking of Belle. Perhaps it was wrong to involve her in the Parksworth affair. It could be just as much a mistake to turn Daisy into a stalking-horse—"

"Only two minutes ago she was a tethered kid—"

"It's not a joking matter!"

"Of course, it's not. I tried only to divert you. You should not be disturbed at such a time—"

"Oh, bother my time!" Sable said shortly. "I'm strong as a horse."

"You paint such an unflattering picture of yourself," he replied gently. "You could not be anything but pleasant to watch however hard you tried. Now that I've told you when we are to force our way into that house—I knew it would be useless to keep it from you—you must try to be patient. It will probably be over in a few minutes and Daisy will be a heroine for life. If your child was a girl, you could not bear the thought, could you, that she meet such as the woman, Miller?"

"No. Oh, no! But it's not a girl. I feel it. I'm sure it's a

293

lusty boy." She wished she had used some other adjective when she saw Adam's expression.

"Well, I hope you're not doomed to disappointment." He smiled wryly.

"It would not matter. I have thought of his name. It should be Adam—the first—"

"Not Adam," he said decisively. "I'd prefer not. I had thought—"

"What?" she persisted. "What have you thought?"

"It's nothing of importance." But his tone belied the assertion. He'd want his own son named after him.

"I don't care for Thomas too well, though it would be good to please your father—"

"He has a second name. Bartholomew."

"That has a good sound to it. Yes, I think I like it—"

"Do not set your heart too much on a boy," Adam warned, moving towards the decanter.

"No. I see it would be foolish."

"And tomorrow you'll compose yourself and have a rest when I go out. I'll take good care of Daisy, never fear."

"I wish I could have come—"

"But you can't," he said decisively. "So you must put it from your mind."

"Yes, Adam," she answered, suspiciously meek. He looked at her keenly, not quite believing in her capitulation. She lowered her eyes so that he should not see the rebellion at the backs of them. She could not really be expected to sit back while her husband and Daisy put themselves into the hands of such people? There must be something she could do.

"Supper, ma'am," the footman said breaking into her thoughts.

"Good," Adam murmured, relieved by her acquiescence and finishing his drink. Sable was not always so amenable to reason.

She smiled at him serenely as they went into the dining room. There was more than one way to vanquish opposition and she'd think of something. She always did.

"Are you quite well?" Adam asked.

"Quite well, my dear," she answered. Quite well, my love, she repeated soundlessly. Quite well, my darling.

There was an article in the news sheet about the newest of London's prisons. Newgate, Sable reflected, sounded more a debtor's prison than a usual criminal abode. Charlotte had told her of some of the horrors in the old prisons. Dank cells where no light ever shone but that of a tallow dip hardly bought.

The people in the house by the theatre would not suffer so much, though they well deserved it. Wilberforce had told her prisons were better places than they used to be and it was plain he believed it. In this case she hoped he was wrong. What these people did was like frost on a tender plant. It was blackened and spoilt. Useless afterwards. Only God knew the nightmares, the twisted relationships that resulted. A good man could make advances to an outwardly pretty and normal girl and be horribly repulsed, unable to understand the reason for her bitter refusal. Her condemnation of what had seemed to him unexceptional, a touch to her breast or thigh, the preliminaries to any lasting courtship, might unleash a terrible response.

Her mind worked unceasingly, forming many plans, most unworkable. But there was one— She bid Adam good-bye, kissing him very thoroughly, as for the last time. It was ridiculous, of course. Adam was indestructible, more machine than man. If only she had not fallen under his indefinable spell, for there seemed little future in it. It was obvious he imagined her affections elsewhere, that she'd go as soon as she had no more need of his protection. And he made it so difficult to be confiding, to whisper the truth. He could turn cold as an icicle quicker than it took to think the chilly word. He made her feel so unworthy. That was the worst obstacle of all.

I hate myself, she thought. Detest my gross, misshapen body, my deception. For, already, she knew she could not sit quietly at home and wait for Adam's return. Somehow or other, she must be there in case she could help.

Sable set aside the news sheet and finished her perfunctory breakfast. Today she was disinterested in everything but the night's doings. Impossible to rest as Adam had advised her. She must be there. Dispassionately, she went over the plan that had seemed the most feasible. It still seemed to hold water. At least she would be there when Daisy arrived, able to do some small thing to avert catastrophe—

She went to her room in the afternoon, to lie on the bed, to let her thoughts flow, but her body lie fallow like one of her father's fields. Adam would not stay for their normal leisurely supper. He'd snatch a bite, look into her room and go, thankful that she was asleep, that there was no need for painful farewells.

All he would see was what she wished him to. A mound under the bedclothes, a shape he'd not dare disturb. A blanket or two could be made into a convincing roll.

What she would do when she got to the house, she could not yet visualize. It would be fraught with difficulties, but when had she ever evaded a challenge?

She prepared the bedchamber after it was cleaned in the early afternoon. The house remained shadowy, unvisited, and where normally she would have chafed under the inaction, today she rejoiced. She found one of her old gowns and the cloak she had worn at Daggleby, both kept out of sentiment, but useful now when she wanted to seem unexceptional, more readily acceptable. She had nothing to lose, nothing, since Morgan had taken it.

Sable was horrified to find herself on the point of tears.

She felt she had failed Adam who never seemed to swerve from the path of duty. Then, there was the crumb of comfort, remembering his behavior when he thought her asleep and unaware. She was married to a man who was all too human, who felt insufficient, who must one day be made aware of his true importance. "I love you," she said by the rolled blankets as she squeezed herself into the old gown and shrouded herself in the cape that served her at Daggleby. She must speak in the old, Yorkshire dialect as though she were still a country wench, or they'd smell a rat.

She let herself out of the house, meeting no one. Earlier, she had asked not to be disturbed until much later, a not too unusual request for a breeding woman. She was able to hire a sedan chair almost immediately and sat in the conveyance, more at peace than the last time she used such a mode of travel.

At the swag shop at the corner seemed the best place to be set down. There was a crowd around the door that would provide concealment, then she could emerge from the throng as if she had been there all along.

She cast a cautious look around her in case any Runners were already installed, but there were so many moving figures both here and further along the road at the lamplit entrance to the theatre that she could pick out no one obviously loitering, but of course, the whole point of the exercise was that they must remain unobtrusive and there were shadows enough.

There were few, if any, women in sight. Just beyond the entrance to the Drury Lane theatre she thought she glimpsed Betty Davies and above the sullen growl of the myriad voices around her she could even imagine she heard the sweet, insistent strains of "The Mistletoe Bough."

Sable moved towards the house with the flawed window. She mounted the single and dirty step and tried the door.

It opened under her touch and she was in a dark, fusty hall with only a tallow dip burning at the other end, enabling her to see a red-and-gold paper at variance with the poor exterior. Someone, upstairs, was weeping quietly. Then, without warning, there was a shadow beyond the light of the dip, the squeak of a protesting floorboard.

Sable moaned and half fell against the wall, aware, between slitted eyelids, that the shadow had become a silhouette, was coming closer. No chance to hide as she had planned.

"What are you doing here?" a voice asked. It was perfectly polite, reasonably well spoken, yet contained an element of hardness that set her on her guard.

Sable mumbled something unintelligible and sank to her knees, clutching at the respectable skirts. Ordinary, Belle had said. Sable had to bite back the need to snarl and shout, to rend at the folds of grey-blue material like some rabid dog. Instead, she pulled herself up and said vaguely, "I'm with child. I felt faint and fell against the door. It could not have been closed. Then I heard someone coming. You'd not deny me a drink of water, ma'am? You've a kind face—" God forgive her for being a sanctimonious hypocrite!

"I was about to go—to a neighbor." The voice was guarded.

"Jesus said we were all neighbors. Brothers—sisters—"

The woman exclaimed impatiently, "A country lass, are you?"

Her accent must have convinced, Sable thought. "Aye. From Yorkshire. But I feel right bad—you must help me."

"Come through, then. There's a sofa you can lie on. Only for a bit, mind you. Let's look at you."

They were in a well-lit room, comfortable enough with table and chairs, the sofa, which looked dingy, and Sable recoiled from imaginings of what had taken place upon it, a dresser and dishes. An oil lamp with a pale orange shade, a picture on the darkest wall of an innocent child with eyes cast heavenwards. The kind of room in which a very young girl would be reassured and flattered.

She allowed herself to be put on the sofa, her head on a cushion that smelt of sweat, her feet on the stuffed arm. "You're kind," she murmured faintly, aware of the clear grey eyes taking in every detail of face and form, resting speculatively on the reticule she held, the string looped through her fingers. Sable was conscious of a twinge of alarm. Before she left the house she had taken the precaution of removing the kitchen knife from the box Adam had bought for her on the way to Cardigan Square. It was sharp. The thought of the shining blade gave her courage. But she could allow no one to search the bag prematurely. She moved her fingers, purposefully entangling the string so that it could not be removed without difficulty. The weeping sound from upstairs had died to a whimper as if someone up there had heard the voices from below and had commanded silence.

The woman moved away, returned with a mug of water. A strong arm was put under Sable's head, tilting it upwards. The water trickled between her lips. She pushed the mug away. "Just leave me. I'll be fine in a few minutes." She closed her eyes and let her head fall back, aware of the woman's indecision. Since there was no doubt about her advanced pregnancy, Deborah Miller could suspect nothing. But she should have been on her way to the theatre to be opportuned by Daisy. Sable had expected some corner where she could remain hidden, from which she could appear if there seemed need, making a diversion. Instead of which, she had been seen immediately and she was hampering the woman, spoiling the whole plan.

Opening her eyelids a crack she saw that Deborah was fastening on a bonnet which she had taken from the table.

299

Her heart leapt. So she was still going out. The woman went out of the room and called from the stair foot. "Davy? Davy! Come here. A problem."

Quick as a wink, Sable had slipped off the string of the reticule, taken out the knife and slid it behind the cushion, then relapsed into her attitude of fainting. The bag fell to the floor with a soft plop just as Deborah came back. The woman dropped to her knees and riffled rapidly through the unspectacular contents. Kerchief, a key, a comb, a few coins of no particular value. Only sufficient to take Sable back in a sedan chair had there been need or if she had changed her mind about participating because of her condition.

Heavy steps thudded down the stairs and someone lumbered through the open doorway. Through her slitted lids Sable saw a large bearlike man fastening up his breeches as if he had been disturbed from bed. She felt immediately sickened, remembering the soft crying that had been stifled. She felt immediately vulnerable and foolish pricked with fear.

"'Oo is it? Got a bun in the oven, ain't she! Pretty, though—" His eyes raked her.

"She stumbled against the door. It wasn't properly shut. That would be you or Jake."

"Jake. I allus shuts the door."

"She's been taken poorly. I can't stop. Late already. I had a look out and there's more doing than for the last week. We need another girl. Those upstairs need attention from Doctor Hays. And will continue to do so if you and Jake don't leave them alone."

"Wot's another slice from the loaf? Doctor hasn't come, 'as 'e? So why not?"

"Makes his job more difficult, that's why. It's virgins they want, not whores. Doctor Hays will be here at any minute. You better be available to let him in. She'll keep. She'll not come round for a bit." Sable could feel the woman's gaze on her supposedly unconscious face. A large finger touched her cheek and wandered down over her chin and down her throat as far as the neck of her gown. She repressed a shudder as Davy continued his investigation.

"Leave her alone, Davy. It's important that those girls be attended to. And I've got to find a fresh one if I stay out all night to do it. Mr. Joiney intends to visit tomorrow and I've promised. Pays well, he does. And none of them up there will do, not so soon. I've just got to find one that'll suit. Actually, now that I thinks of it, that wench on the sofa would make her feel at ease. My cousin from the country. She looks ever so respectable—"

"Mayn't look so respectable if you don't come back soon," Davy warned, his finger venturing further and bursting off the top button of the old gown. "You best hurry."

"Don't be a fool, Davy. I got to get their confidence. A fat chance if I open the door and that silly young cow's screeching her head off. As I say, she's not going to run away, not six months gone and pale as she looks. She'll lose it, most like. Could be real useful after, over at Dora's place. No use here."

"'Cept for Jake and me."

"Well, keep your eyes peeled and be ready to open up for Doctor Hays."

"Be ready to open up for more than Hays! Fancy that wench, bun or no bun."

"I won't tell you again, Davy, there's to be no trouble. I could be back in five minutes with just the ticket for Joiney and you aren't to spoil things. If you were doing your job properly, she wouldn't have been here. She'd have passed out on the street and been picked up where she couldn't come to any harm."

"Aw right. I'll go and see if everyfing's as it should be. Go on, Deb." The heavy tread and the lighter, more decisive footsteps passed from the room. Sable, shivering, sat up cautiously. She must have been mad to think she'd gain entry to such a place without discovery. She could hear Davy padding about, his footfalls ominous. Staring around the room, Sable could see no other exit, though there was a screen in the corner. The front door banged and she knew the procuress had gone.

Rising quietly from the sofa, she retrieved the knife from behind the cushion and tiptoed towards the screen. There was a door. The relief was so great that she swayed for a moment, her head swimming oddly, then she laid her hand on the latch, the dizziness gone. To her horror, the latch moved, rising under her fingers as though of its own volition. She bit back a scream.

She stepped back, her skin goose-pimpled but the door remained fast. There was a bolt set near the bottom and this, she saw belatedly, was pushed home. The latch snapped up and down. "Deb! Davy! Let me in."

Just in time, Sable reached the sofa and lay down. The knife felt cold and she could not imagine using it. But, hidden under the folds of the cloak, it was a defence of sorts. She let her hands hang uselessly as they had done when Deborah left.

The floor shook as Davy hurried across it and pulled the bolt. "Oh, it's you, Hays. Why didn't yer come to t'other door? Usually do."

"I happened to come from the other direction. My God, it's cold. Whoever is that?" The voice was cultured but careless. This man had obviously been educated, but had come down in the world, Sable found herself thinking as she braced herself for a further scrutiny.

"Someone Deb found. Swooned against the door and fell in like a ripe little pigeon."

"Well on, I'd say." The stylish voice came closer, together with the unmistakable smell of brandy. "Overcome by the cold, most probably. She's very white and her hands

302

are cold. Funny about her hands—" He had set his bag upon the table.

"Wot's funny? Got six fingers, 'as she?"

"Very white. Well cared for. Don't quite match the clothes."

"See wot you mean." Davy picked up the reticule and tipped out the contents. "She don't 'ave much rhino." He flicked aside the coins in disgust.

"The kerchief is very clean. Very fine stitching and good linen. She's no serving wench, that's for certain, yet, dressed like that, she'd have to be a housewife. I'd swear she hasn't peeled a turnip in years nor had those hands in a washpot. A mystery, our unexpected visitor. Left her wedding ring at home. There's the mark—"

"Thrown 'er out, 'as 'e?" Davy conjectured. "Or 'as she run away? Don't mind if she stays, to tell the trufe."

"Give me a drink, Davy. Otherwise I'll never be able to do what I've come for. Be generous, man. Ah, that's better."

Sable, venturing another narrow glance, saw that Doctor Hays was tall and slender, dressed in shabby black. His features were hidden, but she knew already that his eyes would be pouched with overindulgence in drink, that he would look pale and unhealthy.

Davy took an enormous swig and set down the pewter mug with a bang.

"You'd best be upstairs when Deb gets back. She's likely caught a bird by now. And don't let them wenches get noisy. Keep Jake with you. I'll stay with her ladyship."

Doctor Hays turned, giving her another curious glance. Sable hated him violently from narrow chin to narrow brow. Perhaps she could stop him for long enough to save those children from his attentions. Already he wondered about her—

She made a small moaning sound and moved one arm, opened her eyes. Doctor Hays bent towards her. She felt

303

his hands on her body, pushing aside the cloak. If he should see the knife! But, mercifully, it had slid with the heavy folds of the material and remained covered, somewhere behind her. Her backbone turned to ice.

"She's not likely to whelp here, is she?" Davy asked, peering over Hays's shoulder.

The competent hands completed their examination. "There's nothing wrong. Child moved, I expect. It's a strong brat, I'd say. Kick like a mule."

"Could I—some water?" Sable said and tried to push herself up against the cushion.

"Brandy might be better. Best give her some, Davy. What are you doing here, girl?" The pouched eyes watched her closely. Suspiciously—

Color ran up into her cheeks. "I—I had to get away. From my husband. I was trying to reach my cousin. She'd have sheltered me—" Her imagination expanded.

"Cruel to you, was he?"

She lowered her eyes. "Yes. He's—a very cruel man."

"You could not always have thought so." He stared at her meaningly, his smile hateful.

"He was always unkind. I cannot go back. Perhaps I should go. I feel better—"

"Didn't take much rhino, did you?" Davy said, jingling her small supply of money.

"He—was mean." She had never told so many lies before. Why could Deborah not come back? She must have met Daisy by now. Fresh horror struck her.

The front door opened on the unwelcome thought. The thin figure of Doctor Hays straightened. Deb's voice, insinuating. Hesitant footsteps. "In there, dearie. You've nothing to fear." Then Daisy, paler than usual, her eyes widening at the sight of Sable. An incautious scream. "Why, my lady!"

"What's this?" Doctor Hays's voice was ugly. "They're in cahoots. You've been had, Deb. You little bitches!" He

304

made a dive for his bag and scrabbled inside. One of the attenuated hands reappeared holding a surgical instrument. Davy was running towards the door behind the screen, but it burst open just before he reached it. The screen toppled and crashed to the floor showing a dark gap through which wisps of fog curled unpleasantly. A figure stood in the space, the cloak gaping to show a glimpse of red, an upraised arm. Davy lurched forward threateningly.

Sable sprang to her feet, the kitchen knife in her hand. Daisy was crouching against the dresser, her mouth an alarmed O, while Deb Miller was already halfway to the front of the house, crying out for Jake to come downstairs or they were all lost.

Doctor Hays came towards Sable. In all the confusion that now reigned, only he had reality. His pallid face was ratlike as he considered the emergency and the fact that she had brought down this calamity upon them. Deborah Miller shrieked like a virago. Jake, unseen and unrecognized, careered down the stairs, mouthing curses. Davy was rolling on the floor with a burly Redbreast, the pair of them thumping and grunting like pigs, legs working and fists pounding like pistons.

"Oh, ma'am!" Daisy was whispering. "Oh, ma'am—" Her hand fumbled about on the dresser, picked up an earthern stewpot, thick and heavy.

Doctor Hays raised his hand and the bright, thin blade flashed in the lamplight. Sable closed her eyes and waited for the blow upon her face. She had thought she could use the knife but it stayed where it was, cold and useless. Her mind shuddered away from what was inevitable. Somewhere she thought she heard Adam's voice, then there was a dreadful thud, a blow upon her shoulder that sent her flying. She opened her eyes as she clung to the stuffed back of the sofa. Doctor Hays lay spread-eagled on the floor, the hand that held the scalpel slashed and bleeding, his

305

head at a queer angle and surrounded by the fractured remains of the stewpot.

"Oh, ma'am," Daisy said, palely. "Oh, ma'am."

There were two Runners astride Davy, punching him into unconsciousness.

Deborah still shrieked her defiance to the night, saying terrible things. And then Adam was there, staring at her disbelievingly. She stumbled towards him.

"So," Thomas said from his place at the foot of the bed. "This is the explanation for that unexpected marriage." His experienced eyes studied the size of the bulge beneath the bedclothes. "No wonder we had not the pleasure of your company at Christmas."

"It *will* be your first grandchild. Hurried though it is."

"You could have lost it. I heard all about your mad behavior from Adam."

"I see now how foolish it was. At the time I thought only of Adam—and Daisy."

"That's what I like about you. Those other minxes at Hunter Hall. Not a thought in their heads but themselves and what they'd get out of my boys. It's not like Adam to be so—precipitate, though." He flung himself into the bedside chair, his broad body out of place in the feminine disorder of the room.

"It is your grandchild. You need have no fears on that score." She knew that her face was flushed.

"So that's the way of it. Adam was always chivalrous. You've the best of the lot. But I suppose you know that already if you were prepared to go into that den of iniquity on his behalf."

"I do know it."

"I'm not spying on you. I had business with Caparty. Thought I'd surprise you."

"It's a pleasant surprise. I feel idiotic lying here. I

think—" She prepared to rise, seizing hold of the bedgown on the counterpane.

"And I think not," Thomas said with kind firmness. "Adam would be furious. You know you've been told to stay where you are for a day or two longer."

"But it seems unnecessary."

"I'm fussed over quite adequately, thank you, by your servants. How's that friend of yours? Lady Agatha?"

"Very well. She's—she's finished with Clara. Miss Caven's not allowed entry to Knowehead again. My little protégée pleases her."

"She's well shot of Clara. I hear she leads a most disreputable life nowadays. Saw her in a carriage yesterday with some painted roué. Made my blood run cold to think it could have been Adam—"

"She must be very unhappy."

"Save your sympathy, my girl," he replied shortly. "Oh, there you are, Daisy. Put the tray here, will you please? Thank you."

"So you're the lass who brained Hays?"

"Oh, sir!" Daisy looked alarmed.

"I won't eat you, child. Not that I mightn't have wanted to years ago."

"Oh, sir." The young voice changed subtly. Daisy was growing up.

"Off you go. I'll look after Mrs. Adam. You've been a good, brave girl. But I'm sure you've been told that already." He turned to pour the thin tea into fragile cups. "Cat's pee," he said unexpectedly and Sable sat up laughing.

"You're a terrible old man!"

"Old? I suppose I am. But I was not always. I had my day—"

"And what is that supposed to mean?" she asked curiously.

"Perhaps—I was not so fortunate as Adam."

"Oh." She had a moment's pity for Sarah. It must be dreadful to be unloved.

"Never thought I was good enough for her," he explained, sipping the watery brew. "But I was young and my parents set on a marriage into a good family. Not really Sarah's fault. She'll come round when she sees the child. Particularly if it looks like—"

"Morgan?"

"Aye, lass. It is his by-blow, isn't it?"

"I want no one to know but you. Adam has his pride—"

"Of course."

"I love Adam. I'd not want him reduced—"

"He shan't be. I should have met you all those years ago. Good for a man's morale, you'd be—"

"Was there no one—?"

His face grew shadowed. The hand that held the cup was still. "Aye. There was a girl. From Ireland, she was." He sat lost in thought and Sable was startled out of her half-lethargy. That story of the pond. A young widow. Aine—

"What became of her?"

"There was some accident. She and Sarah were up at the pond in the wood. I went to find them but there was only Sarah. Aine had fallen and the reeds had hold of her, dragged her down. I couldn't find her. No one ever did."

But he had thought it an accident. Sable had a quite vivid picture of that moment by the pond-side. Sarah, jealous and accusing—Aine amused. A blow struck in anger. The girl falling, sinking, crying out. Sarah frightened now and trying to aid her cousin. She must have tried, mustn't she?

"I'm sorry—"

"At least there was something. And what came after was not all barren. There were the children. One adjusts. We'll be friends, won't we, lass?"

"We are friends."

308

"They'll all come to heel, you'll see. You don't mind if I put something in this stuff, do you?" He took a hip flask from his pocket and added a good splash to the offending tea. "That's better. Now what am I to tell the rest of the family?"

"That I am—four months gone with child. And that I'll send the news in July. You'll take a letter for my mother, won't you, and see that it's read to her?"

"Aye. Now I've promised to dine with Caparty and his wife, so I'll take myself off. Look after yourself."

"Good-bye. What am I to call you? Mr. Hunter sounds so formal."

"Thomas. Why not?"

"Good-bye, Thomas."

The room seemed very empty after he had gone. Sable thought again of the pond, of the young Irish widow. Of Sarah Hunter. And all her previous dislike dissolved into a kind of pity.

Chapter 13

It would have been easier if the child had been a girl who resembled herself. But nothing seemed to come easily. Her life seemed always fraught with difficulties. Yet they were what added the flavor to existence. Problems must always be solved and that unravelling could be as fascinating as a move in chess. Adam could have taken to a daughter with her own looks, transferring some of his obsessive affection to her small counterpart. But the baby was a boy and the image of Morgan.

Adam had ventured a look at him and turned quiet. Against her own inclinations, but seeing that her duty lay with her husband, she'd bound her breasts and given her son to the wet nurse, the nanny, and the nursemaid, all of whom doted on the child. She had suffered by this decisive removal of herself from the son she increasingly adored, but she was Adam's hostess, helpmeet, and social and business companion. She could hardly take an infant to a supper at Holland House or to the homes of Adam's compatriots, or sit on some public platform while Adam addressed his constituents, wondering when little Bartholomew's lusty howls must take her from his side.

Adam seemed in no hurry to return from his bachelor bed in the dressing room. She'd not expected him to for the first few weeks after the baby's birth. But time was slipping by and still he stayed away. Of course, he had much on his mind. A body had been dredged up from the river, rotting and bloated, for it had been disposed of with large stones attached to the feet. He was certain this was Saul West because the man had not been seen again and would never willingly have left his old haunts. There was nothing to connect the deaths of Day and West with either the crew of the *Hyades*, or the West Indian planters who so deplored the revelations of cruelty that aroused increasing revulsion against the slave system and strove to conceal such reports or muzzle the witnesses. Now the *Hyades* was, like the *Janus*, on an extended voyage and could not be searched, nor the captain and crew interviewed for a lengthy period. Nothing would be proved, not this time. But people like Adam were tenacious. One day it would be different.

However, Adam had taken the step of sending for Ben to tell his story in the House and the Negro had arrived last night in time for today's appearance. A thick detachment of dissident West Indian supporters sat noisily together, making their disapproval plain, and Sable from her place in the gallery could see the annoyance on Adam's face, the disturbance on Ben's noble features.

It was very hot and the air inside the chamber was close and disagreeable. She fanned herself as she listened to two uninspiring speeches on tame subjects that aroused only coarse laughter and catcalls. Members really did behave like unruly schoolboys she decided with the unconscious superiority of a woman and mother. The image of Bart's laughing face came to her, filling her with a maternal tenderness, a sense of deprivation.

Wilberforce had been anxious to back up Adam on the subject of the ill-treatment of one defenceless human being by another and his speech was authoritative and almost stern, quite unlike his usual good-natured charm and insousciance. He was heckled as Adam was sure to be, but Sable was much struck by this unexpected facet of the young man's character.

Adam stood up now, elegant as always, his face browner than usual because of the fine weather. She studied his features, conscious of a wave of desire that was as strong as it was unexpected. How surprised most of these overgrown scholars would be if they knew the speaker was at this moment being lusted after by his wife. It did not seem at all respectable, but the thought amused her, making her black eyes sparkle. And Adam, as though he sensed her presence or her so unseemly thoughts, chose this moment to glance in her direction and catch the remnants of the involuntary emotion. He faltered in mid-sentence and several Members, following the line of his momentary distraction, smiled appreciatively at the attractive Mrs. Hunter who could divert more than her husband.

Adam recovered himself and continued with his oration. The House grew quieter and more attentive, though the West Indians harrumphed angrily in places and created diversions with their feet, some coughing disagreeably and others snuffing with unnecessary loudness.

Sable, familiar with his speech, let her mind drift to Betty Davies and her brother Billy, now at Lady Parksworth's home in the country. Billy had needed no second persuasion to work with horses and was popular in the stables. It was he who had coaxed Betty into going there, rather than chancing her luck in Brighton which was too near London for safety. Even Betty seemed to benefit from the change and was becoming increasingly friendly with one of the grooms, a friend of her brother's.

Belle continued to please Lady Chryston and was, herself, happy in her position. And Clara—she had married that old, painted lecher for his money and title and could be seen around town at special functions and important gatherings, her face reflecting a boredom that verged on complete indifference to her surroundings. It was only when she passed the Hunters out riding or in their carriage that something else showed in her eyes and that quality was quite unpleasant. A bad enemy, Sable thought, then told herself that Miss Caven had no power now to hurt her.

There had been a letter from Morgan sent from some port en route asking if his indiscretion over Parksworth was forgotten yet and saying how much he enjoyed the social side of these occasional landings. There was much card playing, dancing, and music. Exotic meals with governors and men of importance. Magnificent scenery. And the sea still compelled him. All that was missing on board was a woman.

Adam had replied to the letter with news of the marriage and nothing about the results of Morgan's visit to Cardigan Square. But the thought must cross his mind, Sable thought, when he arrived back and saw the age and personality of the child. She must face that when it happened and not cross bridges prematurely.

Sarah had visited them for a sight of Bartholomew and, as Thomas had predicted, was smitten immediately by the infant's resemblance to her favorite son. Jane had been friendlier and showed signs of wanting to visit them without her parents in attendance. It had been a successful, if tiring, visit but she was glad when the Hunters left for Yorkshire and the house returned to its usual routine.

Adam sat down to scattered applause and a little booing from the West Indian contingent. He ignored this and spoke quietly to Ben, who stood up to face the still unruly audience. He endured the collective scrutiny of these many strangers with a natural dignity. His deep, warm voice compelled attention. A vast silence encompassed the warm room. There was only this honest and shattering recital and the sleepy buzzing of a fly against the nearest windowpane. He did not speak for too long, and when he took off his white shirt to reveal the scars of the lash on his back and the patch to show his empty eyesocket, there was an instant response in the gasps of dismay and anger that ensued. The West Indians had the good sense to remain quiet at this point.

A ray of sunlight penetrated the chamber just as Ben sat down again, still leaving an uneasy quiet.

Then order papers rustled, feet shuffled, but members seemed disinclined to look at one another, as though they felt some inverted shame.

Sable found herself staring at William Wilberforce who was seated right in the center of the beam of light. Something in his eyes, diamond hard and indestructible, told her that it would not be Adam or Pitt who would batter this cause to its inevitable end, but this small, almost boyish, figure that was so suddenly and surely invested with a purpose almost tangible. He had suffered with Ben, was seared by those same inhuman lashes. At the beginning of his career his word would carry little weight. But later—she went on looking at him as at some savior. It was William who would be remembered, who would labor and despair. But she was sure he'd triumph at the end. She had never felt so certain about anything.

They got home just in time for Bartholomew's evening bath and feed. Sable begged to be excused to participate in the child's bath time as he would, as always, fall asleep hanging on to the breast of the wet nurse, like a replete satyr, almost exuding an aura of infant wickedness.

She left Ben with Adam and William, who had accompanied them, drawn by a compulsion to know more of the slave's trials. Ben would be gone tomorrow, back to the house he considered his home for life. To a mistress he loved. He would take with him gifts and letters for Lady Chryston, Belle, and Tom Dobbs, who was certain to visit there quite soon. Sable had bought Tom some strong shoes for his next travels, thick-soled and silver-buckled, able to carry him for long distances, and a new walking stick with a silver knob.

She was wearing the diamond ring Lady Agatha had given her and the brilliant sparks caught Bart's attention as he lay in the nurse's arms. He chuckled and held out fat little arms to catch the lights, then forgot them as he saw his mother. Young though he was, he knew her. Her body ached with the longing to hold him, to feel his mouth at her breast as any farm girl would have wished and expected as her right.

"Little love," she said unsteadily. "Little—" She bit her lip. She had almost said Morgan. But Morgan no longer meant anything but a dream lost. The child was placed in the china bowl and the water splashed around his firm, pink body. She loved him to distraction. As she would love any child of her own body, she told herself sternly, but knew that parents made their own, inexplicable choices. She must not treat Bart any differently from any others that might come. Adam could not hold out against her for ever. She would not allow it.

Waiting until the little boy fell asleep, she went downstairs to sit at table with Adam, Ben, and William. They were talking of Mansfield and his reluctance to make any firm decisions on slaves and slavery. But for once Sable ignored the challenge of argument and reason, wrapped in

316

her own thoughts, leaving at the proper time, when the port and brandy were passed around, aware of Adam's assessing scrutiny when he thought himself unobserved.

She fell asleep quite quickly for once. It had been a long and quite harrowing day. Her eyes squeezed tight shut and the darkness came. Doctor Hays came out of the gloom to cut her throat with a scalpel and she cried out. She fell into obscure water in which floated the weighted body of Saul West, the fishes nibbling at his eye sockets. She awoke gasping and shuddering, dragging herself against the carved tester, the taste of her dream in her mouth like a noxious flavor.

For a moment she longed to be back at Daggleby where the worst problem would be that of Mistress Perkins, then the spirit flared up in her like a torch. She'd never had any use for weeping and the gnashing of teeth. Everyone had an ill dream sooner or later.

A light appeared in the dressing room and she realized that Adam had probably been wakened from sleep. He pushed open the door and held out the candle, seeing her huddled against the carved head of the bed, her face pale with remembered terrors.

"Sable. What's wrong? You—screamed, I think."

"A nightmare."

He came closer and set down the lighted candle.

"Adam, I'm frightened. Frightened." She wasn't any longer, but it suited her that he should think so.

"You, Sable? You're never afraid."

"I am at this moment. I—dreamed Doctor Hays was here. With that scalpel. And there was no one to prevent him. Then I saw Saul West. He looked—hideous. Bobbing about in a mass of putrefaction. Stay with me, Adam. I'm truly afraid—"

Still he hesitated. She moved across the bed and put her arms around his waist, laid her head against his chest. "Adam. You won't leave me? If—I dream it all over again,

I must know I have some sort of refuge." She pulled at him, feeling his response, seduced by his proximity. "You've stayed there long enough to punish me, haven't you? In that cell of yours."

"Punish you?" He sounded amazed.

"Well, that's what it was, wasn't it?"

"No— It was not that. I imagined you might want to go— Now that Bart's here."

"You're a fool, Adam. I tried to tell you more than once I was finished with adolescent dreaming."

He sat on the side of the bed and stroked her hair almost absently.

"I've been so afraid, Adam. Afraid because I knew you could not bring yourself to love Bartholomew. Fearing you'd never believe I love you. I tried to show you—"

"I thought you were being—kind."

"Damn kindness. Come in beside me, Adam. Please—"

He pushed back the coverlet roughly as though he feared she'd escape him, pulled her down beside him. He kissed her until she felt she'd be smothered, then turned his attentions to the rest of her. Sable had a terrible feeling that the house would go on fire, that some fatality would occur to take him away before he was finished. Whatever is wrong in the world, she thought, dazzled, let it happen somewhere else.

The candle burnt to its odorous end and she was still awake, still triumphant. She'd never lose him now, she reflected drowsily and turned over so that he was curled around her like a shield.